PICTURE
IN THE
SAND

ALSO BY PETER BLAUNER

PICTURE

IN THE

SAND

PETER BLAUNER

MINOTAUR BOOKS
NEW YORK

First published in the United States by Minotaur Books, an imprint of
St. Martin's Publishing Group

PICTURE IN THE SAND. Copyright © 2023 by Peter Blauner. All rights reserved.
Printed in the United States of America. For information, address
St. Martin's Publishing Group, 120 Broadway, New York, NY 10271.

www.minotaurbooks.com

Library of Congress Cataloging-in-Publication Data

Names: Blauner, Peter, author.
Title: Picture in the sand / Peter Blauner.
Description: First Edition. | New York : Minotaur Books, 2023. |
Identifiers: LCCN 2022042896 | ISBN 9781250851017 (hardcover) |
    ISBN 9781250851024 (ebook)
Subjects: LCGFT: Novels.
Classification: LCC PS3552.L3936 P53 2023 | DDC 813/.54—dc23/
    eng/20220909
LC record available at https://lccn.loc.gov/2022042896

Our books may be purchased in bulk for promotional, educational, or business use. Please contact your local bookseller or the Macmillan Corporate and Premium Sales Department at 1-800-221-7945, extension 5442, or by email at MacmillanSpecialMarkets@macmillan.com.

First Edition: 2023

10 9 8 7 6 5 4 3 2 1

To David Denby, for forty years of loyal friendship;

To Richard Pine, my friend and agent, who gave me sensible advice,
watched me ignore it, and then guided me back from the wilderness;

And to Kelley Ragland, who helped rescue this
book and finally gave it a home.

PICTURE
IN THE
SAND

I don't mind the Ten Commandments. I believe in the Ten Commandments. The first one—"I am the Lord, thy God"—is a great commandment. If it's not said by the wrong people.

BOB DYLAN

PROLOGUE

June 9, 2014
To: Bayridgemama475@gmail.com
From: Alexisfire475@gmail.com

Mother,
I'm sorry for what I have to tell you.

Maybe if I was more brave, I would say it to your face. But by the time you read this, I'll be gone.

I realize this will be a shock. You know me only as the quiet, obedient son you and Dad raised me to be. You dressed me and fed me only too well. You sent me to the best schools. You mainly spoke English to me at home, so that I barely learned any Arabic. You helped me with my homework. You tolerated the rap and the heavy metal, the mess in my room, paid for my PS4 and the Sony camcorder, helped me take the tests and fill out the applications to the colleges you assumed I would attend. And I know you hoped I would become a big American success story and make you proud like Dad with his office at Chase or Grandpa with his gas station and his Escalade.

I am sorry I'm going to disappoint you.

But the curtain has been thrown back. The dream is over. What happened to Dad last summer woke me up. Yes, I know the FBI agents who arrested him and held him overnight at the jail have officially "apologized" for mistaking him for a terrorist with the same name. I know that you and Dad are ready to accept this and move on. But I can't.

I now see how easily everything we have can be taken away in an instant. All our savings, Dad's "customer relations" job, the gas pumps Grandpa owns, the big house on Colonial Road. All our assets could have been frozen, our cash spent on defense lawyers. That American flag we fly on our front porch and the little U.S. Constitutions that Grandpa likes to give our guests? They're jokes. We never really belonged here. I've known it for as long as I can remember. In fact, my earliest memory is being at the Fort Hamilton playground with you after those towers came down and having the other kids call me Osama and tell me to go back to the desert.

I remember how you tried to comfort me that day. You told me to dry my tears and hold my head up, that we were as American as anyone else. But we both know that was a lie. These people never wanted us here. And they have no business in the place where we come from. The world is what it is, a battlefield. And we must all choose sides. We must fight to be free men and women, or live and die as slaves and prisoners.

I choose to fight. I won't be going off to Cornell to study chemistry and video production this fall. I'll be learning more valuable lessons on the battlefront, where, God willing, we will find victory or glory in martyrdom.

My life is meaningless without struggle. How could I stand in line buying sweatshirts at the college bookstore or tossing a Frisbee across the quad when other men my age are risking body and soul to confront the enemy? How can I sit in the lecture halls, taking notes and grubbing for grades, when I know my brothers are marching through deserts and valleys with AK-47s slung over their shoulders? How can I hang out on Facebook or go to the library trying to meet girls or be in a dorm with my roommate playing Grand Theft Auto V *when other boys my age are on a desert hilltop with the true power of life and death in their trigger fingers?*

Even as I write this, I find myself imagining your reaction. After the shock subsides, I know there will be tears. And disbelief too. You'll ask yourself what went wrong. What you could have done differently. You'll ask if you should have sent me to a psychiatrist when I started fighting with you and Dad all the time. You'll imagine there are friendships you could have encouraged. Or perhaps discouraged. You'll think I shouldn't have spent so much time alone, in front of screens, getting "radicalized" on the internet. And while it's true that I've spent a lot of time watching martyr videos and talking to my recruiters in Syria about joining the struggle, it's also irrelevant. This journey has been my destiny.

The soul of a warrior has always been within me, even when my only weapon was the shovel in the sandbox, or the joystick I held playing Call of Duty. *I know that the course I've chosen must make no sense to you. But the material life of the present is not enough for me. Something further back in the past is calling out to me, telling me that those other kids were right: I should go back to the desert.*

Please don't grieve. I will always keep you, Dad, Amy, Samantha, and Grandpa in my heart. Insha'Allah we will be together again in a better place someday. Please tell Amy and Samantha to stay out of my room—except to feed my fish. No one wants his little sisters nosing around. Feel free to put all my video games and DVDs out on the sidewalk, though I seriously doubt anyone will want them because most of them are really old.

Try not to be too sad or scared. I know I've never traveled anywhere farther than New Jersey on my own, but I'm totally doing what I need to do.

Your son, Abu Suror (I looked it up. It means "father of joy.")

P.S. I don't want to be called Alex anymore.

July 23, 2014
To: Alexisfire475@gmail.com
From: GrandpaAli71@aol.com

Dear Alex (I'm too old to call you any other name),
I do not use the email very often, but there seems to be no other way
to reach you. Your mother tells me that your cell phone is turned
off and that you have left no forwarding address for regular mail.
Whether this message will ever reach you or whether you will respond
in any way, I have no idea. I pray, Insha'Allah, that you are still alive
to read this.

It has been more than six weeks since any of us have heard from
you. Your mother cries every single day. Often several times in the
course of one meal. Occasionally your two sisters cry as well. But
mostly they just stay in their rooms. Your father is like a zombie.
Since you haven't answered any of your parents' emails, I don't
know if you're aware that he left his job at the bank to devote himself
full-time to searching for you. He has spoken to every taxi service,
every airline, every State Department and embassy official who will
take his phone calls. He flew to Cairo and Istanbul, showing your
picture and spending thousands of dollars on "fixers" trying to track
you down. It appears that you slipped through the fence to Syria to
join these so-called militants fighting the government there under
the black flag. When your father tried to follow your path, he was
detained by the Syrian police, badly beaten, and then sent back to
Turkey. Now he is home, Alhamdulillah, and though your mother
says she doesn't blame him for not finding you, they are not happy the
way they used to be. Which makes me very sad.

There is no real reason for you to respond to me when you haven't
responded to anyone else. Even though I've been part of your life since
the moment you were born, you hardly know me. And I am sure you

would say I hardly know you, even though we've lived under the same roof since your grandmother died and your parents asked me to move in so they could keep an eye on me.

You are a young man who says he is off to fight a battle for his people. I am an old Egyptian with one eye who owns a gas station with a convenience store in Bay Ridge, prays five times a day, roots for the New York Mets, and cries at old movies and misses his wife terribly. You have always played the dutiful polite grandson around me. You have smiled at my tiresome old man jokes, pulled the chair out for me at the dinner table, and covered me with a blanket when I fall asleep snoring in front of the TV. You have shown me respect as the family elder, the father of your father, still working at the age of eighty-five. You have always been patient and said the right things. But I know you have not been very much interested in me.

And why should you be? Someone who has lived what seems to be such a dull complacent life could understand nothing about the great heroic journey you have embarked upon. Except that one thing you said in your letter to your mother caught my attention. You say this journey you have embarked upon is your destiny. You believe that something far back in the past, beyond your parents' comfortable lives, is calling out to you.

I understand this better than you believe.

When I was your age, I went on a similar journey and very nearly did not come back. It's a story that I have never told you. In fact, I have told very little of it to anyone in the United States since I came here more than forty years ago. Even your father, my only child, knows just the broad outlines, because I have always cut him off from asking too many questions. I wanted him to be an American, bright-eyed and hopeful, proud of me as his father, and knowing as little as possible about the past.

Because the truth is that your boring grandfather, Ali Hassan—
the gas station owner with his leathery skin, his old man cologne
and his corny jokes—spent many years in prison for being a violent
criminal, and lost his left eye in the process.

I have always been strict about keeping this secret. But after your
grandmother died, I found myself starting to write things down. Why,
I wasn't sure at first. But when I was a young man, I was a kind of
writer. Or at least I aspired to be. So I began to write my life story.
Not because I believed anyone would ever publish it, but because I
recognized something of my own restlessness in you when you started
having problems with your parents a few years ago. I wanted you to
know me. To know that I had this life, so there would be some record
to pass on. For a while, I thought I might not show it to you, at least
not while I was still alive. But now I feel more urgency to share it. I
don't know if you will have the time or the inclination to read what I
have attached here, if God sees fit to have it reach you. But I hope you
will. Because I know how this movie ends.

                                Yours, with love and compassion,
                                    Grandpa (in Arabic, Gedo.
                        But I prefer you call me what you always have.)

1

As I start to write this story, you, my grandson, are thirteen years old and upstairs in your bedroom with the door closed, not speaking to your parents. I hear the distant percussion of booms and gunshots through the ceiling. You are playing one of your video games. I am in the den, watching an old movie and making a few random notes to myself.

The film is about a silent movie actress trying to be remembered in a world that has forgotten her. I'm afraid you would not like it or understand it. It's in black-and-white, and it's narrated by a dead man. But I wish you would come in and watch a few minutes. Because it would help me begin to explain myself. There is a scene coming up in which the actress goes to see the director who long before made her a star. His name is Cecil B. DeMille. I knew him in real life. He was one of the idols of my youth. And after all these years, it's still hard for me to believe that I spent such a large part of my life behind bars for the crime of trying to destroy him.

But let me come back to that.

I was born in Egypt, between two wars and two worlds. I grew up just down the street from the pyramids, at the foot of the Giza Plateau. The Sphinx was only a short stroll from our front door. But the magnificent absurdity of my life, which led to all my misadventures and blessings, is that I preferred to go to the movies.

Our family lived in a mud brick house directly across the road from the Mena House Hotel, where all the celebrities of the day stayed.

My mother was a chambermaid and my father was a golf caddy for the guests. He was a most excellent golfer himself. He liked to joke that he was the one who broke the Sphinx's nose with a drive from the eighteenth hole.

I was a happy child, and why not? Every morning I would walk to school with my cousin and best friend, Sherif, past wandering chickens and quail in the road; tin roof shacks and smoldering village blacksmith forges; fragrant bakers' ovens in the open air; and the souvenir shop where Sherif's father sold Aladdin slippers, miniature mummies, and crocodile-head backscratchers to the tourists. Every afternoon I would come home to a house full of women: my mother and three older sisters talking gaily to nieces and cousins, conjuring splendid amalgams from room service leftovers, adding spaghetti marinara to traditional *kushari,* Carr's water biscuits to *mish* and *bissara,* London broil to *ful mudammas* while songs like "Begin the Beguine" and "Moonlight Serenade" played on the radio.

I knew we were not rich, but my family treated me like a little prince of Egypt, because I was the only son. My mother brought home silk sheets from the guest rooms for me to sleep on and tailored clothes accidentally left in the hampers. My father let me ride in his golf cart and introduced me proudly to his favorite customers. In the spring, I competed in the pyramid races, somehow beating Sherif to the highest peak, even though he was as lean as a jackal and twice as fierce when he competed. My rewards were the shower of kisses and candies I received from my mother and sisters, and my first Yankee dollars from the tourists who cheered us on.

Sometimes I glimpsed famous guests like Mr. Churchill and Mr. Roosevelt on the hotel veranda. But I was aware of an older, more uncanny world on our side of the road. In those days, before the Aswan High Dam was built, the floodwaters of the Nile would come right up to the paws of the Sphinx. My classroom would be so drenched that I'd have to leap from desk to desk to keep my feet dry and avoid stepping on frogs.

Perhaps you think I exaggerate? Well, I come by it honestly. My neighbors passed down the old legends that had been around since the time of the pharaohs. Well into the middle of the twentieth century, they still believed that the course of daily life was afflicted by jinn and afreet and other invisible spirits in the air, that the evil eye could kill you, that raving unwashed madmen could cure rickets and bilharzia, and that the black cat around the village well transformed into an old crone at midnight who would curse your family if you tried to draw water after sundown. But again, none of those myths stirred me as much as what I saw when my mother started taking me to the movies.

I can still remember settling into the plush velvet seats and looking up at the red damask curtains of the Metro Cinema before the house lights slowly went down, ushering us into the mysteries of the darkness. This was long before TV was common in any Egyptian home, Alex. A celestial white beam shot through a tiny square in the wall behind us, as dragons of cigarette smoke from the orchestra section curled up toward the balcony where I sat with my mother, my two older sisters, and Sherif. That first film was *Fantasia* and, oh, I was overwhelmed, my grandson. It was like watching images from my own unconsciousness being projected onto that giant screen. The wild and florid colors, the cartoon mouse in the wizard's robes, the marching broomsticks, the silhouette of the conductor, the "Rites of Spring" and the dinosaurs, the rising of the dead and the "Ave Maria." I forgot the fact that my mother could only afford one small tub of popcorn for the five of us to share. I wanted to stay for the next showing, and the one after that, so we didn't have to go back to our house, which had no toilet at the time and only intermittent electricity. But Sherif was tugging at her arm and my father was waiting for dinner, so she had to promise we would come back another time.

The next week was even better. We went to a theater called the Avalon. They were showing a British movie called *The Thief of Bagdad*. It was not a cartoon. It had real people in it, doing utterly impossible things. Flying through the air and coaxing genies from bottles. Even more amazing, one of those real people was a brown boy named Sabu, who was even darker than I was! And he wasn't just a silent servant in a scene or two but one of the stars of the picture. When he rode the magic carpet at the end to save the sultan and the princess from the wicked vizier who'd imprisoned them, I was carried away with him, imagining *I*, Ali Hassan, could be the hero rising up from lowly origins to save the day.

After that, I made my mother take me back every week, so we could hold hands and dream together in the dark. Sometimes we would take my cousin and my sisters. Sometimes it would be just the two of us. We saw everything: Egyptian films, French ones, Italian, English, and Spanish. We saw comedies and musicals, romantic melodramas and gangster pictures. But my favorites were American movies. Especially the Westerns with heroic cowboys and black-hatted outlaws having blazing shoot-outs in deserts that vaguely resembled the one we lived in but somehow seemed to be on another planet. Just the names bring me back to those exquisite days of my childhood. *Stagecoach, They Died with Their Boots On, The Plainsman.* The directors' names would appear big as the columns of the Luxor temples before the action, monuments to be worshipped. *Mr. John Ford, Mr. Raoul Walsh,* and the most monumental name of them all, *Mr. Cecil B. DeMille.*

I began to think of how I might rise above my circumstances like Sabu on his magic carpet and eventually become one of them.

But then the houselights would come on and real life would interrupt my dreams.

My village, my city, my country had been spared the worst effects

of the war, until after the battles of El Alamein. Then there was an out-
break of typhus. My aunt Amina, Sherif's mother, fell ill with the fever first. She sweated and could not get out of bed. She complained of
horrible pains in her abdomen. Then she shook and closed her eyes,
and never opened them again. His father, Hamid, the shop owner,
died a few hours after her. The very next day, my sisters, Mariam and
Rana, fell into a swoon and passed within hours of each other. Then
my dear stalwart mother, who'd been running around trying to take
care of them all, and of our neighbors as well, got a raging fever. She
curled up and cried out like she was being stabbed by a hundred invisible knives. I stood by helpless, clutching a damp washcloth. The
hotel doctor could not help her, nor could the village medicine man.
I went with my father to the Al-Hussein Mosque and prayed as hard as
I could, promising Allah I would give anything if he would spare her.

She died anyway.

My world went from color to black-and-white. More than a dozen
in our village died. My father and other men retreated into drinking
and mournful silences at home. I became withdrawn as well, barely
able to pay attention in school. It was Sherif who saved me. My cousin,
only six months older, had always been more like a big brother to me.
He insisted the problem was not that God had failed us but that we had
failed him, by not being devout enough. He started dragging me to our
local mosque every day, showing me where to find solace and explanation in the Holy Koran and the hadith. Faith lightened my burden in
those places, especially when I saw older men who'd suffered in the
plague, praying alongside me.

But that was not enough for Sherif. He always had a talent for pushing things. He declared he was forming a junior promotion of virtue society in our village and appointed me as his vice president. We
would spend hours designing handbills with sayings of the Prophet
Muhammad and then running around like a couple of mischief-makers

slipping papers of hadith under the doors of hotel guests and lecturing our neighbors about the sins of drinking and lasciviousness. To tell you the truth, I rather liked it, because most people received us with tolerant good humor, giving us tea and not reminding Sherif that his father had run a side business selling pornography in the back room of his shop. But then one day, a widow with five children turned on us and started yelling that my mother was to blame for bringing the plague to our village because she supposedly consorted with foreigners as a maid and took us to the movies instead of religious school.

I was hurt and deeply offended, of course. But Sherif actually attacked the widow physically—to the point that I had to hold him back. After that, he became more remote and turned inward. He claimed he was taking private lessons from a local imam, but I suspect that he was just smoking a lot of hashish. He began talking a lot about the need to "do something" to change our country and put us "back on the path toward the one true God"—though I pointed out that our country used to believe in *many* gods. I was secretly relieved when he went off to join a teenage volunteer brigade fighting alongside the Egyptian Army against the common enemy of the Arab world—the newly declared State of Israel. I paid little attention to the fact that the brigade was organized by the Ikhwan, a religious group that was also known as the Muslim Brotherhood. Many people in our country belonged to that movement and shared its objectives. I thought if they could find some use for Sherif's restless urges, it was all to the good.

In his absence, I started working as a busboy at the hotel, using my meager wages to help my father pay bills and occasionally take refuge at the Metro or the Avalon movie theater where I'd spent so many Saturday matinees. Except now that I was older, the cinema became not just my sanctuary but my classroom. I learned about love and courage and success. And it was where I found my own path forward.

After seeing Mr. David Lean's adaptation of *Great Expectations*, I was inspired to put pen to paper to write a review. On a whim, I sent it to Professor Ibrahim Farid, one of the great literary critics of Egypt, whose name I had seen in culture stories in the newspapers. For reasons known only to God, he read it and became convinced that I had insight and promise. He persuaded the admissions office to accept my application into the King Fuad I University in Cairo.

And it was there that my life began again. I formed the student cinema society. I became an entrepreneur, learning how to rent films from my father's golf customers who worked in the movie distribution business. I covered the rental costs by charging the equivalent of twenty cents a ticket for the showings I arranged in the university dining hall. I applied myself to mastering the art of marketing and audience research, with posters and handbills made at the same printer Sherif and I had used for the promotion of virtue society. I discovered that silly comedies with Aly El Kassar and the Three Stooges often sold out. Social dramas like *Life of Darkness* and *I Am a Fugitive from a Chain Gang,* as I've heard you say, "not so much."

But most of all, I discovered my true destiny. In my senior year, I took a chance and rented a French film called *Children of Paradise.* It was a long romantic drama made during the German occupation about four men in love with the same beautiful, unattainable courtesan. I was enraptured by it. My audience was not. People began leaving about halfway through—one at a time and then in droves, until I was absolutely sure I would be alone when the lights came up. I was crestfallen. I'd had a vision and no one else had seen it. I was a fool who would never amount to anything. But when the credits rolled, I heard someone else there, quietly weeping. I turned the lights on and there she was.

She had been sitting in the dark with me the whole time. Just the two of us, sharing *le beau rêve.*

Her name was Mona Salem. I had already noticed her on campus. She was a very striking young woman. She had the dark eyes and complexion of an Egyptian girl, but her curly hair was spun from pale gold. You knew that her parents had come from great distances to find each other and fall in love. She dressed like a Parisienne in white linen and silk scarves, and she moved like she'd had ballet lessons. She seemed like someone from beyond my class, the other side of the road, where the guests at the grand hotel stayed.

"*Ils ont coupé ma mère.*" She sniffled into a cotton handkerchief.

"Someone cut your mother?" I knew a little French from the hotel.

"*Non.*" She shook her head. "*Ils ont coupé les scènes de ma mère du film.*" Then she looked right at me and spoke in Arabic. "They cut my mother's scenes from the film."

It turned out that her mother was a minor French actress, who'd had a few lines of dialogue that were removed. Her father was an Egyptian diplomat who'd fallen in love while assigned to Paris. We stayed up most of the night talking over tea I made in the dining hall kitchen. The more we talked, the more she seemed like someone from my side of the road. She told me how her mother had left her father for a German officer, like the actress in the film, before moving on to a Swiss industrialist. Now Mona had to look after her father, to try to help mend his broken heart. She spoke of how she wanted to be an actress herself, but felt her cheeks were too round, her eyes were too small, and her ankles were too thick. To me, she seemed as enchanting as Miss Ava Gardner or our own golden Miss Egypt, Dalida. She insisted she should have some higher purpose than entertainment. Yet she was still as drawn as I was to that pure white beam from the projector.

By morning, I had a new vision of paradise, and Mona was at the center of it. I hungered for her with my body and my soul, in a way that I had never hungered for a flesh-and-blood woman before. She lit a fire in me. I decided I would find a way to get into the film business, and I would take her with me. I would get a job and make myself an invaluable assistant to one of the famous American filmmakers coming to our part of the world more often in those days. They would be so impressed by my diligence and ingenuity that they would have no choice but to bring me back to the States with them. I would change my name from Ali Hassan to *Al Harrison*! Then I would send for my beloved. She would join me in the real-world paradise of California. And there, beside the aqua-blue Pacific, amid the orange groves and abundant yellow sunshine, we would thrive and become full-fledged Americans.

We would buy a Chevrolet so I could commute to my job on the studio lot and then we would acquire a house in this Pasadena place that I'd read about in the movie magazines. It would have an Olympic-size swimming pool, where Mona could swim laps with the lithe grace of Miss Esther Williams. There would be a guest bungalow so my father could come and play golf in exotic places like Glendale and Alhambra. Then Mona and I would raise a family with natural-born American children who would know nothing about typhus, or starvation, or occupying armies, or any of the other direness that movies had helped us to escape.

I became serious about my ambitions. With Professor Farid's help, I arranged to rent an Arriflex camera. Then I worked extra shifts as a busboy, so I could buy a dozen rolls of Kodak film. I used them to shoot a little ten-minute movie, called *After the Revolution*, starring my beautiful Mona and Sherif, who by then had come back from the war with Israel and been accepted as an engineering student at the university. I pressed my father to tell his customers in the film distribution business about it. Then I cultivated those contacts to get production-assistant jobs on Egyptian and American films. I painted sets. I wrangled animals. I drove the actor Mr. Robert Taylor when he was in *Valley of the Kings*. I tried to assist the screenwriter Mr. William Faulkner when he was researching his script for *Land of the Pharaohs*—though I soon discovered Mr. Faulkner was more interested in researching the hotel bars of Cairo than the course of the river Nile, which he compared unfavorably to his rippling Mississippi.

I put together a résumé and perhaps exaggerated my credits on Egyptian films, on which I was fairly sure the Americans could not easily verify the information. Then finally I got the opportunity I had been waiting for. I learned that in the autumn of 1954, Cecil B. De-Mille himself would be coming to Egypt to make what he announced would be his last and greatest picture, *The Ten Commandments*.

I tell you, Alex, I was such "a fanboy," as you say, that I would have given up my left eye *willingly* to be his assistant. He had made silent films, pioneer pictures, sea adventures, cowboy movies, circus films and, most of all, religious epics like *The King of Kings*, *The Sign of the Cross*, and *Samson and Delilah*—which stirred the mind with their moral lessons and roused other parts with their lavish displays of flesh.

To my disappointment, I was only assigned to the motor pool for the first few days of preproduction, even after I hounded my father to use his contacts to get me a better job. Then on the third night, my father burst in the door with a message from the local studio office that had been left at the Mena House switchboard. I was to show up at ten o'clock sharp the next morning at a brand-new apartment house beside the University Bridge, in my best suit and polished shoes. Mr. DeMille's previous Egyptian assistant had "not worked out" for some unspecified reason, and I was to be the replacement and his personal driver.

And so it came to pass that on a warm October morning in the year of 1954, I was parked along the corniche of the Nile, humming movie music to myself as if the epic motion picture of my life was about to finally begin. I was twenty-four years old then, and I looked quite a bit like you, Alex: a plump-cheeked, slack-bellied, copper-skinned Egyptian boy with an American wardrobe, greasy pomade in his hair and an eager, welcoming grin.

The glass doors swung open and three men came out onto the sidewalk. One was dark, languorous, and heavy lidded in a white, wide-brimmed Borsalino fedora and a linen jacket that looked like he'd slept in it. His unshaven jowls reminded me a little of Mr. Humphrey Bogart in his rougher roles. But his sleepy eyes, long nose, and crooked half smile suggested a more European temperament. He looked like the kind of person who could ridicule you without actually saying anything.

The second man, who held the door, was a more reassuringly familiar figure. He was tall, slender, and craggily handsome with symmetrical features just starting to develop heavy lines and perfectly coiffed silver-gray hair. I realized it was the English actor Mr. Henry Wilcoxon, whose work I had favorably reviewed in *Mrs. Miniver* and *Tarzan Finds a Son!*

The third man was Mr. Cecil B. DeMille.

I once heard a saying, Alex, that great men are the only things in the world that become smaller as they get closer. That was not my experience. Mr. DeMille was seventy-three years old at that time. At fifty paces, he looked like a kindly country doctor. He was bald and wore a blue serge suit with clear horn-rimmed glasses. But he moved with the impatient dynamism of a man half his age. At twenty paces, his jaw hardened and the silver fringes around his temples began to resemble a Roman emperor's laurels. The sun gleamed off his exposed pate and the leather puttees he wore wrapped around his legs looked like the boots of a World War I field marshal. At ten paces, his gentle brown eyes became keen and fierce as they started to form a judgment.

"You're the new assistant?" His hand was on the passenger door before I could open it.

"Yes, sir." I smiled. "Ali Hassan, at your service."

He looked me over. "Going to do a better job than the last one?"

"I hope so, sir."

He grunted skeptically before he got in the back seat.

"Your predecessor had to be sacked because he failed to have Mr. DeMille's shoes polished and his chair ready on the set." Henry Wilcoxon offered a sympathetic smile before he folded himself in after the director. "But don't worry. Someone always gets fired right at the start of a DeMille picture, just to keep everyone else on their toes."

August 4, 2014
To: GrandpaAli71@aol.com
From: Asur@protonmail.com

Gedo,

Okay.

Here are my terms, nonnegotiable.

I will read your story, when I have time. But you may not ask me anything about where I am or who I am with. You cannot ask me what I am doing or what I am planning to do. You cannot ask me to come home. And above all, you may not tell anyone else you've heard back from me. If you do, I swear that I will never communicate with you in any way again.

You will not hear from me often. When you do, it will be from an encrypted email address, like this one. And it won't always be the same one.

But I would like to hear how you wound up in prison and lost your eye. I've always known there were secrets in our family. But did you seriously think I was still such a baby that I couldn't handle the truth?!

Just hit Reply to this email and I'll eventually find a way to get it. And by the way, I am no longer "slack-bellied."

Yours sincerely, in the name of the Merciful and Compassionate,

Abu Suror

August 5, 2014
To: Asur@protonmail.com
From: GrandpaAli71@aol.com

Grandson,
How glad I am to hear from you.
*   I will agree to your terms, for now. Though I hope you will change your mind and at least allow me to tell your mother and father that you are alive and well.*

Love,
Grandpa

2

I got behind the steering wheel and adjusted my mirrors, taking a moment to wipe an errant spit curl off my brow. My assignment was supposed to be simple that day: I was to take Mr. DeMille and his associates to a morning meeting at the production offices near the Egyptian Museum, and then to an afternoon meeting with our new republic's president, General Mohammed Naguib, at Abdeen Palace, one of the *king's* former residences.

The car I was driving that day had been King Farouk's as well. My God, Alex, it was a voluptuous thing. A cherry-red Cadillac Coupe de Ville with flaring rear fins, a V-8 engine, dual-range Hydra-Matic drive, and Dagmar bumpers, meant to evoke the buxom attributes of a certain type of actress. Before the revolution two years earlier, only Farouk had been allowed to have a red car. That way the police would always know it was him, speeding heedlessly through an intersection to see one of his fifty mistresses. But in the summer of 1952, the people finally decided they'd had enough of his corrupt and wasteful ways. We were fed up with the British occupation that had lasted since the building of the Suez Canal. We were suffering and still smarting from the defeat of our ill-equipped military at the hands of our new blood enemies in Israel. So the Free Officers of our army, after months of plotting in secret, had staged a coup and sent the playboy monarch sailing off on his yacht into the Mediterranean sunset.

So now these luxuries belonged to the people. And the son of a hotel maid and a golf caddy was driving the king's Cadillac.

The stone lions flanking the entrance to the Kasr al-Nil Bridge seemed to raise their heads high with pride as I drove past. This was supposed to be a glorious time for our country. For the first time since the pharaohs, Egypt was being ruled by Egyptians again. The Nile sparkled with shattered diamond reflections of the morning light. Feluccas with lateen sails listed in the breeze, like saluting hands on the water. The cars we passed honked their horns with a kind of joyful pointlessness, as if making noise was just a way of saying "Here I am!"

"Welcome to Egypt, Mr. Cecil B. DeMille." I looked over my shoulder. "It is an honor beyond all honors to be in your service, sir."

"Now, *that's* the right attitude." The director leaned forward. "Are the two of you listening?"

"Please permit me to say that I am a very great admirer of the films that you have directed," I added. "And of your contribution to the art of cinema in general."

"Our driver should go far in Hollywood," the man with the sleepy eyes murmured. "He's already mastered the art of flattery."

I did not like the way he referred to me. And I did not care for his accent, which sounded louche with a clipped European intonation that made it hard to tell when he was being sarcastic or merely observant. Mostly, I did not like that he had seen through me.

"Your English is quite good, Mr. Hassan." Mr. DeMille ignored him. "How did you learn it?"

"From your films, Mr. DeMille." I adjusted my mirrors. "And the films of other Americans as well, of course."

"Don't bother mentioning any of the others by name," the sleepy-eyed man chided me. "Thou shalt have no other before thine current director."

"Did I understand correctly from your résumé that you're an aspiring moviemaker yourself, Mr. Hassan?" Mr. DeMille asked.

"Yes, sir. I managed to shoot a short film when I was in school."

I decided not to add that I was a freelance film critic for several local newspapers as well. Cecil B. DeMille's movies were not always very well reviewed.

"It's an impressive achievement for a young man like yourself." Mr. DeMille raised his eyebrows. "Most people in America wouldn't have the audacity to even try."

I was going to tell him more about my movie but decided to hold off on that as well. Just getting it done had been an accomplishment of sorts, but the story was a trifle about a boy and a girl getting lost in the streets after the revolution, and I'd had no idea how to direct my actors or edit my shots together. I would have been embarrassed to show it to my honored guests.

"It was a modest start, sir," I said. "I hope to learn much more from working on this production. In fact, I would love to visit the States someday and see your studio."

"If you ever make it to Los Angeles, call my secretary." Mr. DeMille nodded. "We can set up a tour of Paramount for you."

I beamed, thinking he had already "taken a shine" to me. For all my advanced knowledge about the film industry, I did not yet understand that such tours were available to any visitor with a dollar and fifty cents to buy a ticket.

"Thank you, Mr. DeMille," I said. "May I say that I will be happy to guide you to some of our special locations, which you might want to consider for your production. Not just the pyramids and the Sphinx. I can show you the lake bed that the son of Ibn Tulun had filled with mercury and covered in skins so he could go to sleep on it like a giant mattress every night, while his favorite Koran singers chanted from the shore—"

"Sounds like one of Errol Flynn's wingdings from the good old days," said Henry Wilcoxon with a waggle of his salt-and-pepper eyebrows.

"Thank you, but I think we're all set for our locations, Mr. Hassan," the director said. "If you can get us to our appointments on time, you'll be well ahead of the game."

"Of course, sir."

We crossed the bridge, and I saw that several of the streets near the museum had been blocked off by barricades and military police vehicles. At first I was more disappointed than disconcerted. Like you, Alex, I was a child of the city, and I wanted to show off *my town* to our guests.

Though I yearned to be an American, I still loved Cairo. I loved the call to dawn prayer as the sun was breaking over the minarets, which looked like factory smokestacks. I loved the slight catch in the muezzin's voice as he tried to convince the faithful that prayer was better than sleep. I loved the red municipal buses that stopped in Tahrir Square and the street sweepers straggling out with their warp-thistled brooms to clean the alleyways near the souks. I loved the palm tree fronds that opened like praying hands to the sky. I loved the French gardens and balconies of the yellow and white villas that lined the boulevards like wedding cakes; I even loved the buzzards that landed on the wrought iron railings. I loved the smell of dust in old courtyards and the smell of flavored tobacco from the sidewalk cafés. I loved the voices of Frank Sinatra and Umm Kulthum mingling from opposite doorways as if they were singing a duet in the middle of Soliman Pasha Street. I loved the dancing eyes and white legs of schoolgirls riding bicycles to school. I loved the Nile when it was low in the spring and the riverboats moved slowly; I loved it when it was high before the harvest and the houseboats rocked along the corniche with boisterous parties. I loved the old monuments and landmarks and the stories behind them—the gates of conquest; the sultans' lurid sugar domes; the soaring towers and crumbling ruins left by the dynasties of the Fatimid and the Mamelukes, slaves who became masters and then fell again. I loved the jokes that only true Cairenes would get and the tiny stores where they would only sell you the best gems at a good price if they knew you were a local. I loved the goldsmiths' corners, the tentmakers' canvases, and the saddlemakers' bazaars; the smells of the frankincense sellers and *kushari* shops; the bird and camel markets; and the coffeehouses that stayed open until the small hours, right before dawn prayers when the muezzin yawned and started his chant again.

But I did not love some of the unfamiliar and crooked little streets that we were getting diverted onto that day. I did not love the way that the alleys narrowed so much that the jutting enclosed balconies of the houses were as close as faces about to kiss. And I certainly did not love the way that people seemed to be spilling out onto the streets around us.

We eventually found ourselves in a choked passageway between the Khan al-Khalili bazaar and the Al-Azhar Mosque, a good twenty minutes from where we were supposed to be. I worried that we would be very late for our 10:30 appointment, and then I worried even more as a crowd started to surround us, shouting and shaking their fists.

"What's going on here, Mr. Hassan?" Mr. DeMille leaned forward. "Why are they so upset?"

"I'm not sure yet, sir."

I squinted out my windshield at the signs being waved. One said "English, Get Out!" Another, hastily scrawled, read "BEWARE THE SPIES!" A donkey cart slowly crossed the street in front of us, the beast moving like it had arthritis. I hit the brakes, honked my horn, and looked over my shoulder to see if I could back up quickly. But there was a beggar with a baboon in his arms behind us.

I told you, Alex, that this was a hopeful time for Egypt. But it was also a very volatile time. There had been rumors of struggle among our leaders for months, with different factions vying for control even as Mohammed Naguib tried to unite the nation as its new president. The situation had stabilized for a while, but now the streets were blocked by demonstrations and the detours had forced us into the middle of a major protest with no police in sight.

As I pumped my foot on the brake, waiting for the donkey cart to move in front of us and the beggar-and-baboon show to clear the way behind us, the crowd swelled and fulminated around us. Some were teenagers who should have been in school; others were older and had the hardened, slightly leathery look of fellaheen and manual tradesmen. They were quickly joined by men in mechanics' overalls, shirtsleeves, and dark slacks; women in blouses and pleated skirts; even a few mothers with babies on their hips.

I realized that, as often happens with demonstrations, many causes were converging at once. Some people were protesting the continued presence of English soldiers in the Canal Zone, despite recent talk of an evacuation agreement. Others were waving signs protesting labor conditions. And a few had banners celebrating the recent signing of a treaty with Sudan.

In any event, there were suddenly well over a hundred people in the street, and they were being very loud and vehement. An aggrieved-looking man in a bloody butcher's smock was at the intersection, pointing his knife at the sky as if God himself shared his objection. Others were pointing at the hood of our car, as if they were incensed by its color and remembering that only the king had been allowed to drive a red car. What drew them together was their anger at seeing this symbol of oppression in their midst again, with Westerners in the back seats.

But what was even more ominous to me was another group

jogging up. They were mostly dressed like students and young professionals in Western clothes. Most had mustaches and a few had full beards, which were far less common in Cairo back then. And most wore the tarboosh, the tall red conical caps that Americans call the fez. On the heads of such tightly wound men, they looked like the tops of dynamite sticks and the tassels looked like fuses. From the few meetings I had attended with Sherif, I recognized some as members of the Ikhwan, looking to take advantage of the disorder. They believed any accommodation with the English, even an evacuation treaty, was a surrender. And they were angry that Mohammed Naguib, who they believed to be their ally, had not been seen in public for some time. I slumped behind the wheel, hoping none would recognize me. At first, there were only a half dozen of them; soon there would be more.

The crowd was closing in. Vendors from the nearby stalls gathered around, brandishing fruits and vegetables threateningly. Some of the shouting demonstrators laid hands on another car just ahead of us and began to rock it back and forth. There was a smell of burning rubber and scorched vegetables in the air.

"Oh, dear," Henry Wilcoxon said.

A man jumped out of the white car ahead of us and started to argue with the man in the butcher's smock, before getting grabbed and pulled away by the growing mob.

"What do you think about us getting out of here, Mr. Hassan?" Mr. DeMille said.

"Sir, I would like the same thing. But the situation is becoming very difficult."

People were coming up on all sides. There were children now, too young to be in school, holding their mothers' hands, joining hawkers, street beggars, and tinsmiths. I saw a face upside down on my windshield, and realized it was the beggar's baboon crawling over our roof. I dared not put my foot on the accelerator as voices massed around us. It was so loud that it was as if we were in the middle of a birdcage, sharp beaks and claws ready to attack at every angle. I heard some of the Muslim Brothers chanting Mohammed Naguib's name, but others were calling out a far more dreaded word: *"Ingliz."*

"What are they saying?" Mr. DeMille demanded.

"Sir, they believe that you are the English," I tried to explain.

"Then tell them we're not, goddammit. Except for Henry."

"Mr. DeMille, it's a little late for that," said the sleepy-eyed man.

We were completely surrounded. I could no longer see out my windshield, as hands pounded our hood and roof. There were tarbooshes and swinging tassels on every side of us. All at once, we were lifted up and tilted at an angle, the crowd on one side of the car evidently stronger and more numerous than the other.

"Mr. Hassan, get us the hell out of here," Cecil B. DeMille shouted.

"I will, sir. As soon as I get all four wheels on the ground."

I was trying to sound unflappable like one of my movie heroes, but my heart was pounding so hard that I could feel it in my lungs. Henry Wilcoxon had gone pale and shut his eyes. Mr. DeMille's entire face was scarlet, and his lower teeth were showing.

But for some reason, I found myself watching the sleepy-looking man in my rearview mirror. A hand reached in the window and clawed at his face. Then it seized him by the throat. His eyes opened only a little wider. Then he grabbed the hand that was trying to strangle him, pulled it toward him, and began punching his attacker through the open window with his left hand. He did it five, maybe six times, then wrung his hand like he'd hurt it. People fell back and the other side of the car dropped, tossing the four of us as the wheels hit the ground and the suspension coils squeaked.

"Drive, man! Drive!" Mr. DeMille yelled.

I heard two sharp cracks in the near distance as if someone had fired a gun. I put my foot back on the gas pedal and the car inched forward. The crowd parted ever so slightly. I saw that a pear-shaped older man in a white half beard, spectacles, and a gray galabiya had been standing before us, pushing people out of the way. He had bulbous features and wore a red cap with a white scarf around it that clearly identified him as a religious scholar. But my head was so full of American movie images that all I could think of at that moment was Santa Claus and one of Snow White's seven dwarves.

There was a jolt on my front bumper and a wash of gray across the windshield. Something heavy rolled over our roof.

"For God's sake, keep going," Mr. DeMille cried out. "Don't stop now! They're still trying to kill us, man!"

I stepped harder on the gas and tried to tell myself that we had not been going that fast when we made impact. The crowd before our grille divided as I kept going forward, trying to avoid hitting anyone else, the occasional hand still striking the roof and splaying out a palm on our windows as the white car reappeared.

"What were those gunshots about?" Mr. Wilcoxon asked.

No one answered. I could still hear the suspension quivering from our collision. But somehow the windshield had not broken. I looked in my rearview mirror and saw people behind us gathering in a clump. Then I faced front and saw a pair of mangled spectacles lodged in the recess between the windshield glass and the hood.

"'Astaġfiru-llāha rabbī wa-'atūbu 'ilayh," I began to murmur the istighfar prayer, asking God to forgive me.

"What's that, Mr. Hassan?" Mr. DeMille's hand touched my shoulder.

"Nothing, sir."

I kept my eyes on the road ahead.

To: GrandpaAli71@aol.com
From: Asur@protonmail.com

Gedo,

I don't know what to say about this so far. Except now I assume this is why you went to jail. You shouldn't have hit and run, obviously. Is that where you lost your eye as well?

How did you even put yourself in this terrible position? I know you were naive, but come on! Couldn't you tell that these so-called artists and entertainers came to Egypt to do what outsiders have always done? To exploit us, take our resources. Totally. It's the same whether it's oil or history. The Western hand that pretends to be offered in friendship always winds up wrapped around our throats.

And you're right. I have never heard of this Cecil B. DeMille that you keep talking about. Or most of these movies you mention. But how can you even compare this silly lackey's job you had to the call to duty that I've undertaken!

I only hope that when my courage is tested, I'll do better.

Yours in struggle and faith,
Abu Suror

3

I can still picture the billboard for Camel cigarettes that we pulled in behind a mile from the accident, with its childlike drawings of the dromedary and the pyramids in the background. All four of us got out to inspect the Cadillac. There were scuffs and dozens of handprints, but no permanent dents or shattered glass. Nor was there any blood. But then I saw the broken spectacles by the windshield wipers and my chest tightened.

"Does anyone think we need to say anything about this?" Mr. DeMille spoke first.

"It's possible that no one was seriously hurt," Mr. Wilcoxon replied in a bland transatlantic accent.

"Mr. Garfield?" The director turned to the sleepy-eyed man.

"I wouldn't." He tipped back his hat and pretended to be more interested in studying the gold ring on his bruised left hand.

"What about you, Mr. Hassan?"

Something dripping beneath the hood matched the beat of my pulse.

"Sir, the police here are not like the police in American movies," I said. "I would not go to them voluntarily. But if anyone asks, I would say we were in fear for our lives."

I got down on one knee to look beneath the car to see what was dripping. It was only the air conditioner. I got up, brushed the dust from my pant leg, and disengaged the spectacles from the wipers and put them in my pocket.

We continued to our appointment in silent complicity. I turned on Radio Cairo to see if there was any report on the demonstrations we'd run into. But the station was playing the popular songs of the day by Umm Kulthum and Mohammed Abdel Wahab. And when the news came on, the announcer made a passing reference to a general state of protest rapidly dispersing.

It was well after eleven when we arrived for our 10:30 appointment at the production office downtown. A work crew on ladders was changing the sign as we pulled up in front of the Beaux Arts office building on Soliman Pasha Street. Upstairs, Mr. DeMille gave me a number for a lawyer in Los Angeles named Neil McCarthy and instructed me to pull him out of his budget meeting instantly if I was able to "raise" him on the phone. I did not know the term "Hollywood fixer" at the time, though I understood why I was calling. But there was a ten-hour time difference between Egypt and California; the phone rang and rang without an answer.

Nor could I reach the government liaison whose number was listed on the call sheet. By then, we had to leave for our one o'clock appointment at Abdeen Palace. When we arrived, we were told by the corporal at the front gate that the location of our meeting had been changed.

"President Naguib is no longer available," he said brusquely. "You should have been informed you'll be meeting with other officials."

We were directed to join a military escort consisting of three jeeps with six soldiers heading toward Gezira Island.

"Will someone please tell me what the hell is going on?" I saw Mr. DeMille bare his lower teeth in the rearview mirror.

"I would presume 'no longer available' means the president is under house arrest," replied the sleepy-eyed man he'd referred to as Mr. Garfield.

"Is that true?" Henry Wilcoxon asked.

"Informally, it's possible, sir," I answered as calmly as I could. "There has been, as you say, 'trouble behind the scenes' for some time now."

"Why wasn't I informed of this change of plans before, Mr. Hassan?" Mr. DeMille's jaw hardened.

"Sir," I replied, "I only started working for you today. Someone else should have informed you."

"Yes, why didn't we hear about this change from our contacts at the State Department?" Mr. DeMille turned on Henry Wilcoxon.

"I'll have to ask the new people," the actor said. "Bob McClintock just got assigned to Asia. Apparently, the French left us with some trouble to sort out in Vietnam."

At that instant, I understood why Mr. Wilcoxon—or "Henry," as I came to know him—was no longer a movie star, and had been reduced to acting as DeMille's associate producer with occasional support roles in his films. His face was too blandly handsome to be interesting, and his voice lacked authority. What was worse was that he did not exude the unreasonable confidence that audiences like to see in leading men, and which Mr. DeMille obviously required at that instant. His proud profile at that instant only made me think of a great bird with powerful wings that could not actually fly very far.

Mr. DeMille fell into a deep unsettled silence as we crossed back over the Nile to Gezira Island and saw the streets near the riding clubs lined with almost as many jeeps and tanks as there had been out during the coup two and a half years before.

We pulled in behind our escort at a four-story limestone villa with slightly overgrown gardens and a mooring station for a boat next door. I realized this was another of the king's former residences. The royal yacht was back at the dock, having deposited King Farouk in Naples. Now instead of being festooned with party streamers and flowers that I used to see from the shore, it was being outfitted with machine-gun emplacements.

A captain on duty came out to greet us, tall with an equestrian champion's posture and his hand near the gun in his holster. "Please," he said, yanking open the back passenger door officiously. "Prime Minister Nasser does not like to be kept waiting."

"'Prime Minister Nasser'?" Mr. DeMille sounded alarmed.

He did not get out right away. I suppose he was used to being the one who set everyone else's agenda. But we were surrounded by heavily armed soldiers, not actors and studio executives. And their crackling radios and rigidly blank expressions conveyed that they were not to be trifled with.

"Now, see here," said Henry, fumbling with the latch of an attaché case he'd had on his lap. "We've been in touch with President Naguib's office for months, making arrangements. . . ."

"The government is being purged of Naguib loyalists and all arrangements are subject to review now," said the captain, as his eyes flicked over at me. "You will come as well. Your presence is specifically requested."

The dripping sound I'd heard from beneath the car was in my head now, as I got out with sweaty hands and stiff legs. We were led into a kind of royal museum, from which all signs of opulence had been removed. The vestibule still had a vaulted ceiling and a tiled floor, but the new red, white, and black flag of the republic hung on the wall, with the golden eagle of Saladin replacing the white crescent and three stars of the kingdom's green flag. The stone floor was without Ottoman carpets, and the marble stairs had a stark white strip up the middle, as if a red carpet had recently been ripped away.

The captain brought us to the third floor and deposited us in a large room overlooking the Nile. The heavy wooden doors closed with a forbidding plonk. The room was like a set from *Gone With the Wind* or the Cairo Opera. It had a high white ceiling with gold leaf around its borders, tall Greek Revival windows, red velvet curtains, a half dozen Louis Quatorze chairs of unequal size arranged in the middle of a red Moorish rug with an intricate gold-linked pattern around its border.

"Good God." Mr. DeMille held his arms out. "It's worse turnover than Paramount. Mr. Hassan, tell me about this Nasser, and make it snappy."

"Yes, sir." I swallowed. "He was a lieutenant colonel in the war against Israel and a leader of the Free Officers who deposed the king. But Naguib has been the figurehead. Until now."

"Revolutions are hard to put on storyboards, eh, Mr. DeMille?" said Mr. Garfield.

"We've been in touch with his office as well," Henry said quickly and not very convincingly. "I'm sure everything will be fine."

The doors reopened and two men in khaki uniforms walked in. The first was tall, with strong features and a large, determined jaw. Gamal Abdel Nasser's posture was erect, his shoulders were broad, and he walked like he expected other men to follow him unquestioningly. His mustache was dashing, his black curly hair was silvering at the temples, and there was a small crescent-shaped scar on his large forehead. There was a touch of thuggish arrogance in the way he raised his chin to acknowledge our presence. But when he smiled, skyrockets went off in his eyes and he seemed as much a matinee idol as Emad Hamdy or Clark Gable.

"Prime Minister Nasser, I presume." Cecil B. DeMille offered his hand. "An honor to meet you, sir."

"An honor to meet *you* . . ."

Nasser shook the director's hand politely but then took Henry's grip more firmly, using both his hands.

"And a *great* honor to meet you, Mr. Wilcoxon," he said.

"Well, thank you." Henry looked flustered and disconcerted, like a bridesmaid receiving a proposal from the groom.

"Please allow me to introduce my colleague, General Abdel Hakim Amer." Nasser turned to the officer beside him, whose name I also recognized from the newspapers and café talk.

The general was, like the prime minister, only in his midthirties. If Nasser looked like a leading man, Amer, even with a general's stars on his shoulders, seemed like the skinny comic sidekick with a woebegone mustache who got shot in the second reel, justifying the hero's path of revenge. But he had the eyes of a funeral director and when he looked my way, I felt like he was already figuring out how to bury me.

"And this is Mr. Raymond Garfield, who will be making the documentary that accompanies our main feature," Mr. DeMille said, finishing the introductions.

I had not understood Raymond's role before. Nor did I entirely understand why a documentary was being made.

General Amer gestured for Henry and Mr. DeMille to sit in two chairs in the middle of the room, both velvet backed with curved golden legs. Raymond and I took two smaller chairs behind them and off to one side. That left two seats in the middle, one low and plush with claw feet, the other more thronelike. Nasser started to lower himself into the smaller one, then stopped mid-crouch and signaled to Amer that they should change places, as if he still needed to remember such grand comforts were his due now.

His eyes darted my way. "And you are the representative of our people. Yes?"

"I am just an assistant," I started to say.

"There's no need for false modesty," Mr. DeMille interrupted. "Mr. Hassan has already proved his worth to us."

"*So!*" Nasser slapped his knees. "What is your purpose here?"

Mr. DeMille blanched. The puttees around his legs, which I'd read he wore as protection against snakes in California, squeaked as he leaned forward.

"Our 'purpose'?" The director took a moment to try to regain his composure. "Mr. Prime Minister, we've come halfway around the world to get here. We've been in preproduction for years. *Decades.* We had a deal with the king and then with your predecessor, Mr. Naguib. We're putting *thousands* of your citizens on our payroll. We're spending more money than has ever been spent on any motion picture in history, to make this a reality."

"More than a million dollars a commandment," I heard Raymond Garfield mumble.

"So are you seriously telling me you didn't know about any of these prior arrangements, Mr. Prime Minister?" Mr. DeMille asked almost plaintively.

"But tell me—why *in* Egypt?" Nasser crossed his legs, in no great haste to respond. "Surely you could have built film sets in America."

"Why did *we* come here?" Mr. DeMille threw me a desperate look as if he needed an interpreter. "We came because we wanted to tell the story of Moses and the birth of human freedom in the land where it all really happened. . . ."

The words were from a press release, but his urgency was sincere. I soon learned that despite all his success, he'd had to beg for the funds to mount this extravaganza. He had made a silent version of *The Ten Commandments* in California thirty years before, and famously had buried the set in sand afterward so no one could reuse any part of it. He made no secret that he'd been trying to remake it in Egypt ever since the sound period began. If this was to be his last film, he wanted to get it right.

"But now there is *a problem*," Nasser said.

The skyrockets were fading in his eyes.

"You have come to Egypt at a complicated time," he said, in the slightly stilted English of someone who had learned the language in military school.

"Yes, we understood that you'd gotten rid of the king," Mr. DeMille said. "We have no use for monarchy ourselves. . . ."

"Yes, and like yourselves, we are a relatively new republic." Nasser was no longer smiling. "But now we are surrounded by enemies, seeking to undermine us."

From outside came the voices of men drilling and hammering the king's yacht into service as a warship.

"I myself was wounded fighting against the Israelis in the Negev a few years ago." Nasser knit his brow, creasing the scar. "Now they have spies among us, committing acts of sabotage and subterfuge. And, like yourselves in the States, we have Communist infiltration. But the worst are the Ikhwan, the so-called Muslim Brotherhood. . . ."

His stare lingered on me as he murmured something in Arabic out of the side of his mouth to Amer.

"This is a religious order?" Mr. DeMille asked.

"They're militants and fanatics," Nasser said.

"Not all of them," Amer demurred. "There are a million."

"Enough are crazy and violent that it's a problem." The prime minister's impressively large nostrils flared. "They supported the revolution because they thought Naguib would let them run the country and turn it into a theocracy, with all the men in beards and women in veils. Can you imagine?"

His smile returned for a moment, as if amused by this preposterous vision.

"But now these crazy Muslim Brothers are inflamed," he said, turning serious again. "They were against me to begin with, for being too open to Western influences. Now they're worried that if I can get the British to honor the evacuation agreement, they'll never be rid of me. And just this morning, they're claiming that one of their leaders was killed by someone driving an American car. Sheikh Sirgani. One of the more reasonable ones. They say a driver plowed into him at a demonstration where they were protesting the dismissal of their allies. And now they're going to use this story for their purposes."

I knew the name Sirgani. This man was an imam, a religious scholar. His sermons were broadcast on the radio. He raised money for the poor. He was revered by people I was close to. And his broken glasses were still in my pocket.

"Do any of you know anything about this?" Amer asked.

The four of us who were visiting looked at one another. The tightening of Mr. DeMille's puttees now sounded like the twisting of a hangman's rope.

"Do you think we would be sitting here discussing things so calmly if we did?" the director asked.

Nasser rubbed his mouth. "The point is, your presence in our country represents a major difficulty now," he said. "The biggest Hollywood movie in the world is the symbol of all the Ikhwan despises. So why should I let you stay?"

Mr. DeMille grabbed at his armrests and started to rise out of his seat as Henry began rifling through his attaché case.

"Don't talk to me about contracts." Nasser waved dismissively. "Those were with the previous regime and no longer valid."

"Because we're making another movie as well." Raymond Garfield spoke up, cool and unruffled as he'd been during the attack.

"What's that, sir?" Nasser asked.

"That's right." Mr. DeMille nodded, belatedly picking up the cue. "As part of our original contract, we agreed to make a documentary promoting Egypt as a new beacon of liberty and a land of opportunity in the Middle East. Mr. Garfield, who is an award-winning documentarian, is here to put that together. And I'm sure he'd agree that he has an even better film now that the country has a new leader who looks like a movie star."

"Do you really think I'm as vain as King Farouk?" Nasser pointed at his own face.

"Any leader has to care about the image he projects," Mr. DeMille replied cagily. "And in the modern world, the camera is as important as any other weapon in his arsenal. We intend to show Egypt is thriving under your leadership. Such a film could only help your standing on the world stage."

"You're telling me you're going to make me 'a star'?" Nasser shared a cynical look with his general.

"Mr. DeMille has an uncanny knack for discovering raw talent," Henry pointed out. "He spotted Gary Cooper before anyone else took notice of him."

"Tell me, Mr. Wilcoxon." General Amer leaned forward with a keen, dour expression. "Did you and Mr. DeMille once make a movie called *The Crusades*?"

Mr. DeMille sank back down in his chair. "Not one of our more successful efforts," he admitted.

In, fact, I knew from my studies, its failure had ended Henry's career as a leading man.

"You misunderstand." Amer broke into a grin that made his otherwise grim face look boyish. "We loved that film, when we saw it at the military academy. Especially Mr. Wilcoxon, when he played Richard the Lionheart fighting our hero Saladin. We even used to call the prime minister 'Henry Wilcoxon.' . . ."

"*Khalas.*" Nasser winced. "Enough." He rubbed his imposing chin. "I'm prepared to let your production proceed *for now,* under certain conditions. Number one, we retain the license for this documentary."

"*Done.*" Mr. DeMille nodded with a sly glance at Henry. "That was in the agreement we made with your predecessor."

"Number two." Nasser held up his index and middle fingers. "You do nothing to criticize or embarrass my regime with this film you're making, and do nothing to further inflame this situation by the content of your movie or the behavior of your people in our country. Yes?"

"Yes, of course." Mr. DeMille frowned. "Your censorship office already has a copy of the shooting script—"

"Send another." Amer cut him off with a touch of impatience. "Everyone who was there has been sacked and replaced—as of today."

"And number three . . ."

Nasser looked around, making it clear at this moment that he was the director, setting and controlling the mood of the room.

"Number three," he said. "You promise me that none of you will turn out to have had any connection with what is supposed to have happened to this so-called holy man at the marketplace today."

It was so quiet that I could actually hear people swallowing.

"I need to be clear with you," Nasser said slowly. "This is a matter of national urgency. If any of you caused this death, your movie will be shut down and most of your crew will be expelled. And that's not all. There will be a public trial, and we will make an example of someone."

I tried to imitate the relaxed posture of our guests, the way Raymond slouched and Mr. DeMille fingered his chin. But the habits of human nature seemed suddenly alien. I could hear Nasser saying the words, but I did not believe he meant them. We were all like actors on a set, saying our lines. The only thing that seemed real were the mangled glasses in my pocket.

"So is there anything you need to tell me?" he asked.

Mr. DeMille gave me only a passing glance, but I completely understood the direction he was giving me. I said nothing.

"Please offer our condolences to this holy man's family and followers," Mr. DeMille said, turning back to our hosts. "If you feel it's appropriate, of course."

"I'll save that for now." Nasser smiled again.

"Well, then . . ." Henry closed his attaché case and rose. "I suppose we'll just carry on and look forward to your star turn in Mr. Garfield's film."

"Yes, I look forward to seeing the script for this documentary."

All of us moved toward the door. Then Nasser and Amer paused to give each of us a departing handshake. I was the last to leave. Nasser put a firm hand on my shoulder to detain me.

"Drive safely, please," he said.

August 19, 2014
To: GrandpaAli71@aol.com
From: Asur@protonmail.com

Gedo,

I wonder now if you're putting me on. Of course I have heard of Nasser, al taghout, the dictator. How is it that you never mentioned that you met him? And of course I know about the Muslim Brotherhood. Do you think I'm an idiot? Maybe they were badasses back in your day. But to people my age, they're sellouts. When they got to be in power for like five minutes after the Arab Spring a few years ago, what'd they accomplish? Nada! But I guess they were more radical and righteous back in your day. Or at least more "dangerous" compared to what they became.

Anyway, I'm beginning to understand why you shared your story with me. Yes, some of the same things seem to be happening nowadays with the army seizing power from the Ikhwan again. But to be honest, I don't think I believe in political solutions anymore. I'm still not going to tell you where I was or where I'm going, but I did spend some time in Egypt when I got here, looking for some of the places you've mentioned so far. But they're mostly cheap tourist shops now.

I also want to say that I think it sucks that you didn't come clean about this "accident." God will judge you in the end. Or maybe he's judging you now through the actions he's inspired me to take. I am curious to know how you wound up in prison anyway. And I'm curious to know if you had more dealings with Nasser and the Brothers.

I'm not sure when you'll hear from me again, but I'll keep reading when I have time.

Yours in faith,
Abu Suror

s we walked out of the meeting with Nasser, Mr. DeMille's hand landed on my back. It was not heavy, but it was as firm as Nasser's and it was high enough up that I could feel a slight pressure on the nape of my neck. I believed that he was trying to reassure me that we were in this together now, and our fates were intertwined.

"There was nothing else we could have done," he said in a gentle, gravelly voice before he let me go and climbed into the back seat.

Nothing else was said about the imam's death as we made our rounds. It was as if we suspected a listening device had been planted in the Cadillac, though such things were very uncommon in those days.

I dropped Mr. DeMille off at the apartment house, then took Henry and Raymond Garfield back to the downtown production office, where I learned that we would be traveling to Sinai the next morning to begin filming by the Red Sea.

At precisely four o'clock, I drove over to the lot where I'd picked the Coupe de Ville up that morning. I knew the guard on duty was a wastrel named Fawzi, who had been a customer of my uncle's back room emporium in the old days; he was often drunk and distracted by pornography on the job. I also knew he wouldn't notice when I took the logbook and changed the license plate number on my earlier entry, so it would appear that I'd been driving a Chrysler Windsor. Then I left the Coupe de Ville at the back of the lot, got the keys for a red Fleetwood 75, and used it to pick up a copy of *The Ten Commandments*

shooting script from the studio's production office and bring it over
to the government's censorship office a mile and a half away. It was a
massive document, well over three hundred pages at that point. But
as I riffled through its pages, I could not help noticing that we had
already broken two of the most important commandments that day
and it wasn't even dinnertime.

I returned to the apartment house and waited for DeMille to get
dressed for the welcome event that night on the rooftop of the Semiramis Hotel.

Despite the disturbances in the streets, all of Cairo society turned
out. There were Saudi princes in thobes and headdresses and European princesses in the latest *Harper's Bazaar* haute couture. Army officers showed up without their spouses so they could be free to dance
with whomever they chose. Fresh-faced State Department officials in
Brooks Brothers blazers and rep ties—replacing the ones who'd just
left for Vietnam—stood around, sipping cocktails and ignoring the
advice of the seasoned Arabists trying to explain what they would
need to know here. Actresses and former mistresses of the king flirted
with ambassadors and Texas oilmen on the smorgasbord lines while
an orchestra of our country's finest musicians played "That's Amore!"
and "Three Coins in the Fountain" and Miss Fatima, the famous belly
dancer, spun between the smoldering torches and offered her undu-
lating charms to all.

But for me, there was only one star on the horizon, and she out-
shone all the others. Mona came up to me in a simple black cocktail
dress and pearls, with her yellow hair swept back from her forehead
and gathered in a bun.

At that instant, I was able to put aside my worries, and my joy sang
with the tune the orchestra was beginning at that moment: "See the
pyramids along the Nile / Watch the sun rise on a tropic isle . . ."

She took my hand and pressed her red lips to my cheek. I swear to you, Alex, that I could have died right then and there on that rooftop overlooking the Nile and gone to the afterlife a very happy man.

This was all I had ever fantasized about when I'd stood before my bedroom mirror, practicing the suave dance steps I'd seen in *Royal Wedding* and *An American in Paris* to impress her with my grace. And then we might find a quiet place, where I could finally take her in my arms. In the movies, the screen would fade to black then. But my body ached with hunger for hers and my heart raced like a stallion's as I smelled her perfumed skin, her hair, and pictured all the things that could not be shown then.

"Oh my God, Ali." She brought me back to the present with her French-accented Arabic. "You can't believe how many celebrities are here. Already I've seen Umm Kulthum, Faten Hamama, Shoukry Sarhan, and Laila Mourad—*oh, she's beautiful. . . .*"

I barely heard her as I raised my hand to my cheek in a daze. Although I had known her for several years since the university and had enjoyed passing flirtations in the meantime (well, maybe occasionally more than that, but a grandson only needs to know so much), I was still unsure how to change myself from a friend to a proper subject of a woman's passion.

"And look, there's Michel Shalhoub," Mona said.

She was pointing to the handsome young actor who would soon change his name to Omar Sharif and become an international star. But I froze as I saw he was talking to Henry by the smorgasbord table. I had claimed to have worked closely with Mr. Shalhoub on my résumé, believing the Americans would not bother to check the credit.

"Thank you, Ali." Mona gripped my hand.

"For what?"

"I know you helped me get this job."

"I'm sure you would have found a way to get one on your own."

In fact, I had implored one of my father's contacts in the film industry to interview her for a job assisting the unit publicist, because it would give me more time with her. She succeeded in getting the assignment, thanks to Allah, and perhaps the daringly bare-shouldered photograph she had included with her résumé.

Her father, Nabil, came over in a white dinner jacket, with a champagne glass in hand. "Ah, Ali, *mon ami!*" He kissed me on both cheeks, thinking himself suave. *"Comment allez-vous?"*

I drew back, as a little bit of the champagne spilled on me. I liked Nabil well enough; he was a charming boulevardier with an eye for good clothes and fine jewelry like the Cartier watch he had given his daughter. But he'd been a close associate of the king and was therefore regarded with suspicion by the minions of Naguib. Perhaps he'd come to the party hoping that the shift in power would allow him to find favor again.

"Prenez soin de mon trésor très précieux." His eyes danced from me to his daughter, as he told me to take care of his precious treasure. Then he pulled me closer and whispered in English. "She is a little, how the Americans say, 'a little out of your league,' eh?"

Before I could respond, Mona began patting my arm frantically. "Oh. I almost forgot why I came over."

"It wasn't just to see me?" I affected a pout.

"No, we may have a problem."

"What's the matter?" I asked.

"Professor Farid is here."

As awkward as her father's presence was, the appearance of my former teacher was even more destabilizing. He had not only been closely aligned with the Naguib faction during the revolution, he was known to be an outspoken member of the Ikhwan. There was no telling what he would do or say at an event like this.

"Why is he here?" I asked.

"He just showed up for Mr. DeMille's press conference," Mona said. "We have to make sure he doesn't say anything to upset anyone. . . ."

I looked around frantically until a photographer's flashbulb went off in my eyes and everything went white. As soon as my vision faded back in, I followed Mona across the dance floor to a red-carpeted area, where Mr. DeMille stood before a microphone and a lectern, fielding questions from a gathering of international reporters and photographers in folding chairs.

"Yes, Moses will have more than one love interest in our film," he was telling an Italian woman reporter in a formfitting Chanel outfit. "But remember, Moses was not always an old man. . . ."

The group laughed at the director's sly grin, and I saw Professor Farid standing in the back, with a pen gripped between his fingers like it was a dart he was about to throw.

Although he had been fired from the university several months before and had since become a leader in the intellectual vanguard of the Muslim Brotherhood, my professor still dressed like a Western academician in a tweed jacket with a white shirt and a small bow tie. His mustache was severely trimmed and his hair was severely parted as if he used a stiletto instead of a comb. The downward tilt of the pince-nez perched on his nose emphasized the melancholy droop of his features, as if the world left him in a perpetual state of disappointment.

"Yes, sir." Mr. DeMille peered back at him. "And whom do I have the pleasure of addressing?"

"Professor Ibrahim Farid." His high, stinging voice cut through the frivolous background conversation and the orchestra's rendering of "Satin Doll." "But I am here tonight as the cultural editor of the *Ikhwan al Muslimin* newspaper. . . ."

Bulbs ceased popping, and the reporters looked around at one another, as if they all recognized the name. Mr. DeMille certainly did. His hands came to rest on either side of the lectern for support

"Is yours a religious publication, sir?" he asked.

"Indeed," my professor said in a tone of pedagogic scolding that made it clear he would gladly correct anyone's grammar in English as well as Arabic. "Our periodical covers both spiritual and political issues."

"As will our film, I hope," said Mr. DeMille.

"Quite." The professor cleared his throat and gave me a passing glance that sent a ripple of terror through my bowels. "Mr. DeMille, did I understand you to say that you are grateful for the cooperation of our authorities . . . ?"

"Yes, sir. I had the privilege of meeting your new prime minister, Mr. Nasser, today."

"I see." The professor nodded. "And can you tell us what you discussed?"

The orchestra had ceased playing and the guests let their conversations trail off at the sound of this amplified exchange.

"Obviously, some matters are meant to remain private," Mr. DeMille said. "And I don't want to comment on the state of your country's politics. But I think we all want what's best for Egypt and look forward to maintaining our mutual cooperation—"

"Begging your pardon, Mr. DeMille, but what is your true reason for coming here?" the professor asked, veering sharply.

"Forgive me?" Mr. DeMille cupped a hand behind his ear.

"Why retell this far-fetched story now?" Professor Farid asked. "Your timing is highly suspect, to say the least."

"How so?"

"This *Ten Commandments* movie of yours is all too convenient right now. Especially so soon after territory was stolen from us in our war with Israel, in which so many of your Jewish colleagues in the movie industry supported our enemy. Is it mere coincidence you come here now to join forces with our new apostate government to make a film that legitimizes this theft—"

"We're here to celebrate the birth of human freedom," Mr. DeMille said.

"But whose freedom?" the professor challenged him. "Surely not the Egyptian people's. These lies are used to subjugate us and deny *our* freedom. You're not even using any of our major actors in your film."

The unit publicist, Mr. Condon, came up to Mona and started whispering furiously in her ear. She turned to me and clutched my arm. "You were his favorite," she said quietly. "Get him to stop."

There was no reason to believe he would listen to me. But this was a plea from my most cherished. I crept toward my teacher like a dog-catcher getting ready to seize an overexcited dachshund. He halted me in my tracks with his unblinking glare. This man was more than my mentor and sponsor, my teacher, my *ostazi*. He had been, at times, like a second father. He had seen some promise in me, believed I had talent when few others did.

But I was working for Cecil B. DeMille now. He was the one who could protect me if, as Nasser said, there was a public trial for the imam's death and someone needed to be left to the scorpions. Just as important, Mr. DeMille could open the golden doorway onto the beautiful American life I dreamed of having with my one and only.

"But, *professor*," I said, "what you refer to as a myth is actually one of the central aspects of our own Holy Koran. You can open it randomly and find Moses within a few pages. His story is our story as well. You cannot accept one without the other. I've heard you say so yourself."

My teacher slowly lowered his eyes, as if he were just noticing a knife that had been stuck into his gut.

"Why don't we wait to see the finished film before we pass judgment?" I asked.

Professor Farid shook his head, more in sorrow than anger. "Evidently Mr. DeMille is gifted not just at creating movie spectacles but at molding impressionable young minds."

"Excuse me, sir," said Mr. DeMille. "Is there another question?"

The professor stared at me and shook his head. "No, Mr. DeMille. There is no other question at all."

The director smiled and adjusted his cummerbund, like a sheriff in one of his Westerns hitching up his gun belt after a shoot-out.

"That's enough scholarly debate for one evening," he intoned into the microphone. "Everyone eat, drink, and be merry. Tomorrow we set out for the desert."

Henry cued the orchestra to begin playing again, guests flooded onto the dance floor, and the professor stalked off.

Mona shooed me with her hands to tell me to go after him and make sure he didn't cause more problems. I caught up to him by the smorgasbord.

"Professor Farid." I was breathless as he filled his plate with carrots and hummus. "I'm surprised to see you here."

"Sadly, I can't say the same for you, Ali *bey*." His pince-nez slid down his nose a little. "Instead of embarrassing me, you have embarrassed yourself. There are a lot of hadiths about betrayal, but all I can think of right now is, 'How sharper than a serpent's tooth it is to have a thankless child.'"

How typical it was for him to remind me of my debt with a quote from *King Lear,* one of the works of Western literature he'd taught me to love. But now he had changed, and so had I. After the revolution, the State Department had sponsored him to spend a year abroad, as a visiting professor at Indiana University, in the hope that he would bring notions of democracy back to our homeland. Instead, there were rumors of drinking, an unrequited love interest, and a public scene he made at a showing of *Gentlemen Prefer Blondes*. On returning from America, he declared the West in a state of *jahiliyya*, a moral and spiritual disaster zone, full of sickness and hypocrisy, which had to be opposed vigorously on all fronts. His stridency had cost him his job at the university, and now I was ashamed that I hadn't done more to stay in touch.

"I know your parents were hotel workers, Ali Hassan, but this is going too far with the business of hospitality. Can't you see that Cecil B. DeMille is just the latest in the long line of occupiers?"

"No, professor, he's a great artist."

"If you believe that, then I've failed you as a teacher of cultural discernment as well as moral judgment. He's a sentimental *vulgarian*, Ali. You should read the reprehensible collection of lies in this script."

"How did you see it?"

"At the government censorship office, before I got fired. I was working there to make up for my lost salary at the university. But today, they purged me with all the other Naguib allies."

"I'm sorry, professor. I hadn't heard—"

"This film you're supporting is going to be an abomination, Ali Hassan." He poked me in the chest with his unusually long forefinger. "They mean to show a prophet cavorting with wanton women. They propose to create miracles on a screen that only God could create in life. Worst of all, they're going to use this medium as a weapon to make Egyptians look like villains in the eyes of the world at a time when we need to rescue the revolution from this infidel, Nasser."

"Well, we don't know that for sure, do we?"

"I believe I can say it with some certainty." He dropped his voice. "Did you hear what happened to Sheikh Sirgani today?"

"No."

"He was run down in the street by a bunch of Westerners. . . ."

For a few seconds, his voice faded in my ears, and all I could hear was the inanities of the other guests and the senseless swelling of the orchestra playing popular dance songs.

"We're trying to find out more," the professor was saying as I tuned back in. "But Nasser's people are rounding up witnesses and threatening them into silence. It's plain that he's trying to sell us out to the Americans. Who are just as bad as the Romans, the French, Turks, the English, or any of the others before them. I tell you, we have to fight them and resist them at every turn. If you have the courage, walk out with me."

"I can't," I said, struggling to get back my bearings.

"Why not?"

"I'm supposed to accompany Mr. DeMille out to Sinai tomorrow."

"Oh, so now you're *his chauffeur*?" He probed under his lenses and rubbed his eyes with his fingertips. "I must say, I expected more from you, Ali *bey*." I winced at the mocking honorific. "You had so much promise as a student."

He turned on his heel and walked away.

I looked after him, worrying that I might have made the wrong choice. Nasser's grip on power seemed tenuous. If Naguib retook the palace with the help of the Brotherhood, there would be no defending myself in court. My head could wind up on an actual chopping block, as if we were across the Gulf of Aqaba, in Saudi Arabia, where justice was dispensed with the blade. I started to run after him to explain myself, but Miss Fatima blocked me with her tangerine scarves and the winking zircon in her navel. When she moved, the professor was gone. Instead, I found myself gaping at what Mona was doing.

To my horror, the mistress of my desires was dancing with another man. Her fair calves and ankles were bared as her dress twirled and lifted. Her head was resting against the side of his shoulder and the balance of the universe was imperiled by the way she swayed her hips.

When they swung around, I recognized that it was the actor Charlton Heston, who would be playing Moses. I had seen the early publicity stills of him in costume, with his long white beard and flowing hair, strikingly like Michelangelo's sculpture of the prophet of Sinai. But here he looked young, tawny, and virile, with a corona of reddish-brown hair and a touch of a hunter's cruelty in his steely white smile.

I went up to Mona and tapped her on the shoulder.

"Ali, what's the matter?" She turned around as if I'd woken her from a blissful trance.

"I thought you were working."

"The press conference is over. Have you met Charlton Heston?"

The actor widened his grin and gave me a hand grip that would buckle the knees of an ox. "How're you doing there, buddy? Call me Chuck."

Chuck. My fear was instantly subsumed by jealousy.

"No, I haven't," I said. "Mona, I need to talk to you."

"Why? What's the matter?"

My eyes scanned the guests, looking for an excuse to pull her away. Nabil was at the bar with a fresh flute of champagne, having an animated discussion with General Amer, who must have arrived during the press conference.

"Your father may be in trouble," I blurted out. "I think he needs your help."

Of course, at just that moment, her father said something that caused the general to give a wan smile and shake Nabil's hand.

"He seems fine now." She gave me a searching look. "Are you sure that's why you came over?"

"Yes, *Alhamdulillah.*" I touched my hands to my heart. "Thank God that it's been sorted out."

"Chuck was suggesting that I join all of you on your trip to Sinai tomorrow," she said.

"That's right." The actor grinned. "I was hoping you could show me the sights and high points of local interest." He looked down at her, his high sunburned forehead gleaming with what I took to be lust.

"But you already have a job in publicity," I pointed out. "They need you here."

"No, they don't. Mr. DeMille's going to be in Sinai. Nothing's going to happen until he gets back."

I noticed how her hand lingered on the interloper's arm, far longer than it had rested on my hand earlier.

"Besides, there hasn't been that much for me to do so far," she said. "Chuck was saying I could come and be his assistant when he needed one, or maybe help Raymond with his documentary."

Now it was "Raymond" too? All this first-name familiarity with foreigners was disconcerting to me. Especially when I saw this Raymond by the bandstand, filming the party with a small handheld camera. He stared back at me as he rewound. Already there was too much of the wrong kind of knowledge between us.

"You always said you wanted me to learn more about filmmaking," Mona reminded me.

Of course, I was being unreasonably possessive. *Yes*, she was not yet what Americans would call "my sweetheart." But in my soul, I was already betrothed to her. Our mutual love of movies had bridged the gap in our social stations, and I truly believed that our eternal union was as ordained by the stars as the lapping of the oceans on the shores.

But the longer her hand stayed on Chuck's arm, the more certain I became that I would have to keep my eye on her if she went to Sinai with us.

"I could talk to Mr. DeMille, if you're uncomfortable about it," Chuck said.

"It's all right, I'll speak to him." I forced a smile. "I think he trusts me, at this point."

I noticed at that moment that Mr. DeMille and Henry were watching me carefully from a breezeway.

"Good, then it's settled." She finally took her hand back. "Bring extra clothes," she said. "The desert gets cold at night."

I tried to argue again, but my voice was lost in the swell of the orchestra playing a familiar tune and the sound of her father drunkenly commandeering the microphone.

"'Mona Lisa, Mona Lisa, men have named you,'" he crooned as she tried to hide behind me. "'You're so like the lady with the mystic smile.'"

Such was the way Allah interfered with the affairs of men and women that night. With smoking torches on the roof, the Nile rolling on silently beneath us, and a father singing a song made famous by Mr. Nat King Cole in loving tribute to his daughter.

August 28, 2014
To: GrandpaAli71@aol.com
From: Asur@protonmail.com

Gedo,
I must write back immediately, even though it is the middle of the night where I am.

Surely you now know that you were on the wrong side of history. Ibrahim Farid was right about these Americans. Since I read the last chapter, I looked up some of his writing online. He was a great visionary, well ahead of his time, and a martyr, blessings be upon his name. I cannot believe you knew this man. And I cannot believe you didn't learn more from his example. Did no one else in Egypt, besides the Ikhwan, recognize how we were being used? Welcoming these invaders on bended knee, when it sounds like there was not a single

Egyptian actor in the main cast? These days that would not go—no way, no how. Did you not know the words "inclusion" and "diversity"?

Maybe I'm being too harsh. You are my grandfather and you were only a few years older than I am now. You didn't have the advantages of video games and social media to educate you about how the world works.

Yours in mercy and compassion,
Abu Suror

P.S. I cut you some slack because of this girl you liked. I've been pretty confused by them myself back in the States. But the brothers who are helping me on my journey tell me we're going to get that straightened out and find me a pious wife who will do what she's supposed to.

August 29, 2014
To: Asur@protonmail.com
From: GrandpaAli71@aol.com

Alex,
I notice you are making more and more religious references. I wonder if you're becoming a zealot yourself, and my story is sending you the exact opposite message than I intended. And I wonder who are these brothers that you mention.

With love and misgivings,
Your grandfather

5

It was after ten o'clock when I arrived back at the house I shared with my father. Some of his friends were still on the porches of their own homes, smoking hookahs and playing backgammon. I waved as I passed them, then removed my shoes by the thatched welcome mat. The door was unlocked, as always, and his golf clubs were by the papyrus plant just inside the entrance. Right above them was a plate with the *"Ahlan wa Sahlan"* greeting in calligraphy and an autographed photo of the American golfer Byron Nelson swinging a nine iron with the pyramids in the background. My father claimed he'd been Nelson's caddy that day, but he was nowhere to be seen in the picture.

Somehow, the rooms seemed smaller, instead of larger, with my mother and my sisters gone. Or maybe it was simply that my father and I were less skilled at folding ourselves neatly into corners. The front room was a mixture of old family furniture and pieces that my parents had "liberated" from the hotel over the years. They wouldn't have considered it stealing; they were simply encouraging management to replace and upgrade old items. So now the towels in our humble home were terry cloth ones my mother had collected from the maids' pantry. There were lampshades, curtains, and tablecloths, also from the hotel, which she had taken the trouble to dye in tea, so they wouldn't yellow with age. How typical of her to anticipate how the world would look after she departed from it.

My father was by the coal-black stove, in his Lacoste polo shirt and green pants, his back bent from a hard day's labor carrying guests' clubs. He was cooking his customary late meal of *kushari*. I could smell a history of our country in the mingled odors of rice, onions, lentils, and macaroni overladen with garlic vinegar and tomato sauce.

"How was your first day, my son?"

"Fine." I fumbled with the knot of my tie. "Uneventful."

"Was there a lot of traffic in town?" he asked. "Some of my customers were complaining."

"You didn't hear the rumor that Mohammed Naguib was put under house arrest?"

"You know how I am, *habibi*." He briefly looked back over his shoulder from stirring the sizzling onions. "I don't pay attention to politics. When I'm out on the fairway, I put my head down and don't think about anything except the game. By the way, did you have a chance to ask Mr. DeMille if he's interested in a tee time?"

"No, Father. I'm not even sure he *plays* golf."

"He won't find a better course in all of Egypt. . . ."

I reached into my pockets to empty them and found I still had Sheikh Sirgani's broken glasses. I looked around for the wastebasket, thinking the time had come to stop torturing myself and finally throw them away. But the basket was overflowing with papers obscuring an empty bottle of Johnny Whittaker Red, a cheap local imitation of the whiskey my father's customers drank.

"Please, *baba*," I said. "He has much more important things on his mind."

"You seem like you have something on *your* mind, my son. What's the matter?"

"Nothing," I twitched like a dog with fleas. "I'm sorry, Daddy. I've just been tense, trying not to make mistakes. Mr. DeMille is a very demanding employer."

I stretched and arched my back until my spine cracked. My hands ached from how tightly I'd been gripping the wheel. Even as I stood still, my balance was questionable, as if my body was only now catching up to the fact that we'd been on the verge of overturning.

"Can I tell you a joke to make you smile?" my father asked.

"Can I stop you?"

In truth, I loved my father's jokes, and pretending to be annoyed by them was a routine with us.

"It's very funny. I promise." He rubbed his hands together. "If you like it, you can tell it to Mr. DeMille."

"I'm not sure he appreciates Egyptian humor. . . ."

My father plunged ahead, as sure of his audience as Kish Kish Bey. "A salesman drives downtown, trying to make a deal to save his dying business. But everywhere he looks, there's nowhere to park his car."

I heard a car pull up outside and saw a pair of headlights swing through our front windows.

"So now it's getting later and later, and this businessman becomes afraid he's going to miss his meeting and lose everything," my father continued. "Even though he's never been religious, he starts to pray. He says, 'O Allah, please help me to find parking! If you do, I'll dedicate the rest of my life to you. I'll pray five times a day. I'll send all four of my sons to the Al-Azhar, I'll never commit another indecent act.'"

"I thought you said this joke was 'very short.'" I mimed a yawn as I heard the car door slam and men talking right outside our door.

"Just then, a car pulls out in front of him, leaving an empty space to park in." Daddy clapped his hands and grinned. "And then the businessman looks up and says, 'Never mind, God, I found a spot.'"

A knock on the door interrupted us. My father gave me an odd look. It was too late for visitors. I went over to open the door. My cousin Sherif burst in and threw his arms around me.

"*Assalaam alaikum*, my brother." He pressed his bearded chin to the side of my neck, crushed me in his embrace, and then kissed my forehead with a loud smack. "Too long, too long."

It *had* been at least two weeks since we had seen each other. He was often away these days in Aswan, working with government engineering crews evaluating the High Dam project. When he was in town, he was occupied with a new wife and a baby boy in the neighborhood called Shoubra. I was glad to see him, but uneasy. Because there's something perhaps I should have mentioned when I was describing the meeting at Nasser's office: Sherif was an acolyte of Professor Farid's too, and a member of the Muslim Brothers' labor division.

"How are you, my cousin?" I asked. "What are you doing here?"

"I am well, *Alhamdulillah*." He patted my cheek and limped over to kiss my father as well. "But things in general are not good. You must know that already."

I closed my hand around the glasses still in my pocket. "What are you talking about?" I asked.

"We're in a state of total *jahiliyya*," he said. "You heard about Mohammed Naguib, didn't you?"

"Yes, I just did." I nodded gravely. "It's hard to keep up with all the changes, isn't it?"

"Yes, as God is my witness, I've been saying for months that son of a mongrel whore Nasser couldn't be trusted," my cousin said.

My father rolled his eyes and went back to his cooking. His patience for my cousin was almost as limited as his patience for politics. He could not understand how his own brother Hamid, reputedly the funniest man in our village, could have produced an offspring who was so fiery and sincere that he didn't even realize when he was being funny himself.

"It's a calamity." Sherif flopped down on the old Edwardian-era couch that our fathers had taken from one of the hotel's sitting rooms and began pulling on the beard that somehow made him more look like a stained glass Jesus than the devout Muslim he really was. "They're already purging Naguib loyalists and members of the Ikhwan from every level of the government. They've forgotten who supported them and made this revolution possible."

I loved and envied my cousin. And, to be honest, I had always been a bit afraid of him. His eyes had a kindly, soulful quality that drew people to him and made it look as if he was always on the verge of saying something sweet or generous. But those were mere appearances that he had inherited from his parents. Sherif himself wasn't really like that. His true gifts were courage and commitment. And the longer I live, the more I realize that there are very few real believers in the world, but they intimidate everyone else.

My cousin was one of those rare people who make the leap of faith every day and then look back across the gap to ask the rest of us, "Why can't you follow?" Perhaps Moses, if he existed, was such a man. In his way, maybe Mr. DeMille was as well. When people like this don't ascend to mountaintops or commandeer movie cameras, they often end up on pulpits or in madhouses. But you can never doubt their authenticity. Once they are in your lives, you can never be entirely free of their influence.

From the time I was young, I had measured everything about myself against my cousin. And more often than I liked to admit, I found myself wanting. Sherif was among the first to join the uprising on that July afternoon known as Black Saturday. He had fought against the king's soldiers in the streets as bravely and honorably as he had fought with the Muslim Brotherhood's youth brigade in the War of 1948, when an Israeli soldier's bullet shattered his left leg. He was a true rebel and a revolutionary. And at that moment, I was a former movie critic who'd accidentally hit a holy man with a Cadillac and then drove away in a puff of tailpipe exhaust.

"Don't you think things will calm down?" I asked.

"Not if I have anything to say about it." My cousin propped up his injured leg on a puffy ottoman. "We should be out in the streets every minute of every day, protesting."

"Except that some of us have jobs," my father mumbled.

Sherif looked at my father and sighed as if he felt sorry for him. Then he stared at me and began pulling harder on his beard, hand over hand, like a man climbing a rope.

"I didn't even tell you the worst of it yet," Sherif said. "They're refusing to let us hold a martyr's funeral for Sheikh Sirgani."

"The imam?" My father glanced over his shoulder. "He died?"

"Run down in the street by a bunch of foreigners." Sherif closed his fist around his beard. "He left a young wife and six children behind. I tell you, he was the finest of men. Not just a scholar but a near saint. He opened schools and took food off his family's table to feed the poor. And they ran him over like a dog. In a red car like one of the king's fifty, no less. Ali, have you heard anything about that?"

"No, of course not," I said, a bit too emphatically. "I mean, I saw the professor tonight and he told me about the accident, but I haven't heard any other details."

"Who said it was an 'accident'?" Sherif stopped pulling on his facial hair.

"Well, the professor made it sound that way."

"Really?" Sherif began stroking his beard more thoughtfully. "He didn't speak about it that way to me."

I smelled my father's tomato sauce starting to get scorched, a sweet odor turning pungent that reminded me of the burning odor I'd smelled in the streets that afternoon.

"I must have just misunderstood." I shrugged. "But it's hard to believe anyone would do such a terrible thing deliberately."

"Why is it so hard to believe?" Sherif raised his chin. "These *khawagat* have treated us like dogs for generations. What's a learned man like the imam to them? Someone needs to teach them a lesson."

The more he spoke, the more I found myself reliving the sensation of being halfway off the ground with my wheels spinning.

"Sherif, I need to ask you something." My father took his pot off the flame. "You said they're purging all the Naguib loyalists and Ikhwan from their government jobs. But what's going to happen to you?"

"They already fired me."

My father and I exchanged a look. We both knew my cousin was not a man who did well with time on his hands. In his fallow periods, he was no stranger to depression and what we now call substance abuse issues. I suspected that he drank in secret, despite his professed religious principles. He certainly smoked hashish, but it did not make him calm or peaceful as it did for most people. But what could we do? Family is a blessing and a curse, a comfort at the best of times, and a trap at the worst of them. You can try to get away, but you can never really escape.

"Don't worry," Sherif said. "God will provide for me. In fact, he already has."

"How is that?" My father laid the steaming pot on the table, red sauce dribbling down the side.

"I already have another job," Sherif said. "Thanks to Allah and Ali."

"What did *I* have to do with it?" My voice broke.

Sherif came over and put an arm around my shoulders. "I went by the film production office, right after you left this afternoon." He smiled and tightened his hold on me. "They're hiring by the hundreds to get everything ready, especially anyone with experience in construction. I told them you'd vouch for me, so they wouldn't have to call my references. It worked out perfectly. I'll be going to Sinai with you."

September 2, 2014
To: GrandpaAli71@aol.com
From: Asur@protonmail.com

Gedo,

Finally I know why the blood of martyrs runs hot in my veins. Finally I understand why I'm stirred to the call of battle. Why did no one tell me before of this heroic relative, Sherif? High school would have been so much easier. I would have walked through the hall with my head held high, instead of getting elbowed aside by the jocks and ignored by the prettiest girls. I could have talked back to the teachers who distorted our history and ignored our achievements. I could have felt some pride about where I come from.

Now it makes sense, this journey I'm on. Getting ready to fight in a greater battle. I don't know if you will ever understand this. But if your cousin Sherif is anything like you say, I think he would take my side. In fact, if he's still alive, please ask him to contact me.

In the meantime, I want to ask you about something and I don't want you to tell Mom or Dad that I mentioned this. I was wondering if you could send me some money. It's really important to me to get where I need to be asap. If you can't do it, I guess I'll understand.

Forgive me if this puts you in a bad spot, but ask your cousin if he's still around. I think he would get it.

Yours in faith,
Abu Suror

September 3, 2014
To: Asur@protonmail.com
From: GrandpaAli71@aol.com

Alex,
I'm afraid that I can't do what you ask, sending you money without telling your parents. That does not seem right. I am sorry if this is not what you hoped for. All I can offer you right now is my story.

Love,
Grandpa

6

Our caravan left before dawn the next day, crossing over the Suez Canal Zone as the sun rose. The oil globes, the cargo ships, the control stations, the rows of half-empty British Army barracks, and the drooping Union Jack on its flagpole receded behind us. The English had finally agreed to leave, and the fingerprints of the old empire were fading as we followed parts of the haphazard road they'd carved out into the Sinai Desert during the last great war.

The winds picked up as our motorcade headed inland along the twisting mountain ridges and then south toward the coastline. I was trying to drive a canvas-covered British Army Land Rover with proper confidence, even though I'd never been behind the wheel of such a vehicle before. A vague brownish haze filled the air, only blurring the landscape slightly at first. But by nine a.m. as the gusts grew stronger, it began to look like a buzz saw was cutting through the peninsula, throwing up such spumes of sand that the cars ahead of us disappeared for seconds and then minutes at a time. Whenever the frenzy subsided and the air cleared, the cliffs and hills around us looked like piles of sawdust. Every half hour or so, all the vehicles would stop and a man wearing a dust mask would climb out of a truck in front of us, find a large boulder, and splash white paint all over it, to mark the trail so we might eventually find our way back.

But as I looked around at rising dust and the black exhaust smoke in my side mirrors, all I could think about was what was coming up behind me. By now, news of Naguib's ouster and the sheikh's death were spreading across the country.

I was glad to be getting out of Cairo. But I was also aware that there were four military police officers in a covered jeep directly ahead of us, ostensibly assigned by Nasser to help with our security. And somewhere behind them, Sherif was riding in one of the crew trucks.

I'd been up most of the night, picking over the conversation we'd had in my father's kitchen. I was not completely naïve about my cousin. I knew that his using my name to get a job on the film would not be a good thing for me. But I was hemmed in, since he'd already been hired without anyone asking me. I just had to hope that he didn't indulge his habit of getting into petty fights or, worse, make an issue of his involvement with the anti-Nasser resistance.

"You're doing a fine job, Mr. Hassan." Cecil B. DeMille said from the back seat. "Just stay the course."

"Thank you, sir."

I worked the gear shift and throttle as I tried to stay on what passed for a road in Sinai. The Land Rover rattled and shook as we went over gravel and uneven ground. "Who said it was an 'accident'?" I heard Sherif's question again and pictured the way he stopped pulling on his beard as he asked it.

Could he know?

The possibility was too terrible for me to contemplate. But I found myself making excuses anyway. We'd been under attack from all sides. I had only been following orders when I'd stepped on the gas. The fact was that it *had* been a matter of pure survival to get out of there. But it was also a fact that I'd left a widow without her husband, and six children without their father. As much as I struggled to steady the wheel the wind kept pushing the Land Rover toward the edge of the road, where a steep escarpment appeared.

In our religion, Alex, there is a story that two recording angels will come to your graveside on the day of your death: Munkar and Nakir. Before you are laid to your rest, they ask you a series of questions to determine your final destination. One is "Who is your Lord?" Another is "What is your religion?" And the last is "Who is the one true messenger?" If you answer correctly, you will eventually pass into Paradise, *aljana,* with its green fields and waterfalls. If you don't, you will be squeezed until your ribs interlock and your insides ooze out through the gaps, until the Final Day when you are cast into hell, where your body will burn for eternity.

I pictured the recording angels seated right behind me as we rumbled along.

In reality, it was Henry Wilcoxon and "Chuck" Heston squeezed between Mr. DeMille and Mona, the four of them somehow not throwing up as we swerved and skidded.

Raymond was beside me in the front, hat brim tipped back as he laconically wound and unwound the homely little combat camera that he called an Eyemo, occasionally pointing its three lenses out the window to film the rippling, inconstant landscape.

"Just don't run into anything," he said in that dry martini way that was starting to drive me to distraction.

"I know what I'm doing," I replied.

I still did not like or trust him, even though we were now bound together by a secret. And I could not help but notice that he was looking at Mona in his mirror while no longer wearing the wedding band he'd had on when he was punching the man through the window.

The jeep stopped short before us and I had to hit my brakes to avoid a multicar pileup. My springs yelped, my passengers were tossed, and sand sprayed over our windshield as I turned into the skid, just barely avoiding a head-on collision.

"Easy there," Mr. DeMille said. "I know you're a skillful driver, Mr.

Hassan, but if we get in another accident, there won't be *any* commandments."

"'Another' accident?" Mona asked.

"Figure of speech." He deflected her with a showman's grin.

I tapped on the brake as we began to skid into a long shallow ditch. The sand made a hissing sound as I spun my tires, trying to back out, the heat inside the vehicle beginning to rise.

"Christ, how much farther?" Chuck said, perspiring in his open-collared khaki shirt.

"I'm afraid it will be several hours, at least," I said. "It's not how far but how hard the road is ahead of us."

"And to think I could be doing Shakespeare on Broadway." Chuck gritted his teeth.

"Could you?" Raymond asked.

"Or with my hunting gun, out in the Michigan woods," Chuck replied with a bolt-action snap.

"Oh, now, boys," said Mona.

"I'm just kidding." Chuck patted her knee. "But seriously, driver—I'm sorry, I've forgotten your name—could you ease up on the brake pedal? I'd like to get there this century."

"I'm doing my best, *sir*." I watched the red needles on my gauges shake.

I considered running away. Just dropping my honored guests off at the base of Moses's mountain and then slipping away like a thief in the night. I imagined myself driving across the desert until dawn and taking my refuge among the Bedouins. Far beyond the reach of Nasser, the Muslim Brotherhood, and anyone seeking vengeance. The only difficulty was how to get all the way through the borders of Israel on a tank of gas to reach Jordan or Saudi Arabia, when I had absolutely no money or contacts anywhere else in the world to help me.

In my rearview mirror, I saw Mona turn the beam of her attention onto Chuck's shining face like a klieg light. I told myself that I couldn't run away and let him take advantage of her. Nor could I abandon my father, when he'd lost almost everything else that was dear to him.

"Mr. Hassan, I have a question," Mr. DeMille said suddenly. "Who on earth was that rude bastard at the press conference last night? That tweedy son of a bitch who was giving me a hard time."

"Oh, that was Professor Farid." Mona tagged me with a touch on the shoulder. "He was a teacher at the university. Ali was his pet student."

"*Was* he, now?" Mr. DeMille glanced out the window at the sand seething around us.

"Oh, I don't know if I would say I was his '*pet*.'" I tried to shoot her a warning look not to get me in even more trouble.

"That's why I asked Ali to intervene at the press conference," Mona said. "I knew the professor wouldn't listen to anyone else."

"Who is he, anyway?" Raymond craned his neck to look back at her.

"He's a famous academic and cultural critic," she said. "He's angry because he just lost his job at the government censorship office—"

"Sounds like a righteous pain in the neck." Chuck grimaced in my rearview mirror.

"And he's one of these Muslim Brothers?" Mr. DeMille raised his eyebrows.

A clot of sand hit our windshield like a fist. Mona and I started answering simultaneously.

"He wasn't so doctrinaire when he was my instructor," I hastened to explain.

"He never liked me," Mona interjected tartly. "Because I'm a woman. And because my family are Christians."

"But I saw you were still talking to him after the press conference, Mr. Hassan," Mr. DeMille said with a lingering edge of suspicion.

"Ali used to write unsigned movie reviews for him at the newspaper," Mona said, not very helpfully. "They were usually very perceptive."

"I see." Mr. DeMille just sat there, breathing, for a long time. "Then do I understand, Mr. Hassan, that you were the movie critic for the Muslim Brothers' newspaper?"

"Well, only in a manner of speaking, sir."

"And were you also a member of this organization?"

"Never officially, sir." I checked the dial to make sure the engine wasn't overheating. "Certainly not now."

Mr. DeMille rolled his lips in and out of his mouth. "I don't recall seeing that on your résumé. Was it there?"

Our Land Rover was trembling in the face of the oncoming khamsin wind.

"I didn't think it was relevant, Mr. DeMille."

"Hmm." He looked out the window again. "Things can change in a hurry, can't they?"

"Yes, sir."

The sandstorm was upon us. Day was turning into night. The vehicles before us were barely visible. I knew that I had lost a measure of Mr. DeMille's trust, and to survive I needed to get it back.

"And do you still agree with the aims of this Muslim Brothers organization?" Mr. DeMille asked. "And with what your professor said last night?"

"I would not be working for you, if I did, Mr. DeMille."

"Hey, what's going on here?" Chuck asked irritably. "Is this something I need to know about?"

"That remains to be seen," Mr. DeMille said.

The weather inside and outside the vehicle was deteriorating rapidly. My right front wheel struck a stone, causing the chassis to shudder and reminding me of what had happened at the market. I knew I had to do more to stay on the road.

"Mr. DeMille," I said as calmly as I could. "You heard me tell the professor to wait until he saw the movie before he passed judgment. That was not easy for me to say publicly to such a respected man."

"Perhaps not," he allowed. "But I like to make sure I have the complete loyalty of my crew. Especially when we're entering into difficult circumstances."

"Mr. DeMille, having a movie reviewer as a driver is not quite the same as having a traitor among us," Raymond said, defending me unexpectedly.

"Spoken like a critics' darling," Mr. DeMille replied acidly. "Allow me to remind you that we're not making some little documentary for the Venice Film Festival jury, Mr. Garfield. This is a major motion picture. I need to know where everyone stands."

"Are we still really just talking about the movie here?" Chuck asked. "Or did we switch tracks when I didn't notice?"

"Mr. DeMille, you have my utmost loyalty," I said, feeling the car start to rock again.

"That better be the case, fella," he grumbled.

I understood I needed to do something to reassure him and stabilize our situation. "By the way, you know that I reviewed your last film," I said.

"*The Greatest Show on Earth*?" Mr. DeMille looked up. "The circus picture?"

"I would have shown you the clip, but it was in Arabic," I replied. "This was a wonderful spectacle. The color, the movement, the crowd scenes. I singled out Mr. Heston's performance as the circus manager for special notice."

It was a ridiculous gambit. We had been talking about matters of life and death, and I was attempting to distract them with cotton candy. I hadn't even reviewed the movie, though they had no way of knowing that. But anyone is susceptible to praise if it's offered at just the right moment.

"Chuck *was* very good." Mr. DeMille nodded. "He wouldn't be here playing Moses if he wasn't."

"Didn't that circus picture end with a train wreck and all the animals escaping?" Raymond asked.

"Did you know it won the Academy Award for Best Picture, Mr. Hassan?" Henry asked, seizing the chance to try to change the mood.

"But not Best Director." Mr. DeMille stared out his window. "I guess that picture must have directed itself."

"Surely that oversight will be corrected after this film," I said.

"From your lips to God's ear," Mr. DeMille replied gloomily. "Because He knows it hasn't happened yet."

The cars in front of us stopped short again, forcing me to stomp on the brakes and jolt all my passengers.

"Whoa, bucko." Chuck grabbed my shoulder, more fondly now that he believed I'd given him a good review. "I almost lost my breakfast again."

"Would you like someone else to drive?" Raymond asked.

"*Kos omak,*" I muttered under my breath. "You think you could do better?"

Two military police officers got out of their jeep, shielding their faces against the flying dirt.

"Oh, for the love of Christ, what now?" Mr. DeMille exclaimed from the back seat. "Henry, give me my goddamn pith helmet, will you?"

He climbed out of the vehicle, keeping the hat on top of his head with one hand while shielding his eyes with the other as he staggered toward a group of Bedouins idling beside the track on camelback, looking at our cars, trailers, and equipment trucks curiously.

I watched how Raymond wound and aimed his camera at Mr. DeMille, trying to stay upright and keep his helmet on as he shouted furiously and pointed while the Bedouins held their camels' reins and looked on bemused.

"Don't tell me." Raymond pressed the button to let the film run. "He's ordering them to make the wind stop."

"Well." Chuck cleared his throat. "He *is* Cecil B. DeMille."

September 21, 2014
To: GrandpaAli71@aol.com
From: Asur@protonmail.com

Gedo,
Right now, it is still dark outside the two small windows of the little room where I'm sleeping with a bunch of other dudes close to my age. Soon the first light will appear in the eastern sky, which will slowly spread across the width of the horizon. Then will come the call to dawn prayer, the fajr, *and the voice of the muezzin from the minaret down the street, telling us that prayer is better than sleep. It will be the first time in my life that I have heard a live human chanting these words, instead of a recording from a storefront masjid barely audible above the traffic on Fourth Avenue.*

I have decided to proceed to the next leg of the journey, even though you wouldn't give me the money to buy my ticket. I guess I understand, but I found another way to get it. How, I'd rather not say.

I won't tell you where we are either, not because I'm mad that you didn't wire me the money, but because we are still in a place with a lot of nonbelievers and potential spies.

It's okay, though. I feel serene and strong in my purpose. Like I am drawing closer to where I should be. Today we will be crossing a border like you did. We've been warned that some of us may not make it. But as the sun starts to rise, I find myself not worrying but thinking of you.

Anyway, it may be a while until you hear from me again.

Abu Suror

7

We drove without stopping for several more hours, some-how arriving in one piece at the first location, which was an old British Petroleum camp on the Red Sea coastline, just before sunset. Although the film's main set was just outside Cairo, our schedule called for us to get the difficult journey to Sinai out of the way first. Mr. DeMille believed the rugged and unforgiving land-scape would give a necessary flavor of authenticity to his Bible story.

The original plan was to sleep at the base camp by the shore, shoot some footage in the morning, then pack up and head for Mount Sinai for a more extended sequence. But Mr. DeMille was out of the Land Rover before I had the engine off, yelling for Henry and Chuck to get out and get a move on, as I grabbed a pen, a walkie-talkie, and a clipboard to run after him, trying to take notes in English and Arabic.

"Come on, get to it!" he shouted. "We're losing the light!"

He summoned the first and second assistant directors. He called for the wardrobe mistress and makeup artists to get Chuck ready. He ran up to the camera truck and started remonstrating with propeller-like arms. Then he went up to the cinematographer and began exco-riating him about an outcropping of rock overlooking the water and how the idiot location scouts should have done a better job framing up the advance photos they'd sent.

"On the double, on the double!" He clapped his hands, becoming more and more energized by his own anger. "We're losing money by the minute."

The crew scattered like ants after crumbs. They brought out the cameras and cables. They started laying track along the sand that led to the water's edge. They held up light meters and tape measures as I ran back and forth with setting numbers that Mr. DeMille dictated to me. Yet nothing we did—or how fast we did it—seemed to satisfy him.

"What's going on?" Mona trailed after me. "Why all the hurrying? I thought we weren't going to begin filming until sunrise."

"Of course, he wants to start sooner." Raymond walked up between us, camera in hand. "It's golden hour. When everyone looks like a god. Instead of just thinking they are one."

My walkie-talkie blared and Mr. DeMille's voice crackled over the static, even though he was standing just a few yards away. "Mr. Hassan, get yourself over here right away," he said. "I need you to have a word with some of your countrymen."

I found him waving his hands furiously at three Egyptians outside a production truck. One was a former bodybuilder named Mustafa and another was a longshoreman named Lofty. I'd briefly met both at Brotherhood meetings. The third was Sherif.

My cousin looked at me, then he looked at Mona. Though they had starred together in my student film, they were not friends.

"What's the matter, Mr. DeMille?" I asked.

"I need you to ask these . . . *gentlemen* to get a set of brooms off the truck and start sweeping up the sand," he said.

"*Sweep up the sand?*" Sherif asked, whose English was rather good.

"Yes." Spittle flew from Mr. DeMille's mouth. "I don't want my cameras seeing these dark unsightly mounds in the background. Smooth them out, dammit. Chop-chop."

He went off in search of someone else to upbraid while the shot got set up. My cousin looked at Mustafa and Lofty, and then at me, as he started to pull on his beard "'Chop-chop'?" he said. "Does he think we're in a Charlie Chan movie?"

"He's the director," Mona replied. "You better do as he says."

Reluctantly, my cousin and his friends went to get brooms. All around us, walkie-talkies blazed with English and Arabic. We were facing the open sea, but the air was thick with people asserting their own importance.

"Mr. Hassan," Henry called out through a bullhorn. "Get Mr. DeMille's chair ready. It's in the two-banger."

I ran for the trailer just as our leading man came striding out. If it wasn't for the advance publicity photos I'd seen, I would scarcely have recognized the man who asked to be called "Chuck." He had long gray hair and a long gray beard. He wore a sack-like brown robe with leather straps on his wrists and a big red cloak with the Levite stripes over his shoulders. He carried a gnarled wooden staff that was taller than he was. The crew stopped their work and stared. He looked very much like Michelangelo's sculpture of Moses—except for the horns. Even Sherif leaned on his broom with his mouth agape.

"Let's go right into it." Mr. DeMille started clapping his hands again as he walked back and forth like a caged lion. "Marking rehearsal and then I want to *shoot*. No stand-ins, no last looks. We need to beat the sun."

Chuck stepped out onto the rock some fifty yards away. Two massive VistaVision cameras slid up on the angled tracks that had been laid behind him. An Egyptian assistant knelt by the star's feet. His abject servitude was embarrassing until I realized he was just putting colored strips of tape down by Chuck's sandals so the actor could know his marks.

I got the director's chair and saw my cousin sweeping the sand, his disgust wafting toward me as palpably as the wind off the water.

The sun was getting low in the sky. A man with a fur-covered microphone at the end of a long boom was creeping out along the rocks behind Chuck, while another man was crouching with a big reel-to-reel tape recorder behind him. Raymond was off to the side, filming the filmmakers with his more modest device. Mr. DeMille howled at all of them to stay back and get the hell out of his shot.

He bent his knees and sat back into the air. Somehow I managed to run around behind him, unfold the canvas seat, and straighten his name on the back before his rear end planted itself on the throne.

Several people laughed and he whipped his head around.

"Quiet on my set," he said with a snarl. "Anyone who can't follow directions can leave right now."

Henry came up to me in an agitated state. "Get his bullhorn, for God's sake. Come on, man. Move. I won't be able to save you every day."

Time stood still as I ran for the director's trailer, my importance on the set diminishing with each step. I'd been hired to be Cecil B. DeMille's assistant and confidant, and now I was dashing to get his chair and his megaphone. I made a conscious effort not to meet my cousin's eye as I handed the director his horn.

"All right, the first shot of the production will be the last shot of the day." Mr. DeMille stood up, his voice echoing down the beach. "Everyone settle. We're about to make movie history. Moses is about to part the Red Sea. Chuck, are you ready?"

The actor adjusted the wig on his head, fussed with his cloak and then lifted his staff. "Ready when you are, Mr. DeMille," he called out.

"And . . . *action.*"

The actor nodded solemnly and looked down, as if trying to find inspiration at his feet. Then he turned and raised his staff to the setting sun.

"Behold his mighty hand!" he bellowed, a salt breeze off the water carrying his lines back to us.

And then the whole crew stood absolutely still as if something really momentous was occurring. But it was just a late afternoon on the coastline. The water was mostly flat. I could even see an oil tanker in the near distance.

"What's happening?" Mona whispered. "Why's everyone acting like there's a miracle?"

"I don't know." I shrugged. "Maybe they're going to add something special in postproduction."

"I said, 'Quiet.'" Mr. DeMille glared over his shoulder, though our voices had been no louder than the breeze. "I won't tell you again."

After a fourth take of Chuck holding up his staff on the rocks, Mr. DeMille called out, "Check the gate!" and the crew began breaking down the set as quickly as they'd put it together.

As I took Mr. DeMille's dinner order and ran his chair back to the trailer, I saw Sherif still slouching over his broom and talking sullenly to his friends.

"They didn't even use it," he said as I passed.

"What?"

"The work we did." He pointed to the smoothed-out sand. "I have a degree in civil engineering. Now I'm sweeping sand for a bunch of *khawagat*. And they don't even bother turning the camera around to look at it."

"This is the movie business." I shrugged.

"It's just another big man throwing his weight around." He turned away in disgust.

When next I saw Chuck he was out of his makeup and into a pair of tight red swimming trunks. He seemed very proud of his athletic physique as he charged into the water. Several others in the American crew, eager to cool down after the long hot drive, began stripping off their shoes, socks, shirts, and pants as they waded in after him.

Then came Henry and Mr. DeMille, who had taken off his suit, pith helmet, and glasses, in favor of black bathing trunks. His build was good for a man of his age, but his age remained seventy-three.

Even in the dusk, I could see the varicose veins standing out in the backs of his legs as he went jogging past me. But he was still Cecil B. DeMille, and he displaced a lot of water when he dove into the Red Sea.

"They act like it's all theirs, don't they?" Sherif came over with his broom and started sweeping around my feet. "Can you believe the arrogance?"

"You know you don't have to keep doing that," I said, trying to get out of his way. "They're not filming anymore."

"It helps me to stay busy." He refused to look up as he started sweeping more intensely. "Otherwise, I think I'll have to hit someone."

Mona came up to me on my other side. She was wrapped in a white terry cloth beach towel and wearing a white rubber bathing cap like Esther Williams.

"Ali, are you going in?" she asked.

I could not answer right away, because I could not breathe. Her legs were naked beneath the towel. Her toenails were painted the same shade of red as her lipstick. When she adjusted the towel, I could see the full shape of her bosom in her white Catalina swimsuit. One did not often see that much of a woman in those days. Especially not in our part of the world. I became erotically anxious, with no idea what to do about it. I had not packed a bathing suit because I didn't own one.

"In a minute," I said. "I need to speak to my cousin first."

"You're missing out," she warned me.

She handed me her towel and ran toward the shore, tossing a coquettish look over her shoulder as if she was tempting me to follow sooner. Or maybe just teasing Sherif, whom she found an insufferably high-minded bore. In the name of all that is holy and eternal, this was far more sexual voltage than I'd ever encountered in my uncle's den of iniquity. The glimpse of her shining bare shoulders, the swaying of her ample hips, the bounty of her backside in that white bathing suit. And, praise God, her unhesitating grace when leaping into the water, where the dying sun dripped molten ore on the rippling surface.

"You know you're an idiot," Sherif said.

"What makes you say that?"

"You can't see what she really is. She's just using you."

"And what exactly are you doing?" I asked. "Why did you follow me out here?"

He piled his hands atop the broom handle. "If there's a battlefront, I'm going to be there."

"What battlefront?" I said. "It's a movie set."

"Oh, it's more than that. And we both know it, Ali. First, they come here to claim our stories for their Bible. Then they want our women and our land. Now they want our oil." He looked back at the derricks. "We need to draw the line."

"I don't know what you're getting at."

"You don't?"

Sherif was, as I've said, my flesh and blood, my comfort in my time of greatest sorrow, and—until fairly recently—the best friend I'd ever had. But now as his lips parted in a semblance of a grin, it was as if I'd never really seen his teeth before.

"I know you were the driver," he said softly.

I stared at him, breathless, trying to tell myself that I couldn't have heard him correctly.

Someone ran up behind me, tapped me lightly on the shoulder, and then kept going. I saw Raymond's pale white body streak past me, clad in just a pair of khaki shorts. To my jealous dismay, his skinniness was revealed to be wiriness. I worried how Mona would respond when she saw he had a baseball player's ropy arms, a long muscular back, and springy pistonlike legs. He jumped in the water and began splashing around, joining Chuck and Mr. DeMille in a loose circle around Mona.

"Ali." Her voice rang out like a bell. "Come in with us. The water is *heavenly."*

Sherif smirked. "Go ahead. Let's see how brave you are."

Of course he knew that I'd never had swimming lessons. What choice did I have? I just needed to get away from him and what he'd said. I took off my navy blazer, kicked off my shoes, pulled down the white duck pants I was wearing, and shed the rest of my clothes down to my trunks-like plaid boxer shorts. I was depending on the cover of darkness to shield my less than toned body from stares that would make me self-conscious. Then I strode toward the shore like I was Johnny Weissmuller playing Tarzan. The undertow threatened to pull my feet out from under me. I shivered in the evening wind. Torches and tents were being set up on the beach behind me. But I couldn't go back and warm up. Because in the darkness, I heard more splashing and then giggling and then a woman's voice saying, *"Stop."*

And then Raymond asking, "Do you really want me to?"

I forced myself to wade in. The water was surprisingly warm, like a milky bath. I went in up to my knees easily. But then I suddenly stepped off a steep ledge and found myself up to my chin. I started doing a kind of frantic dog paddle that I had taught myself during the flood season. The Red Sea has high saline content and it would have been relatively easy to float, but water is water, and once you're in deep enough, you can drown.

I paddled in the direction of Mona's sighs and giggles, trying to get as far from my cousin as I could. I kicked my legs and flailed my arms to keep from sinking. Chuck swam past me easily, pulling handfuls of water as he did a relaxed, manly crawl. In the movie, he was playing Moses, the most humble of all men; in reality he was a rangy Midwesterner showing off for Mona and the others. I maneuvered around him like a tugboat, then found myself directly in the lane of Mr. DeMille.

"Hey there, fella—watch where you're going." He paused before me, barely expending any effort to keep himself afloat.

"Forgive me, Mr. DeMille." I breathed heavily, my arms and legs doing more work under the surface than I wanted him to know. "I didn't mean to get in your way."

"It's all right. Maybe I should be the one asking to be forgiven. I got a little snippy with you, I know. But I'm an old man, and it's been a long journey already."

"Sir?"

"Maybe I should just say thank you." He swam close so I could feel the power of his motion all around me. "I appreciate your discretion so far."

"What would I say, Mr. DeMille?" I took in a gulp of salty water and spat it out. "It isn't in anyone's interest to speak about what happened, is it?"

I looked back toward the shore, but I no longer saw Sherif. *I know you were the driver,* he'd said.

"Have you heard much talk about the accident?" Mr. DeMille asked.

"Some, sir."

I tried to tell myself that "I know you were the driver" could refer to other things. But none came to mind at that moment.

"People are upset, naturally, Mr. DeMille. This was a revered man, who left behind a large family. He had a lot of followers."

"Yes, of course." He nodded as he kept treading water. "I feel terrible about it. And I wish I could do something for his wife and children. But how can I, without drawing the wrong kind of attention?"

"You can't. We just have to swallow this for as long as we can." The taste of salt was still burning in my mouth. "As disagreeable as it is."

"Yes." He looked up at the darkening sky. "It's a bitter pill. But as I said, there was nothing else we could have done. Those people meant to kill us, didn't they?"

He sounded like he needed me to agree. But I knew someone like my cousin would not accept this as an answer.

"I'm not sure if that was their specific intent, Mr. DeMille." I worked harder to keep my head above water. "But they were in an angry state. We had to get out of there."

"I believe you're right," he said. "The question is, where do we stand now? Nothing can be allowed to cancel this picture. I've worked too hard to get here. Thousands of people are depending on its success. Its message needs to be heard. Sometimes I feel like Moses. Just an old man trying to stay upright long enough to climb the mountain and tell the story."

I finally found a place to stand, but it turned out to be a jagged edge of coral that scraped the bottom of my foot so badly that I had to move off it.

"What do you think about this man, Nasser?" he asked. "How much can we trust him?"

"Until the tide turns, Mr. DeMille." I paddled a little more desperately. "He needs to keep the Muslim Brothers under control."

"Here's what I want to know." He wiped the salt from his eyes with the heels of his palms. "Will the dam hold?"

"I'm not sure I understand the nature of your question." A fish brushed the side of my leg.

"We have another three weeks of shooting ahead of us. Including the Exodus scene back near Cairo, which involves ten thousand human extras and ten thousand animals and a set that cost two million dollars. Can Nasser keep a lid on things until it's time for us to go back to America?"

"Only God can predict the future," I said. "But at the moment, I would say our interests aligned. You would like to see your picture done, he would like to stay in power, and I would like to stay out of prison."

I was getting tired from treading water, with my arms and legs whirling frantically beneath the surface. I could see my cousin again in the torchlight on the beach, gesturing for his friends Mustafa and Lofty to come over and watch us. I heard Mona's voice pitched high on the water close by, as if she was in some kind of peril.

"You'll let me know if you start seeing danger signals?" Mr. DeMille asked.

"Yes, sir. Of course. But right now will you excuse me?"

"Okay, and next time you'll tell me about the movies you want to make. . . ."

I swam toward where I'd heard Mona crying out. But my arms and legs quickly grew weary from moving against the current. Seaweed clung to my feet and ankles, slowing me down. I began gasping and swallowing more water as I lost my sense of direction. The torches on the beach were no longer in sight. I could not tell the shore from the horizon.

I thrashed around, but only succeeding in exhausting myself further, as salt stung my eyes, my nose, the back of my throat.

"Musaeda!" The cry for help escaped from my blubbering lips.

I sank beneath the surface, just as I heard Mona laughing. Down below, the world was black, cold, and airless. I bobbed back up again, my lungs seizing. Someone was grabbing me. I spat out a mouthful of water. A hand yanked my hair and then an arm went under my arms.

"Is he all right?" I heard Mona ask as water ran out of my ears.

I was being pulled back toward the shore, the lit torches coming into view under the star-choked sky.

"You going to be okay, amigo?" Chuck was swimming along on my right, his big white teeth visible in the dark.

Mr. DeMille was swimming along on my left, as my escort.

"Kick," I heard Raymond say. "Help me out a little, buddy."

He had a good grip on me as he dragged me through the water with one arm. He must have been some kind of lifeguard in his youth. The beach was within twenty yards. I knew my cousin would be there with the others, watching this interloper rescue me. As soon as I was sure we were in the shallows, I broke free of him so I could walk the rest of the way on my own.

"Thank you, that wasn't necessary," I muttered.

"Ali . . ." Mona began to admonish me for my rudeness.

"He's probably right, you know." Raymond shook out his arms. "Hardly anyone drowns in the Red Sea."

8

Afterward, I sat on a rock, wrapped in a towel, dripping and humiliated. My clothes were sandy from being dropped on the beach. There was a buffet being served over by the tents, but I didn't feel like eating. Mona came strolling over, after a respectable interval. She was barefoot on the sand and wearing a heavy red sweater now, with a white fringed shawl over her shoulders. Unlike me, she knew enough to bring the exact right wardrobe for the coastline.

"Are you all right?" she asked shyly.

"Yes, of course." I threw the towel aside. "I told you I could have made it back to shore easily on my own. I was more worried for you."

"For me?" She laughed. "I've been swimming all my life. My father arranged private lessons for me when I was at the lycée. There was an Olympic-size pool with a diving board at the Lido Club. . . ."

Her voice trailed off in the breeze; perhaps she knew that bringing up her father's private club was no comfort to me. She held out a plate that was heaped with more food than I'd ever seen her consume at one time.

"I thought you might be hungry," she said. "It would be good to get something warm into you. They have lentil soup as well."

"I don't want any lentils."

"Are you sure?"

I was about to ask her what she was doing, swimming out that far with strange men. Didn't she know how people would talk?

My cousin came over, holding a plate down at his side as if he had just licked it clean. He and Mona regarded each other with the same quality of mutual caution that made them unconvincing as lovers in my student film.

"Did you enjoy your swim, Miss Mona?" His fingers pressed into his beard, as if in search of roots.

"I did." She stuck out her chest. "Too bad you didn't come in."

They were back to the way they'd been during the production, trying to unnerve each other. Him with his piety and her with her co-quettishness. The Muslim Brother and the French actress's daughter.

"Why would I do something so stupid?" Sherif scoffed. "I saw how Ali nearly drowned going after you."

"It was just a misunderstanding." I tilted my head, trying to get the water out of my ears. "She was fine and I was fine. No one needed to save me."

"You're very comfortable showing men your body, aren't you?" He took his hand from his beard and reached out as if he was about to yank at the silver cross hanging just above her cleavage. "That must serve you well as an actress."

"There's nothing in my religion that says I can't go swimming where I want." She pulled the shawl more snugly around her shoulders.

"It seems disrespectful," he said. "To God, and to yourself as a woman."

"I can speak for myself 'as a woman,' Sherif," she replied tartly. "And I wasn't aware that God needed *you* as his spokesman."

His hand returned to his beard like it was a pet that needed comforting. "Anyone with eyes in his head knows what's haram and what isn't."

"Then why not keep your eyes to yourself?" Her lashes fluttered.

If they had simmered this expressively when I was directing them, my film would have been a smashing success.

"This is a stupid conversation about a stupid subject," Sherif said.

"I agree," said Mona. "Remind me who started it."

Sherif gave me one of his soulful martyr looks. "Ali, you and I have more serious things to discuss," he said. "But this isn't the right time."

A breeze off the sea put the chill back in my bones. I shivered as he walked away.

"What does that mean?" Mona asked.

"Oh, you know how he is." I looked after him and rubbed my hands together. "He always wants to discuss serious things."

"I'll tell you." She clicked her tongue. "There is one thing I like about your cousin. But *only* one thing."

"What's that?"

"The fact that he loves you as much as he does. Otherwise, Sherif can *va au diable*. He can go to hell."

Perhaps you're used to cursing in your generation, Alex. It was not so common in my time. Especially not from nice Christian girls who had gone to the lycée. I was so surprised to hear her speaking so bluntly that I momentarily forgot my fears about the imam and the Cadillac.

"Sometimes I think he's just jealous of you," she said.

"Jealous of *me*? Why?"

"I don't know." She wrinkled her nose. "But I noticed it when we were making your movie. Just the way I'd see him looking at you sometimes when you were laughing or happy about an angle you'd found. Like he didn't want you to be able to do something that *he* couldn't do."

I looked down the beach, trying to see where Sherif had gone and whether he was still watching us.

"I'm sure that you're mistaken," I said. "My cousin does the kind of things that men like me only make movies about. And I wish you could try to get along with him."

My attitude toward Sherif had begun to shift. Before I had merely been intimidated by him. Now, because of what he'd said about my being "the driver," I was starting to be truly afraid.

Mona turned her back to the Red Sea as the wind started blowing harder. "I'll try to be more civil with him. For your sake. But I tell you, he's hard. I was arguing with him when I was getting dinner just now."

"Over what?" I tried to shield my eyes from flying sand.

"He says I shouldn't have been allowed to come out on this trip. That I'm a 'bad influence' on you. And now he's saying you almost drowned because of me. That's not true, is it?"

"No, of course not." I tilted my head the other way. "No one made me get in the water."

"He's only happy when he's fighting, your cousin. And then he accuses *me* of taking advantage of you."

"Of course, that's unfair." I tried to placate her.

"But why is *he* here?" she asked. "I thought he had no interest in film."

I had been wondering the same thing since that night in my father's kitchen. It couldn't have been a simple coincidence that he applied so soon after the imam's death. Using my name, so he wouldn't be vetted too closely. But the alternative explanation, that he might be deliberately stalking me, as an agent of the Brotherhood, made me feel like my lungs were filling with water again.

"He needs a job," I said. "That's all."

I tried to imagine what would happen if they started talking when I wasn't around to referee them. Sniping at each other and trading insults. How long would it be until he repeated what he'd said about my being the driver?

"Well, I'm glad he walked away." She sighed and started winding the tassels of her shawl tightly around her slender fingers. "Because there's something else I want to say to you."

The wind began to die off, to the point that I could fully open my eyes again and wipe the grit from the corners.

"What's that?" I asked.

"I want to thank you for what you've done for me." She put her shawl over her head like the convent girl she'd once wanted to be.

"What did I do?"

"You gave me a chance to work. And meet these people and come out to this place. I've always wanted to see this shore at sunset."

The water rolled in and then receded, its gentle rhythm helping me relax a little.

"All I did was forward your résumé to Mr. DeMille's office," I said. "I'm certain you could have done the same and gotten the work on your own."

"Maybe," she allowed. "But I'm not just talking about *The Ten Commandments*. I'm talking about when you let me work on your movie."

"Oh my goodness." I winced, remembering all my mistakes. "I hardly knew what I was doing. You were doing me a favor by acting in it, for no money."

"It wasn't just the acting and posing in front of the camera. I liked it when you let me help you carry the lights and the camera gear."

"You did?"

I remembered her struggling through the streets in her plain dress and flat shoes, looking overwhelmed with the heavy equipment and then sweet-talking the police officers who threatened to arrest us for filming without a permit.

"It made me feel . . . *purposeful.*" She smiled at finding the right word.

"Why?" It seemed a peculiar thing to say.

"You let me feel like I was part of a crew, capable and strong, not just this fragile little ornamental thing that my mother raised me to be."

"You're not exactly cut out to be a grip or a gaffer," I pointed out.

"Yes, she wanted me to just be an empty-headed girl in a party dress." She rubbed her wrist. "You know, once, she even introduced me to the king. At a party on his yacht . . ."

I noticed that beneath her hand she was wearing the Cartier watch that she'd taken off for swimming.

"Why would she let you anywhere near that scoundrel?" I asked.

"Why do you think, Ali? So I could get back the status she'd lost when she married my father."

"How old were you?"

"I was thirteen."

She looked at the watch and then dropped her hand to her side like she had no more use for it. It occurred to me that maybe this wasn't a gift from her father, as she had previously told me, but from the king. And that there was more to this story than I wanted to know.

"But you made me feel different, Ali," she said. "You made me—what's the word?—*ordinaire.*"

"You're thanking me for making you feel ordinary?" Now I was really confused.

"*Yes,*" she said emphatically. "Because I didn't want to be this pretty fragile thing that couldn't be handled. I don't want to live in a jewel box. I don't want to be up on anyone's pedestal. I want to have my feet on the ground and bury my toes in the sand. I want to live a life that's real. I don't want to be caught up in any more lies."

I looked down at her feet, surprisingly near mine, then stepped back as the water surged around our ankles. I felt unworthy to be near her. Especially with Sherif so close by.

"Do you think there's a chance he'll take us back to America with him?" Mona asked.

"Who? Mr. DeMille?"

"He seems to like you. The others do as well. Like Chuck and Raymond."

"Well, I don't know," I muttered, my mood darkening again at the mention of those other men's names.

"Why not?"

I looked down and saw my clothes had gotten wet with the tide coming in.

"These people are not what they pretend to be." I snatched them up in disgust.

"What do you think they're pretending to be?" she asked with a sort of amused curiosity.

I wrung my clothes out and threw them on a rock to dry. "They're making a religious film, but they don't always behave so religiously offscreen."

"And thank God for that!" She giggled, a little coquettishly.

"What do you mean?"

I thought of how Chuck had been dancing with her at the party. Then I thought of how she had been thrashing in the water with Raymond. But then I thought of how fast the Cadillac had been going when I hit the imam and I heard my cousin's words again in my head: *I know you were the driver.*

"You know, this Chuck is married," I warned her, trying to control my growing agitation. "And this Raymond was wearing a wedding ring when he first got here. But then he took it off!"

"Yes, I know he was married." She held her chin up. "He t all about it. But now he's getting a divorce."

"Why was he talking to you about it?" My jealousy was running amuck.

"Why shouldn't he? He's a free man."

"And you're worried about Sherif taking advantage of me? I'm worried that it's you who's going to be taken advantage of."

"Is that so?" Her voice went flat. "Do you really think that I don't know what I'm doing, Ali?"

All at once, she was not the person I'd made up in my head, whose lines and actions I could script. She was going to do exactly as she pleased, whether it broke my heart or not.

"You should stay away from Chuck, and from this Raymond as well," I warned her. "They're going to corrupt you."

"Maybe I want to be corrupted." She took the shawl off her head and shook out her curls.

"You don't mean that. You don't know your mind."

"Maybe I *changed* my mind."

"But don't you see . . ." I was losing control. "What about your reputation?"

"My 'reputation'? You know who you sound like now, Ali? You sound like your cousin."

I sputtered. "Well, maybe he has a point sometimes."

"God, what's the matter with you?" she asked. "I came over to see if you're all right and you're pushing me away."

"Maybe I just need to be alone," I admitted. "I have a lot on my mind."

"I see that. And I hope you get it sorted out. But right now I think it's time for me to get back to the others."

She walked away before I could call after her, swinging her hips as she dropped the shawl to her waist, and the soles of her feet kicked up sand in her wake.

October 11, 2014
To: GrandpaAli71@aol.com
From: Asur@protonmail.com

Gedo,
I must admit that I'm very confused, as you must have been. Who was playing who here? It seems like everyone, except for you, had a hidden agenda.

I also feel sad about how you talk about this woman you loved, Miss Mona. I must confess that I have never been in love. Though there were some close calls in high school. Especially Katy Almontasir. Women, if you must know, confuse me as well.

I feel far safer where I am now, with my brothers and our hardware. And the goals we have ahead of us. They have promised me an obedient and devoted wife when we get there. Well, they don't use the word "wife," but it's pretty much the same thing.

Anyway, I can't say much more about what we're doing, because it's supposed to be secret. It will be daylight soon and they don't know that I still have my old alternative phone with me. But it's funny that I'm reading about you taking this journey with Mr. DeMille and the others, when I'm about to embark on a journey of my own, Insha'Allah.

I think I am beginning to understand why you're relating this history to me. At first, I thought you were just trying to "guilt" me into coming back to America or dissuade me from my mission with some useless life lesson. Now I think it's something different. I think you're trying to speak to me through the past, to show me who you were and how we were perhaps not so different. Maybe you just want to feel closer to me now that I'm gone. But I'm not sure if we have that much in common anymore except for a bloodline.

> *Yours in the Name of the Merciful and the Compassionate,*
> *Abu Suror*

October 12, 2014
To: Asur@protonmail.com
From: GrandpaAli71@aol.com

Alex,
I'm glad you're still reading my book, but please don't endanger yourself by looking at your phone too much and angering your superior officers.

It concerns me, though, that you're talking about finding an "obedient" wife. I wouldn't have described your grandmother that way, but I was very happy with her for many years. My advice to you is to be gentle with women and go slowly with money. And be careful of who you call your brother.

I am still praying for your safe return.

> *Yours in faith and "bloodline,"*
> *Grandpa*

9

After the restless night camped on the shore of the Red Sea, Mr. DeMille captured a few more shots of Chuck in beard and costume with the morning light shining its beams in his face. Then our caravan continued inland through the endless Sinai wilderness, dotted only by crags and the occasional shrubland. With so little to look at outside, I found myself brooding on what was going on beneath the Land Rover's hood: the humming of the engine, the grinding of the gears, the currents from the alternator. I tried to stay on track as my mind veered back and forth, worrying about my conversations by the Red Sea and what my cousin would do with the knowledge he had about the imam.

By midafternoon, we reached St. Catherine's Monastery, the fourteen-hundred-year-old Christian compound that sat at the foot of what the locals call Moses's Mountain and everyone else calls Mount Sinai. We were there to film the sequence in which Moses goes up the mountain to receive the commandments directly from God.

After a meal with the abbot in the refectory and a few hours of sleep, we disassembled the gear and brought it up the mountain on camelback to begin shooting. All day long, I ran around with the bullhorn and the director's chair, tripping over rocks and trying to snap the seat open in time to capture Mr. DeMille's descending backside before he shouted, *"Action!"* and Chuck with his beard and staff would begin his long sweaty climb to the summit, where I assumed special effects would be added in postproduction to show God some-how giving Moses the tablets.

Over and over, I watched Chuck fall to his knees in the dirt and cry out, "Lord, Lord! Why do You not hear the cry of your children in the bondage of Egypt . . . ?" until Mr. DeMille was satisfied and yelled, *"Cut!"* Then Mr. Chico Day, the assistant director, would du-tifully call out, "On the good gate-in, turning around on Moses," and a substitute for Chuck would stand in dressed in an identical wig and beard and red robe, to be surrounded by technicians with tape mea-sures and light meters.

All my life, I had wanted to be on the set of a Cecil B. DeMille pic-ture. But now that it was finally happening, it was hard for me to enjoy it. For one thing, the director would yell in increasingly bad temper whenever he saw me talking to the cinematographer and the camera-men, trying to understand how they were shaping the light and why they were framing the shots in a certain way, instead of bringing him a bottle of water or an umbrella to block the sun.

For another, Sherif kept drifting into view, carrying pieces of track for the cameras to glide on or special heavy covers to keep sand from getting in the gears of the cameras.

I was still haunted by what he'd said about me being the driver. How could he have known I was there? Who would have told him? Every time I tried to think through the consequences, my mind went white. I decided there was nothing I could do about it now, so I tried to be like an actor and pretend I had no troubles looming.

Once the sun dropped into the valley, it started to get very cold. The Americans made campfires amid the tents near the mountain-top. Flames cast flickering shadows on the rocks as they finished eating lamb and goat on skewers, so that each wavering silhouette looked like someone's true self set free to dance wildly behind them.

I found myself in a circle of crew members around a campfire, facing Chuck and Mr. DeMille across the flames and contemplating the judgment that might lie ahead.

"I have a question," Chuck said. "In the burning bush scene that's coming up, whose voice will we hear talking to Moses?"

The director took off his glasses, exposing the fine lines and folds of his age in the firelight. "You mean, which actor should we use in post?"

"It's an important decision, don't you think?" Chuck rested an elbow on his knee, more frontiersman than Moses in this pose.

"Are you asking me who will play God?" Mr. DeMille said.

"I had a thought." Henry interrupted. "What if we had a different actor dub the voice in every country where the film is shown? We'd have God speaking in the native tongue no matter where we are."

"And the biggest confusion since the Tower of Babel," Mr. DeMille replied. "No, Henry, that's your worst idea yet. Which is really saying something."

"I was thinking *I* should do it," Chuck broke in.

"*You?* You've already got a pretty good part," Mr. DeMille shot back. "You want more dialogue?"

The fire jumped again, its intensified glow defining silhouettes within the tents that had been set up around the plateau, turning each canvas into something like a small cinema screen.

"I don't think I'm just being an egotistical actor," Chuck said.

"*I'll* be the judge of that." Mr. DeMille angled his glasses.

I looked around for Mona, realizing it had been hours since I'd seen her.

"I've thought about this seriously," Chuck insisted. "Don't you think God speaks in subtler ways? Isn't it possible that he talks to us through our own thoughts in our own voices?"

"I don't know if that's right," I said, wondering how my cousin would react if he was close enough to hear this.

They all stopped talking.

"Or rather, I don't think that's right," I tried again. "I think people of faith might be offended if you suggest that God is just a psychological condition. To them, God is not just a state of mind. God is real. He gives consequences to all our actions."

A chunk of burnt wood fell and fiery cinders rose into the air.

"Mr. Hassan, I think you're taking Chuck a little too literally." Mr. DeMille squinted. "All he's saying is that we need to find a way to represent man's faith. We all agree that we can't show the face of the Almighty. But should he not be present in our film at all? Should we just have silence when the Lord speaks to Moses?"

"Why not?" asked Henry.

"So a prophet of three faiths will be shown talking to himself?" I asked, looking for clarity.

I noticed the light in one tent about twenty yards away seemed to blaze up with a special brightness, like the screen when a monster finally appears in a horror movie.

"Mr. Hassan, we're just trying to come up with a visual solution to a practical problem," Mr. DeMille said with rising irritation.

"But you were asking me before how my people might perceive this production more gladly," I said, swatting a burnt flake from my face. "In Islam, there is a belief that visual representations of God are haram and that some things can only be seen with the spiritual eye—"

"Well, I'm not making this film through the spiritual eye, I'm making it in VistaVision," Mr. DeMille cut me off.

I looked around again, wondering where Mona could have gone. "I understand that, sir, but such things can give offense—intentionally or not."

"You know, I'm getting a little sick and tired of having my motives impugned over and over by some freelance movie critic—"

"I don't think Mr. Hassan is impugning anything," Chuck said. "He's just putting in his two cents."

"Then here's *my* two cents, in United States currency." The director got to his feet, legs looking like they were strangulating in their tight puttee wrappings. "If you don't like it, lump it."

"Forgive me, Mr. DeMille." I jumped up. "I didn't mean to insult you."

But the fire was inside him now. "You know, you've been getting on my nerves this whole trip, you and your ilk. Nothing's ever good enough for you, is it?"

"With respect, Mr. DeMille." I put my hands out like he was about to charge at me. "I thought we were just having an idle conversation."

"I don't allow 'idle conversation' on my set, mister. And I don't like this constant carping about how we're not telling the story the way you want it told or how we're carrying out a secret mission for the Jews in Israel or whatever other nonsense you've been spewing."

There was no point in trying to explain to him that it was Professor Farid who had hurled some of those accusations, not me. De-Mille was in a blind fury, his temper feeding on itself, and I was the nearest target.

"Why don't you go make your own goddamn movie?" he said. "You think you're some hotshot young filmmaker, don't you?"

"Sir, that would hardly be practical." I tried to smile. "I'm not Cecil B. DeMille."

"Oh, so it's personal? You know, I've had it with all this bellyaching and second-guessing. And I'm not going to put up with it. You understand? You can get lost right now."

His fists were clenched and his face was so contorted that he was barely recognizable as the solicitous old man floating beside me in the Red Sea. He wanted to punish me, to make an example of me for the others. To strip my skin off in public. I saw Henry and Chuck look away, embarrassed.

"Henry, I'm going to need another assistant," the director said. "What's that other boy's name? Idris? Eddie?"

"Yes, Mr. DeMille, we call him 'Eddie.'" Henry got to his feet. "But do we want to make a hasty decision like this when we're this tired and tempers are this frayed?"

"My temper is fine and my judgment is sound," Mr. DeMille replied. "I want Mr. Hassan off my mountain."

"*Your mountain*, sir?" I stared, not sure he could be serious.

"How soon can we ship him back to Cairo?" the director said. "I want another driver as well. One who actually knows how to drive."

I took his words like a slap to the face. Tears came to my eyes. He was blaming me for the accident. After I had followed his orders to get us out of there and then betrayed my teacher publicly to defend him at the press conference.

"Come, now, we can't just throw him off the mountain in the middle of the night," Henry tried to reason with him. "Especially after what he's done for us—"

"I don't care what he's done or hasn't done, or what he's said or hasn't said." Mr. DeMille lashed back at him. "Mr. Hassan, I would like you gone by first light."

He stalked off, leaving the rest of us in stunned and awkward silence. No one would meet my eye. And then, one by one, they started mumbling excuses to get away, until it was just Chuck and myself.

"I've got lines to learn and a letter to write to Lydia." The actor got to his feet and stretched his long legs. "I'm sorry, Mr. Hassan. Obviously, the stress is getting to the old man. Good luck with wherever you end up."

I sank down slowly into a squat, asking myself what had just happened. I had believed that we were in this together. That one of us could not go down without taking the other with him. But I'd been half blinded by my idolatry. He had fired me because he *could*. And I was powerless to stop him. I could not hurt his picture without sticking my own head in a noose. Because what was I to him? Less than a speck of sand in the desert.

I stared into the flames. A woman was laughing somewhere close by. Mocking me. I looked around and saw silhouettes moving within the canvas tents that had been set up, figures in the shadow play of my imagination. Then I heard the smooth rumble of a man's voice, trying to talk her into something. But it couldn't be Chuck. He had stopped to join a group of crew members, watching four shepherds enact the ancient ritual of the wolf stalking the sheep around another fire on the landing.

"The story never changes." I heard my cousin's voice. "The interloper tries to steal in and raid the flock, and has to be chased away."

"Oh my God, Sherif." I turned to face him. "Why do you have to keep tormenting me? Why couldn't you have just stayed in Cairo?"

"Oh, I always wanted to come back to Sinai." He yawned and rubbed the sides of his beard with a look of contentment. "The best times of my life were here."

"That sounds like madness," I said. "This is one of the places where we lost the war with Israel. And where you were wounded."

"The hard places make us who we are." My cousin rested a hand on my shoulder. "Yes, it's a parched wilderness, where hardly anyone lives and hardly anything grows. But I couldn't wait to get back here. Married life is nothing compared with the closeness I had with my brothers here and in the Negev, and all the other places we were. How am I supposed to care about whether the baby's diapers get changed after we survived four months in the pocket of Al-Falujah with our supply lines cut and that incompetent moron Nasser in charge? After I've seen the villages raided, the people killed, and the land stolen by these Israeli interlopers—"

I knew he was telling me something important, but all I could focus on was the sound of the woman's lightly scandalized laughter. I recognized the suavely insinuating accent of the man in the tent with her.

"Excuse me, Sherif." I started to get up. "But I have something I need to do—"

"*Don't.*" He grabbed my arm. "I *told* you she's not worth it."

"You don't know where I'm going." I tried to pull away.

"Of course I do. You're going to see what that Coptic whore is doing with that fucking Jew. And I'm telling you not to do it."

I barely heard him as I watched the figures behind the screen merge and then come apart. It was like witnessing my own murder.

"I tried to warn you, didn't I?" Sherif said in a husky growl. "I could see what she was when we made that idiotic movie together. But you wouldn't listen. She's a user."

"It's not true." I tried to deny the evidence from my own eyes.

"You let her blind you," he taunted me. "And she isn't even that good-looking—"

"Shut up." I yanked my arm from him. "Do you have a knife?"

"Why?" He gave a small laugh. "So you can cut her throat? Or yours?"

"I don't know." I started to sob. "I don't have anything left to live for anyway—"

"*Stop it.*" He suddenly seized me by the ears. "Be a man and get a hold of yourself."

"Sherif, you're hurting me." The shock of physical pain refocused my attention.

"You're a disgrace," he said. "And you've brought it upon yourself."

"How can you talk to me that way?" I blinked back my tears in astonishment. "You're my cousin. Can't you see I'm in pain?"

"You should be in worse pain." He pulled harder on my ears. "In fact, there are people who want to murder you right now."

"What are you talking about?"

"I told you before. I know you were the driver. You killed Sheikh Sirgani."

My knees started to go weak. And then everything inside me collapsed. I could not remember how to breathe or swallow properly. All I could do to defend myself was make a vague croaking sound.

"Don't bother to deny it." Sherif fingered my ears more tenderly. "When the people who'd been in the crowd described the driver of the red car, I knew it was you."

"They were trying to kill us, Sherif. You weren't there. They were starting to turn the car over—"

"Don't make excuses." He twisted my ears so savagely that I thought he would rip them off the sides of my head. "*You* chose to be there. You chose to work for these *kufar*. You chose to be behind that wheel. Not someone else. *You* caused the death of a holy man who was important to our movement. And then *you* helped these infidels cover it up. A lot of people are saying you should be punished by death. In fact, the real reason I came out here was to protect you. Mustafa and Lofty still want to beat you within an inch of your life and leave you crippled."

"Mustafa and Lofty know as well?" I asked, trying to catch the wind that had just been knocked out of me.

"Of course. Lofty's cousin was in the crowd that day."

"But what can I do to make up for it?" I asked desperately. "You know I meant no harm—"

He pressed his forehead against mine and began to roll it back and forth, as he spoke to me with a tenderness that I had not heard from him in many years.

"Apologies are not enough," he said. "You need to do actions. If you want to make real amends, and not just talk. Don't you know that you've said enough empty words to last a lifetime?"

I let him continue rolling his brow over mine as I wept for forgiveness. It felt like he was trying to change the shape of my forehead. He was right. I had chosen the wrong dream. Every prayer I had skipped in favor of a matinee, every film magazine I had opened instead of the Koran, every belittlement I had endured from a foreigner had led me to the wrong path. I knew now there would never be a swimming pool and I would never change my name to Al Harrison, and Mona would never ride beside me down the Pacific Coast Highway in a Chevrolet convertible with the top down. Because I would never be a real American. I was just a brown man in a white man's world.

"Please, Sherif. Direct me. Tell me what to do."

"Don't worry." He finally let go of my ears and hugged me. "No harm will come to you as long as you stay on the rightful path. But first, I need to know that you're willing to commit to your faith and to being a soldier in this war we're fighting."

"Which war?"

"We're going to take our country back from Nasser," he said. "His grip isn't as strong as he believes. There are members of the Revolutionary Command Council who are still with us. They just need a sign that we're willing and able to do whatever it takes."

It was not as extreme an idea as it may sound now, Alex. After all, Naguib still had the title of president and there were more than a million Muslim Brothers in the country. If they were inspired to rise up in revolt, he might regain power and put Nasser in chains. Even in my hopeless fallen state, I recognized my own self-interest in this.

Under a new Ikhwan-backed regime, I might be marked for death as a traitor. Unless I could show some value as an asset.

"You've never had to be really courageous, Ali, but I've told the others something in you is worth saving." Sherif held me close, allowing me to huddle against him for warmth. "I used to see it when you'd beat me to the top in the pyramid races. But your commitment needs to be absolute. Will you swear that you are one of us and Islam is your constitution?"

It's true, my grandson, that I could still have found a way down that night. I could have turned myself in; thrown myself on the mercy of Nasser's associates; informed on my cousin; done my time; and perhaps lived a quieter, more anonymous life after I got out. But it wasn't just fear or cowardice that stopped me. I wanted a role. I wanted to fight. I wanted to be part of something bigger than the life I was living. And if it wasn't Hollywood, it would have to be the war my cousin was promising me a role in. Everything I had been before burned up in the fire on the mountain that night.

"I don't know what use I can be, Sherif. The only thing I've ever really done before is run the student cinema society."

"Forget all that." He kissed me on the forehead and released me. "Your true life starts now."

"Okay." I used my wrist to blot my tears. "But first can you get me a ride back to Cairo?"

10

As the sun cast its first rays the next morning and slowly warmed the mountaintop, I was looking at the world through changed eyes. I do not mean to say that I became a jihadi overnight, Alex. But when I took a deep breath and pulled back my shoulders, the ache in my side from sleeping on the ground went away.

I brushed off my white canvas trousers, dealt with my bodily functions behind some tall boulders, and decided to try to renew my faith with the *fajr* prayer to greet the day.

But once I took off my shoes, I discovered a problem. No water. Not a drop to wash my hands, feet, ears, and nose as prescribed. The sun streamed through a gap in the stones, drying up whatever moisture was in the air. I remembered the lessons of the school I used to go to with Sherif. My teacher would say it was twice as blessed to pray in the desert because Allah could hear your voice more clearly in the wilderness. He reminded us that the Prophet Muhammad had no sinks or cisterns. One could perform *tayammum,* the act of purification, when no water was available. So I got down on my knees and touched the cleanest part of the sand with both hands before I pressed my brow to the ground.

"What are you doing, Ali?"

Mona's voice startled me.

"Nothing that concerns you." I hurt my back by straightening up too fast. "I thought I was alone."

"It looks like you're praying." Her hip jutted out like the curve of a question mark.

"I am." My wounded pride forced my eyes down. "What of it?"

"You don't need to do it in a mosque with a running fountain?" she asked.

"My faith doesn't require plumbing. I can find God with my hands in the dirt as easily as you can find it in a church with a domed ceiling."

"Then I envy you," she said. "I wish I could feel things that way myself. Plain and simple."

"Do you?"

The sun was in my eyes and my heart was shriveling up in my chest as I spoke to her. She really didn't have a clue about how I felt.

"It's all gotten so complicated," she said wistfully.

I gathered two fistfuls of sand, dimly aware that there was something else she wanted to tell me. But I had started on another journey, and I wasn't looking back.

"What do you want from me, Mona?"

She put her feet together, remembering her duty. "Mr. DeMille wants to start filming on one of the lower ledges before the sun gets too strong. He asked me to help find everyone in the crew."

"Except I'm no longer in the crew. He fired me last night."

"He did? I had no idea."

"Of course not. You were busy. In your tent."

"Oh no." She folded an arm across her chest, as if I'd wounded her. "What happened?"

"It's what I told you. These people are not what they pretend to be."

"I'll speak to Mr. DeMille about taking you back," she said hastily. "I think he likes me."

"I'm sure he does," I replied. "You've found favor with the others, haven't you?"

"You make it sound like this is my fault, Ali." She stepped back, stumbling over a stone. "I'm trying to help you."

"I don't need your help. I need you to leave me alone."

The arm she'd had stretched across her chest dropped to her midsection. It was the first time in my life that I had brought tears to a woman's eyes. I regretted my words immediately, but in the rising desert heat they seemed to hang in the air for a very long time.

"I should go get the others," she said. "Tell Raymond that Mr. DeMille is looking for him as well."

I watched her turn and walk away as the sun sharpened its exacting blades. I threw away the fists of dirt I'd been holding and looked for a place to wipe my hands. I was disgusted with her but more disgusted with myself. I needed to clean up and start over. To be the unbowed and untainted warrior that my cousin had challenged me to be. But how? I needed a sign of Providence, a direction to take.

Just then, I swear, something ran over one of my feet. I looked down and saw a homely little porcupine scurrying away, quills bristling as it dodged through a gap in two boulders. I was wondering how it had managed to climb so high when I heard scuffling and groaning sounds from the other side, distinctly human.

I went over to peer between the stones and found Raymond lying on a flat outcropping with his camera in his hands.

"What do you think you're doing?" I asked.

He didn't even bother taking his eye from the viewfinder. "Getting an establishing shot."

"Establishing what?"

There was nothing below. Just miles and miles of endless Sinai emptiness. Hard-packed desert—brown sugar and coffee grounds—with just occasional scrubby vegetation. The only signs of life were the man-made caves in some of the surrounding cliffsides. I could almost picture dissident cults hiding in these warrens back in ancient times, feverishly writing alternative gospels and secret histories of man and God on papyrus scrolls. Except the caves looked as if they'd been carved with modern tools.

"What are you filming here, anyway?" I crept up behind him with a tingle in my hamstrings. "It looks like another ridiculous waste of good film stock."

He looked back over his shoulder again. "Why don't you let me worry about that? But in the meantime, would you mind holding my ankles? I seem to have gone out a little farther than I realized, and I don't want to have the camera slip from my hands," he said, not sounding so suave or seductive anymore.

Just beyond the precipice, there was a single spindly branch and then a steep drop of at least sixty feet. If he fell, he would be smashed on jagged boulders, and his shattered bloody remains would drip down the mountainside.

It occurred to me that this was the sign I had just asked for. My rival laid out before me, twelve inches from the edge of the precipice. Just a little nudge would send him plummeting. But I needed one more sign to give me the confidence.

A single white cloud drifted like a lost lamb over the neighboring mountain ranges, and a bluebottle fly harassed one of my ears.

"Take your shot," I said. "I have you."

I noticed he was wearing black silk socks with his cowhide desert boots. How frivolous and hedonistic, this man. Spending money on clothing that no one would see.

"Could you at least try to get a better grip?" he asked. "I feel myself slipping a little."

"Your wish is my command," I said, like the genie in one of those Hollywood Oriental movies I'd once loved.

I gripped him more tightly, giving him the confidence to push himself out a little more. His elbows were less than six inches from the edge now. My foot slipped, kicking loose a handful of gravel that rolled out into the abyss. The little stones made loud *pock* sounds for several seconds as they echoed down into the void.

"Watch yourself," he said. "I don't want you going over the side here yourself."

"It's okay. I'm on more solid ground."

He crawled out a little farther, so that his torso was at almost a forty-five-degree angle, with most of the strain on his abdomen.

"This is amazing." He turned the silver crank and raised the camera to his eye again. "If you can, try to take a look over my shoulder."

I forced myself to rise into a half crouch, my stomach dropping as my eyes found nothing but open air. Suddenly I had vertigo, after a childhood spent running up and down pyramids with my cousin.

On the ledge twenty yards below us, two full-grown rams were facing each other. I could see their flanks going in and out rapidly as they breathed. On some predetermined animal signal, they ran straight at each other and collided head-on. Their horns made a hollow knocking sound that resonated in the pit of my stomach.

"That's one way to settle differences," Raymond said.

The rams backed off and prepared to charge again.

It would have been easy enough just to let go of Raymond's ankles and let gravity have its way. But what if he managed to grab a ledge or a branch and hang on? Would I have the nerve to stand over him and grind down on his knuckles with my heel, like the villain in a Hitchcock movie?

"Mr. Hassan, are you all right?" He chanced another look over his shoulder. "It feels like your grip has loosened a little the last few seconds."

"Don't worry. I'm not going to let you go. I owe you, don't I? You saved me in front of everyone."

"Do I detect a note of resentment?"

He tried to push back and replant his elbows.

"Not at all." I put my knee behind the sole of one of his boots.

"Then what's eating you?"

"What's 'eating' me is what should be eating you, Raymond."

"Which is?"

"That we were involved in a terrible thing."

"We're talking about the accident again?" I could hear him sucking his teeth as he looked down.

"We've barely talked about it at all. In fact, we've done everything possible to avoid taking any responsibility."

"Ali, let me remind you of something." It was the first time he had addressed me in this more familiar way. "We were surrounded by a mob that was trying to kill us. We did what we had to do. In America, it would be justified as self-defense."

"But we're not *in* America now."

"Thank you. I noticed."

"Tell me something." I turned to wipe my sweating face on my shoulder. "Does this seem right to you? That some of us keep going along, living the good life, making movies, and chasing women like it doesn't matter?"

"Is that what this is about?" He took another quick look back, his normally pale face turning salmon colored. "A woman?"

"Not at all."

"Look, my good man, I would be happy to have a philosophical conversation with you under almost any other circumstances." He was straining to sound calm. "But right now, I'm asking you to just get a better grip. Okay? It would not be good for your career or mine if you let me fall."

I pulled him back a little as the rams collided again.

"I don't have a career anymore, Raymond. Mr. DeMille fired me."

"Well, he's damn well not going to hire you back, if you drop me off the cliff when I'm trying to make the documentary Nasser wants," he said.

"You're the one who chose to go out this far, Raymond."

"Understood."

I could do it now. I could just lift his ankles a few inches and tip him forward. He would lose his balance like an overloaded wheelbarrow and disappear over the side.

"Do you believe in God, Raymond?"

"What?"

"Do you believe in the God who sees our actions and gives us consequences?"

According to Sherif, I would be more than justified in letting him fall. This man was more than my romantic rival. He was a Jew, an infidel, a representative of the greater enemy. Killing him would be my first real act as a jihadi. Maybe the first real thing I'd ever done in my life.

"No, I do not," he said in a steely tone through gritted teeth. "And I will gladly tell you why another time."

"Then what do you think holds you up, if you don't believe in God?"

"I thought *you* were holding me," he said. "But right now, I'm not that sure. If you're not going to get a more solid grip, can you please pull me back a little so I can get this shot without falling."

I could have done it then. I had the right anger. But God did not grant me the sign I was asking for. Instead, I looked over Raymond's shoulder and saw the two rams walking past each other, as if they'd lost interest in continuing their fight or had just finished airing their differences.

I pulled Raymond back half a foot so he could wind his camera.

"That's more like it," he said, pressing the button to get his shot.

Then I dragged him back another yard, making sure to scrape his elbows and chest. He got up and brushed himself off nonchalantly as if he were getting dressed after a massage. But for all his sangfroid, he was still a little ashen faced from being so close to the edge.

"Thank you," he said. "By the way, I didn't know the woman was anything special to you."

"Never mind." I wiped my hands on my shirt and started to turn away. "Just remember: we're even now."

December 23, 2014
To: Asur@protonmail.com
From: GrandpaAli71@aol.com

Alex,
It's been quite some time since I've heard from you. Is everything all right?
*   Please drop your aged grandfather a line. Even if it's just to say you've stopped reading. I don't mind. I only want to know that you're okay.*

Love,
Grandpa

11

I did not tell my father that I had been fired from the picture. After I got back to Cairo, I just kept getting up every day before dawn, as if I still had the job. I would comb the pomade into my hair and iron my shirts as if I were going to pick up Cecil B. DeMille from the brand-new apartment house where he was staying by the Nile and take him to the set. Every night, I would come home late and tired, so I didn't have to answer too many questions.

What did I do with the rest of my day?

I walked the streets, looking for new direction. I tried to get a job with the government work crews changing the street signs from the names of old kings to dates of the revolution. I went to Cairo Station and watched the trains come and go, wishing I could afford a ticket to get on one and go somewhere, anywhere, and never come back. I sat on benches beside the Nile, reading the Koran and watching the river flow. I hoped no one I knew would see me and ask what I was doing. Then I waited until after sunset to go home and make up gossip to tell my father about my friendly American bosses and how important I was to them.

We were still under the same roof, but I was living in isolation, becoming a stranger to him. I was not just lost but lonely and pining. I missed Mona. I missed having a little money to go to the movies and an evening meal or two at Café Riche, with leftovers I could bring home to my father. And most of all, I missed the fragile hopes that had sustained me, that wonderful faith I'd had that the curtain was just drawing back and the grand epic of my life story was about to begin.

After a week of this, my cousin showed up at the house. He arrived just before sunrise and pretended for my father's sake that he was going to give me a ride to the set fifteen miles outside Cairo, near a quarry village called Beni Youssef.

Ironically—no, *preposterously*—Sherif still had his job working on *The Ten Commandments* after I had been so unceremoniously sacked. Instead of taking me to the set, he took me to an old Mameluke-era mosque that I'd never been to before, near the Brothers' headquarters in Helmiya. It had threadbare red carpets, mold on its columns, and gold paint peeling from its grand vaulted ceiling.

Some of the men made a place for me among them in the front row near the mihrab, the rounded niche in the wall that faces Mecca, where our true faith lies.

They all knew I'd been driving the king's car that day. Yet they nodded and touched their hands to their hearts, like they were happy to have me there. Then I realized that the four very young boys at the back, who were being given special attention by the older men, were special guests as well.

"Those are Sheikh Sirgani's sons," my cousin murmured. "He had two daughters as well."

"Oh my God. What are they doing here?"

It wasn't even the mosque where their father normally preached.

"They wanted to see you."

"Why?" As in the prophecy, the two sides of my rib cage began to close in on me. "Do they want to kill me?"

"I wouldn't think so. Look at them."

I glanced over my shoulder. Not a one of them was older than ten. The imam must have started fatherhood late in life.

"Listen." My cousin rested a hand on my arm. "Our God is a

benevolent God. And our religion believes in forgiveness for those who pray."

The smallest of them, a pie-faced boy who wore glasses like his father's, gave me a shy wave.

"What's going to become of them?" I faced forward again.

"We're collecting money. And looking for a new husband for his widow. Now come on. Say the words."

I tried to regain my composure and remember the *fajr.* From disuse, the old gestures and words had turned into fragments of dry parchment on my tongue. But then I stood upright and looked toward the shrine of al-Ka'bah in Mecca, the most sacred site in Islam, placing my right hand atop my left hand on my chest and acknowledging Allah is greatest and there is no god but God.

The imam this day was a man not much older than myself, with a weak voice and a beard like seaweed clinging to his chin. But as I began my *rakats,* I was reminded, Alex, that there is no compulsion in our religion. There is joy. When I knelt and prostrated myself with the others, asking Allah to take me back onto the straight path and not the one that had led me astray, something began to unfold within me. A road through the moral chaos, a sense of clarity that had eluded me when I had foundered in the wilderness.

This was not some abstraction or hollow routine dressed up in velvet robes and ancient forgotten languages. It was true focused engagement, as real as the stone floor beneath the carpet I knelt on or the steering wheel that had been in my hands when that terrible accident happened. Faith, of the kind my cousin had, was alive and real: a cause to fight for and defend, a place to stand tall and be fully in the world.

"Subhanaka allahumma wa bi hamdika wa tabara kasmuka wa ta'ala jadduka wa la ilaha ghairuka."

I melded my voice with the others rendering praise to God and acknowledging no other was worthy of worship, a little stream joining the greater tributaries that led to the wider river of faith. I began to feel more substantial, like there might be a way for my life to be worth living again.

"A'udhu billahi minash shaitnir rajim."

I sought refuge from Satan, the accursed. Then I made a silent addition, asking forgiveness for my transgressions and asking God to show me the true steps toward redemption. Sheikh Sirgani's sons all lined up to shake my hand afterward. When the small one who had given me the shy wave reached up and put his arms around my neck, I started to faint and fall on top of him.

The next day, Sherif took me for a short run after prayer services and before he had to drive to the set. My wind was pathetic and my legs were gelatinous, but it was good to start moving again. After we were done, I drank water until my bladder threatened to burst.

The day after, I could run a little farther without needing to stop and squat to catch my breath every quarter mile.

On the third day, Sherif suggested that we try to re-create the old pyramid races we used to run as boys.

Those stone triangles are more immense than you can imagine up close. Each step is a challenge to the thigh muscles. We started at a light trot on the dirt road leading out of the village and past the hotel. The sun wasn't even up, but I was already sweating in my undershirt and the one pair of shorts that I owned. By the time my foot was on the first step of Khufu's pyramid, my lungs were tight and wheezing like an accordion with a bullet hole. My cousin bounded on ahead of me, using his one good leg to vault upward and hoist the one wounded in the war onto the next step. I gritted my teeth and put my head down, trying to forget the fear of heights I'd suddenly developed looking over Raymond's shoulder on Mount Sinai. My knees pumped harder, ignoring the cramping of my leg muscles and my gut. I grew dizzy as my heart pounded. I was afraid I might fall, but I was more afraid of my cousin beating me to the top of the pyramid.

I pulled into my core and raised my feet higher as the steps turned steeper and rougher. Sherif grunted and slipped. He fell on his face ahead of me. I reached down and tried to pull him up as I started to pass, but he cursed under his breath and turned his head in bitter refusal of any aid.

The capstone was high above us, half hiding the sun. Elbows tucked in at my sides, I lifted my knees and asked Allah to give me strength to reach the summit. My thighs were rubbing together and my calf muscles were shredding. But God straightened my back and allowed me to maintain the integrity of my gut. As I neared the top I heard Sherif give a high-pitched yelp behind me, and I knew I had him. I stepped onto the capstone and raised my arms, as the white eye of the sun offered me the forgiveness of its widening aperture.

Sherif limped up the rest of the way, his beard not quite concealing the same look of disgruntlement he'd worn when I beat him as a boy. Things were different now, of course. He'd been wounded fighting in the Negev while I was in my soft velvet seat watching John Wayne movies. But he threw his arms around me and embraced me with all his might.

"You did it, my cousin," he said. "I knew you still had it in you."

On the fourth day, he brought me to an old gymnasium in Dokki after his work on the set was done. There were several Brothers I vaguely recognized waiting there, as well as his friend, Mustafa, who wore a blue wrestler's singlet that plunged and gripped him in ways that I found very uncomfortable to behold.

"What are we doing here?" I asked Sherif. "I'm not a fighter."

"But now you *have* to be." He pinched my cheek and gave it a playful slap. "Or else you're a *khaser*."

The equivalent English word would be "loser," Alex. But that doesn't convey the full disgust and abasement of how my cousin said it in Arabic, or the way the old mats at that gym reeked from the sweaty, frustrated helplessness of the men who'd been pinned on them over the years.

Mustafa shook out his heavy arms and grinned as he beckoned for me to engage with him in the faded white circles at the center of a canvas. He was a large man with a short neck and a massive, proud-looking chest. He had a pale complexion and a reddish tinge to his hair and beard which he attributed to one of his ancestors being a member of a legion of lost Crusaders who had converted to Islam. The more likely story, shared among Brothers, was that his mother had an assignation with a Scotsman, which explained his father's absence and his defensive temperament. More dauntingly, Mustafa—the Americans on the crew called him "Big Mo"—had been a runner-up to be Egypt's entry in the Mr. Universe bodybuilding contest several years before, while my own experience of physical competition was limited to grappling with Sherif when we were schoolboys.

"Go on," my cousin said. "We have to build you up again."

"I promise I'll go easy." Mustafa rolled his head around on his broad shoulders until there was a crack. "But not too easy."

The others laughed as I held my arms out stiffly, not even sure how I should try to grab him. Mustafa seized me and put me in a headlock. Then he started to walk me around the room with my chin clamped onto his hip, proudly displaying me like a pet goat to the others as they doubled over with laughter. But, as I said, I was still wearing a good deal of pomade in my hair. It allowed me to slip out of the half nelson and dance away to show he hadn't hurt me.

As he came at me again, I noticed the awkward way he crossed his feet. Not like an experienced wrestler. It occurred to me that his impressive physique might not actually be that strong. When he grabbed me again and threw me down to the mat, I decided to resist. I stayed on my stomach, refusing to let him roll me over and pin me.

"Submit," he said under his breath, as he tried to bulldoze me onto my back. "Come on. Get it over with."

At first his strength was so overwhelming that I might as well have been grappling with a jeep or a three-hundred-pound tiger. But the longer I made him struggle, the heavier his breaths became. I kept my knees and elbows locked and my center of gravity low. When he tried to grab me by the hair, I suddenly jerked my head back and smashed it into his jaw. I heard his teeth come together like castanets. He slapped me and let out a childish yelp as if he'd bitten his tongue. I jumped up and pulled free of him just as I heard my cousin blow a whistle.

"Okay." Sherif clapped his hands. "That's enough for now."

Mustafa looked at me, grunting and panting, his face even redder than his beard. To this day, I don't know if he'd held back to help me build my confidence, or if he was simply not as good as he claimed to be.

After I toweled off and showered, we went to Professor Farid's houseboat, docked near University Bridge, for evening prayers and the intellectual salon. It was really not much more than a floating living room with thatched rugs, rickety furniture, and a tiny galley. I had spent many happy evenings there, expanding my mind before we had our break. As I stepped aboard for the first time in months, the deck beneath me and the smell of bilge water filled my nostrils. I almost hit my head while entering the low-ceilinged cabin and I felt a little seasick.

I suppose I was scared that I had been lured onto the boat to be attacked as an apostate. But Brothers whom I had never met before stood up to shake my hand, and the professor himself, who was not given to physical displays of warmth, put his arms around me and embraced me in a way that he never had before. Instead of talking about Western literature and film as we had in the old days, we talked about suras and respect for the laws of our religion. I do not remember all that was said, but I realized what I had been missing for so long when I was chasing my movie mirages. Here was a sense of belonging, of being at home in the family of my Brothers, of what Mona had called a *purpose*.

"I don't like very much about the Christian Bible anymore," the professor said, taking a moment to embrace both Sherif and me after the meeting. "But I have always loved that story of the prodigal son. What was lost is now found."

So I was more than a little surprised when my cousin came up to me on the pier afterward and told me that the next day we would be driving out to the set in Beni Youseff and I would be working on *The Ten Commandments* again.

"What are you talking about?" I asked. "What you're suggesting isn't even remotely possible. Mr. DeMille fired me personally."

"It doesn't matter." My cousin shrugged. "He's fired and rehired at least three people since I've been on the set. That seems to be how it is with these movie people."

I nodded, having seen the same volatility on Egyptian productions as well. We even had an expression for it: "Gone with the wind, back with a belch."

"Anyway, they've agreed to give you another chance," Sherif explained. "Just not at the same level. You'll have to work your way back up."

"'Not at the same level'?" My voice cracked. "How much lower can you get than carrying a man's chair around for him?"

"You're going to need to work two jobs for less money, to get back into"—he stopped to search for the right English—"'the good graces of Cecil B.'"

"You're not joking?"

"Your father's the one who tells jokes." He shook his head in disapproval. "But listen. I've arranged for you to be in a crew with me two days a week, helping with the rigging and painting. The other three days you'll be with Miss Mona and this Jew she's working with, carrying gear for their documentary."

I could scarcely tell the seething in my head from the lapping of the river against the dock.

"Who even suggested this?" I asked. "I'd sooner have Mustafa's sweaty stomach in my face."

"It was my idea," Sherif said. "And Miss Mona was all for it when I spoke to her."

"*You* spoke to Mona?"

"Yes." He started pulling on his beard. "For you, I can try to get along with her. I always said I was a better actor than you gave me credit for."

"And what did she say?" I asked.

"I was able to take advantage of her guilt." He gave a little laugh behind his hand. "She feels bad because you got her hired for this film and now you don't have a job on it. She said she'd speak to this Jew Mr. Raymond and convince him to go along with it as well. Even though he's a little reluctant."

"I'm sure he is!"

Yes, I had ostensibly saved him from falling off a cliff, but he had more than enough cause to be uneasy around me.

"I don't know, Sherif," I said. "But why would I even want this again? You told me yourself I was wasting my life and hurting our cause just by associating with these infidels."

"Are you joking?" He smirked. "You'll be given unprecedented access as part of the documentary unit. You'll be filming air force bases, army installations, the Egyptian mint, and Nasser's personal office. You'll be able to report back to us when they're planning to make their move against the Ikhwan. Which our sources say they are."

"Why would Nasser let me see any of that?" I asked.

"Don't underestimate yourself, Ali. You can be very persuasive when you want. I saw how you lied to get the assistant's job in the first place."

"That was different." I blushed, embarrassed. "That was convincing a bunch of American movie people I was qualified. Nasser is in charge of the whole military and intelligence operations."

My cousin grabbed my ears again and mashed his prayer-callused forehead against my still-unblemished one. "Have faith in God and trust in your Brothers. You won't be alone."

As he said this, other Brothers were stepping off the houseboat and coming up to shake my hand. I liked the way they slapped my back and shoulders, welcoming me into the fold and letting me know in gesture as well as word that I was now one of them.

"I still don't understand how I could have gotten rehired after Mr. DeMille himself fired me. Mona asking Raymond couldn't have been enough."

"It wasn't," Sherif admitted. "I had to get involved in convincing some people as well."

"You? How?"

"I talked to this Mr. Chuck, who's playing Moussa the prophet. He said he didn't like you at first either, but then he felt bad about how you'd been let go."

"Wait—You've gotten to be friends with *Charlton Heston*?"

"In a way." Instead of pulling on his beard, Sherif smoothed it with a touch of pride. I told him I'd been a soldier and we started talking about guns. He's very knowledgeable, you know."

"Yes, be careful. He said he's a hunter."

"We talked about that as well." My cousin grinned. "To be honest, he's not such a bad fellow when you get to know him."

January 13, 2015
To: GrandpaAli71@aol.com
From: landocal@protonmail.com

Grandpa,
I told you that you wouldn't be hearing from me for a while, didn't
I? But I suppose it's natural for you to worry. So I wanted to use this
new email address to let you know that I'm all right for now.
  I can't write for very long, or tell you anything about where I am
and what I'm doing. But trust in Allah that I am with my brothers
and happy in my sense of purpose. I'm glad your book has taken a
turn. I was beginning to question why I still was reading it. But now
I'm starting to see why you say you were on the same path before me.
  I was specially interested to read about you trying to get into
better shape, because I've been doing the same thing. You would
scarcely recognize me now! I've lost, like, twenty pounds in fat and
regained it in muscle, because I've stopped eating crappy American
junk food and started exercising. Every day since we've arrived, I've
been running five miles a day with the others. I can do nearly fifty
push-ups without running out of breath or stopping because my
muscles are exhausted, the way they did when I flunked phys ed and
had to make up the credits to graduate. We've been climbing ropes
and lifting weights, and next week we continue our intensive weapons
training. Soon they tell me I will be introduced to my bride.
  Anyway, I guess you can tell Mom and Dad I'm fine. But please
remind them that I'm never coming back and they need to accept
that.

                              Yours, with respect,
                              Abu Suror

12

Sherif picked me up early the next day, but instead of going to prayers we drove out past the golf course and the pyramids until sand stretched out into infinity on both sides of the road, striated lightly with the distant memory of having been underwater many millennia ago. In my obsessive sorrow and yearning for Mona, I began to see womanly curves in the berms and dunes, as if God practiced the notion of the feminine on this landscape before putting it into human form.

I was about to ask Sherif if we were going the wrong way to *The Ten Commandments* set when, fifteen miles outside Cairo, a giant pharaonic city loomed up from the sand, like a battleship suddenly appearing in the middle of the desert.

An avenue lined by sixteen ivory-white sphinxes led to a pair of gates that were at least eleven stories high and a quarter-mile wide. I looked up at them as if King Kong's foot were about to come down and crush me. Flat-roofed pylons pushed back a nearly purple sky, their façades painted in brilliant hues of yellow and blue, depicting scenes of royal hunts and kings in chariots firing arrows at the sun. There were identical black marble pharaohs on either side of the entrance, thirty-five feet tall, seated and staring out placidly as if they could see clear to the end of time.

The gates opened and a line of horse-drawn chariots burst forth as if from the pages of a children's storybook. White and brown chargers hauled golden-wheeled baskets, with the whips of men in brass helmets and breastplates flashing in the dust. They came right at us, links in an endless chain, then abruptly veered away. A white Ford pickup truck was in hot pursuit, with Cecil B. DeMille hanging out a side window and hectically shouting directions through a megaphone while my Egyptian replacement translated.

"Go get them! Ride, goddamn it, ride. Ride like your job depends on it!"

"What's going on?" I asked.

"It's just another rehearsal." My cousin hit the brake to avoid getting us caught in the middle of it. "For this big Exodus chase scene with all the people they're filming next week."

One of the soldiers fell off the back of a chariot and went rolling off the track, his helmet rolling off in the opposite direction. He wound up facedown and motionless in the sand. The chase went on without him and no one appeared to look back.

"Allah!" I turned to Sherif. "Why doesn't anyone go to help him? He looks like he could be seriously hurt."

"This is how it goes. He's not the first. They'll take him to the hospital, but not before the rehearsal is over."

I recognized the actor Yul Brynner bringing up the rear of the chase, in a chariot that was much bigger and more ornate than the others. He was wearing a white T-shirt, and his completely hairless head was gleaming in the sun. He was smoking a cigarette and holding on to the side of his wagon like it was a cruising yacht while an Egyptian in a modern cavalry officer's uniform whipped the horses for him.

"This shaven-headed one is playing the pharaoh Rameses the Second," Sherif said. "If you end up working with him, make sure you always have a pack of cigarettes ready."

I was still a little shaken as we parked behind the façade, among the trailers, trucks, and regular cars. Henry, the assistant director Chico Day, and some of the others whom I'd worked with before my

firing nodded and smiled, cautiously welcoming me back as we made
our way through a small industrial city that had been set up near the
ancient quarries.

We passed a huge commissary tent with outdoor grills and dozens of picnic tables, a makeup tent where extras were getting their
bodies bronzed with makeup, and yet another tent where scenic artists were painting pieces of kelp that would appear on the dry bed
that was supposed to be the parted Red Sea at yet another location. I
smelled fire from the forges of a blacksmith's hut where artisans were
busy soldering and hammering shields and helmets. Just behind a
half-dozen wardrobe trailers were two massive derricks digging wells to
provide water for the thousands of extras and animals who were already
starting to show up. Not to mention the full-sized corral for the horses
and a legion of gasoline-powered generators with step-down transform-
ers on poles hidden just behind the façade of the pharaoh's city.

Less than a week before, I would have been enchanted and enraptured by all that had been wrought in Cecil B. DeMille's mighty
name. But now I was enraged. *How dare they?* I finally understood
why the professor and the others had turned against these outsiders.
The Americans had spent millions of dollars to create this extrava-
gant mirage, when villagers nearby were starving. They stood to reap
millions from their illusion while paying a pittance to the sweating,
straining, hardworking Egyptian bodies that risked permanent injury
and disfigurement, if not actual death, to help them do it. My salary
had been reduced from twenty dollars a day to five dollars a day, for
doing twice as much work. Others were getting even less and getting
thrown from moving chariots.

All at once, I detested everything about these *kufar* from the smell
of their hamburgers grilling in the commissary tent to the way they
gave everyone nicknames ("*What's the scoop, Ali Oop?*"). I told myself
that I would have eventually turned against them anyway, even with-

out the harsh lessons of Sinai. But as I followed Sherif up a series of ladders behind the façade, I became sick to my stomach. And not just because of the fear of heights I'd discovered in Sinai. I was disgusted with myself for having shamelessly aped these outsiders for so long, without noticing they were blatantly laughing behind my back.

"Hey, buddy, looking good."

The sound of Sherif's voice singing out in English startled me. Down below, Chuck, in his Moses beard and wig, aimed his staff up at us like a rifle and pretended to fire.

"See? He really does think that we're friends," my cousin muttered in Arabic. "I really am a better actor than he is."

I shook my head in wonder as I joined him on a platform some eighty feet above the ground. Sherif had constructed a persona that was completely at odds with who he had always been: a cheerful happy-go-lucky laborer in denim overalls who whistled while he worked. And one of the peculiarities of our situation is the more serious our operation became, the more he relaxed and developed a sense of humor.

"Look around," he said, hands on hips. "What do you see?"

Now that the chariot-race rehearsal was over and medics had taken away the fallen man, there was another large-scale rehearsal going on at the right side of the gate. Hundreds of Egyptians, who looked to my eye like village peasants, had been dressed up in rags like slaves of olden days. Perspiring and mostly shirtless, they were using ropes and push poles to drag a giant obelisk toward a square-shaped hole in the ground. The pickup truck carrying DeMille swung around and the director climbed out with his megaphone in his hand, not missing a beat as he transitioned toward rehearsing this sequence.

"Push harder, you Jews!" he shouted as an Egyptian assistant director tried to keep up with simultaneous translation through a smaller bullhorn. "Harder! Strain your backs, show your muscles. Pull, you mud turtles, pull! Put your backs into it. This is the bitter brine of affliction! Chico, get some more overseers out there, for Chrissakes. Let's see some real acting! Some emotion! It looks like you're all posing for a Sears, Roebuck catalogue. . . ."

Idris, the production assistant who had replaced me, ran up behind him with the director's chair. I must confess that it hurt my pride more than a little when he opened it just in time for Mr. DeMille to be seated.

"What I see is people making a movie." I answered Sherif's question. "A very expensive movie."

"Good. That's all you're meant to see. A pack of filthy lies meant to make us the villains and the Jews the heroes of this libelous fairy tale."

"Okay." I had heard this before from the professor. "What *else* am I supposed to be seeing?"

For once, Sherif's smile overwhelmed his beard. "We're going to make our own movie, inside their movie. Only it's going to be much bigger and better than Cecil B. DeMille's, because it's going to be real."

I picked up a hammer someone had left lying on the platform. "Sherif, what are you talking about?"

I happened to glance down at that moment and saw Raymond and Mona off to the side of the obelisk rehearsal. He was handing her his ugly little camera with its revolving lenses and showing her how to turn its crank and look through the viewfinder. I had to restrain myself from dropping the hammer on them.

"Ali, forget them." My cousin touched the yellow-painted wall we were standing next to. "Look at this."

"What about it?"

"It's just painted wood panel on massive scaffolding," he explained. "Eleven stories of space. I've had them put sandbags at the bottom of the pylons to help stabilize the whole structure so it doesn't sway too much when the wind blows."

"And?"

"You didn't ask me what's *inside* the sandbags."

"Sand, I'm guessing."

"TNT and ammonium nitrate. From the ammunition dumps the British left behind in Sinai and the Western Desert."

I abruptly became very self-conscious about the vibrations we could set off with any large movement or loud word.

"Don't worry." Sherif nudged me. "They're not hooked up to any kind of fuse yet."

"Sherif, we're not talking about blowing up the set. Are we?"

"Of course we are. Why do you think I brought you up here?"

"But what purpose would it serve? It's only a movie."

"A very big movie. A very big movie that our enemy Nasser has chosen to support. That the Americans have spent truckloads of money on already." He was clearly enjoying slipping back into his familiar childhood role of being the one to lecture me. "If Nasser can't protect them with their massive investments, then the foreigners will take their money and go home."

"I suppose that's possible," I allowed.

"Of course it is. Nasser's regime will be destabilized and collapse within days. Mohammed Naguib will be brought back into power and the Ikhwan will have a seat at the table. In fact, we'll *own* the table, because Naguib will owe us everything."

I grew dizzy, realizing how far we could fall. "But do you really think the people will be with us, Sherif?" I asked. "It sounds like hundreds could be hurt."

"Don't be stupid, Ali. We're not going to do it when there are bystanders and risk casualties." My cousin took me by both shoulders and shook me. "Think, man. We're going to set off the charges in the middle of the night, when there's no one minding the set, except our people in the security ranks, and we can get everything we need into place. It'll send up a fireball that they'll be able to see all the way back in Cairo, fifteen miles away. Can't you just picture it against the black night sky?"

He put his hands up, framing the shot like a director so I could visualize it.

"I'm seeing the great Cecil B. DeMille sleeping peacefully in his king-sized bed in the penthouse beside the Nile." Sherif moved his hands like he was locked into a panning shot. "In the meantime, Nasser is in his bed at general headquarters. Suddenly they both hear a massive boom. In their different locations, they both throw back the sheets and roll out of bed in alarm." His voice grew thick with portent, as if he were narrating a newsreel. "Through their windows, they see the glorious red eruption like a volcano in the desert night. Oh my, Ali. It will take the heart out of them. Like God himself has decreed their defeat."

The more he talked, the less far-fetched it seemed. I should explain, Alex, that this was long before the time when suicide bombers and the massive killing of civilians in peacetime were regular news events. But we'd both been out on the street during the revolution just over two years before, and had seen how the king had been deposed after the foreigners' hotels and businesses were set ablaze with minimal casualties.

"Will it work?" I asked.

"What do you mean, 'Will it work'?" Sherif frowned, with the kind of withering condescension DeMille sometimes showed his assistants.

"Don't explosions need something to *push* against?"

"It *will* have something to push against." He stopped and sighed as if he needed to remember to be patient with those of lesser vision. "This structure will be closed up before they start filming. Don't you see? We can use what they've built against them. And do you know where we first got the notion?"

"Not at all."

"From the Jews themselves." He pointed in the general direction of Israel. "When they got rid of the British."

It took me a moment to understand what he was referring to. Eight years before, our enemies in Jerusalem had their own war to free themselves of the English mandate. Zionists from the Irgun terror group bombed the King David Hotel, where the foreign authorities had their headquarters. They snuck in disguised as Arab workers and waiters, and killed nearly a hundred people. Publicly, most people I knew in Egypt called it "terrorism"; privately, some, especially in the Muslim Brotherhood, admired the boldness and ingenuity.

"They put the bombs in milk cans by the support columns," Sherif said, yanking on his beard as his excitement grew. "We'll use the gasoline in the generators below as kicker charges. It's brilliant, if I don't say so myself. The explosion will ignite the material we've embedded up here and—*boom*—if we time it all correctly, the whole thing will collapse under its own weight and burst into the conflagration. Without anyone getting so much as a splinter in the process."

I could see how much he wanted my admiration, just as he had when we were boys with our virtue society.

"It could work," I admitted. "I see you've thought it through."

In a way, my cousin was a man ahead of his time. He was envisioning exactly the kind of staged act of destruction that could be filmed and shown over and over on twenty-four-hour news networks and the internet.

"It will be just like this stupid movie you dragged me to," he said, wanting to share his enthusiasm. "The one where the blind man tears down the pillars and the temple collapses—"

"*Samson and Delilah*? Mr. DeMille's movie?"

"He made that?" My cousin threw his head back and for the first time I could remember gave a full-throated laugh. "Oh my God, this is even better. This makes it perfect."

"It would be ironic," I admitted.

"You know, this won't even stop him from making this moronic Moses movie," Sherif said in a musing voice. "He just won't be able to do it *here*. He'll probably just take the insurance money and go back to Hollywood."

I must have looked sad when he mentioned that faraway place because he cupped my chin in his hand and squeezed it.

"Oh, poor Al Harrison," he said. "You weren't still thinking they were going to take you with them, were you, *Al Harrison*?"

I pushed his hand away. "I should have never told you about that."

Down below, Mona was aiming the camera up at us with Raymond hanging over her shoulder.

I grimaced and bit my lips as I turned back toward the façade. It was better to think about my cousin's operation. I wanted to feel strong instead of broken. I pictured high-velocity shock waves erupting from the hidden places, knocking out the base on one side of the gate and then the other, destabilizing the structure and causing it to come crashing down, flimsy as a house of matchsticks, nails and planks flying, the giant brought to its knees, collapsing in a mighty thundercloud and leaving only smoldering wreckage.

My pulse began to quicken as I imagined being part of something so momentous and devastating. I would not have to think of myself as a loser who had disgraced himself in Sinai. Who wouldn't want to be a warrior instead?

"But what is it you need *me* for?" I asked. "I have no ordnance training."

"Don't you see? That's the beauty of it. No offense, Ali. But everyone thinks you're a harmless toady who works for movie people."

"Oh, thank you for that." I looked up at the boiling clouds, knowing the sarcasm would be lost on him.

"Don't be so sensitive," he said. "You're not on anybody's security watch list, like some of the others in the Ikhwan. So after work tonight, you'll go by the Mena House switchboard. There will be an envelope in your name left with the concierge, with money and an address inside. It will be an out-of-the-way place."

"What will happen when I get there?"

"There's an English soldier who says he's willing to work with us—for a price. He claims he has access to time pencils."

"What are those?"

"Fuses for the explosives." He saw me look at him blankly and dropped his voice. "Instead of long fuses leading to detonators, they're just compact devices that you can time to go off."

"How much trouble could I get into if I'm caught?"

"It's not going to be a problem. There probably won't be any security officers around to see you. We've planned a distraction event. We finally got the permits, so they'll be watching the march we're having in the streets to recognize the martyrdom of the imam. And what you're buying aren't explosives anyway. They need to be connected to blasting caps to set off the explosives. They can't arrest you for having them. I just need someone I can trust not to run away with the money."

The platform we were standing on was no longer swaying in the wind. But my interior scaffolding was still vibrating. Especially when I looked down again and saw Raymond put his hands on Mona's shoulders and turn her like a piece of equipment, to film something else.

"And you really think we can pull this off?" I asked.

Sherif put a hand over his heart. "Look, Ali, from the time we were small you've said you wanted to be like the cowboys and the soldiers in the movies. Now is your chance. You can help bring down this hypocrite Nasser. And when the histories of this time are written and our names can be revealed as the victors, you'll be remembered as a hero."

"I wish I could be as certain as you are."

"Our side will prevail," Sherif assured me. "We'll be celebrated. Despite themselves, the Americans will even make a movie of it."

"About this attack? You think they'd show their own set in flames?"

"Definitely." He nodded. "They'll show it all over the world, like that zeppelin that blew up." He walked toward the ladder to begin the long climb down. "Trust me. If there's money to be made from blowing things up, they'll sell tickets."

February 3, 2015
To: GrandpaAli71@aol.com
From: landocalr@protonmail.com

Grandpa,
I wish that you and Sherif could see where I am now. It is truly a paradise.

All armed resistance has been pushed aside and the pharaoh's soldiers have melted away like the cowards they are. We have come into this town, which I still am not permitted to name, and we have changed it almost overnight. The black flag of our militia flies over the town square. Like your cousin, I am working the Promotion of Virtue unit for now. All the haram places that sold liquor under the counter have been shut down. So have the stores that sold CDs and DVDs with Western depravity. Now the voice of the muezzin rings out from the minarets, and the songs of Jay-Z and Beyoncé have been silenced. The men have all started to grow beards and the women now cover themselves from head to foot in burka and niqab. You can no longer even see a quarter inch of bare ankle! When I finally meet the bride I've been promised next week, I will make sure she dresses this modestly.

We have laid claim to some of the American-made military equipment that the army abandoned in Iraq and our rivals brought over here. It's insane. My comrades, who come from all over the world, are having a great time firing off artillery and driving tanks in circles. My turn is supposed to come soon.

And, yes, we have closed down all the movie theaters. No one will be seeing Thor or Captain America here soon, I can personally assure you. I broke into the projection both, with the others, and watched the confiscation and burning of the prints.

It's funny, though, that you mention your friend Mustafa. It's a common enough name here, but my American upbringing was so corrupting that I keep reading it as "Mufasa," like the father from that silly Disney Lion King cartoon. Thank Allah that I'm beginning to forget all of that.

I hope you don't mind, but I have shared some of what you've written with my brothers in the struggle.

To be honest with you, a lot of them were down on you at first. As you know, anyone not involved in the struggle is the enemy of faith. I don't need to add that some of the decisions you made would bring shame on any family. But now that the story is turning toward the path of righteousness, I can see that you did try to redeem yourself by doing something of significance with your cousin.

I also took the chance to show some sections to some of my commanders, who have otherwise strictly forbidden communication with outsiders. But when I told them that you'd been involved in qisas, the principle of equal retaliation, they were interested in hearing more. So I have been allowed to stop by the internet café in the nearest town (which I am not permitted to name) and print out a few of the pages you have written for the censor to review. Thanks to God, we can continue our exchange.

P.S. Some of my friends are totally into reading this out loud. Especially when too many people are using Call of Duty or Grand Theft Auto IV on the lame PlayStation setup they have at the house we took over. I think some of them may just be doing it to embarrass me, though. :)

Yours in triumphant conquest,
Abu Suror

February 4, 2015
To: landocalr@protonmail.com
From: GrandpaAli71@aol.com

Grandson,

I am concerned to see you starting to sound like a fanatic. And it saddens me to hear you renounce so much of your old life. Especially since I so enjoyed the hours we spent watching The Lion King over and over when you were a very small child sitting on my lap.

But your message also reminds me of how I was when I started to get caught up. It's painful and deeply unsettling how much I recognize of myself in you. I wish something I could say would make a difference. But sometimes I think the old trying to talk to the young is like the dead talking to the living.

Thank you, at least, for letting me know you're still okay. Please take care and write again.

Yours in sorrow and compassion,
Grandpa

13

All at once, my pointless and servile life had significance. I had become a secret agent, like in one of the English spy novels my father read. After my day of work on the set, I went back into the house to change into a blazer with a red pocket square, as Sherif had told me to wear, then strolled over to the Mena House front desk to pick up the money and address where I was to meet the English contact.

There was money in the envelope that had been left in my name—fifteen hundred Egyptian pounds, to be exact. But instead of the obscure location that my cousin had promised, a short handwritten note told me that the original spot had been compromised and instead I should proceed immediately to the Auberge des Pyramides nightclub just down the road.

This seemed like both a good and a terrible idea. On the one hand, a lot of people went there. On the other hand, a lot of people went there. The club had been a favorite destination for King Farouk. It was said that Egyptian men did not like to bring their wives there, lest the monarch cast his eye on them and demand their company. But it was also frequented by tourists and expatriates, so I would not attract undue attention meeting with a foreigner.

I decided to stick my head in to assess the risk. It was after eight o'clock, and L'Auberge was already so crowded that hardly anyone looked at me when I appeared in the entrance. The club was set up in such a way that there was an outdoor courtyard used for drinking and performances in the summer and an indoor area with tables, chairs, a bar, a waterfall, and a dance floor that could be electronically raised as a stage. On this night, the interior area was filled with musicians in sunglasses and red vests who were performing Egyptian and American popular tunes to a *beladi* rhythm. A beaded curtain parted and Miss Fatima, the belly dancer who had been at the Semiramis, appeared. Her bare arms, adorned with golden asp bracelets, were held out from her sides, and she stood stock-still, letting the waves of our anticipation build as she presented the lush and only occasionally veiled body she was about to deploy for our entertainment.

All eyes were on her. Except for a pale, wrecked-looking man wearing a cockeyed fez and a water-rat mustache. He was waving to me from a side booth as if he were mortally wounded and I was an ambulance driver.

"*Oi, oi, oi,*" he called out. "Over here, lad."

Two or three heads turned, even as Miss Fatima cocked a hip once to the left and twice to the right. I realized I would draw more notice for leaving right away, so I headed over to him.

"Are you Mr. Abdul?" he asked only a little more sedately.

This was the unfortunate code name that Sherif had given me, along with the instruction to display the red pocket square.

"You can call me Neville." He took a long draw off a hookah he had set up on his table. "As in Chamberlain. Though that's not me real name either."

"Sir, do you not think it would be good to do this at another time, in a different place?"

"Not bloody likely, Abdul." He exhaled, wafting orange-flavored smoke and whiskey stench at me. "I'm not meeting you in some dark alley where I can get me head coshed in. It's now or never, lad. Have a seat."

I slid into the booth opposite him as the musicians began to play an Arabized version of the theme from *The Third Man* that was popular then.

"You're a writer, then, are you?" Neville asked.

"Sir?"

I was a little stunned that he would have so much of my biography. Sherif had told me this would be a clandestine business.

"I assume you're a writer because you're interested in 'writing implements,'" he said more deliberately, as if he were addressing a slow-witted child.

It took me a half second to understand he meant the time pencils.

"Yes, sir," I said. "I'm interested in writing, but I do have a deadline."

"You don't fancy a drink first?" He reached up for his fez as it started to topple off his head. "Or are you one of those Moslem temperance league types who won't touch a drop?"

"No, sir." I slouched down in the booth. "I've just seen the sorrows that alcohol can bring and would prefer to do our business in a state of sobriety."

"'Ship me somewhere east of Suez.'" The Englishman raised his glass, which was half full of brown liquid. "'Where the best is like the worst. Where there aren't no Ten Commandments an' a man can raise a thirst.'"

I glanced down at my watch, disconcerted by the looks I was getting from two men at a table by the waterfall. They were both wearing suits that appeared to have been cut and sewn by hardworking tailors with no true understanding of how clothes were supposed to hang.

"Don't know your Kipling, do you?" Neville asked.

"Yes, I know who Rudyard Kipling is, sir," I snapped. "Do you have a package for me?"

"Steady on." His mustache drooped as if I had hurt his feelings. "You have something for me as well?"

I took the envelope from my pocket and put it on my lap. "How shall we do this?" I asked.

"Show me yours and I'll show you mine." He finished his drink in one gulp and then held up his glass to a passing waiter. *"Un autre, garçon, s'il vous plaît. Et ghayarlee il hagar low samaht."*

"You have the writing implements ready?" I asked, losing patience.

"You have my shekels?"

I started to reach for the money, raised by the Brotherhood's charity division to help widows and orphans and then diverted to the so-called secret apparatus for militant operations. The envelope slid off my lap. Just then I saw, at the bar just to the right of the waterfall, my father.

He was still wearing his Lacoste shirt and green pants from the golf course and was talking to two pink-faced men whom I recognized as customers from America. With them were two women in false eyelashes and garish makeup, who I was equally certain were Egyptian prostitutes.

This is a part that grieves me still to talk about, Alex. But if I am making my full testament before God and my descendants, I am compelled to tell the whole truth. I had long suspected that when my father did not earn enough from his meager salary and tips on the golf course to pay for our food, my books at school, and all the necessary clothes for my work, he had a side business introducing his customers to such women. My cousin, whose father I believed had also done such things, had alluded to it several times over the years. But this was the first time I had witnessed such sinful behavior with my own eyes.

I tried to look away and pretend I hadn't seen them, as the Americans and the women laughed with forced gaiety. But my father did not join them. His eyes found mine in the smoked mirror above the bar and then skittered sideways with shame.

"Let's get this over with," I said to the Englishman. "The longer we stay here, the greater the risk. You pass your package beneath the table, and then I'll give you my envelope."

"'Here's your hat, what's your hurry,' eh?"

There was a commotion near the entrance to the club, more clacking of beaded curtains and a raising of voices. I saw a shaved head and the lit end of a cigarette being held high above a gathering crowd. Yul Brynner had walked into the room, his shaved head as conspicuous as a hundred-watt light bulb screwed into the socket of his black turtleneck. He was accompanied not only by Henry and two of the second assistant directors I'd seen on the set but, bringing up the rear, Raymond and Mona.

I slouched down even farther, so that my knees wound up touching the Englishman's.

"What's all this then, guv'nor?" Neville stiffened.

"I'm just trying to be discreet, sir." I peered around cautiously as Yul Brynner and the rest of the crew were shown to a table right in the middle of the room.

"*Yanks.*" Neville huffed his pipe sourly. "They think they own your whole bloody country, now, don't they?"

From the corner of my eye, I saw my father hastily exit the club, leaving a trail of shame as vivid to me as the perfume and flavored tobacco in the air.

"Let's get this over with," I said, turning back to the Englishman. "On the count of three, I'll pass what I have to you and you'll pass what you have to me."

"As you like . . ."

He used a cotton napkin to honk his spongy-looking nose while he slipped a package wrapped in newspaper under the table in exchange for the envelope with the money.

"There you go, old son," he said. "A dozen British writing implements straight from the supply dumps in Sudan."

My cousin had explained these were copper rods that acted as fuses or, more accurately, delay switches. When bent at a certain angle, they released acid that within ten minutes struck a firing pin, triggering the blasting cap and a massive explosion. I started to rise.

"Hang on there, Abdul. You're not leaving till I count the filthy lucre and my fingers. You lot have a reputation for stealing anything that isn't nailed down."

"I was about to say the same about the British, sir."

We were interrupted by rustling and clanging. Miss Fatima had left the stage and glided over to waggle her supple belly at me, urging me to get up and dance with her.

I put a hand up to cover the side of my face and tried to ignore the bewitchment of her hips. But I heard laughter and handclaps. Yul Brynner and his American friends were enjoying her play at seduction. This was a calamity beyond all imagining. Especially when Mona saw me.

I wanted to tell her that I was truly not here for wanton purposes. That even after all that had happened, there was no other woman I would ever desire more than her. But then Miss Fatima's cool damp belly brushed my cheek, she reached for my hand, and Mona looked away as if she was ashamed for me.

"I'll tell you, lad, they don't do the hoochie-coo like that on the Brighton Pier." Neville clapped his horny hands and added his throaty roar to the mess.

I shook my head at Miss Fatima and she pouted seductively as she spun away toward Mona's table, finger cymbals chiming with wild abandon.

"Our business is done," I said.

Miss Fatima was trying to get Mona to get up and dance with her, while everyone else was stomping their feet and whistling.

After much vehement urging from the men around, Mona stood

and faced the belly dancer. She had her hair back, and she wore a beige linen dress that looked very modest in these demimonde surroundings. She swayed her hips and shook her shoulders in appropriate rhythm, but I recognized the look on her face. She was trying to have a good time, or at least trying to make all the men around her believe she was having a good time. But she was making herself do something that she did not wish to do. As her eyes stayed on mine longer than they had to, I had the oddest feeling that she was asking me to forgive her.

"I need to go." I stood up, with the package under my coat.

"Off with you, then." Neville put the pipe stem back in his mouth. "Enjoy your next revolution. One good turn deserves another, eh?"

I walked out briskly, trying to make sure I hadn't been followed by the men in the ill-fitting suits. Then I went over to the Mena House and had two glasses of wine at the bar, to try to calm myself, even as I kept the package under my elbow.

I moved gingerly as I walked home through the desert chill, lest the fuses snap and set my sleeve on fire. A half-moon shone down on the Sphinx. I could hear the whispers of ancient intrigues in the shifting sands. A group of my father's friends were in the courtyard outside the house, playing dominoes and smoking hookahs of their own. Gentle souls who worked during the day as waiters and bellhops at the Mena House, who'd helped the family after my mother died. But on this night, I scarcely gave them a nod as I took off my shoes and went inside, the whistle of a teakettle in the kitchen greeting me.

"*Ali*, is that you?" my father called out. "Can you bring me in the pot? I'm in the bath and the water's getting cold."

"Just a moment."

I went into my bedroom and hid the package beneath a loose floorboard under my mattress, then got the whistling teakettle from the kitchen. My father was sprawled and shrunken in the tub, his brown eyes barely open under lids the size of mushroom caps, shoulders slumped from carrying golf bags all day.

"Just pour it right in," he said. "My entire body is aching."

I did as he asked, a little bit at a time, trying not to notice another half-empty bottle of Johnny Whittaker Red sitting behind the tub.

"How was your evening, Ali?"

"Fine," I said. "How was yours?"

He sank a little lower in the water. "I had a good day today. Mr. Lawrence McCauley from the Standard Oil Company was playing against two gentlemen from Ohio Welding. He scored an eagle on the eleventh hole. He tipped me ten Egyptian pounds afterward—"

"Father, stop your prattling." I cut him off. "I saw you tonight. And I know you saw me."

He tried to raise himself up by holding the sides of the tub. "There's nothing wrong with socializing with customers off the fairway, *ya ibni*. These are my friends."

"They're *not* your friends. They're your customers."

I was filled with disgust. For more than thirty years, this humble man had been handing clubs to players without an eighth of his talent on the course, complimenting them on their atrocious techniques, and thanking them for their stingy tips. Never even complaining when one of their wives heedlessly ran over his right foot with a golf cart, leaving two of his toes permanently mangled. In America, he might have someday been as rich as his heroes, Bobby Jones and Ben Hogan. His arms were thin, almost spindly looking, but when he swung a club the ball arced high above the pyramids until it disappeared against the sun, before touching down within putting distance. Then he would finish the job with small, finely calibrated strokes, like an artist with a brush. How many times had I watched him on the course, befuddled by his patience and frustrated by the slowness of the game, but wishing I could find a calling that would bring me as much sense of dedication and satisfaction?

Now I had found such a calling, and it caused me to look down on him.

"And I saw the women you were with at the club tonight, Father. I know what they are."

He went still in the water. "It's not what you think—"

"It's *exactly* what I think," I said, with disgust. "Are you just the procurer, or are you one of the customers as well?"

"Don't talk to me that way, Ali."

"I'll speak to you any damn way I like."

"Don't you dare." His eyes blazed. "You haven't the right."

I shut my mouth. I was a little stunned to hear him speak this way. Through all our hardships, I had never truly seen him lose his temper before. It was a frightening thing to behold, because he'd been holding on to it for so long, and now it was as explosive as the fuses I'd hidden under the floorboards.

"You know, it's totally haram to be a pimp." I tried to recover. "How could you even do this?"

"I did it for you, *habibi*." He simmered, refusing to look at me.

"Oh, don't try to put it on me. You probably use the extra money to pay for that alcohol you drink. You know, it's not even top-shelf."

"I don't do it for the alcohol. I don't drink that much."

"*Fine*. Keep lying to yourself. Look where that's got you. Selling our women's bodies to foreigners—"

"I did it to help you."

He smacked the water with both hands, splashing my face and pants.

"That's nonsense!" I jumped back. "You're making excuses because you don't have the nerve to ask for more money in tips."

"No, Ali. I don't do it for myself. I do it because I'm trying to earn enough money to help you go to America."

"That's another lie."

"It's *not* a lie." He looked up, the fury in his eyes becoming colder and harder. "I do it to get contacts that can help you. Some of my customers are in the film business. Why do you think they helped you get those jobs? Because I advise them on what putter to use?"

I grabbed a ragged hand towel to wipe myself off. "Then I don't want you to do it anymore. It's sinful."

"Since when do you talk that way?"

"Since I woke up." I threw the towel down and then picked it up to put it properly on a rack. "I don't need these contacts anymore anyway. I can help myself."

I went to the linen closet and brought back two fresh towels for him to dry off with. They were from the collection that my mother had brought over from the Mena House Hotel years before. Another disgrace. We had some of the best cotton and the best weavers in the world, and then we let foreigners put their monograms on it.

"By the way, who was that I saw you with at the club?" my father asked more evenly.

"Never mind, Father. It was no one of any importance. No one you need to know about."

"It looked like a very serious conversation."

"He's a producer, okay? A film producer. I'm already looking for my next job after this one."

He looked up at me with his liquid brown eyes, no longer angry but sad. He knew I was lying to him as surely as he knew he had been lying to me.

"That's good," he said. "Maybe that will lead to another opportunity. If things don't work out with Mr. DeMille."

I nodded. He was a simple man, but not a foolish one.

He reached up and grabbed my wrist as firmly as he gripped his nine iron. "Don't worry, Ali," he said. "I think things will work out for you in the end."

I tried to pull free, but he was too strong. "What makes you so sure?" I asked.

"Because you're not like your cousin." He held firm for another second before he released me. "You're a good boy. You know how to be happy and contented. I remember how you were as a child and your mother would take you to see the pictures. I'd like to see you smile like that again."

"That was a long time ago, Father." I offered him another towel to dry off. "Here. You'd better get out before the water gets too cold."

March 17, 2015
To: GrandpaAli71@aol.com
From: Sureshot@protonmail.com

Grandpa,

I'm sorry it's been a while since you've heard from me. Access to the internet has become a little problematic. One of the rival groups attacked us and damaged our power lines. I am fine, Alhamdulillah, and we captured several of these infidels.

But there is also good news. Because of my background with computers and the sections that I've shown from your book, my commanders have transferred me to the media production and editing unit. Which is awesome! Just as you and your cousin did in your day, we recognize that we need to use modern means to send our message, and the camera can be as potent a weapon as the cannon.

So, just like you and this Raymond, we're going to be making documentaries. Kind of. My video unit has been assigned to go around the town we've taken over, getting interviews with the residents about how life is under our regime. We're supposed to be getting candid man on the street interviews (the women are all inside the houses, naturally).

To be real, it's a little tough so far. Most people we talk to seem too scared to say anything interesting. They just get this glassy look and keep saying, "Yes, it's better now. I can't wait for the caliphate." I think they're afraid they'll be punished for saying the wrong thing.

So thanks for giving me the confidence to apply with your story. You may not have realized it, but your book is serving as a kind of reference letter for me.

And by the way, I finally got my bride the other day. Her name is Shayma. She is young. Really young. And not so easy to understand. I'll tell you more about her later.

Yours truly,

Abu Suror

March 18, 2015

To: Sureshot@protonmail.com

From: GrandpaAli71@aol.com

I'm sure you can understand my chagrin at your last message, Alex. This is not at all what I intended when I sent you my book. But my story is in your hands now and your fate is in God's hands, so, Insha'Allah, somehow we'll all find our way to a happy ending. Including your new "bride," who I would like to hear more about.

Yours,

Grandpa

14

I was already in a heightened state of tension on the first morning that I worked as a driver for the documentary unit. There were army officers on the veranda of the Mena House Hotel when I went to pick up Raymond that morning. One of them took out a notepad and made no effort to hide the fact that he was writing down the license plate number of the red Ford Crestline I was driving, signaling there would be no evading responsibility for accidents from now on.

Nor did it ease my mind when Mona came out of the lobby, looking a bit like a glamorous nun in a white headscarf, bright red lipstick, and Foster Grant sunglasses. A Chanel pocketbook slung over her shoulder and a tripod under her arm furthered the impression of a woman between two worlds. Raymond came out after her, wearing sunglasses as well. I began to feel a little sick. They had both told me in Sinai that nothing romantic was going on between them. But she was supposed to be living at her father's villa in Garden City more than thirteen miles away. How could she have gotten here so early if she hadn't spent the night at the hotel?

It did not help that they both got in back together, as if I was just their chauffeur now. "Good morning, Mr. Hassan," Raymond said. "How did you enjoy your evening?"

"Fine, sir." I bristled at him resuming the formal way of address after I'd saved his life. "How did you enjoy yours?"

"Very well." He yawned. "I saw you at the club last night. You didn't seem to be having a good time with our belly dancer."

"Perhaps I wasn't in the right frame of mind." I started the engine. "I just wanted to be left alone."

"Then why come to a nightclub, eh?" He pushed his sunglasses down his nose.

I made a sharp turn onto the Pyramid Road, to throw him off balance. In my rearview mirror, Mona was turned toward her window with a preoccupied expression, her ruby lips pressed together, her brow furrowed.

"That's okay." Raymond lightly elbowed her. "You're not the only one who was put off. Miss Mona was not terribly amused either."

"It was all right." She looked through her pocketbook perfunctorily. "I just don't like when an art form is treated like a burlesque show, with men ogling and whistling. I prefer to appreciate the aesthetics of the performance without being pressured to join in."

"You don't think Yul and the others appreciated Miss Fatima's aesthetics?" Raymond teased her.

"Maybe it's just cheap titillation to you." She snapped the clasp shut. "But there's a craft to what we do in this country. Ali taught me to appreciate that."

In my rearview mirror, I saw her face forward, as if she was looking at the back of my head. Her lips twitched as if there was something more that she wanted to say to me. There was an ache in my chest, a crack threatening to let hope seep back in under the armature my cousin had just given me. In my distraction, I almost plowed into an oncoming production truck and realized that I had to pay stricter attention to what was directly in front of me.

Our first assignment that morning was to film Nasser performing a speech Mr. DeMille had prepared for him at general headquarters. As soon as we crossed the bridge to Gezira Island, I noticed the ramped-up security measures. There were twice as many jeeps and soldiers as there had been on the streets for our first visit. There were new barricades set up in front of the former royal mooring house and a line of cars delayed by guards, closely inspecting every identification card and then passing a mirror on a pole beneath every vehicle.

"What are they looking for, bombs?" Mona asked.

"'Uneasy lies the head that wears the crown,'" Raymond replied, with his sardonic half smile.

"I hadn't heard about any direct threats." Mona took off her scarf and glasses. "Ali, have you?"

I shook my head, worried my voice would betray me if I spoke. My cousin would be asking detailed questions about all the new procedures in place. Once our papers were examined and our identities verified, we were directed to a parking space near the entrance. When we got out, two male soldiers frisked Raymond and myself, while a woman in civilian clothes searched Mona. It was hard to conceive of anyone bringing weapons into such an environment, without being on a suicide mission.

An escort led us upstairs with our gear and brought us into the prime minister's office, just down the hall from the much larger room where we had met with Nasser before. A crew from the main *Ten Commandments* had been sent over to help give the scene a more professional look and sound than the rest of the documentary. Two large Mitchell cameras sat on tripods. A boom operator dangled a Shure microphone just above the frame line, which contained dozens of the medals and military citations that he had already collected on the wall behind him. A gaffer adjusted thousand-watt lights with Fresnel lenses while an electrician looked for additional power outlets. But Nasser was not yet present. Instead, General Amer sat behind the desk, reading through script pages and making slashing marks with a pen.

As we walked in, Amer stared at me with his woebegone expression as if he was sad about what would become of me. Then he stood up and shook my hand firmly like we were old friends.

"Ali Hassan, so good to see you again." He held on longer than seemed necessary. "I was becoming concerned about you."

"About *me*, General?" I tried to smile through his surprisingly powerful grip.

"Yes, we had heard you were no longer with the film," he said. "We were relieved when we were told that you had returned. We were worried that your attitude toward our project might have changed."

"I had no idea you'd been following my work so closely," I said.

As I took my throbbing hand back, I wondered what else they knew.

"I noticed there are more guns and security around than the last time," Raymond said, looking up from polishing a lens.

"With good reason." Amer tugged self-consciously on the hem of his uniform jacket. "You may have heard that those Muslim Brothers we told you about last time tried to stage a march to memorialize one of their so-called martyrs last night. This imam, Sheikh Sirgani—"

"The one who was killed?" asked Mona.

Raymond and I studiously avoided exchanging a look.

"Yes," said Amer. "We had initially granted the permit and then decided to deny it at the last second, because we saw signs the people were getting too stirred up again. Now our sources are telling us that they're threatening to retaliate."

"These are crazy people," Mona muttered.

"Yes, there's a lot going on." Amer thumbed his lower lip dolefully. "Not just with Ikhwan but with the Israelis and their spy network. We locked up a group of them who were planning to plant more bombs and create more instability. We'll have a trial to make examples of them as well."

"'As well' as what?" asked Mona.

The general set the script pages aside and studied her. His interest did not seem warm or even romantic. He looked disturbed and aggrieved, as if she had betrayed him personally by choosing to speak up. It was becoming more and more obvious that Nasser's not being here was a deliberate strategy of some kind. Amer picked up a bulky brown file that had been lying on a large desk and began to page through it as if he was impatient to find a certain item.

"Forgive me, Miss Salem," he said. "You were not here last time, and we weren't properly introduced. So perhaps you're not aware of all that was discussed among us."

He raised his eyes from the file and looked at me in such a way that there could be no mistake about what he was referring to.

"General, with all due respect." Raymond breathed on the camera lens. "Is there not a danger you're just adding fuel to the fire?"

"What do you mean by that, Mr. Garfield?" Amer closed the file.

"It's perfectly understandable that you would be in a state of heightened vigilance." Raymond removed a handkerchief from his breast pocket to wipe away the fog he had created. "But isn't it possible that this is exactly what your enemies want? To provoke the prime minister into acting like a dictator, to justify their own violent response?"

"You have to appreciate the difficulty of our situation," the general replied. "The prime minister is trying to move Egypt from being a monarchy to being a republic in less than a generation. When they did this in France, they had the guillotine." He struck the edge of the file against a corner of the desk with a loud *thwap*. "Even in the glorious United States of America, there was a bloody revolution. Here, we are trying to use the velvet glove. And your movie camera. But sometimes it's necessary to show you're still willing to bring down the iron fist."

I noticed the other technicians had left the room and it was now just the four of us—Mona, Raymond, Amer with his file, and myself—in the heat of the thousand-watt lights. And, of course, Nasser, who pulled off the movie star's trick of making his presence seem much bigger by virtue of his absence.

"That's why we've had to increase security measures the last few days." Amer took his time looking at each of us, the funeral director taking measurements. "Our enemies believe we'll fall if they keep the pressure up. And then they can take over in the power vacuum. That's why we have to be more cautious with the people we allow to get close. I've asked our intelligence service to take a closer look at the backgrounds of those Mr. DeMille has hired. It seems that Moham-med Naguib did not do a thorough enough job."

He reopened the file and began to page through it more quickly. Fear began to eat away at my composure.

"You're not suggesting that a member of our crew is under suspicion, are you?" Raymond asked.

"We're asking questions that should have been asked before." Amer stopped turning pages and lifted the file toward his face. "Miss Mona." He affected a quizzical expression. "Your father, Nabil Salem, was close with the previous regime, wasn't he?"

I flinched like a man before the firing squad who had just seen someone next to him get shot unexpectedly. Mona, who was normally very graceful, wobbled a little on her high heels.

"If you mean King Farouk, he was," she said, after taking a moment to remember her English. "But he has repledged his loyalty to the Revolutionary Command Council. He still has diplomatic contacts in France that will be helpful to your administration."

"And where do your loyalties lie?" the general asked. "To your father or to your country?"

"I don't believe there's any contradiction." She covered the Cartier watch on her wrist. "We're all for Egypt. Aren't we?"

"Are we?" Amer did not appear convinced as he turned to another page. "And what about you, Mr. Garfield?"

"What's the question?" Raymond ceased his polishing.

"Was your name always Garfield?" The general stared at him more keenly. "The State Department was not able to furnish us with your birth certificate. And your passport is only from 1952."

"Because I was born in Germany," Raymond replied. "And my original name was Gorfein. I changed it, as many people in the film industry do. Kirk Douglas was Issur Danielovitch Demsky. Paul Muni was originally a Weisenfreund. Jean Harlow was—"

"We don't do that in this country." Amer cut him off. "People are what they say they are. And if they change their identities, we like to know the reason. Especially before we allow them into our country."

"There was no attempt to deceive anyone, General." Raymond put the handkerchief back in his pocket. "I was a last-minute replacement for another filmmaker whom Mr. DeMille decided to fire. I presented all the documents I was asked for."

"Still, I wonder." Amer returned his attention to the file. "It says here that you served in the United States Army Signal Corps during the war with Germany. How is that possible if you were born in Germany?"

"I immigrated long before the war." Raymond straightened up as if he was parodying Prussian rectitude. "Out of necessity. Then I joined the army in gratitude to my new country, as many others did as well."

I was not sure where this was going, or why Amer was insisting on scrutinizing our backgrounds so intently at this late stage. Or how much of this had been scripted in advance by Nasser and left for his sidekick to deliver and keep his own hands clean. All I knew was that the room was beginning to feel unbearably stuffy. And that in this atmosphere of growing suspicion, it was only a matter of time before this form of the evil eye found its way back onto me.

"And what about you, Mr. Hassan?" Amer asked. "I see no record of any military service from you. Why is that?"

"I was in school during our conflict with Israel, General," I said, my voice thick with embarrassment.

"At King Fuad University, yes?" I noticed he did not need to consult a file to know that detail.

"Yes, sir."

It was obvious that he had most of his answers and was making a point by asking me these questions in a certain way. To lead me up a path and into a corner.

Nasser finally came into the room, making a late dramatic entrance in his dress uniform and medals. He did not smile or try to shake hands with any of us. His mood seemed more brusque and official than it did the last time. I noticed he was carrying a file of his own. It was noticeably thinner and more orderly than the one Amer was holding.

"You founded the student cinema society there?" Amer continued his questions. "In 1948?"

"That's correct, sir."

I was sure General Amer was about to ask about Professor Farid's support for my club and my level of contact with my teacher these days.

"You were showing movies, when your countrymen were serving and sacrificing their lives?" Amer asked.

I heard a tut-tut sound and saw Nasser shaking his head in disapproval as he looked down at the file he had brought in. I knew he was in possession of a report from the men who'd been watching me at L'Auberge the night before.

"Let's not be too hard on our young friend," Nasser said to Amer, pretending to chide him. "We all have our roles to play."

My mouth went dry. I still could not tell what his purpose was. But I was no longer consumed with jealousy over Mona and Raymond. I was more concerned about whether I would be able to walk out of this room as a free man.

Mona looked at her watch. "Perhaps we should start filming? We were told the prime minister could spare us only twenty minutes."

Nasser put his hand up, refusing to be rushed. "We have brought all this up to make a point. This is a historic moment for Egypt. Next Tuesday, I will be formally announcing the signing of the Evacuation Treaty for Britain to withdraw its troops from Egypt."

"Allah," I exclaimed. "Finally."

I may not have trusted Nasser, especially at that moment. But like every Egyptian I could not wait to have the boot heels of the colonizers off the backs of our necks.

"I'll be speaking to a quarter of a million people in Alexandria," Nasser said. "And the speech will be carried live on our national radio system."

"Sounds like quite the event," Raymond said. "Are you going to frisk everyone who comes to hear you?"

"That would hardly be practical." Nasser's eyes began their familiar glittering. "But we need to be vigilant. These reports we're receiving from our intelligence service show our various enemies are becoming more violent in their plans."

"Are there specific warnings you're passing on?" Raymond asked.

"I do not want to reveal what we know or don't know yet," Nasser said. "We have our sources."

"Then what *are* you asking, Mr. Prime Minister?" Raymond inquired.

"We always want more eyes and ears," Nasser said, looking around. "Can I trust you all to be part of it?"

The floor felt like it was swaying beneath me, like I was back up on the platform with my cousin discussing his plans. I remembered Raymond's camera tilting up and finding us on the scaffold at a crucial stage. If the explosives were found on the set, that footage would be enough to send Sherif and me to the gallows. With a sinking heart, I realized I needed to try to stay on my rival's good side.

"Prime Minister, we're only filmmakers." Mona brushed her fingers through her hair. "What can we do?"

"We've given you access to military bases, government agricultural areas, and even the mint where we make our money," Nasser noted. "You do remember that as part of our cooperation agreement you are expected to report on any counterrevolutionary activities that you observe or overhear?"

"Are you offering to hire us as members of your intelligence service?" Raymond held his arms out. "What's the per diem?"

"This is serious." The natural effervescence of Nasser's gaze became flintlike. "Anyone who knows about such activities and doesn't report them will be considered an accomplice. Do we understand each other?"

Mona's complexion, which usually had olive undertones, became pale. "I don't know anyone involved in such things."

"Nor do I." Raymond went back behind the camera he'd set up.

Nasser stared back at me. I could see many things had changed in a short time. He was no longer the man who had hesitated to sit in the big chair. He had become more like the man who expected the chair to be ready when he decided to sit down.

"What about you?" he asked.

"You would know if I knew anything." It was hard to keep my eyes off my shoe tops. "But I'll continue to be on alert."

"Shall we begin filming?" Raymond prompted. "Mr. Prime Minister, do you have the script pages Mr. DeMille wrote for you?"

"Yes, but I've decided not to use them." Nasser took several sheets out of the folder he had brought in and laid them flat on his desk.

The crossed-out script pages were covered with Arabic handwriting on the back.

"I wrote my own speech instead." He grinned, pleased with himself. "I think it's better."

April 2, 2015
To: GrandpaAli71@aol.com
From: Sureshot@protonmail.com

Gedo, Grandpa,
I've continued sharing your book with my commander and some of the other warriors I'm with. We just got done reading the part where Nasser was trying to menace you guys and scare you in his office. What a dick. There are a lot of arguments among us about what he was really up to, but there's a general consensus that it would have been better if you'd had a gun instead of a camera with you that day.

I also wanted to let you know that our own big project is going pretty well. I think I told you before that my video interviews didn't go so well, but now we're onto something way bigger than a Hollywood movie. We're developing an online video game called Kill the Crusader. It's a first-person shooter that allows thousands of people all over the world to be playing at the same time on their computers. We call it an RPG about RPGs (role-playing game about rocket-propelled grenades, get it?). And since a lot of the people who play these games are kids between the ages of twelve and twenty-four, it's like the best recruitment tool we've ever had. It's pretty crude, but I got the idea from that Crusades movie you mentioned earlier.

So thanks. I changed my mind about what I said before. I am actually starting to feel closer to you from reading this.

Yours,
Alex

P.S. Things aren't working out so well with me and my "wife." But I'll tell you about that when I have more time.

15

When we drove to the main set to report to Mr. DeMille at the end of the day, I found Sherif and went behind the façade to tell him what I had observed at general head-quarters.

"I think Nasser may be onto us," I said. "He was saying that anyone who knows about subversive activities must report them—"

"Stop and breathe in." He gave me an encouraging pound on both shoulders. "He would say that to anyone. He's becoming paranoid and frightened. And that's a good thing. It means he's about to make a mistake."

"He has good reason to be paranoid. He knows a lot of people are trying to bring him down. I'm afraid who could be watching us."

"Okay, calm down. No one is looking right now." Sherif glanced up at an army plane passing low overhead. "I'm going to need you to provide us with the number of guards he had on duty and sketches of the rooms you were in."

"Why?" I asked. "Are we planning something else besides what you told me about?"

He looked around as the wardrobe assistants trundled by with racks of slave costumes and pharaoh's army tunics.

"The less you know, the better." He lowered his voice. "We don't want to jeopardize any part of the operation."

I used the collar of my T-shirt to mop at the perspiration stinging my eyes. "Sherif, I think he may know we're up to something bigger," I said.

"Why?" He grabbed me by the elbows. "Did you say something you shouldn't have?"

"No, but he was asking a lot of questions. And he said they had sources who were watching us closely."

"That doesn't mean anything—necessarily." He tried to laugh. "By the way, are you sure that you weren't followed after you bought the 'writing implements' at the club?"

"I took every precaution that we talked about, and then some."

"But you still met with this Englishman after he changed the location?"

"Are you saying I shouldn't have?"

"No, no, of course not." He squeezed my arms more tightly. "I'm just trying to be careful."

"I wasn't followed," I said so emphatically that pigeons in a nearby coop fluttered. "I would have noticed."

"I'm sure you would have." He threw a fake cowboy punch at my jaw, to reassure me. "And you didn't say anything to anyone either, did you?"

I had not told him about seeing my father, Mona, and Raymond at the club. Nor did I mention Henry, Yul Brynner, or the two men in ugly suits who had been watching me.

"Of course not," I said, afraid of what he would do if he believed my mistakes had hurt the operation.

Before he could ask me more, I heard a voice on a bullhorn summoning all hands back to the set. Chico Day, the assistant director, was calling out that all crew members were needed on the double. Mr. DeMille had decided he did not like the color of the Per-Rameses gates and wanted them painted again.

"I'll talk to you later," Sherif said with an exasperated sigh. "This business never stops."

T he next day I was not on the schedule for the documentary or crew work on the main set. But a pickup truck pulled up in front of my father's house and idled for several minutes, as if it was waiting for me. When I came out to see what was happening, my cousin's friend Mustafa leaned out the driver's window with his pale sweaty face and red beard.

"Get in the back," he said.

I saw he had two other men in front with him. A calf was standing up in the back, blinking and making little bleating sounds.

"What's going on?" I asked.

"Your cousin wants to see you."

"Why? I just talked to him yesterday."

"He's concerned about something you said." Mustafa stuck a finger in his ear and glanced back at the calf. "We need to adjust some of our preparations."

"Okay, just let me tell my father." I was already formulating a plan to get away. "We were going to play golf this morning."

"It's better if we go right away." Mustafa leaned back, so I could plainly see that he had a handgun lying on the passenger seat beside him. "Don't bother your father."

We took a long twisting route out into the Western Desert, the calf swaying and continuing its bleating beside me, its flanks twitching anxiously the whole way.

The midmorning sun was a glaring inspection light as we arrived at a desolate spot I'd never seen before. A single acacia tree was standing like a lonely prophet in the wilderness. It had a thin, crooked trunk, thorny branches, and dry gray-green leaves.

"Where's Sherif?" I asked.

"He'll join us later, if he can." Mustafa came around to the back with the others, the gun plainly displayed outside his tucked-in shirttails now.

"What are we doing all the way out here without him?" I asked.

The hatch dropped.

"Testing the operation." Mustafa grunted as he carried the squirming calf off in his massive arms. "It's getting late for mistakes."

One of the others helped me down. I realized I had met him before, through my cousin. He was a former Cairo police officer named Osman who had a finicky, exacting look, as if he was constantly smelling something disagreeable. He was a prodigious hashish smoker, like my cousin, and a harsh critic of the drugs, which he never found good enough. He moved with exaggerated efficiency, showing off as he carried a gray package over to the tree and then cracked the neck of one of the time pencils I had bought from the Englishman.

"We want to see if this works," he called out. "Or if we have to torture you for bringing us duds. Heh, heh."

The rest of them joined in his laughter.

At that point, I had only a rudimentary understanding of how long it would take for the acid inside the rod to release the firing pin or how powerful the blast would be once the pin struck.

"Drop and give me twenty-five push-ups right now." Mustafa shoved me roughly.

"What? Why?"

"Do as I tell you. We need to see what you're made of. Osman was a police officer. And Ramzy was in the Egyptian Navy." He pointed to the other man, who was trim and as taut as a length of hemp. "But you need to prove yourself."

"Does Sherif at least know what we're doing out here?"

"He ordered it," Mustafa said. "Now get down and give me twenty-five. And be prepared to do a lot more."

After four sets of twenty-five push-ups, they had me run a quarter mile full speed, until I was wrung out and on the verge of collapse. Then I heard a boom and looked up to see the tree disappear in a cloud of smoke and dust. When it all cleared, the acacia was split almost down the middle, with its limbs blown off and the twisted remains of its trunk smoldering.

The three of them shouted and clapped one another on the back like the Egyptian national soccer team after a goal. The calf, now tied to the back of the truck, stared at me unhappily.

"What did I tell you?" Mustafa socked me hard on the arm as I got up to watch the smoke clear. "In the Koran, it says the reward for patience is doubled. Eight minutes and fifty-two seconds. *Allah Akbar*."

I rubbed the place where he had hit me, thinking he was paying me back for not being able to pin my shoulders to the wrestling mat.

He took the gun from his waistband and pointed it at my face.

"What are you doing, my brother?" I put my hands up. "What's the matter?"

"What would you imagine the matter is, '*my brother*'?"

It's odd what you notice at such frightening moments, my grandson. The revolver was the kind British carried on the streets of our childhood, an Enfield Number 2 with a top break. Then I fixated on the redness of his beard and the way he mocked my speech, like a man with something to prove.

"I've done everything I've been asked to do so far," I said.

"There was an arrest made late last night," Ramzy, the navy man, said. "The authorities took in the English soldier you gave our money to."

"'Took in'?" I gave each of them a searching look. "Is he officially under arrest?"

"We don't know yet." The sun was shining on Mustafa's outstretched arm as his muscles and sinews tensed. "But we know someone talked."

"Why suspect *me*?" I asked in an indignant squawk. "That man's a drunken lout. He could have said anything to anyone."

"He's already in custody and our sources tell he's not talking," said Osman the former policeman. "His embassy is trying to claim they have jurisdiction and get him sent back to England."

"You're the weak link among us," Ramzy said with the special contempt that experienced seamen have for landlubbers.

"How would it even be serving my interests to speak to the authorities?" I asked, trying to appeal to their logic.

"You're already in trouble because of what happened to the imam," Mustafa retorted. "So now you're trying to find a way to save your own skin."

The muzzle of his pistol pressed into my forehead, a cold metal circle imprinting itself where more devout men had their prayer calluses.

"It still makes no sense, what you're saying." I shut my eyes. "Think about it. Nasser can't be trusted. Even if I told him all that I know, he would have no reason not to use me and throw me away. He'd gladly make me a scapegoat for the imam's death, if it was convenient. The Brothers are my family now. I could never betray my cousin. Do you think I went to university so I could choose the losing side?"

"So you believe we'll win?" Mustafa asked.

I swallowed and nodded, still not opening my eyes.

"Why?" he asked.

"They have the numbers and the money, but we have the belief," I said. "And nothing is more powerful."

In the silence that followed, I smelled the burnt wood of the exploded acacia and heard the calf's forlorn baying. After a few seconds, the pressure of the barrel lessened against the front of my skull.

"So you've said nothing to anyone?" Mustafa asked.

"Of course not." I pried my eyes open. "I know what can happen to traitors."

"Do you?" Mustafa asked. "Then prove it."

"How?" I rubbed my forehead where I could still feel the muzzle's stamp.

"With this." He shoved the gun at me. "Use it."

"On who?"

My brow felt sore, and so did my pride. I realized this had been a game of some kind and they were all laughing at me a little.

"Show us that you're one of us." Mustafa nudged me with the gun again, his crimson beard a contrast with the sand around us. "That you're ready to do what it takes to protect the operation if you find out who has been talking."

"Are you testing me to see if I could shoot an informant?"

"Could you?" Mustafa placed the grip firmly into my palm. "Could you look someone in the eye and pull the trigger?"

"If I had to," I said, not very convincingly.

"Then do it." Mustafa folded my fingers around the grip. "Let us see that you really have the heart of a warrior."

He stood back, revealing the calf dipping its head and staring at me curiously.

It was dusk by the time we got back to Cairo. Sunlight had just faded on the Nile, replaced by the cherry neon flash of a Coca-Cola sign on the black rippling surface. We had taken a byzantine route back from the desert to make sure we hadn't been followed. We made a stop at a butcher shop in Faiyum to deliver the remains of the calf who had to give her life in order for me to demonstrate my loyalty. Then we continued to the city and the professor's houseboat, rocking gently on the evening current.

I heard him speaking in the main cabin as I stepped off the dock, his voice high and straining with didacticism as if he were back in the classroom. But as I stepped through the beaded curtains into his salon, with Mustafa and the others right behind me, I was brought up short.

A camera had been set up in the living room. Professor Farid sat erect and a little overwhelmed by the large pillows on his couch while Raymond filmed him and Mona held out a boom microphone.

"Yes, the title of this song was truly 'Diamonds Are a Girl's Best Friend.'" My teacher wagged a finger, the sound of his pained outrage filling the cabin. "I could not believe my own eyes when I saw the film. Not just base animal lust, *but pure material desire*! Sung by this blond *harlot* in a hot-pink gown that barely covered her breasts. I ask you, what could more epitomize the diseased foreign state that's trying to impose its will on the peoples it hopes to subjugate? We've given the world the pyramids, the library at Alexandria, the temples of Karnak and Luxor, and what do you give us? *Marilyn Monroe!* You see? This is why we resist you."

His voice trailed off as he glanced toward those of us just arriving.

"Cut." Raymond took his eye from the viewfinder. "I think we got it that time. Mona, don't bother with the slate. We're ready to check the gate and pack up."

"What is this?" I asked.

It was as confusing as walking in on the middle of a feature or finding a Christmas tree in the middle of the Al-Hussein Mosque's courtyard. These things simply could not coexist. Especially not when I had Mustafa, Osman, and Ramzy at my back, eager for an excuse to take me back out to the Western Desert again.

"Mr. DeMille wanted us to include as much of Egypt as possible," Raymond said with a sporting shrug. "He thought Professor Farid would appreciate having the *Ikhwan Muslimin* point of view represented in the documentary."

"He's been very impressive," Mona added. "Especially as a counterpoint to what we already have."

"Excellent." I nodded, with a sickly smile.

The floor rocked beneath us, from the wake of a passing motorboat. Who could have possibly suggested that this was a good idea? Yes, I could imagine DeMille thinking he might placate and flatter a troublesome critic by putting him in front of a camera. But why would he have risked Nasser's wrath by giving a known Muslim Brotherhood spokesman such a platform?

"Did you ever think you would see me in the movies, Ali *bey*?" The professor offered me one of his rare smiles.

His teeth were still in a state of anarchy, incisors and canines facing one another like rioters. He told me that he'd bolted from a dentist's chair in America because he feared the gas that he'd been given was altering his thoughts. He had no idea how bad they would look on film, and now I was in no position to warn him.

"Miss Mona says that you're next bound for Alexandria," the professor said.

"*Ostazi?*" I reverted to the old honorific.

"To film our glorious new leader's propaganda speech to the masses," he said sarcastically. "It should be quite the show."

I looked from him to Mona, still trying to get my sea legs as the boat kept rocking. Everyone appeared to be acting contrary to their normal best interests. The professor referring respectfully to Mona, when I knew he disdained her as much as he disdained all of his other female students. Mr. DeMille handing over screen time to a known enemy of Nasser's in a film he was producing for the prime minister. And Mustafa, whom I had overheard speaking offhandedly about using the pretext of another uprising to burn down the Ben Ezra Synagogue in Old Cairo and attack known Jews on the street, nodding pleasantly at Raymond.

"Yes, I hope to be part of the crew at the Stock Exchange," I said. "Though we haven't really discussed the schedule yet."

"Of course you'll be there," Raymond said brusquely. "We'll need to take extra hands for an event of this scale. We just didn't need you tonight, because it was such a simple setup."

"Of course." Though for some reason, his words rang false in my ears.

I assisted them in putting the rest of the gear away and helped Mona step off the boat. But the professor held on to my arm as I started to get off after her.

"Stay," he said. "There's something we need to discuss."

He guided me back into the cabin, where Mustafa was once again taking the gun from his waistband and holding it out by the barrel.

"You need to bring this with you when you drive to Alexandria tomorrow," the professor said.

"No. I cannot." I crossed my arms to tuck my hands under my armpits. "What if I'm searched?"

"They won't search you if you're part of the film crew," Mustafa said, as he kept thrusting the weapon at me. "And they'll let you get close to the stage."

I turned away, sickened all over again. "It's impossible. I was barely able to shoot that animal from three feet away."

"Don't be an idiot." Osman gave a spiteful little laugh. "We wouldn't trust you to pull the trigger. I'll find you once we're allowed near the VIP area, and you just slip it to me. I'll take care of the rest."

"It won't work," I said. "Nasser and Amer are already on high alert. And what happened to the plan to blow up the set?"

"We decided to put it on hold while we have this opportunity," the professor explained. "How many times will we have a chance where the pharaoh is appearing before a quarter of a million people in Mansheya Square?"

"And what if I say no?"

They all stared. I heard a sloshing sound and smelled noxious odor. For a moment, I thought both were coming from inside me. Then I realized it was bilge water that had collected in the houseboat's side boards.

"Ali, effendi." The professor came over and laid a hand on my chest. "You have a father who is still alive, don't you?"

"Yes."

He smiled up at me with his snaggled teeth. "Your cousin tells me that he's been involved in some sordid business with women. Is that true?"

I stiffened. "He works at the hotel golf course. That's all I know."

Mustafa and Osman knocked into each other and smiled as the boat rocked. No doubt they had known sordid business with women themselves.

"You need to open your eyes," the professor said. "One way or the other, Nasser will be deposed and Naguib will be put back in charge. And when that happens, we will rule with shariah, our laws will come from the Koran and the hadiths and there will be severe penalties for anyone found to be involved in the exploitation of women and their bodies. Do you understand this?"

"You're not seriously threatening a member of my family, *ostazi*, are you?" I was nearly pleading with him to tell me that I'd misunderstood.

"I'm just telling you what's *likely* to happen." He tapped the center of my chest. "Unless there were mitigating circumstances to earn your father special dispensation."

I held his wrist to make him stop. "But how can you justify this?"

"Easily." He pulled away. "You can find justification on every page of religious text ever written, if you twist the words enough. But this is different. We're fighting against the dominion of man over man, when it should be only God over man."

"I still think this is a terrible mistake," I said, though I knew it was useless.

One thing I have learned from living in both America and the Middle East: You can never change anyone's heart or mind when they are confident that they have bullets in their gun and God on their side.

Mustafa stuck the Enfield in my waistband. "Don't break any traffic laws this time. *Insha'Allah*, all will go as it's supposed to, and tomorrow the pharaoh will die."

April 3, 2015
To: GrandpaAli71@aol.com
From: SeekerAL@protonmail.com

Grandpa,
I'll have to make this short because I don't have much time. I'm using a different encrypted address because I need to ask your advice about something.

Things are not working out with me and my wife. Shayma is only, like, fourteen. She's Yazidi. She and her younger sister got picked up by one of our rival groups near a place called Mount Sinjar near the Syrian border and then sold to us. I guess in the States they'd call this kidnapping. Now she's supposed to be, like, my sex slave. My commanders cite all kinds of verses from the Koran and hadiths to justify it, but I don't know if that's what the Messenger really meant.

Long story short, Shayma just sits on the mattress, crying all day. She doesn't speak any English, but I think she really misses her

family. When I go near to try to comfort her, she shrinks away like
I'm some kind of monster. So now I feel bad for her. In fact, I don't
even want to touch her. But I don't want to reject her as a bride,
because I'm afraid of what the others will do to her instead.

What do you think I should do?

Yours in haste,
Alex

16

W hat's wrong?" Mona asked me from the back seat.

It was the next day, midafternoon, and we were on the long desert road to Alexandria with our camera gear, and the green fields and water-lifting seesaw shadoofs of the Nile Delta were no longer in sight.

"Why do you ask?" I adjusted the rearview.

"You keep looking back." She turned around, her knees on the seat. "Is something bothering you?"

There had been a red car behind us for the last hour at *least*. It never appeared to speed up or slow down. It just maintained the exact same quarter-mile distance from us, whether my foot was on or off the gas.

"We seem to have an escort." Raymond barely glanced up from making his shot list. "They've been on our tail ever since we left Cairo."

"Who are they?" Mona asked.

"Probably studio accountants, minding the expenses," Raymond answered, drawing a swift line across a page.

"Or someone else coming to see Nasser's speech." I tried to sound unbothered even as I pressed on the accelerator and went up to sixty-five miles an hour.

The red car matched my speed exactly, staying just far enough away that I couldn't see what the model was or how many people were inside but close enough that it could catch us within seconds.

The color said that it could be one of the king's old cars, which were under the control of Nasser's government. After our conversation at headquarters, I was sure that Amer would have someone tailing us. But then it occurred to me that there were enough other red cars available these days that it could also have been a backup team from the Ikhwan making sure I was still heading in the right direction.

The Enfield was tucked into my waistband, its trigger guard digging into my side. No matter how I shifted position, I could not get used to it.

A motorcycle came out of nowhere, ripping the air with ferocious velocity and nearly taking off my side mirror. A family of four was on board: a skinny father with a wife in a headscarf and two wide-eyed children, as well as a few sacks of belongings and a freshly slaughtered goat strapped to the back, spattering blood on the dusty road ahead of us.

"How much do I love this country?" Raymond asked, leaning half his wiry body out the window to film them.

"I don't know, Raymond," I shouted above the wind. "How much?"

"Enough to break your neck, filming it." Mona pulled at the back of his jacket, trying to get him to come back inside. "What's wrong with you?"

"You're a lucky man, Ali." Raymond settled back into his seat with a strangely sated expression.

"Why do you say that?"

"To be from here must be a gift. Everywhere you look, there's a picture worth savoring. The past and the present are happening at the same time."

"It's a blessing and a curse," I murmured.

"Doesn't everyone feel that way about their country?" Mona asked.

"What?" I glanced back over my shoulder at her.

"That where they're from is a blessing and a curse."

There was a sound of regret in her voice that made me look back again. But she had turned to look out her open window, her tied-back hair resisting the wind's incitement to riot.

I kept my hands on the wheel, fighting its tiny shifts and the buffeting of the wind as the blood trail dribbled out and the pressure of the revolver gave me the urge to urinate. I started thinking about where I might find a bathroom and almost missed the turnoff for Alexandria a half hour later, then proceeded to get us lost in the back streets of that old coastal city that you were named after, my grandson, the red car maintaining its distance behind us.

I had been to the city countless times before, and had admired its feeling of nostalgic melancholy. Even as a Cairene, I had affection for its bone-white villas, its dusky Mediterranean beaches, its old world cafés where Cavafy wrote his odes to lost Greek glory. But it was different tonight. I could feel the excitement in the air before we even reached the city center, where the streets were jammed with mobs heading toward the Stock Exchange in Mansheya Square.

It was like a scene from one of Mr. DeMille's epics, set in modern times. There were not just thousands of people but literally tens of thousands. As we passed them, they were smiling and waving jubilantly, the exact opposite of what we'd encountered that terrible day the imam died in Cairo.

There were beggars and bank clerks, seamstresses and secretaries, waiters and maids, the petite bourgeoisie and the fellaheen, women with babies and men on bicycles, frail elderly couples who'd been waiting for this night since they were teenagers, bureaucrats in their work suits loosening their ties and hollering like madmen, fishermen in turbans and greasy smocks holding bamboo poles aloft, middle-aged women with harvest moon faces swathed in hijabs trilling the *zaghareet,* girls in tulip-pink scarves giggling while thick-lipped boys in colonial school blazers chased after them, vendors giving away macadamia nuts and corncobs they'd been roasting on sidewalk grills, and hawkers handing out tiny golden flags on sticks instead of selling them.

They were in such a joyful state of anticipation about Nasser's speech declaring our independence that I almost didn't notice the red car was no longer behind me. But I could not escape the feeling that hostile eyes were still on us. Even more worryingly, I couldn't think of a way to get rid of the gun I was carrying without endangering myself or my father.

As we crawled toward Mansheya Square, the crowds grew even thicker and more enthusiastic. Speaker cones hung from acacia and banyan trees along the malls, so people far away could hear as well. This was not just going to be an announcement of an evacuation agreement but a coronation, a public acknowledgment that Nasser had not only forced the last of our occupiers to leave, he had also vanquished his old ally Naguib. He was now officially *El Rayyis,* the Boss.

I realized what the Ikhwan was attempting to accomplish here was like trying to swim against the tide in the Red Sea. The odds against success were overwhelming; anyone who raised a hand against Nasser, let alone a pistol, would be surrounded and torn to pieces.

When we parked the car, I bent over to tie my shoe. Then I slipped the Enfield under the driver's seat and got out to help the others with the gear.

A stage had been set up on the roof of the Alexandria Stock Exchange, which stood on the border of the square. There was a giant golden eagle flag draped banner-style over the taller building directly behind it. Folding metal chairs for visiting dignitaries had been set up toward the back of the stage, and microphones for the state broadcasting system were arranged toward the front, so that people all around the country could hear the speech live on their radios.

There was so much celebration around us that, for a few seconds, I managed to forget my creeping apprehension and need for a bathroom. The air smelled like sea breezes and cordite from actual fireworks being shot off. This was a night for the Egyptians, and no one else. People were shouting out expressions of thanks and joy, *"Mutshakreen!"* and *"Ana mabsoot,"* provoking laughter, nods of grudging acknowledgment, marveling headshakes, and sincere touches of hands to hearts. I wanted to join in, to be part of this feeling, but then I remembered that Osman would be coming up to me shortly and looking for the gun. A quake of fear went through me, as I thought about what would happen when he discovered it was not in my possession.

Mona showed our letter from the Ministry of National Guidance to the guard at the main entrance, and General Amer was summoned on the radio to escort us to our camera position. With an out-of-body sensation, like I was watching myself in a film, I put the tripod over my shoulder and followed Raymond with the camera and Mona with the boom microphone. Three soldiers accompanied us to a roped-off area some twenty-five rows back from the stage, where four members of a local film crew were waiting to assist us with the setup.

I spotted Osman, a dozen rows ahead of us, pacing back and forth restlessly while preliminary speeches were made on the stage just above him. Already, a half-dozen military police officers were around him in red berets. He was drawing too much attention to himself with his nervous energy. It did not help that he kept making his fussy, bad smell face and squinting over at me like I was a waiter who had forgotten his champagne order.

I turned away and found Raymond having an argument with Amer.

"But this is absurd, General." Raymond pointed at the rope and the guards surrounding us. "You have us *miles* from the stage. There's no room for us to lay track or dolly in for close-ups."

"I'm sorry, sir, but for safety and purposes of national security you will not be having any close-ups," Amer replied blandly. "And I'm not sure what 'dolly in' is, but you won't be doing that either."

It dawned on me why the professor had wanted to make sure I was coming in with the camera crew. Like my cousin with his plan to blow up the set, he was thinking of the camera as a weapon in the modern arsenal and wanting his spectacle to be captured on film.

"Mr. DeMille is not going to be happy about this," Raymond warned.

"Sir, you keep forgetting that Mr. DeMille is just a guest in our country." Amer pointed a finger. "As are you."

"*Honored* guests." Mona fluttered between them, a dove trying to make peace.

"Yes." Amer raised his chin. "And we treat our honored guests with courtesy and respect, but they do not make the rules."

I'd lost sight of Osman in the meantime, but his restlessness haunted me as much as the red car that had been following us. Soon the opening speeches wound up and Nasser joined several other officials taking seats in folding chairs on the stage.

The crowd started to murmur and point while I tried to stay busy, helping the technicians unspool their cables and change the camera batteries. We were surrounded by miles of human acreage, ready to close in on us like the waters of the parted sea.

One of the government ministers got up to make the introduction. It was drowned out as Nasser rose and threw his arms wide open as if to embrace everyone and everything. The crowd roared in one voice with a quarter of a million microtones. I watched Raymond pivot the Mitchell camera that I'd helped set up on its tripod, trying to take it all in. Now would have been the perfect time to have a crane shot rising above the crowds or, better yet, be in a helicopter looking down like Allah on the full epic of the gathered humanity. I was just an ant among ants. But Nasser was incandescent, posing under a globe light on a wire above his head, a true star, a hundred times more handsome and charismatic than he'd been in his office.

It was more than a mirage. In his proud but humble bearing, he was unmistakably *one of us*. Not a scion from a royal family, or a French or an English politician, not even a pasha from a wealthy dynasty. He looked like what he was—the son of a postman, a child from a village like myself. But somehow he had transcended. He had risen above his station, on his own magic carpet. He had fought his way into military school; climbed up through the army ranks; done battle in the trenches like my cousin; and, most improbable of all, had led the coup that rid us of the monarchy once and for all. If he could accomplish all this before the age of forty, anything was possible.

The crowd began to chant *"Ya'ish Gamal, ya'ish Gamal!"* Long live Gamal, long live Gamal.

Nasser clenched his fists and held them aloft before the golden eagle. This was his picture-perfect moment, the freeze-frame before the credit roll, the instant just before the promise of freedom gives way to the sordid compromises and betrayals of governing. He became an even bigger man right before my eyes, his chest pumping up from all the hope and adulation he was receiving.

But at the same time, I could hear the pockets of silence. I could see stray dissatisfied men standing here and there with their arms folded. Not necessarily members of our conspiracy—though there were certainly more of those in the crowd than I knew—but unbelievers who could not or *would not* be persuaded and won over so easily. I saw Raymond pan over briefly, filming them as well.

"My countrymen, welcome," Nasser began in his common man's Arabic as the crowd settled down. "It is good to be here in Alexandria—"

A new cheer went up with the mention of the city's name. Why do people cheer for a place where they already are, Alex? To this day, I still don't know.

"It was in this same square, when I was a small boy, that I participated in my first demonstration—"

I looked around for Osman, having lost sight of him once the speech started. I noticed soldiers and police officers roaming up and down the aisles, like they were searching for something.

"It was against the British," Nasser said.

He paused, giving the masses another chance to respond. Even at this tense moment, with the dammed-up piss about to burst from my bladder, the critic in me admired his fine natural instinct for escalating the drama in his voice and then knowing just when to let a thing stand on its own. If, by some miracle, this assassination plan did come off, I could not imagine Mohammed Naguib, Professor Farid, or anyone else associated with the Brotherhood being able to supplant him.

"In this square for the first time I saw men being hit over the head." Nasser pointed to the scar on his brow. "I saw Egyptians shooting down their fellow Egyptians."

Someone was passing very close to me, touching my arm.

"It's off," I heard Osman say. "There are too many police. Someone talked."

None of the people I was with noticed. Raymond was too preoccupied as he hunched over his camera, and Mona was inching forward with the boom microphone and headphones.

"But I am alive today." Nasser thrust out his jaw and held his arms up higher. "I am alive and helping free my country. I am alive and—"

I heard two quick pops and saw people onstage dive from their folding chairs. A tall man in a white shirt and black pants had come down the center aisle, firing a handgun. Nasser remained upright at the microphone, as if he did not understand what was happening. There was a third shot. A fraction of a second later, the globe light over Nasser's head exploded and glass rained down. He took cover as the man in the white shirt kept firing, with one hand on the grip instead of two, somehow not hitting anyone or anything.

I dove on top of Mona. A metal chair fell on us and someone ran across it, compressing us together like a sandwich. Mona stiffened with the weight of our sudden forced intimacy. Her knee came up between my legs as she rolled as if she meant to throw me off.

But then her arms went around my neck. Her warm breath was in my ear. And somehow, in the midst of this utter chaos, with the gunshots and screaming in the background, I felt I was finally safe, warm, and where I belonged.

Meanwhile, the world above us was all writhing confusion. A high heel grazed the side of my head and someone in sandals stepped on my ankle, almost breaking it. But I managed to raise my head up just enough to see the tall man in front of the stage, being surrounded by people beating him with fists and folded chairs. His arm was swinging wildly, with his hand still holding the gun. A man in a blue galabiya was gnawing on his wrist, trying to get him to let go of the weapon. Most other people had dropped to the ground to avoid getting shot. But Raymond remained behind his camera, like the captain staying at the helm of his ship.

"I'm sorry." Mona squirmed out from beneath me, trying to catch her breath.

"For what?" I stared up at her.

She looked disheveled and disoriented, with her hair in her eyes and her blouse untucked.

"I thought I might have hurt you," she said.

I had the strangest feeling, in the middle of this mayhem, that she meant to tell me something else. That our accidental contact had elicited an unexpected rush of feeling in her.

But the chance to say more disappeared in the rush of soldiers running past our position to try to extract the shooter from the mob enveloping him. Nasser was back at the microphone, speaking rapidly and forcefully. He was trying to calm everyone down, but the sound system kept cutting in and out, so it was hard to catch all his words.

I watched Mona straighten herself up and pick up the boom mic. Then I uttered a silent prayer of thanks to Allah. Surely the Creator of Days had shown me his mercy and compassion by arranging things just so. Allowing the plot to fail without implicating me, or giving the Brothers a reason to punish me or my father. Only the Divine could have allowed this gunman to stand right before the stage and fire at least eight shots without striking anyone. And only Allah could have found a way to briefly deliver me into the arms of my most loved amid such chaos.

Osman walked past me again. "You goddamn son of a whoremonger," he cursed me under his breath. "You told someone what we're up to. You'll pay for this."

It happened so quickly with so many other things going on that there was no reason for anyone else to have noticed. The crowd was still shouting, Nasser was still waving his arms, and the police were dragging the shooter away as he struggled and shrieked like a madman.

But Mona looked after Osman, registering that she'd seen him before. Then she turned back and stared at me as if we had suddenly become strangers.

April 4, 2015
To: SeekerAL@protonmail.com
From: GrandpaAli71@aol.com

Alex,
I was very concerned by the last email you sent. You must take care that nothing bad happens to this poor girl or yourself.

I believe that you're right that you must not appear to reject her as your wife. The others who are with you may not be so gentle with her. But you must not take advantage of her as if she was your tillage or a piece of property. She is, as you say, just a child who has been forcibly separated from her family and sold as a slave. To touch her as a bride would be a grave sin. If your group is as respectful of true Islam as they claim, they know there will be eternal consequences.

But this is the world as it is. If you tell the others that she shrinks when you try to touch her, they may give her to another man as a slave or maybe even do worse. So my advice for now is this: nothing. Do nothing to her. Leave her be. Be an actor and tell the others that she is being a compliant wife. When they ask when she will give you a child, say that you are trying. Then when you have the opportunity, help her get away.

I know it won't be easy. And there will be great risk to both of you. But you asked for my guidance, and this is the best I have to offer you.
May Allah watch over both of you and protect you,

Yours, in compassion,
Grandpa Ali

17

W e quickly packed up our gear, found our car outside Mansheya Square, and started back to Cairo. The night-shrouded streets were filled with people still celebrating the courage of the new national hero. When I stopped short to avoid hitting an elderly couple at an intersection, the pistol that I'd stashed beneath my seat slid forward and came to rest with its grip against my Achilles tendon.

With the seat moved forward to make room for the gear in back, I could not move my leg enough to get free of it. Nor was there room for me to reach down and move it without anyone else noticing.

The car was jammed with equipment and my mind was full of confusing images that I needed to sort through as soon as possible. Why had there been a suddenly increased police presence right before Nasser's speech? Who had tipped them off? And where had this other shooter come from after Osman walked away? All I could be certain of was that Mustafa and the others were right. The traitor among us had known of the plan in advance, which meant that none of us were safe now.

I turned on the car radio, hoping to find a music station to calm my nerves and give me time to think with "Mr. Sandman" or "If I Give My Heart to You." Instead, I heard Nasser's voice, high with emotion but fully in command as the crowd yelled hysterically in the background.

"O free men, let everyone stay in his place," he shouted in Arabic.

"This is Gamal Abdel Nasser speaking to you. This is Gamal Abdel Nasser. My blood is your blood. My life is yours. You are all Gamal Abdel Nassers. If I had been killed, it would have made no difference, for you would have carried on the struggle. You are all Gamal Abdel Nassers."

"Turn that up," said Raymond from the back seat. "Is that supposed to have been recorded earlier?"

A news announcer came on, saying that the recording had indeed been made at the Stock Exchange, where a Muslim Brother named Mahmoud Abdul Latif had been put under arrest for the attempted assassination. Coconspirators were being actively sought.

"Did you hear him say any of that right after the gunshots were fired?" Raymond twisted around to look at Mona.

"No." She took a tissue out of her handbag to wipe the smeared mascara from her eyes. "But the microphones were malfunctioning, so we missed a lot of it because of the bad sound."

"Those sound like some pretty flowery words for someone who'd just been shot at," Raymond said. "Most people would just say 'Get him' or 'Am I hit?'"

"What are you saying?" Mona asked. "That it was written down ahead of time?"

His white face brooded in my rearview mirror. "Did anyone else notice the delay before the globe above his head exploded?"

Mona leaned back from him. "Raymond, are you trying to suggest that this was all staged?"

"It *would* serve a purpose, wouldn't it? Remember what he was saying about the Muslim Brothers in his office?"

A military police checkpoint had been set up just ahead. I slowed down and halted before the wooden barricades that had been erected. A middle-aged sergeant with the clamped-down, swollen-looking mouth of someone who'd had to keep too many complaints to himself approached my window. When I stepped on the brake, the Enfield had slid forward and was now at an angle where a corner of the grip was cutting into my ankle.

"*Wa'if hassib hena, min fadlak.*" The sergeant shone a flashlight into my eyes. "Your identification, please."

"Is there a problem?" Raymond asked.

Another officer came out with another flashlight to examine our license plate. Then he aimed the beam into the interior, blinding each of us for a few seconds.

"You will get out now, please," the sergeant said.

"Is there a problem?" I asked.

"Just do as I say." He put the light in my eyes again. "Pull over, and let the other cars get by."

The other officer had taken a radio off his hip and was speaking into it too rapidly for me to catch what he was saying.

"Sir, there's been a mistake." Mona started to rummage through her bag. "Do you know who we are?"

"There's no mistake." The sergeant pointed his light at her. "Now pull over and get out. And don't make me ask again."

I edged off toward the sidewalk and cut the engine, trying to kick the gun back under my seat before I got out. Instead, it fell forward on the floor mat when I moved my foot. Streetlight gleamed off the barrel as I got out and slammed the door after me.

The three of us were directed by the sergeant to go stand on the sidewalk and produce our identification papers, as cars went streaming past, honking their horns and blinking their red brake lights like part of a vast nervous system. After a few minutes, an army jeep pulled up and General Amer got out with two soldiers trailing, looking even more determinedly doleful than before.

"General, why have we been detained?" Raymond asked, as if they were still in the middle of the argument they'd been having before the shooting started.

"Because we're now in a state of national emergency." Amer looked up at him. "There was an attempt on the prime minister's life tonight, and immediate security measures are being put into place. We would like the film you shot tonight."

"For what purpose?" Raymond glanced at the rest of us, to see if we were equally confused.

Amer's face was like a closed wallet, giving nothing away. "Is there a problem?"

"I'm asking, what do you need it for?" said Raymond.

"Because I'm giving you an order," Amer said. "That should be enough."

"I'm not resisting, General. I'm asking you a simple question."

I didn't know if it was natural-born insolence or bullheaded resistance to authority that was causing Raymond to talk back. But my legs were starting to vibrate from fear and the prodigious amount of piss I was still struggling to contain.

"Are you refusing to cooperate?" Amer looked at Mona as if he needed help with translation.

"I'm just curious as to why getting our footage is such a priority under these circumstances," Raymond said.

Five soldiers were around us, and at least two of them were looking through the windows of the car.

"Mr. Garfield, the man who tried to kill the prime minister may have had accomplices," Amer said, struggling to maintain his composure. "We need to examine your film as evidence. Now will you help us or do we need to search the vehicle ourselves?"

I looked up at the star-filled sky and sent a desperate message.

Please, I asked the Divine. If you're going to punish me, at least let it be for my own sins, not for someone else's.

"Raymond, please don't argue." Mona started to reach for his arm. "It's not your country."

"I'm aware of that."

He stood back from her, without jerking away or making a show of it. Whatever heat had existed between them was now quickly cooling. I would have taken heart if I wasn't doing a little dance to keep from disgracing myself.

"And it's our documentary," Amer said accurately. "That was part of our cooperation agreement. Now will you give us that footage, or do we need to take control of your vehicle?"

Raymond looked over at me and sighed. "Mr. Hassan, may I please have the keys to the trunk?" he said with a sort of theatrical formality. "If we have to turn over the film, can we at least make sure it doesn't get exposed and ruined?"

Within a few minutes, the rolls were relinquished and we were passing over the Mahmoudiya Canal. We lost the signal for the news on the radio, and soon the city on the Mediterranean was just a memory. Wind beat against the sides of the car like the hands of a hundred drummers. And one headlight shone in the rearview mirror from behind me, a lone car following us on the desert road, never gaining on us or falling too far behind. But simply letting us know it was still there.

"I think I might not have been the only one who noticed the timing of when that globe exploded," Raymond grumbled.

Nothing else was said. I think we were all too aware that from that point on, we were being watched and listened to.

I needed to get out of the country. And I needed to get my father out as well. Whether Mona would come with us, I had no idea. But when I remembered her warm body pressing against mine and her eyelashes fluttering against my cheek in the chaos, my heart lifted a little.

At the end of our two-and-a-half-hour drive back to Cairo, the car radio faded back in with more news. A crackdown was already under way. There had been a raid on the Ikhwan headquarters in Helimaya. Several dozen Brothers had been arrested and charged with being part of the plot to kill Nasser and free Naguib from house arrest. Hidden caches of arms and explosives had allegedly been discovered in mosques and graveyards just outside town. Whether any of this was true or not, I didn't know. But plainly someone within the organization was disgorging names and locations.

By the time we got downtown, there were roadblocks everywhere, as if we were in a state of siege, as well as army jeeps in Tahrir Square and soldiers alongside the lion statues of the Kasr al-Nil Bridge.

I dropped Raymond off at his hotel, then drove Mona to her father's villa in Garden City. But I was so nervous about the gun that was still under my seat that I was unable to make conversation with her. She must have interpreted my silence as sulking. When she thanked me for trying to protect her and kissed me on the cheek to say good night, it barely registered.

Then I drove down to the Nile, and once I was sure no one else was in the immediate vicinity, I finally relieved my bladder. Then I tossed the gun toward the river. But unlike the acid that had been backing up in my body, I never heard it splash.

It was long past midnight by the time I returned the car and took the tram back to Mena House, looking over my shoulder the whole way. But the red lights and sirens were far off, in the more populous parts of the city. I stopped on the threshold, took off my shoes, and gave a silent thanks to God for protecting me from harm. But then I opened the front door and heard two voices talking.

"Don't pick your head up so much," my father said.

"Please. I know what I am doing."

As I came into the living room, I saw my father wearing the look of patient consternation he wore when caddying for tourists. One of the teacups my mother had liberated from the Mena House Hotel kitchen lay on the threadbare rug with a Titleist golf ball a foot and a half away. Sherif was hunched over with his hands around the grip of my father's favorite putter.

"What's going on?" I asked.

"Your cousin says his house has been overrun by pests and vermin," my father said. "He asked if he could stay here awhile."

I understood this to mean that it was not safe for Sherif to go back to his home in Shoubra or Ikhwan headquarters, because the police were there.

"But, Father, do we have enough room?" I asked. "We have only two beds."

"We can share one like we did when we were children." Sherif gave a playful swing and smiled like he was watching the ball sail off into the horizon. "It will be just like the old days."

April 6, 2015
To: GrandpaAli71@aol.com
From: CecilBAbdul@protonmail.com

Yo, Grandpa,

Excuse me for addressing you this way, and from a new encrypted address, but I now feel an even greater kinship. And forgive me if I no longer think of you as just my old grandfather, but as my brother.

I looked on Google and saw there was stuff about the Brotherhood trying to kill Nasser in Alexandria. Amazing that you were part of that, even if it was just part of some setup. I can't wait to find out what was really going on.

My commanders are okay, for now, with my reading the book out loud to the others and communicating with you—as long as it's under their supervision. They definitely don't like what the Muslim Brothers have become, as a semi-legit political party, but they can respect that our family has a tradition in jihad.

Also, they're giving me a lot of cred because you worked for this famous American movie director, and they're allowing me to move up in the media section. Our Kill the Crusader game is getting a lot of traction online. It helps that we have Brothers who were game developers and graphic designers for a big video game company in Sweden. Our site is sometimes a little glitchy because of where we are and how we have to keep changing our location settings, but we have awesome visuals because of the live-action videos we've incorporated into the cutscenes. (Don't worry about it if you don't know what those are.)

At last count, we had more than eight thousand people playing around the world, in places like Australia, Denmark, Dagestan, and even Texas. It's been a totally sick recruitment tool, because people play and then want to get more involved. We're starting to get real media attention. A guy who says he writes for The New York Times Magazine *sent us an email, asking if he could interview us. So we'll see how that turns out!*

So thanks for inspiring all that. Even though it might not be what you were thinking when you sent me the book.☺

Yours,
Abu Suror (I'm back to using my war name)

P.S. That situation I was worried about before has resolved itself. She's not around anymore.

April 7, 2015
To: CecilBAbdul@protonmail.com
From: Caddygrandaddy71@aol.com

Alex,

My heart is troubled by your responses. I realize that there are some things you cannot write about freely because of where you are. But I wish I knew what you meant by "not around anymore." I hope no harm has befallen your wife.

I had difficulty sleeping last night because of the pains in my chest. Your mother is taking me to a doctor today. But, as I said, my story is in your hands and you'll make of it what you will. I just pray that you'll keep reading and eventually find something beyond inspiration for "cutscenes."

Your grandfather—not your Brother—Ali Hassan

had hoped to go into hiding until the trouble blew over from Alexandria. But Sherif's presence in my father's house made that impossible.

I kept thinking my cousin would come to his senses and realize the time had come to abandon all plans. But instead, the botched assassination had the exact opposite effect. It made him more determined to go ahead and show "we" were unbowed and undaunted.

At times, Sherif insisted that the effort to kill Nasser had simply been badly conceived and poorly executed. No one had consulted him about the operation—but if they had, he would have had maps and reconnaissance photos well in advance. He would have chosen superior marksmen and had a better escape plan. He sounded like a producer distancing himself from a failed film he'd worked on. But at other times, Sherif agreed wholeheartedly with what Raymond had been intimating: the whole assassination business was a setup, staged by Nasser himself to justify the crackdown on the Brothers.

"Probably he had help from these Hollywood people," Sherif said. "Maybe your Mr. DeMille came to Egypt to direct the eight bullets instead of *The Ten Commandments*."

His own plot would be more authentic and ambitious. In this instance, he would truly outdo even Cecil B. DeMille.

"We're going to kill them all," he said after my father went to work the next day.

"What are you saying to me?"

"*All of them.* As many as we can. We're still going to blow up the gates with the explosives and the time pencils. Only now while they're filming this great big Exodus scene, in the daytime."

"Are you out of your mind?" I reared back. "There'll be thousands of people and animals around. If they don't get crushed by the wreckage, they'll get crushed in the stampede afterward."

"Exactly."

"But you said that's what we had to *avoid*." I grabbed him by the shirt. "We'll be guilty of mass murder. Hundreds of Egyptians will die with the Americans. The people will turn on us for sure."

"The people like to go with whoever the winner is." He shoved me backward into my father's personal set of golf clubs. "You'll see."

I tried to tell myself that he couldn't mean it. That he wasn't himself. He was barely sleeping and was smoking hashish every hour. He was acting erratic, exhausted, and a little removed from reality. He claimed he could not go home to see his new wife and child in Shoubra because the neighbors said the police were still around. But the more he talked, the more I became convinced that he didn't want to go home. Family life was not for him. He found it a chore to care for his son and his wife, both of whom he spoke of with little affection or interest. I remembered what Mona had said about Sherif. And I wondered if he had just married the kind of woman that men who do not really like women end up marrying.

He hung around my father's house all through the day and refused to let me out of his sight. He had a loaded Webley Mark IV revolver that he wasn't afraid to wave in my face. He told me in no uncertain terms that if I somehow got away from him, he was prepared to walk a quarter mile down the road and shoot my father in front of his customers on the golf course.

"I love you, my cousin," he said, "but I'll go to my judgment gladly before I let you get in the way."

That night, he slept with the pistol under his pillow and his arm around my shoulders, so he'd know if I so much as tried to go to the bathroom without him.

When he wasn't high from the hashish, he was as mean and snappish as a crocodile, complaining about my father's liquor bottles and questioning me furiously about who could be informing on our group. He was suspicious of Mustafa, Osman, and Ramzy. My father was a possibility as well. And of course, I was still at the top of the list, despite all protests and appeals to common sense.

"You've never really been one of us," he insisted. "You've still never shown what you're willing to sacrifice."

He was in thrall to his own vision. He drew sketches and diagrams like a director storyboarding a scene and then set them on fire in the kitchen sink before I could study them. He left empty clay jugs on the porch with crumpled-up messages inside, which mysteriously disappeared within a few hours. Then other Brothers, whom I'd never met before, showed up behind the house for quick clandestine meetings and left small packages. When Sherif was distracted, I looked inside one and found it, puzzlingly, full of cherries and apricots.

I could not track any of this. We had suddenly escalated from destruction of property to destruction of life on a scale that was rarely seen outside war zones. I kept thinking that the informant or God would force a change in plans, but as the time drew near, no diversion was appearing.

On the night before the operation, I found that I could not take it anymore. I begged Sherif to let me go somewhere, anywhere, even with him, hoping to slow his momentum or somehow slip away myself. But every suggestion I made was met with furious dismissal. No, we couldn't go for a walk down any street, because an informant might recognize us. The mosques were out of bounds as well, since Nasser's police would be watching them. Even a stroll to the Sphinx was out of the question.

But to my surprise, he agreed when I asked if we could go to the movies, like we did when we were younger. "No one would believe we'd waste our time in this insipid way."

An American film, *On the Waterfront*, had just opened at the Metro, on a double bill with a Japanese monster movie called *Gojira*. We paid a pound each to sit in the balcony. Sherif brought the loaded Webley to keep me from running and a bag of fruit to eat instead of popcorn from the concession stand. He spat pits and grunted his displeasure at each name in the first film's credits: the lead actor had the Italian name of "Brando," the main actress was called "Eva Marie Saint," the director Kazan was either a Greek or a Turk, and the writer was evidently a Jew. Sherif briefly fell asleep, and I studied his profile in the theater's gloom, thinking about trying to grab the gun and run out. But then Sherif woke up just as Marlon Brando was in the back of the taxicab with his brother near the climax, agonizing over all the chances he'd missed to be the man he could have been.

"'I coulda been a contenda.'" Sherif imitated the actor's American mumble with a couple of apricot pits in his cheeks. "How absurd that was."

"Why do you say that?"

"That the gang didn't kill him as soon as he became a cooperator," he said. "They should have cut his head off and hung it on a wall, so everyone would see what happens."

The Japanese monster film, however, was much more to my cousin's liking. He actually laughed and rocked in his seat as the terrible lizard stomped on the power lines and set Tokyo on fire with his breath.

"Now, *that* should get the Academy Award," he said.

I had run out of time to dissuade him or escape. When I stepped out of the house in the middle of the night, just to clear my head and look at the stars, he was right behind me, and two Brothers I didn't know were sitting where my father's friends usually smoked and played backgammon. Within two hours, we were on a bus with several dozen other crew members heading out toward the set.

As we sat in the back, Sherif confided some of the final details of the plan, which he had been withholding until then. He claimed that a member of the Ikhwan's secret apparatus had infiltrated the production's transportation unit months before. Lately, this Brother had been working as the driver of a fuel truck providing gasoline to the electrical generators on the set. On this day, Sherif said, he would be parking just behind the façade of the pharaoh's city, and once the time pencils were attached to the explosive materials embedded within the scenery and cracked by their necks, there would be a flaming spectacle the likes of which the world had never seen.

In the wake of Alexandria, there was an increased security presence around the perimeter of the set, with army jeeps and military police vehicles checking the identification of drivers allowed through. But it was okay, Sherif assured me. Key officers were actually part of the secret apparatus as well. They were passive participants so far, but once it looked like we might succeed, they would become more active and lethal.

Our bus arrived at the main gate at quarter to five in the morning, and we were waved through. There were simply too many people working on the film to check every single ID. After we parked and got off, Sherif turned to me one more time.

"If you say anything to anyone now, I won't just kill you. I'll make sure your father is tortured and humiliated in the worst way possible before he's publicly executed. I never liked his jokes, you know."

He sprinted off into the gray scrim of dawn before I could ask detailed questions.

But I could see the fuel truck he had described parked right behind the gates, where the generators were rumbling.

The hills around us were still black heaps against the gray remains of the night. I recognized at least a half-dozen Brothers from Professor Farid's salons emerging from the darkness to help unload crates from the equipment trucks, their actions so far unremarkable among all the other preparations going on. There were small flickerings of fire and bestial lowings among the dunes, as I realized that thousands of tribespeople had camped out overnight, with their animals, so they would be ready to work as extras at dawn. The moon was waning through the pharaoh's great archway. Dozens of horses whinnied in their stables; goats and sheep brayed in pens; and hundreds of pigeons fluttered in their wooden coops, awaiting their star turns before the cameras.

As the sky lightened, wardrobe mistresses opened up their tents, and propmasters loaded oxcarts and put together bundles for the extras to carry: their worldly possessions in the Exodus.

A lone stooped figure in a wide-brimmed hat looked up at the façade and then stared over at me. The fixed quality of his attention made my heart stop. I feared it was someone from state security who'd been surveilling me since Alexandria. But as the sky grew slightly brighter, I saw that it was Mr. DeMille.

He turned back toward the façade and raised a viewfinder to his eye like a jeweler using a loupe to inspect a gem for flaws. Then he took a step to the left to get a different perspective, oblivious to all the movement around him.

His head turned just a fraction of an inch so that he was staring up at one side of the gate, the area where I'd been working with Sherif during the rehearsal period.

"What is that?" he said loudly. "For the love of God, can someone tell me, please?"

I swallowed hard when I saw what he was looking at. A thin thread-like black electrical wire, barely visible in the twilight, was hanging down from the platform. Somehow it had gotten out from behind one of the painted panels.

"I think it's for the sound system, to amplify your voice when you want to address the entire set, Mr. DeMille," I said. "I'll talk to someone on the rigging crew about making sure it gets tucked out of sight."

"Unbelievable." He shook his head. "I've spent most of my working life trying to get this picture made the right way, and people don't care enough to keep a cable out of sight. It makes you wonder, doesn't it?"

"It *is* unbelievable." I squinted, not sure how the old man's vision had been keen enough to spot a loose wire while missing the larger conspiracy going on behind the scenery.

He looked me up and down. "Tell me, Mr. Hassan, were you planning to be in the scene today?"

"Why do you ask, sir?"

"You look like you're already in costume. And we could use as many bodies as possible."

I hadn't shaved since Alexandria, and I was wearing a galabiya that Sherif had made me borrow in order to blend in among the extras. "Well, I hadn't considered that, sir."

"Just honoring your traditions, are you?" He grinned. "Perhaps our journey to Sinai made a lasting impression."

"More than you can possibly know, sir."

He looked up at the gate again, the first rays of the sun reflecting off his glasses. "So what do you think now?"

"Of what, Mr. DeMille?"

"Of *this*. The whole undertaking."

"Truly it is beyond words."

He stared at the side of my face as the wind ruffled through my clothes.

"Are you thinking, 'Was it worth it?'" he asked.

"Sir?"

"You know." He lowered his voice. "Everything we went through. The unfortunate events before we left for Sinai—"

"Such things are hard on one's conscience," I conceded.

"I'm sure you might have been tempted to say something after I fired you."

"Is that why you hired me back, sir?" I turned, finally granting myself the privilege of showing him my true anger. "To make sure I'd stay quiet?"

The wound inflicted in Sinai was still burning. He had humiliated me and made me feel I was nothing—*less than* nothing. No man should be able to make another man feel so worthless, I told myself. Back when my cousin was only talking about destroying DeMille's set, I was able to go along with it, because I wanted to send him back to America without a usable frame of his film. I wanted to deprive him of his final and greatest achievement, the one that he dreamed would be his monument.

"I hope you don't think it was that cynical and calculated." Mr. DeMille tipped back his pith helmet, showing me more of his sunburnt and heavily lined face.

"Why would I, sir?"

"Because I *am* cynical and calculating sometimes. I have to be, on a picture of this magnitude. A director has to be a dictator. Otherwise, there would be chaos. But I *did* see something in you, Mr. Hassan. And that's the real reason I wanted to give you another chance."

"Yes, Mr. DeMille. I appreciate that."

I wanted to believe him, but I'd seen behind his façade as well.

"So I've been meaning to say that I've had my eye on you since you've been back. Whether you're aware of it or not." He hitched up his belt. "And I know what you've been up to."

My eyes went to his waistband, where I saw there was a silver handle tucked over to the side a little, near his hip.

"Sir . . . ?"

There could be no mistake now. Cecil B. DeMille was carrying a gun on his set.

"I've seen you doing two jobs," he said. "Burning the candle at both ends. Don't think that it's escaped my attention."

"I don't, Mr. DeMille."

While he was speaking my cousin had ascended the platform and was watching us from six stories above.

"Hard work to make up for lost time will always be rewarded on my movie sets," Mr. DeMille was saying. "I see a bright future for you, young man. In fact . . ." He reached inside his jacket and pulled out a business card. "I don't know if you're planning to visit the West Coast of America, but if you ever make it that far, please call my office number."

"For the studio tour, sir?" By then, I understood the terms better.

"No. To talk about your prospects. I'm impressed by your grit. Lesser men wouldn't have taken the lesser job. I can't make any promises if you come and see me, but I could certainly try to arrange for you to talk to someone on the Paramount lot. They see plenty of spoiled Hollywood kids out there. I think they might enjoy meeting someone who's willing to take a few hard knocks and keep hustling for his breaks."

"I am most obliged, sir." I slipped the card into a pocket of my galabiya.

The sun was rising higher now, revealing more of what had been constructed for him: the giant black marble pharaohs flanking the gates, the immensity of the obelisk, the re-creations of the hiero-glyphics and cartouches on the walls, the chariots with their golden wheels and leopard-skin interiors, the villagers leading their cattle and camels over the hillsides.

But for some reason, he kept looking up at the platform where my cousin was now trying to tuck the errant wire out of sight.

"Hey, fella." Mr. DeMille shaded his eyes as he looked up at him. "Make sure that one of the gaffers from the American team goes up to double-check your work."

"Nothing will be left to chance, sir." Sherif waved back down at him.

I waited until Sherif was distracted by other workers climbing up onto the platform with him before I turned back to the director.

"Mr. DeMille, sir, I need to tell you something."

I knew that he would think I was insane if I told him he needed to shut down his set immediately. He looked at his watch as Henry Wilcoxon, who was dressed in a breastplate and kilt like one of the pharaoh's soldiers, approached with Chico Day, who was armed with a clipboard.

"Make it fast," Mr. DeMille said. "We're falling behind already."

My tongue lay flat. If I warned him, I would be sentencing my father and myself to certain death. If I failed to speak up, many more would die.

"I think you should reconsider your schedule for today," I said. "Something could go wrong."

"'Something could go wrong'? Mr. Hassan, we have gathered ten thousand extras and fifteen thousand animals for today's shooting. We can't afford to have *anything* go wrong."

"I know that, sir. But you need to be careful. You heard what happened to Prime Minister Nasser in Alexandria the other night—"

"Yes, yes." He was already losing patience and turning away to consult with his aides. "I sent him a cable to congratulate him on surviving. Now I must look after our setups—"

"Sir, there are rumors of sabotage," I said more strenuously.

"What is your source of information?" asked Henry, smoothing his skirt down over his bony English legs.

I hesitated, seeing my cousin was no longer on the platform. "There's been talk among the workmen," I said.

"Why on earth would anyone want to spoil our production?" Mr. DeMille demanded. "We're not involved in politics. All we're doing is making a movie."

It was far too much to explain in too little time. The imam, my cousin, the Ikhwan, Nasser and Naguib; once I started, I'd have to go through the whole history of Egypt to make him understand.

"Mr. DeMille, we gotta go." Chico waved his clipboard. "We've got less than ten hours to get this scene before it gets too hot to have all these extras out in the sun."

I started to say more, but a hand clamped on my shoulder. Sherif had come down off the platform to see what was going on.

"Mr. DeMille," he said, like they were old, dear friends. "I just wanted to wish you luck today. What do they say in English? 'Break a leg,' sir."

"That's exactly what you're *not* supposed to say." Henry sniffed as a wardrobe assistant handed him a shiny headdress to put on.

"It's the thought that counts. Good luck yourself, fella." Mr. De-Mille headed toward his tent, then looked back at Sherif and me. "Hey, Chico," he called out. "Try to get these two characters into proper costumes and makeup before we roll. They've got a good look for the scene."

19

What did you say to him?"

Sherif waited until he had me back up on the platform, in our wardrobe costumes and sandals.

"Nothing." I went about collecting tools and tarps. "He just wanted to know what I thought of the film so far."

"All this time it took to give him your opinion?" He kept staring at me. "Did you give the plan away?"

"No, of course not."

He followed me around as I grabbed a broom to sweep away the candy wrappers and cigarette butts as part of the final preparations.

"I swear, Ali." He seized the broom to stop me. "I'll have you tied between two horses and torn in half if I find out you're lying."

"I haven't said anything. If I had, wouldn't we both be under arrest by now?"

He ignored me and looked at his pocket watch. In the last ten minutes, the military presence on the set had tripled. From our vertigo-inducing perch, we could see beyond the Avenue of Sphinxes to the berm where twenty or thirty air force officers were servicing and guarding the silver Spitfires that had been set up as wind machines for the Exodus. Several dozen more army officers and military policemen were roaming the areas just outside the fences on either side of the sphinx gauntlet, keeping a careful eye on the animals and villagers penned in within the frame lines.

When I turned toward the rear of the set, I saw no fewer than forty extra cavalry officers arriving on horseback to talk to their colleagues wearing the costumes of the pharaoh's army back by the corrals.

"Sherif," I said, "we're surrounded by soldiers. Even if these explosions go off as you say they will, don't you think we'll be caught and arrested right away?"

"Not a chance." He picked up a stray screwdriver. "There are thousands waiting for our signal to attack general headquarters and take Nasser into custody."

"Yes, but if someone from the Brotherhood is talking already, they'll name you and me. We'll both go to prison forever."

"*Insha'Allah,* it won't come to pass that way," he said, turning his attention to the swarm below. "Many of these soldiers here today belong to the secret apparatus."

"I still don't believe that."

"You'll see. Once the explosions start to go off, they'll use their rifles to shoot the legs out from under people trying to run away. One shot to the legs and then one shot to the head to finish them off. Like pigs in a pen."

"Oh my God." I laced my hands on top of my head. "How can you even talk this way?"

I was beginning to realize that terrorists, dictators, and Hollywood filmmakers were alike in not accepting the world as it really existed, but insisting that the terms be changed for them, that logic be bent to their purposes, and that life as everyone else knew it be broken down and remade according to their expectations.

"You have to imagine it before it happens." Sherif used the screwdriver to draw a picture in the air. "Allah gave the Messenger the idea to fight against all odds in the Battle of Badr. And then he gave him an impossible victory. Surely he can give us another against Nasser and Hollywood. If it wasn't permissible, he would have found a way to stop us by now."

Down below, I heard voices getting louder. A group of American set dressers were on their way up the ladder to do "last looks" and make sure everything was as it should be before the outer scaffolding was rolled back.

"I can't be part of this." I moved toward the ladder, wanting to find my way down. "I won't go to Judgment Day with all this weighing on my heart."

"Ali, look down there." Sherif pointed with the gleaming end of his screwdriver. "The third sphinx on the left. What do you see?"

In the middle distance and the blowing sand, I could just barely discern a woman dressed like a Hebrew slave in a burlap sack dress and a headscarf. I was too far away to see her features or the tendrils of yellow hair that were probably poking out from beneath the scarf, but there was no mistaking the self-mocking way she posed for the photographers who were crowding around the crouching man-beasts, with a hand on her hip and head thrown back in a pantomime of sun-dazed rapture.

"You know what I always thought?" Sherif smirked. "She could have never been an actress, even in Egyptian films. Her face is too broad and her ass is too fat."

"Shut up."

"I never could understand what you saw in her." He flicked the screwdriver playfully past the end of my nose. "Dumb faithless cow. Look. They've already lost interest in her. . . ."

One or two of the photographers had peeled away and begun moving toward another woman, who was walking down the Avenue of Sphinxes with Mr. DeMille. This one wore an eye-catching broad-brimmed floppy white hat; big sunglasses; a white blouse; a black skirt; and, judging from the marks in the sand, two-inch stiletto heels. Yet somehow she moved as if she were on a fashion runway. When she took off her hat and sunglasses, I could see it was the American actress Yvonne De Carlo, who was scheduled to appear as one of Moses's wives in the film. Immediately, all the other photographers left Mona and ran over to her. She threw back her ebony hair and posed effortlessly, with cheekbones I could see from on high catching the sun perfectly.

My eyes swung back and caught Mona crossing her arms awkwardly and looking around, trying to be gracious about another woman's having taken the spotlight from her. A woman who was thinner, paler, more American, and, perhaps to Western eyes, more attractive.

I think many of us have a moment in our lives when we realize that we will not ever be who we hoped to be. I think this was hers. She would never be a star, or even a minor actress like her mother. Her dream was fading, just as mine had faded a few weeks before. But she tried to smile bravely, as if it didn't matter. Which caused me to realize that I was still very much in love with her.

"She's a whore and an infidel." Sherif aimed the screwdriver between my eyes. "But nothing will happen to her if you do what you should."

"How can I believe that?" I pushed the tool from my face. "You've been lying to me all along. Haven't you?"

The mask had dropped. I realized that a part of him had always held me in contempt. I had failed to see it because I assumed he loved me as a cousin.

He tucked the screwdriver into his pocket and handed me three of the time pencils I'd acquired from the Englishman.

"Connect the rest of these," he said. "Then you won't have to worry about anyone coming up and slitting her throat."

He patted me on the back to send me on my way. As I descended the ladder, I passed the set dressers assigned by Mr. DeMille to double-check our work. By the time I reached the ground, I was having what people now call a panic attack. Reality whirled around me, like horses on a merry-go-round.

I looked for Mona, but she'd already disappeared through the pack of photographers swarming Yvonne De Carlo.

Instead I saw Mr. DeMille headed toward the director's tent with Henry striding after him in his costume and headdress, so he could both act in the scene and position the extras as needed. I ran after him, thinking if I could show him the primers in my hand he would understand the danger. But a young baby-faced military police officer moved into my path, his substantial frame more than compensating for the lack of experience in his face.

"It's forbidden," he said. "No one else is allowed in."

"Please, sir. It's urgent."

I could only just see what was inside the tent. It was like the lodge of a Hollywood emperor transplanted to North Africa. An Ottoman carpet was laid over boards on the sand, Oriental tapestries hung from four sides, and a half-dozen deck chairs surrounded a linen-covered table, where an intricately detailed model of the entire set lay, complete with miniature versions of the sphinxes and hundreds of figurines enacting the scenario about to be staged. Mr. DeMille was smoking a pipe and moving a group of little chariots into place while assistants made notes in their well-thumbed copies of the shooting script.

"I promise it will only take a few seconds," I said.

I was going to hand the director the primers and leave the rest up to God, but then I turned and saw two other policemen go by in a jeep and realized that one of them was my cousin's friend Osman. Somehow I had assumed he'd been arrested in the crackdown.

"It's an emergency," I pleaded, as a Sudanese waiter in a white jacket stepped past me and disappeared inside the tent with breakfast and tea service on a tray.

"I warned you nicely." The officer guarding the tent raised his rifle. "Go away before I smash your teeth in and arrest you."

I scuttled off, already tasting blood in my mouth. I pictured thousands of people fleeing the explosions, then getting shot in the legs and heads by Osman and the others. I ran toward the commissary tent, asking Allah to help me prevent this catastrophe. I would accept any sign what to do, any help from any source, without hesitation or question.

The answer to my prayers came in the slouching form of Raymond Garfield as he came ambling out of the commissary in his fedora and sunglasses. He paused to try to light a French cigarette in the blazing sun. His match hand was so unsteady that he must have been hungover. How he could have hoped to handle a camera later, I don't know.

"I have to speak to you." I ran up. "A terrible thing is happening."

He lowered his sunglasses and aimed his bloodshot eyes down his nose. "I know you fancy yourself a critic, Ali, but don't you think you should keep your opinion of Mr. DeMille's directing to yourself?"

"I'm not joking, Raymond. There's going to be another attack today. A lot of people could get hurt."

He dropped his cigarette and sighed. "Could you be more specific?"

"There are explosives inside the scenery. You need to tell Mr. DeMille."

"Oh, for God's sake . . ." He took off his sunglasses and tucked them in his breast pocket. "Do you have any proof?"

I showed him one of the time pencils. "Do you know what this is?"

He took it gingerly between his thumb and forefinger. "Where did you get this?"

"I can't tell you."

As he studied it, he looked very different from the man he had been just moments before. "This is a number ten delay switch, made by the British."

"Yes, I know."

"It's not from the prop department, is it?" He inspected me as closely as he'd inspected the fuse.

"So you *do* recognize it?" For some reason, it struck me as odd that he knew the exact name.

"Yes, from the Army Signal Corps."

"But I thought you were in the *United States* Army—"

"Oh for God's sakes, Ali," he cut me off irritably. "This is serious business." His eyes were no longer sleepy. "Whoever you got this from isn't kidding around."

"That's what I've been trying to tell you." I threw my hands up. "*Now* will you tell Mr. DeMille he needs to shut the set down?"

He groaned and put his sunglasses back on.

"Raymond, we need to hurry. . . ."

Without another word, he began to walk briskly toward the director's tent. I exhaled in relief. But then two military police officers came up alongside him and each took him by an arm. I realized they must have been watching us since I'd left Mr. DeMille's tent. As they started to lead Raymond away, he let the time pencil slip from his fingers. But one of the officers stopped and plucked it from the sand.

"*La-a-a . . .*" He wagged it in Raymond's face and grinned. "No, no," he said in English. "Naughty, naughty."

I watched in astonishment as they dragged him toward the back of the set, past the horses at their troughs and the costumers on their hands and knees before the pharaoh's soldiers, fixing hemlines and tying sandal straps. How could Allah have permitted this? At the very moment that I'd been forced to put my trust in this outsider, he was getting taken into custody.

I looked inside the commissary tent to see if there was anyone else I could ask for help. It was filled with extras whom I didn't know. Real-life soldiers from the modern Egyptian cavalry were dressed like Henry, in the finery of ancient charioteers, while having scrambled eggs and *ful mademas* alongside several distinguished Egyptian theater actors I recognized who were dressed as Hebrew slaves.

But then I saw a familiar face behind the smoke rising from the grill.

Professor Farid was wearing the white cap and jacket of a line cook. He looked down when he saw me staring. I first tried to tell myself it was the pride of a learned man reduced to menial circumstances. But then through the smoke, I saw him take off his glasses and wipe his eyes as if signaling we should acknowledge each other.

Someone came up behind me and put a hand on my shoulder. I spun around with a raised fist as Mona stepped back.

"Easy, Ali," she said. "I was just going to tell you that Mr. DeMille is about to call 'Action.' If we want to be in the scene, we have to go."

May 5, 2015
To: GrandpaAli71@aol.com
From: CecilBAbdul@protonmail.com

Grandpa,
Just a quick note to say that if it turns out that you're telling me this whole story and the point is to run down Ibrahim Farid, I'm throwing the rest of this book away.

We've been studying his work and that dude was a real deal visionary who laid the groundwork for a lot of what we believe in now. If you're trying to discredit him to turn me around, I'm not buying in. And neither are my commanders.

Just saying . . .

By the way, I told the others that I didn't want Shayma as a wife because I don't like her looks. She's been assigned instead to be a laundress for the fighters. Now every time I pass her, she keeps looking at me like she wants me to do something for her. But even though she's learned a few words of English lately, I can't understand her.

Anyway, I'm more concerned to hear about those chest pains you mentioned a few weeks ago. Did Mom take you to see the doctor?

Yours,
Abu Suror

20

A s we walked away from the tent, Mona casually looped her arm through mine, which she had never done before.

"We have to get away from here." I was in such a state that I hardly registered the fresh intimacy of the gesture. "Right now."

"What are you talking about?" She started to take my hand and then stopped. "They're about to roll."

"It's all going to blow up." I sneaked a glance back at the gates.

"What is?"

Sherif was looking down on us from on high, a hand to his side where I knew he was still carrying the gun under his galabiya. He waved and pointed at Mona like he was going to make her a star.

"Oh, so now he thinks *he's* the great director?" she said.

"Please listen to me." I put my hands up close to her face. "Sherif is going to try to do something terrible—"

"Miss Mona, can I get your help for a second?" Mr. Condon, the main unit publicist, was calling out to her. "Some of the press photographers need to be shown to their area so they don't get in Mr. DeMille's shot."

"Don't go anywhere, Ali." She squeezed my wrist. "I'll be right back."

I looked after her forlornly. Everything was going too fast to stop now. The cameras were in place: One in the far distance, just beyond the Avenue of Sphinxes, mounted on the back of a flatbed truck. Two others placed strategically along the route, to catch the procession.

A fourth was positioned on top of the gate of Per-Rameses, for the God's-eye point of view shot.

All that was needed was for Mr. DeMille to climb the ladder to the top of the gates and call "Action." Assistant directors wearing slave costumes waded in among the masses gathered between the sphinxes below, making sure bundles were secured, wagons were sufficiently differentiated, and people wearing similar colors did not stand too close together. A little girl in green rags banged a timbrel on her hip, shivering its bells. A boy in a beige robe knelt by the pigeon cages, tenderly blowing air into the baby birds' mouths and stroking their frail throats to get them to open wide for food. A withered old man in the robes of a village headman glanced both ways and then borrowed a slingshot from another boy to ping pebbles off the high buttocks of the wardrobe mistress.

A shining metallic figure walked out of the gates and the crowd parted for him, pointing and shouting. It was Yul Brynner again. But instead of the black turtleneck I'd seen him wearing at the nightclub, he wore a turquoise war helmet and ivory bracelets on his well-oiled biceps. He was like a museum exhibit come to life in his golden breastplate, gold belt, gold sandals, and a white kilt like Rameses II. A royal chariot pulled up with golden wheels, a leopard-skin interior, and a cavalry officer in period costume lashing a fine white Arabian charger. Yul climbed aboard and held up two fingers in a V sign. I wondered if this was some pharaonic gesture from hieroglyphics that he was trying to bring to life after close research for the role. But then an American production assistant ran out with a cigarette and lit it so the pharaoh could enjoy a smoke before he started chasing the runaway Hebrews.

Amid all the excitement, few of us noticed that Mr. DeMille had finally ascended to the top of the gate and was standing next to the A camera operator.

"Chico, get that woman in red away from the Levites on the right."
He called out through his megaphone. "The Levites on *my* right. Put
her with the Nubians and Benjaminites instead. Now get those geese
and camels centered, for crying out loud!"

I could not believe this man was still fussing with the elements at
this late stage, unaware he was standing on several hundred pounds
of explosives packed into the structure. I saw Sherif come down off
the platform just below him as a soldier walked along the fence peri-
meters on the sides of the frame line, his rifle pointing down.

An army jeep pulled up in front of the gate and a group of officers
got out quickly, carrying carbine rifles, and began to survey the area.
Gamal Abdel Nasser disembarked after them—his medals, smile,
and lightly silvered temples on full display. Whether the attempt on
his life had been fake or real, *El Rayyis* was going to show the world
that he was unafraid. Mr. DeMille waved to him from the top of the
gate and then indicated a space at his side, to show this was where
men of their stature belonged.

Nasser waved back and put a hand to his heart, pretending to be
humbled.

I looked around for Mona. If Sherif had already crimped the necks
on all the time pencils, then the detonation train had started, and
within minutes, maybe even seconds, the walls would come tumbling down.

Carpenters were nailing the last of the painted boards into place
on the wooden scaffolding, closing up the sides of the façade. Each
hammer blow resounded in my chest, vibrations that could set off the
charges prematurely. Soon, the workers would be enclosing the right
side as well. Chico Day came over to my cousin and began pushing
him in the direction of a lopsided cart that had a wheel coming off,
to fix it.

A tremendous unearthly screech cut through the cacophony, a

sound so high and piercing that people had to cover their ears and even the beasts were stunned into silence, except for the pigeons in the cages back by the gates, which fluttered their wings restlessly. A voice spoke from above.

"People of Egypt!"

Cecil B. DeMille had a microphone now, instead of the bullhorn. His voice was being piped through loudspeakers to the sides of the gates.

"This is the day you've been waiting for all of your lives. . . ."

He was speaking the way he did when he provided the narration in his movies, slowly and significantly, as if his words were meant to be carved into stone. All movement ceased; humans and animals eyed one another nervously, as if Allah himself had chosen this moment to address all of his living creations.

"Today is the birth of human freedom. . . ."

A Sudanese goatherd beside me, a very dark man with skinny blue-black arms extending from green and red tribal robes, turned his palms up toward heaven. Why would God be speaking to them in the language of colonists? But then a second voice broke in, offering Arabic translation.

"Ala-youm milad horreyet al-ensan. . . ."

I looked up and saw Nasser was on top of the gate, beside Mr. DeMille, speaking through the microphone, which he then handed back to the director.

"When we give the signal, I want to see every single one of you *acting*, every one of you emoting, giving me everything you've got," the director said, sweeping his arm over the masses. "I want you to follow this man Moses into history."

The crowd parted and I saw Chuck at the front of the pack in his beard and robes, waving his staff high in the air. A burble of awe went through the masses: *"Moussa! Moussa! Moussa!"*

"Remember"—Mr. DeMille's voice echoed between sky and sand—"you have been slaves for generations, ruled over by tyrants. But this is the morning of your liberation. *Carpe diem!* Seize the day for all it's worth! I want to see every single one of you acting like you're up for an Academy Award!"

The goatherd shook his head as Nasser took the mic to attempt to translate this part as well. But no matter. Just because people lived in mud huts and didn't know about the Oscars, it didn't mean they were ignorant. They knew there would always be a pharaoh.

"Now go out there and become a light among nations!" Mr. DeMille declared, after taking the mic back. "Let freedom ring from mountaintop to mountaintop! Hear, O Israel, remember this day! You are God's chosen!"

"Allahu Akbar!" Nasser called out as Mr. DeMille handed him the mic one more time. *"Haz sa'eed!"*

Again, I searched the crowd for Mona. Soon it would be too late. I caught sight of Sherif, still trying to fix the wheel on the oxcart, and used the moment of his distraction to run back toward the gates.

"I think I left a torch inside," I said as I brushed by the carpenters and riggers who had completed their last looks.

I wedged myself into the narrow opening at the bottom of the north pylon. It was the strangest feeling, being behind the scenery. It was like being inside history, without being able to see what it looked like from the outside. I could hear the voices of all the extras and the *thonk* of boots and shoes on the platform high above me and the wind sifting sand against the sides. I could smell the animals in the sun and the gasoline from the generators powering all the electrical equipment. I could feel the claustrophobic closeness of the air and the desert heat around the enclosure, trying to get in.

But then the sun shifted for a second, so that a thin seam of light came through the slats of the façade. It was just enough that I could see the piles of sandbags that had been there before were either gone or torn open. And what was spilling out was not TNT or ammonium nitrate, but plain light-beige sand. The time pencils and blasting caps were gone as well.

"Ali, where are our bags?" my cousin screamed like someone was squeezing him by the balls.

He had trailed me inside with his screwdriver in hand and was looking around in a frenzy.

"There were five hundred pounds in here a few minutes ago," he yelled, as Mr. DeMille and Nasser kept speaking above us. "What have you done with them all? Did you take the ones out of the camera truck as well?"

"I didn't touch anything."

"You liar! I'll fucking kill you!"

I bolted out into daylight, trying to get away from him. I ran straight into a pack of female villagers with small children, and accidentally bumped into a squat peasant woman, who started screaming that I'd tried to touch her improperly. I tried to go backward, but lowing steer got in the way.

Assistant directors began yelling for everyone to move back toward the middle so the mob would look bigger, and I was carried back with the tide, toward where my cousin was searching for me among the oxcarts, treasure sledges, and camels braying like old toothless derelicts. I looked desperately for Mona, calling out her name, as Sherif spotted me and started to come toward me, sun glinting off the screwdriver in his hand.

"Someone get rid of the tool that man is holding," I heard Mr. DeMille cry out. "It's a total anachronism."

The hordes shifted again, lifting me off my feet and shoving me back toward the gate among flocks of rams and oxen; screaming swaddled babies and braying goats; swarms of Egyptian tribes disguised as the Children of Israel; a groaning, howling, bleating Tower of Babel moving sideways.

Nasser had come down off the gates and was already being driven off the set in a jeep. In the meantime, a group of his soldiers, dressed in the costumes of antiquity, had started to roll out in their chariots, sun flashing off their helmets, shields, and javelins. Yul Brynner was in the front chariot without his cigarette. A cavalry major was holding the reins.

"Ali, come back." Sherif was still trying to fight his way over, his intention to stab me as plain as the light flashing off his screwdriver. "I need to speak to you."

I began pushing past sledges loaded with golden idols, my eyes swimming, thinking I'd glimpsed Mona up near Chuck at the front, but then the sound of a gunshot stopped me. My back spasmed. My cousin had taken out his gun and shot me, I was convinced. However, I looked back toward the gate and saw Mr. DeMille at the top of the arch, pointing at the sun, gray smoke trailing from the starter's pistol he had just fired.

"Action!" he called out through his microphone while his Egyptian assistant translated through a megaphone.

Thousands of voices erupted around me, all repeating the same word in English and Arabic, as the pigeons were released from the gate and flew around wildly like torn pages caught in a jet stream.

Under any other circumstances, it would have been a glorious parade. An ocean of color and movement across the sand. Men and women of every possible age and hue in orange, purple, and green robes. They carried golden pots and idols on palanquins and hoisted shrunken elders in dirty sling sacks suspended from wooden poles; they wielded scythes and palm fronds, swung smoldering censers and wineskins off long sticks. Wind-blasted women in crow-black scarves balanced wooden birdcages and baskets of unleavened bread on top of their heads. Camels carried fig trees on their humps and small children bounced up and down on cattle backs like they were trampolines. Greased-up men with barrel chests tugged straw carts and hauled boats made out of olive wood and painted rhino hide. Pioneer women in full burkas stuck their heads out of covered wagons, giving the *zaghareet* and ululating wildly behind their face veils, the beating of their tongues to the roofs of their mouths unfurling a carpet of sound.

It had been orchestrated piece by piece by a master director with an eye almost as meticulous as Allah's. But the only things I could think of at that moment were the explosives in the camera truck that my cousin had mentioned and the glimpse I had caught of Mona's scarf as she walked right behind Chuck, heading straight toward it.

"*Bomb!*" I yelled at the top of my lungs. "*Qunbula!*"

Only a few people heard me at first; my voice was too faint against the shouting and the lamentations of livestock and the whirring propellers of the airplanes in the distance.

There were bushels of wheat, rivers of sheep, cracked earthen jars, sleds full of statues, opulent facial hair, vegetables and grain sacks, blue-and-gold tribal standards, flaming torches, hands clapping, and moving walls of sweating skin. Barefoot girls urged ducks along with sticks while little boys chased after runaway goats that chanted "*yam*" over and over. A musclebound man with an immense black beard ambled along with a net full of dates dangling from a stick on his shoulder, unaware that a camel directly behind him was picking the cluster clean with huge crooked teeth. A woman no bigger than Shirley Temple in a purple sack somehow balanced a wooden yoke on her shoulders, with a basket of bricks on one side and a small child sleeping on the other. A black donkey stopped in the middle of the pack and started to sit down, threatening to create a major traffic pileup. A boy about six years old pulled on the lead rope and two little girls of equal size shoved him from behind until the ass straightened up and started moving again.

I yelled "*Qunbula*" again and the extras just ahead of me looked back, almost dropping a mummy on a pallet that was supposed to be the patriarch Joseph.

I broke into a run, maize stalks and flour sacks flying as I pushed toward the front of the crowd where I'd seen Mona.

"There's a bomb about to go off!" I shouted in English like my chest was on fire. "*Qunbula!* We're all going to die!"

People began to push against one another trying to scatter. I saw some of the production assistants wade into the crowd from either side, trying to prevent a stampede.

All I was thinking now was to save my beloved. My feet sank into the sand as I ran toward where I'd last seen her, trying to will strength into my limbs to find her. *No God but God, no God but God.* Lungs bursting, I clenched my jaw and prayed for my muscles not to fail. Up ahead, the pack was thinning out as the solitary man with the staff walked toward the camera on the flatbed truck going about twelve miles an hour. I screamed out Mona's name again as I ran toward him, pushing people out of the way.

From the corner of my eye, I saw Henry in his chariot racing outside the frame line, holding on for dear life as a cavalry officer whipped the horses.

"Ali, you're ruining our shot!" he yowled though his bullhorn. "Please leave the scene."

I kicked my way through ducks and chickens, seeing Mona and then losing sight of her again. I glanced back and saw a surge of people coming toward me, threatening to run me over like a tsunami, as the gates of Per-Rameses quivered in the heat waves like they were getting ready to fly to pieces.

My ill-fitting wardrobe sandals were slowing me down, so I let them fly off as I ran on, the hot sand burning the soles of my feet. I called out Mona's name with all the air I had left in my lungs. As if in a nightmare, she finally stopped and turned, just as I found myself surrounded by furious assistants and security officers aiming guns at my head. Henry came riding up in his chariot to berate me as I saw my cousin try to recede into the crowd.

I dropped to my knees and raised my arms in surrender, submitting to the Master of All Destiny. I knew I was in trouble, but at least Mona and the rest of the crowd were far enough away from any remaining explosives to be safe. And for that, I gave thanks.

But then I heard Henry's walkie-talkie crackle. "We have to cut," I heard Chico's voice through the static.

Henry, his two-way radio incongruous with his pharaonic soldier's costume, clicked his talk button. "What's the matter?"

I heard a group of confused voices trying to speak over the airwaves all at once.

"Mr. DeMille has collapsed," Chico shouted, trying to be heard above the fray. "He appears to be having a heart attack."

Sherif was thrown down beside me, with a soldier's boot on the back of his neck and his screwdriver finally pried from his grip. As they handcuffed him, he managed to turn his sand-encrusted beard toward me and started to laugh.

"You think something's funny?" I asked, trying to catch my breath.

"I do," he said. "Because it worked."

"What worked?"

"Never mind." He rested his cheek in the sand and closed his eyes, like a tired child ready for his nap. "With God, all things are possible."

May 6, 2015
To: CecilBAbdul@protonmail.com
From: GrandpaAli71@aol.com

Alex,
I am glad to hear your wife is well. I am well too, Alhamdulillah, though the doctor wants to order more tests. What would help my heart the most would be to hear that you are finally coming back to your senses and on a plane flying home.
*   Until then.*

Yours in abiding faith,
Grandpa

21

The two of us were then grabbed up and frog-marched back toward the gates of Per-Rameses. I saw Mr. DeMille on a stretcher, being carried like an emperor on a royal palanquin. How they got him down from a height of eleven stories, I still don't know. He was alive but in poor shape. He looked pale and fragile as he was loaded into the back of an ambulance. I wanted to call out to him and apologize for ruining his shot, but my guards punched me in the back of the head and kicked me in the buttocks, as they forced me to climb into the back of a covered truck with my hands shackled behind me.

I smelled the fear and desperation of the men already seated inside, as the soldiers climbed in after me and started the business of beating me in earnest. They started with fists and batons, then knocked me on the floor and stomped me with heavy boots. When I tried to roll onto my side and curl up like a shrimp, a corporal kept me pinned on my back with a knee on my chest, as he slapped me over and over and demanded to know where the rest of my explosives and accomplices were.

The engine started and the truck lurched forward. My eyes blurred with tears and my head swam with nausea. I turned my face so I wouldn't gag on my own vomit. My cousin and Mustafa, whom I had not seen earlier in the day, sat on a side bench in handcuffs. Professor Farid was opposite them, still in his cook's clothes. How they had all been captured so quickly, I did not know. Nor did I understand where the explosive material had gone or why my cousin had been laughing. All I could be sure of was that the informant had done his job well. A kick to the underside of my chin rolled my eyes back into my head and paused my speculations.

After a few minutes, the beating began to slow to an occasional rabbit punch and side kick, as if the officers had tired themselves out. They hauled me up and shoved me between Sherif and Mustafa, grinning dishearteningly at the three of us. We rode for nearly an hour in silence. My ribs were almost caved in, and blood from my sinuses drained down the back of my throat. But what was most painful was the way Sherif and Professor Farid would look at me every few minutes. Of course, I had not named any names, but I knew it would go hard for me if we were locked up together.

Radios belched and blurted fragments of information about several other simultaneous plots being interrupted in other parts of the country. At least twenty other Muslim Brothers had been arrested for conspiracies to take over general headquarters, the Egyptian Mint, and the Egyptian Broadcasting Company.

The truck came to a halt and the back doors were flung open. I realized that we had been taken to the Citadel, Saladin's medieval compound beneath the Mukattam Hills. How many times had I played with Sherif in the shade of these battlements? Back then we were just two boys pretending to be warriors fighting in the Crusades. Sherif being Saladin, me being Richard the Lionheart, like Henry in *The Crusades*. Now we were arriving in chains. We were helped down from the truck and led out onto the cobblestoned passageways. I looked up at the old castle towers and imagined I could still hear eight hundred years of anguished voices crying out from the barred windows.

The number of officers surrounding us doubled and then tripled as we were brought through a courtyard and up a flight of granite steps, soldiers wanting to share in the reflected glory.

"We are going to die here," Sherif muttered.

"No," said Professor Farid. "We won't be that lucky."

It was late afternoon, the sun slanting bleached white rays straight into the line of cells we were nearing. Faces came to the rusting bars to watch us pass: sunken-eyed, hollow-cheeked men in their twenties and thirties. They couldn't have been here long—the crackdown on the Ikhwan had only begun after the aborted assassination attempt— but already their spirits were broken. Nasser's minions had worked quickly.

The officers stopped before an empty cell, opened the door, and shoved me in, slamming the bars behind me before they moved off with Sherif and the others.

I sank into a squat in the corner of the cell and clasped my hands under my chin, asking for Allah to find me and protect me within the confines of my tiny cell. But all I saw was a single drip of water running between the crumbling bricks, thinning strips of light between the bars of my cage, and a cloud of insects already beginning to assemble and feast on my exposed skin. Then I looked across the way and saw Raymond's hooded eyes staring back at me from the opposite cell.

"So, Mr. Hassan," he said, "I guess you're off the picture as well."

May 12, 2015
To: GrandpaAli71@aol.com
From: callFate28@protonmail.com

Grandpa,
It's hard for me to know what to say about this turn in the story. You were wrong to turn against your Brothers at that late stage in the plan. If you still don't know that in this life, I think you'll find out

in the next one. May God have mercy on you for your mistakes of judgment and loss of nerve.

Obviously, my commanders are forbidding me to continue our communication. I had to beg them to let me send you a final farewell. They believe that you tried to play a trick on me by sending me your book. Some stories are instructive, and some are corrupting. I would like to believe that was not your intent, but I don't know what was in your heart. I only know I will not be following the same path.

I do want you to know that I still care what happens to you. I hope your follow-up appointments go well. I would say I'll be in touch to check in, but I won't. I mean, I can't. My commanders are shutting down this server. But I will be thinking of you. In fact, I was reminded of you by the guy who came to interview us the other day about the video game. He said he used to watch The Ten Commandments *all the time with his family back home. But never mind all that. What's done is done.*

May Allah show compassion for your immortal soul,
Abu Suror

P.S. It turns out that what Shayma wanted was for me to help her get back to her family. That's so not happening.

fter spending a long, cold night at the Citadel, I found myself among the dozens of prisoners being transferred on a caravan of exhaust-spewing buses to a former British military installation known as the Al Siggn Al Harbi. The base had been converted into a prison, just outside Cairo, to the east of the Nile. When they realized where we were headed on the bus, several of my fellow detainees began to weep openly.

I was sick to my stomach and deeply confused by the situation I was in. Yes, I comprehended all too well that I had been caught up in the crackdown against all of Nasser's perceived enemies. But I did not understand why my attempt to foil my cousin's plot had not earned me at least some consideration. Nor did I understand why Mr. DeMille had suffered a heart attack at the crucial moment of the filming. But from Sherif's reaction I strongly suspected that it was not a coincidence. And finally, no one had explained why Raymond had been locked up with the rest of us. Yes, he had been caught with the time pencil I had given him. But it was impossible for anyone to believe that this Jew had played a role in a Muslim Brothers conspiracy.

And yet here he was standing to my immediate right, still wearing the clothes he was arrested in, among four rows of ten inmates apiece in the prison yard, listening to the welcoming speech of the deputy warden.

"Gentlemen, there are days when the course of a man's life changes forever. Sometimes, it's the day he leaves his parents' home. Sometimes, it's the day of his wedding. Sometimes, it's the birth of his first child. And sometimes, it's the day that he knows will be his last on earth." The deputy warden paused to let the notion sink in. "*Gentlemen*, today will be such a day for all of you."

He was a short man with a high voice, squinting eyes, and a small troutlike mouth with a gray-white sprig of a mustache. He derived his authority solely from the stripes on his uniform sleeves and the sentries aiming high-powered rifles down at the thirty-nine other prisoners joining him in the inner courtyard.

The Siggn itself was a disheartening place, made up of five large gray cement-block structures surrounded by thirty-foot-high granite walls, coils of razor-ribbon barbed wire, and a ring of soldiers at the base. Each building operated as a prison within the prison, two tiers with a courtyard in the middle and guard towers in the corners. There were twenty officers on hand to greet the new arrivals in the yard— one for every two inmates—large, thuggish men who moved in a more slovenly way than regular soldiers, smirked at the new arrivals, and spoke in rough rural accents. As the deputy warden spoke, they waded in among us, pulling men out of line for imaginary infractions, putting them against the walls of the cellblock, and then striking them on the arms and kicking their legs while frisking them for contraband.

"You have all been brought here because you are considered enemies of the state," the deputy warden continued. "You do not have the same rights as normal prisoners. You are not subject to civilian law. You have no right to a speedy trial. You have no right to see a lawyer. You have no right to unmonitored visits. In fact, you have no right to even hear the reasons for your detention. If you are given any of these things, you should bow down to Gamal Abdel Nasser and give thanks. . . ."

The deputy warden stopped in front of me and chucked me under the chin, giving a sidelong glance to Sherif, who was to my immediate left. My cousin had still not spoken to me since our arrest.

"If you are given a chance to go to court or face a military tribunal, you will stand in a cage, like the dirty animals you are, and hear the charges read against you. I would advise you to plead for mercy and admit the nature of your disloyalty at the first opportunity." He leaned close to me and sniffed, a dreadful insult, since I took great care with my personal hygiene. "Enjoy your stay. We're glad to have you."

A sergeant grabbed my arms, cuffed my hands behind my back, and led me into the Block 2 building. Hope died in a long hot corridor lined with iron cell doors on each side, bloodshot eyes strafing me from three-inch slits, crazed voices erupting from within, from men trapped too long with their most dire ruminations and fears. An empty five-by-eight cell was waiting at the end of the hall. I was pushed in and the door slammed behind me, leaving me alone with a naked bulb radiating gray-blue light on a stone floor. Odors of mildew, shit, and ammonia attacked, bypassing my nostrils and going straight to the pit of my stomach.

Through watering eyes, I saw a waterlogged straw mattress in one corner and a rubber bucket in the other that smelled like it had been recently used as a toilet. A snapped-off loop of rope was knotted around a sagging part of a wooden beam, as if something had recently been dangling from it. A series of dark spots formed an almost-solid line halfway up a gouged stone wall. At first, they appeared to be deliberate marks that could have been made by a former resident, counting off the days of his sentence. Closer examination showed that they were bodies of blood-fattened bugs that had been methodically squashed one by one.

I stared at the pattern until it became a code to be deciphered. What was to become of me? Less than three weeks before, my beautiful American dream had seemed almost within reach. Now I pictured my father hearing news of my arrest on the putting green at the edge of the desert, a bag of clubs slipping off his shoulder while customers moved on to the next hole. That's if he knew where I was. Then I remembered how Mona had stared after me as I was being led away from the Exodus march. I could still taste the grit in my mouth from the soldiers driving my face into the sand while the cameras rolled. No wonder my cousin laughed at me; I tried to play the hero but wound up acting the fool.

Out in the courtyard, a bugler from a nearby training camp kept practicing his call to arms over and over, hitting a wrong note in the same place each time and then starting over.

I raised my eyes to the high barred window, finding a dull sliver of the sun behind a gray cloud, like an old coin half hidden under a man's shoe. Over the next few hours, I watched it slowly dim, until everything else went dark and I was left with just the singing radiance of the bulb above me and the army bugler practicing his scales outside.

Just after dusk, the cell door opened and a tall fleshy man came in wearing the uniform of a brigadier emir, with two guards accompanying him.

"Good evening, Ali Hassan," he said. "I am Hafez Digwi, the warden of this facility. I trust everything is as it should be."

"Yes, sir." I had heard the name already in the hallways, from men who tended to spit on the ground and cough into the crook of their elbows after they said it.

"I am informed that you are one of our more educated inmates. Perhaps when we get more accustomed to each other, we can discuss improving programs for the population here. It could be very good for morale."

Contrary to his reputation, the warden showed a rather sincere and humane expression. When I spoke, he thrust his head forward and cocked it to the side, as if he was honestly interested in what complaints a common prisoner might have. Every few seconds, his gray-brown eyes half closed into what looked like a wince of sympathy, as if he was truly pained by the wails and complaints of prisoners in adjoining cells. But in repose, there was a sullenness to his features that made him appear coarse and much less intelligent.

"There is a problem in our facility, though, I must confess," the warden said. "Many of our guards are poor men. They don't read books or go to nightclubs like L'Auberge. They resent anyone who has had a superior education and often treat them quite brutally. May I ask where you attended school?"

"King Fuad University in Cairo, Warden." The wiser choice would have been to lie, but I had not yet learned to rid myself of pride.

"I expect that you might have a very difficult time, then." The warden inclined his head kindly, but I was shaken by his apparent reference to that night I'd met with the Englishman.

"It would be in your interest to make your stay as brief as possible," he said. "Do you follow my meaning?"

"Why wouldn't I?"

"I'm saying your best decision would be to start cooperating immediately." He took great care to enunciate each word. "If I were you, I would provide a full confession and information about your friends from the Muslim Brothers, so that we can expedite your sentence before the military tribunals."

"But, Warden." I attempted a smile, even though my face was still sore from the beating in the truck. "Surely you know that if the Brothers even imagine I'm cooperating, great harm could befall not only me but my loved ones outside these walls."

"Yes, we can all see why that would be a concern." The warden shared a nod with the other officers in the room. "Which is why we must make a sincere effort to persuade you to see that our way would be easiest."

One of the guards stepped forward, a sergeant about six and a half feet tall with a small bluebird tattoo near the corner of his right eye that indicated he was from one of the mystically inclined tribes of Upper Egypt.

He pulled off his belt as two more guards entered the room. They seized me by the arms and held me down.

"Give him the baton," the warden said.

I squeezed my buttocks, to keep them from violating me.

Instead, the tattooed sergeant stunned me with a slap. Someone else wrapped the belt around my head, just above the eyebrows.

"What's happening?" I yelled.

One of the other officers pulled the belt tight and buckled it snugly. Then he inserted the baton into the space between the belt and my forehead. He started to turn it, so that the leather tightened and the metal studs of the belt began to press agonizingly into my skull.

"In the name of all that is holy, *stop*!" I shrieked.

Instead, they twisted the baton again, and I heard a cracking sound inside my head.

"You're going to kill me!" I yelled. "It's too much pressure."

"It doesn't have to be like this," the warden said.

I gritted my teeth, praying the top of my head wasn't about to pop off like a section of squeezed sausage.

"What good can I do you if my brains are coming out of my ears?" I cried out.

There was some discussion among them. The bluebird sergeant stunned me with another slap. The belt was pulled away and a blind-fold went around my eyes. A rope was tied under my arms and used to hoist me up toward the ceiling. They spun me around, laughing hysterically as they kept beating me like a Mexican piñata. I was on the verge of spewing everything inside me into every corner of the cell. Each blow was a shock because I couldn't see it coming. The out-of-tune bugler added to my nightmarish delirium. Finally, they let me down and undid the blindfold. My vision gradually returned from pitch-black to charcoal gray. The sergeant with the bluebird tattoo uncuffed my wrists as the warden stood before me, holding his arms out.

"You see?" He blinked twice. "We're all reasonable men here."

I was too sick and swollen to eat breakfast the next morning, having been kept up the majority of the night by guards bursting into my cell, yelling and clanging pots to keep me from sleeping, and then insects feasting on my ankles. I was in a zombie state for most of the day, staggering out for head counts and exercise times, and at the end of the day answering the bugle call to join the dinner line. An ovenlike heat remained constant in the air, promising no surcease for the evening and a long rich afterlife for bad smells. The stench of unwashed bodies and dust from crumbling cement walls filled the air. Dun-colored smoke wafted from the prison incinerator, making a brown film over the sun. Rats frolicked near the shower shed, enjoying a freedom denied to the humans in the facility.

I looked around, recognizing few of the men in line. Some of them may have been part of other Ikhwan plots I was kept ignorant about. But from the predatory way they sized me up and smiled at one another, I knew most were probably just common criminals. Plainly, I'd been set down among them to make cooperation a more attractive option.

At the head of the line, a trustee with jaundice-yellow skin and a hacking cough was dispensing soapy broth from a giant steaming tureen, while armed guards stood watch on either side. Every time an inmate's metal bowl was half filled with the viscous liquid, guards would order the man back to his cell on the double, brandishing bull-whips.

"'Eddie," who had so unceremoniously replaced me as Mr. De-Mille's personal assistant and chair boy, limped by. On the set, he'd been a fashion plate in a seersucker jacket and a bow tie. Now patches of his hair were already falling out and two front teeth were conspicuously missing. To this day, I have no idea if he was a part of any conspiracy. I rather doubt it. He was probably just a cinema enthusiast like myself. But he had been placed here as another lamb among the wolves. As he tried to hurry back into the cellblock, Eddie had to pass a long double gauntlet of guards on either side. I watched them take turns sticking out their shoulders and legs to trip him and jar him for sport until the tall sergeant with the bluebird tattoo stepped forward and shoved him hard with both hands, knocking the bowl from the lad's hands. Eddie fell to his knees, tear streaks visible on his smudged face as he looked up in hunger and confusion. The sergeant spat on him and the other guards laughed as the boy got up, collected the empty bowl, and ran back to his cell.

My stomach bowed in toward my spine. It had been more than a day since I had eaten, and I had been counting on this meager sustenance to get me through. I reached the front of the line and tried to steady my bowl with both hands. The trustee ladled in two spoonfuls, spattering drops on my wrists, which I wasted no time in licking off.

"On your way." The lieutenant at the front of the line kicked my backside, eliciting more laughter from the watchtowers. "Run."

Another thimbleful of broth spilled over the side, scalding my thumb. Three-quarters of the way down the line, I saw the sergeant doing knee bends and windmilling his arms, getting ready. I limped toward him, girding myself, hands tenderly cupping the bowl, protecting my nourishment, but with each step my balance was more precarious. The sergeant moved directly into my path with his fists on his hips.

I lowered my shoulders and braced for impact, but then right before the collision, Allah guided me differently. I veered close to the
sergeant and then stepped back, causing him to stumble past me, just
missing me as I danced out of reach, like Mr. Gene Kelly avoiding the
police officer in *Singin' in the Rain*. Even the other guards laughed as
he fell against a wall to steady himself.

I finally reached the cellblock entrance. Another gauntlet awaited
me there. This one was made up of the common criminals, *baltagiyas*,
who'd already been fed and were waiting to prey on others passing
by, especially members of the Ikhwan, whom they greatly despised.
I tried to move past them quickly, raising my bowl to avoid the hands
trying to swat it away. Mustafa stepped out from near the end of the
line, ready to avenge his failure to pin me to the wrestling mat. He
planted himself like a brick wall, waiting to meet me head-on. I hobbled toward him, eyes stinging at the sight of a so-called Brother taking part in this organized sadism. Perhaps the prison governor had
already started rumors that I'd been cooperating. But then I saw how
Mustafa flexed his muscles and posed like he was back on the platform in one of the Mr. Universe competitions. I realized that the truth
was even simpler: Big Mo never much liked me to begin with, and in
prison, Brothers were under no obligation to be brothers.

I slowed my step as I saw him raise his fists, ready to club me into
bloody submission. But then another prisoner moved into his way,
blocking him and forcing him back into line with a sweeping broom.

"Look out," Raymond called out. "Hot stuff coming through."

I hurried by, my bowl of tepid broth still mostly intact. I got back
to my cell, closed the door before the guards could, and drank the
soup as if it were part of the five-course meal I'd once served to King
Farouk himself in the Mena House dining room. I savored each curd
like caviar and licked the residue from the sides of the bowl like the

sweetest juice of pomegranates. Then I dropped the bowl to the floor with a satisfying clatter and silently gave thanks to God, Gene Kelly, and the mysterious deeds of men.

May 23, 2015
To: GrandpaAli71@aol.com
From: Nosleeptiljihad@protonmail.com

Grandpa,
I know I said you would probably never hear from me again. But we've had to reopen the server so we can keep recruiting with the video game (which, I admit, is still just a really primitive prototype with lousy graphics) and communicate some of our new demands to the Americans.

One of the new "guests" we have in our midst had a picture on his phone that reminded me of you. I wanted to check in. How did your follow-up with the doctor go? How is your health?

Hit me back, a-right? I'm taking a big chance writing to you again. Our rivals are supposedly headed our way and the Americans have been flying their Predator drones overhead. My commanders say there will be serious punishment for anyone they catch on email without correct authorization. One of my comrades has already felt the lash. Publicly. But some things are worth the risk.

Yours,
Abu Suror

P.S. Shayma tried to run away and get back to her family on her own. It didn't go so well.

23

Early the next morning, I was awakened with a deluge of ice-cold water cascading over my face and the sound of Umm Kulthum on a radio down the hall, singing a newly composed ode to Nasser's courage in leading our nation. Two of the guards who'd beaten me the previous day were back in my cell, standing over me and laughing with a halo of flies around them.

"Get up and get a move on, you worthless swine," the sergeant with the bluebird tattoo said as he kicked me. "You have a visitor instead of breakfast today."

They shackled my hands and ankles again. But I noticed that they struck me more half-heartedly on the back and shoulders with their batons as I staggered past the other cells, as if they were losing enthusiasm for distributing pain as the rest of us became more inured to it. They deposited me in the warden's office in the building closest to the main gate, where I found my father dressed in his white cardigan, green pants, and golf shoes.

"Oh my God." I stopped on the threshold. "What are you doing here?"

"I don't know." He hunched his shoulders. "I've been making phone calls and writing letters for days, trying to get in to see you. But then this morning, agents from the Mukhabarat suddenly showed up on the putting green and said I had to go with them. Right before tee time. My customers must be very confused about where I've gone."

I was pushed in and the door slammed behind me. I saw the warden had pictures of Nasser and General Amer in his office as well as the flag of our glorious new republic, photos of what the prison looked like when it was a British installation, and many military decorations. Some of which, on closer examination, could not have been the warden's. They came from other branches of the service and had probably been confiscated from inmates upon entering the facility.

"What happened, Ali?" my father asked. "They said you were involved in something terrible on this movie set. But I told them it couldn't be. You've always been such a good boy—"

"Father, we have to be very careful what we say here." I looked toward the door. "People are just outside listening."

"But they think you're one of these crazy Muslim Brothers. I told them they had you mixed up with Sherif. You love John Wayne and Shoukry Sarhan—"

"Please don't say anything else to them. I need to get a lawyer."

I sat down in a chair by an empty birdcage and the chessboard. I had seen little of Sherif or Professor Farid since I'd arrived at the prison, and I was only slowly piecing together what was going on outside the prison walls. The crackdown had gone way beyond the supposed events in Alexandria. As near as I could tell, anyone suspected of terrorism, sedition, or jeopardizing public safety had been rounded up and arrested. Not just Muslim Brothers but anyone suspected of being a malignant influence. Under emergency security measures, the jails were bulging with so-called bad actors. Brothers from the secret apparatus; Communists and their sympathizers; alleged Israeli operatives; as well as pickpockets, hoodlums, drug fiends, and, yes, I'm afraid, pimps like my father—your great-grandfather.

And now that we were all in custody, the authorities were scrambling to find a pretext to keep us there. Apparently, their informant had either stopped cooperating or was not giving them enough information to hold us all at the same time.

"I've been trying to hire a lawyer for you, *abnee*." My father grimaced a little as he reached back and touched his lower lumbar. "But it's difficult. The best attorneys are expensive, and most of them don't want to take a case like this because they're afraid of getting Nasser angry."

"Of course." I tried to smile, even as my tongue found a tooth knocked loose from the beating in my cell. "*El Rayyis* must not be crossed."

"But I'm not giving up." My father patted my knee. "A foursome is coming to the course tomorrow with two lawyers who work at the American consulate. I'm going to ask if they can help."

"I'll be fine." I tried to make a show of good cheer.

"I was thinking of asking the movie people for help, but most of them have left the country already."

"Have they?" I had lost any sense of the shooting schedule once I was arrested.

"Yes, Mr. DeMille got sick on the set," my father said. "People think it might have been food poisoning. Or the water. You know how hard it is on some tourists' stomachs."

"Right . . ." I tried to maintain a neutral expression. "Do you have word of his condition?"

"No. It was very strange. None of the crew people were talking much at the Mena House bar that night. One of them said something about a special American doctor being rushed over to see Mr. De-Mille at the penthouse where he was staying, and then Mr. Heston told him to shut up about it and walked out. He seemed very upset."

"I'm sure he doesn't want anything said that could jeopardize the production," I muttered bitterly. "This was the role of a lifetime for him."

"I'm sure he's just worried about Mr. DeMille," my father countered. "It's hard to understand what could have happened so suddenly."

I said nothing, having confided my suspicions about my cousin and the professor to no one. As in one of Mr. Cagney's gangster movies, I knew my ability to keep my mouth closed was keeping the Muslim Brothers from killing me or harming my father.

"The cast and crew packed their bags and left the next day, before I could contact any of them," my father said. "But I'm going to write to the American embassy, to remind them what a good job you've done driving for all the VIPs. . . ."

His eyes gleamed with that same naïve excitement he had always had when it came to believing foreigners appreciated his work. But this time it just made me more desperate and upset as I tried to make sense of what was going on around me.

"Father, I need to ask you something that's been on my mind," I said in a husky whisper. "And I need you to keep your voice down when you answer."

"What is it?"

"Have you been talking to anyone about me or Sherif?"

"You mean the authorities?" His voice rose, despite my warning. "Why would I do that, habibi? You're my flesh and blood."

"I know. But you saw me talking to that Englishman at the Auberge des Pyramides nightclub. And I saw you. With those women."

His lips moved a little, as if he needed to talk through the scenario to understand it. "You think I would go and inform on my own son?"

"The Englishman I was talking to was arrested the very next day. Someone who was there that night must have alerted the authorities."

"And you think it was me?"

I instantly felt ashamed of myself, but unable to relinquish my suspicions. "It was someone who saw me that night or knew I would be there. I'm sure of it."

"It breaks my heart, Ali, if you could believe I would ever do such a thing to you."

The pain in his voice pierced through the paranoia that had been swarming me like fruit flies. Tears were brimming in the corners of his eyes. There are a lot of people in this world who are skilled at acting and deception, Alex. Your great-grandfather was not one of them.

"Forget I said anything." I shook my head. "I know it wasn't you. It's just the circumstances we're in. None of us are at our best in here."

"Maybe if I were a more important man, I could have changed the circumstances—"

"Father, there's no time for that," I interrupted. "I need you to do some things for me."

"What, my son? You know I'd do anything for you."

"I need you to start asking your customers for another fifteen percent in tips."

"How?" His sun-beaten face sagged. "Why?"

"Because I want you to use the extra money to buy a bottle of real Scottish whisky and bring it to the warden here. He'll treat me better if you do."

"Okay." He nodded. "What else?"

"I need you to go to where Sherif's father kept his pornography collection and distribute it to the guards here. Don't pretend you don't know what I'm talking about."

He hung his head. "I won't."

"And then I need you to do one more thing for me."

"What's that?"

"Tell me one of your jokes," I said. "I could use a good laugh right now."

"No, *habibi*. I'm too worried for jokes. I haven't slept for even an hour since they told me you'd been arrested."

"If you can give the warden alcohol and the guards sexy pictures, then you can give me something funny to say to the other people here."

My father cast a worried look toward the door. "But I don't know if the guards would think this was funny."

"Never mind the guards," I said. "If they were going to arrest you, they would have done it already."

He rubbed his face with hands clad in leather golf gloves. "I don't think your cousin and his friends in the Muslim Brothers would like this joke either," he said. "Even I didn't like it when I first heard it . . ."

"Then you *have* to tell me," I insisted.

If my torturers were going to get liquor and pornography, I needed to get something to maintain my dignity.

"Okay, I heard this right before you were arrested," my father said, unable to resist his natural impulse to perform. "So Nasser notices his favorite pen has gone missing."

"I love it already."

"So he mentions it to the secret police."

We both heard a cough and looked toward the door; the guards outside were plainly listening.

"Go on," I said.

"Are you sure, Ali?"

"Yes, Father, you are the greatest of all joke tellers and I am your faithful audience. Nothing will change that."

"Okay." He squared his shoulders. "So then they round up all our glorious leader's enemies and they torture them to try to get them to confess. Then they throw them in a black hole without food and water for thirty days. . . ." He hesitated, like he was stopping in the middle of his swing. "Ali, I told you, I don't like this joke."

I glared hard at the door, thinking about how they laughed when they beat me.

These people, these so-called officers, believed they had broken me with their belts and their batons. And, yes, I would stoop to bribery to earn better treatment. But *Alhamdulillah*, I would not let them keep my father from telling one of his beloved jokes.

"Please, Daddy." I forced a smile. "I *need* to hear the punch line now."

"Okay." He prepared himself like he was about to drive the ball down the fairway. "So then they force Egypt's greatest artisans to study photos, find the molds, and make a perfect copy of the pen that's gone missing."

"Don't stop," I said, cackling like a lunatic. "And then what?"

"Yes, because when they bring it to the Supreme Leader, he says, 'Never mind. I just remembered it was in my other pocket.'"

I threw back my head and laughed until tears ran down my face, and then the officers rushed into the room and dragged me away. If I did not see my father again, this was how I wanted him to remember me.

"Don't lose faith, Daddy," I called out. "I'll see you at the Masters Tournament in Georgia when this is all over."

May 24, 2015
To: Nosleeptiljihad@protonmail.com
From: GrandpaAli71@aol.com

Dear Abu Suror,
Thank you for inquiring about my follow-up at the doctor's. I am fine, thank God, though they want to keep testing and making adjustments to my diet. I think mostly they want to keep billing my insurance company.

I am much more worried about these emails I am receiving from you. All this talk about Predators, public lashings, and photos you've found in your guest's phone makes me very nervous. And when you talk about your commanders punishing you for emailing me, it makes it hard for me to sleep. And I am already very tired.

What happened to Shayma? And what are these demands that you're making of the Americans?

Just come home. I beg you. For God's sake and for your family's. I don't know how much longer I can hang on.

Love,
Grandpa

24

A few days after my father's visit, I was brought without explanation into the warden's office. The guards cuffed me more tightly than usual and refused to look at me as they marched me down the hall. My attempt to bribe them had evidently backfired, and now there would be consequences. But when the door opened, Mona sat waiting under the slow-turning fan. She was wearing a very modest long white cotton dress that covered her arms and legs, flat shoes, and a black headscarf. But my blood throbbed in the same parts of my body as when I saw her at the Red Sea in her swimsuit.

"What are you doing here?" My knees locked as I stood on the threshold, oblivious to the guards taking off my shackles.

"My father was brought here yesterday," she said as they pushed me in and withdrew. "They arrested him even after they said they wouldn't and accused him of being part of a plot to overthrow Nasser."

"*They think your father would put down his cocktail shaker long enough to join a conspiracy?*" I looked over my shoulder as the door slammed behind me. "Are they really getting that desperate?"

"They must be, if they're going back on their word like that."

Her father was no more a dissident than he was a French poodle. He was a playboy without a portfolio, a roué, and maybe even a grifter, because he ran up bills and always managed to be away from the table when the check arrived. But he was the furthest thing from a revolutionary, or even a counterrevolutionary. Yes, he wanted to keep getting his pastries from J. Groppi, his cocktails at L'Amphitryon, and his silk shirts imported from the best tailor on the Rue de Richelieu without tariffs. But he wasn't about to spill his drink or wrinkle his collar in order to hold on to them.

"Yes," Mona said. "It's madness. They're locking everyone up now, for anything. They even have Raymond here."

"Yes, I know he's here." I rubbed my sore wrists. "Is that who you really came to see?"

"No." She started to untie her scarf and then stopped. "After I saw my father, they told me I could see only one other prisoner. So I asked to see you."

"You did?" I walked to a chair and sat down stiffly.

I hoped she wouldn't see how much I was limping. Or notice my broken sandals and the dirt on my feet. Or smell how infrequently I was allowed to wash.

"Raymond doesn't need my help." She looked down at her watch, the Cartier piece incongruous with the rest of what she was wearing. "The American embassy is already starting to make some inquiries on his behalf, and . . ."

I saw dampness in the corners of her eyes and dared to have hope. Where there is water, there can be life. Or maybe the stench of my body odor was getting to her. She took out a tissue.

"What is it?" I asked. "You know you can always speak plainly to me."

"He's not as likely to be put to death as you." She blew her nose daintily.

"Oh." I scratched a flea bite on the back of my neck. "I see."

She looked down as if the business of folding and refolding her tissue into smaller and smaller squares was an all-consuming task, and more important than what she'd just said.

My brave face began to fall. It was not, strictly speaking, new in-formation. I had overheard other prisoners in the yard talk about the possibility of death sentences. But these were abstractions, shadows on the wall. Hearing the words from Mona's lips made them as real as the hemp oval of a noose dangling just above my head.

"You already knew that," she said. "Didn't you?"

"Well . . ." My mouth was full of tar. "I had hoped there would be some consideration for the warnings I tried to give. . . ."

"I hoped that too. I tried to tell them this is all a misunderstanding. You don't hate the Americans. You love them—"

"I *admired* some of them," I said, embarrassed by my past sycophancy.

"Oh, please. You mooned over Mr. DeMille like a schoolboy when he first got here."

"I wasn't *that* obvious." I held my head up. "Was I?"

"Wouldn't it be better to say that you were?" Her voice softened. "I tried to speak to him or Henry before they left Egypt, but you know, they were in such a rush."

"So I've heard."

She cast a frightened glance at the door. "You know, there's a rumor he was poisoned."

"Is there?"

"The military police want to hush up the whole incident, so foreign investors don't get unnerved. But I've heard that they found ground-up cherry pits in his teacup." She leaned close, so I could feel her exhale onto my face. "They say each one has only a little bit of cyanide. But if you put a bunch in at once, it can cause someone to have a heart attack."

"*Allah* . . ."

It was starting to make sense now. The fruit that came in the envelope when we were in hiding, my cousin spitting the pit into his palm, the professor working in the commissary tent. For all the clandestine coordination and feverish plotting with explosives, it all came down to dropping a handful of crushed pits into a teacup at just the right moment. And all I'd done with my running around and yelling was to create a useful diversion.

"I am a fool," I said flatly.

"No, you're not. It's not your fault at all."

"Then whose fault is it?" I put my face in my hands. "Oh my God. Why didn't I see what was really going on around me? I thought I was being so careful and smart—"

"It's not your fault." She raised her voice. "Because it's my fault."

Her gentle brown eyes alighted on my face and then, after a moment or two, turned away.

"Mona, how could any of this be *your* fault?"

"Because I was the one talking to them."

I turned my ear toward her, sure I could not have heard her correctly.

"Talking to whom?"

"You know. . . ."

She stared down at her feet, which were shod in small red velvet slippers with a faded gold geometric pattern.

"Mona, you're not making any sense."

"Listen to what I'm telling you." She put her head down and spoke in a rapid murmur as if she were praying in solitude. "I've been telling the government people what I thought you and the others were up to."

"That can't be true." I wagged my chin, refusing to accept the testimony my ears were providing. "Can it?"

Her head stayed covered and bent, but she gave the tiniest of nods.

My mind stopped functioning in a logical way. Instead, it went to the strangest place.

I pictured myself walking along the banks of the Nile the day after my mother died. I was holding my father's hand when we came upon a banyan tree full of birds. Only I couldn't see the birds, because the branches and leaves were in the way; I could only hear them screaming. I remember looking up and thinking it was the tree itself crying out, as if nature had gone wild with grief.

What Mona was telling me at that moment made no more sense than that shrieking tree.

"They've been using me the whole time to spy on everyone," she continued in a low and fervent voice. "I should have told you much sooner."

"Why?" I struggled to recover the wind that had been knocked out of me. "Why would you even agree to do such a thing?"

"To keep my father out of prison." Her thumb rubbed absently over the dial of the watch he had supposedly given her. "They've been holding that over me, ever since Naguib was in charge. I've been going to parties and public events for almost two years and reporting everything I see—"

She kept talking for a while, but I could not follow what she was saying. Everything was muffled and blurred, like I was drowning in the Red Sea again.

Her voice gradually faded back in. "Now that I've stopped cooperating, they've arrested my father to try to force me to keep spying for them. But I'm done with all that. I decided I had to stop talking after they arrested you."

"But this can't be true." I found myself getting very cold and still. "It doesn't add up. Someone else must be the informant. You're not even related to anyone in the Ikhwan."

"They may have had others. But I won't use that as an excuse. I'm the one who's responsible."

As I started to rewind the movie in my head, it all began to make a kind of terrible, inevitable sense. She was familiar with Sherif and the professor from our days at the university. She was aware that each of us were involved with the Brothers to some degree. She'd had ample opportunity to observe what we were doing in the operation. She'd been the one pointing Raymond's camera when I was up on the platform with Sherif. She had seen me at the table buying the time pencils from the Englishman right before he was arrested. She had even been in attendance on the professor's houseboat to see me with Osman and Mustafa before the alleged assassination attempt in Alexandria.

"But *why*?" I asked, astonished. "Why would you do this to me?"

"It wasn't to hurt you. I was just trying to help my father. You can understand that, can't you?"

I pictured Nabil drunkenly warbling "Mona Lisa" in front of the rooftop orchestra. Then I remembered him whispering in my ear that she was a little bit out of my "league." I had thought it was an insult. Now I realized it was a warning.

"You would have done the same for your father," she said. "Wouldn't you?"

A hot, prickling anger came over me. "So you were just using me as well? For the whole time I've known you?"

"It wasn't like that," she started to say.

"And why should I believe you?" I raised my voice. "Because *now* you're not acting?"

Sherif had been right about her. I didn't know whether to be more disgusted with her or with myself for not seeing through the ruse.

"It's a shame that Cecil B. DeMille didn't give you more time in front of the camera," I said through front teeth that were chipped from the beatings I had taken. "Because you're a better actress than I gave you credit for."

"That's unworthy of you, Ali," she replied in a small wounded voice.

"You're in no position to tell me what's worthy and what isn't," I

shouted. "I'm the one who's bound for the gallows. Or did you conveniently forget that?"

"No. I didn't forget."

A cough outside the door reminded me the guards were still out
there and ready to come in. I took a breath, trying to collect myself.
She was right about one thing, of course. I would have done the same
thing if it had meant keeping my own father out of prison.

"Please, I need to try to make this right." She reached for my hand.

"How?" I drew it away. "Are you going to try to climb into Nasser's
bed?"

"That's not very nice."

"Neither is being an informant," I said.

She began fussing with the scarf's knot under her chin. "I'm going
to try to raise money to get a lawyer for you."

"Don't bother." I sniffed. "My father is trying to do that. But most
of the attorneys are afraid to get on Nasser's bad side."

"Then I'll go to America and try to speak to Cecil B. DeMille."

"That's the most ridiculous thing you've said yet."

"Why?"

I gestured haplessly at the locked door, the bars on the windows,
and the warden's stolen citations on the wall, trying to convey how
futile the situation was.

"Mr. DeMille has been deathly ill," I reminded her. "Even if he re-
covers, I very much doubt that he would agree to see you. Especially
not on my behalf."

"*Néanmoins*, I'll make him see me," she said with a touch of Gallic
arrogance. "I'll sit outside his office until he comes out. I'll make him
understand."

"I'm sure he has a long line of other failed actresses waiting."

"I know I deserve that." She nodded with a heavy sigh. "But I'm
not giving up. This is my cause now."

"Oh, that's what I am to you? 'A cause'?" I shoved back from her, my chair legs making a grunting sound. "No thank you, Mona. I don't need anyone feeling sorry for me."

"I'm not doing it because I feel sorry for you." Her jaw became firm. "I'm doing it because I want to."

"Why? I've already served my purpose. Haven't I?"

"That's not how it was. I didn't mean for you to get hurt."

"That sounds like a line from a movie I took you to. Was it Laila Mourad or Bette Davis who said it originally?"

I was still trying to wound her, because that's all I could do. If I was going to die soon with no other way to leave my mark on the world, I might as well be someone's bad memory.

"I'm going to make it up to you," she insisted.

"Oh please." I sneered. "You want to light your candles and get your absolution, like you're still the good-hearted girl in your Christian school. Leave me alone, Mona. I'm not the one to give you absolution."

"That's not what I came for."

"Then why *did* you come?"

My sneer hurt me. My top lip was so dry and cracked from dehydration that it began to bleed a little.

"I told you. I came because I wanted to see you."

She reached out and wiped tenderly at the trickle.

"I don't believe you." I shook my head. "I'm a dead man and we both know it."

"Don't say that. They can't hang everyone. I'm going to fight for your life."

"Good luck—Even if they spare me, I'll be in prison for most of it."

"Then I'll wait for you."

"Please, Mona." I sucked my cut lip. "That's just your guilt talking. It won't last."

"No." She put a soft hand over my mouth. "I've felt this way all along. Ever since you showed me *Children of Paradise* and it ended up just the two of us alone in the dark."

This time I did not pull away. The comfort of her touch, the perfumed smell of her skin, the faint pulse under her palm. My body shuddered with the promise of joy, even as my mind told me this was all just another illusion.

"Come on." I tilted my head back. "I never had enough money for you, and we both know it."

The Cartier watch was still on her wrist, inches from my eyes.

"That's what I thought as well." She touched the clasp self-consciously. "But now I know better."

"Wouldn't you rather wait for Raymond?" I asked.

"You're not serious, are you?" She looked at me sideways. "That was just a passing fancy."

I squinted. "You're actually saying you would wait for me to get out of prison?"

"Yes."

I ached inside, wanting to believe her.

"It could be years before I get out," I said, testing her. *"Many* years."

"It doesn't matter."

"How could it not matter? You're a young woman."

"I've told you, I always wanted to devote myself to something. With all my heart. I used to think I could be a nun. Then that I could be an actress. Now I know I want to devote myself to you."

I tried to remember that I'd believed in mirages and performances before and had wound up in chains.

"It's not rational, what you're saying." My tongue touched the spot of drying blood on my lip. "Your entire life is ahead of you."

She might not have been Yvonne De Carlo, but there were still many in Cairo who would have gladly married her. Army officers, businessmen, even foreign diplomats who could have taken her far away from Egypt on their next assignment and given her a life of leisure in another land.

I asked, "What about money? What about your social standing?"

"I used to think I cared about those things." She undid the unclasp of her timepiece. "I don't anymore." She held the watch out to me. "Here. Take this. Maybe you can use it to gain favor with the warden and the guards."

"No, it'll just get taken from me." I shook my head. "Is this what you really want?"

"More than I've ever wanted anything," she said.

I closed one eye, like I was about to look through a microscope. "But is it what *I* really want?"

"It's up to you, Ali. I'm here only for you."

She spoke so quietly and so modestly that I thought I might have misheard her. I hunched forward in my chair and opened both eyes, trying to make sure that she was speaking in earnest and no longer acting. The better part of my life passed in the two seconds before her eyes stared straight back into mine.

I remembered something else about that day I'd walked along the Nile with my father. There had been a great fluttering among the branches of the banyan, and then the birds all flew out at once. I think they might have been swallows, which in the olden times were supposed to represent the souls of the dead. They had massed over the river at sunset and then slowly spread out like an unwinding thread against the darkening sky.

And as they did, I remembered my mother and my sisters, and my spirit lifted just a little. I recalled wanting to ask my father how life could be so beautiful and cruel at the same time, but I did not have the words.

Finally I did have the words, but what good could they do? The woman I loved was saying she longed for me. Yet I was in a cage and she was one of those who'd helped put me there.

The door opened and the warden appeared in the doorway, apparently having heard more than enough.

"Your time is done," he said. "Stand up and put your hands behind your back. You have to be handcuffed again."

I did as he asked while Mona looked up at me.

"I'd like to come see you again before I go to California." She held up the watch on her wrist. "I'm going to sell this piece to get some of the money for the ticket. I told my mother she has to give me the rest or I'll never speak to her again. Is that all right?"

"I'm your captive." I managed to smile as the warden put the manacles on my wrists again.

She kissed me right on the mouth. It was not a movie kiss, meant to be seen, not felt. It was the kind of kiss you never recover from. My legs started to go out from under me. I put my hand on her shoulder to steady myself and the warden cleared his throat.

"Now I'm *your* captive," Mona said.

Then she walked out without giving him so much as a nod.

25

For days after that, I dared to have hope. There was a new lightness in my step. Whenever I saw the sergeant with that tattoo by his eye, I would whistle "Zip-a-Dee-Doo-Dah" and sing the words "Mr. Bluebird on my shoulder" to myself. The beatings ceased and my body began to heal. Along with some of the others who'd been arrested with me, I was designated a "political prisoner" and allowed to wear my own clothes again. Then I was given extra hours in the exercise yard, where I was permitted to see the sun and join the circle of my fellow inmates humming to themselves while walking counterclockwise around an empty chair.

It was there that Professor Farid finally approached me, after weeks of ignoring me since our arrival at the Siggn.

"You see that?" He thrust his fragile-looking chin at the vacant seat.

"See what?"

"It's where Mahmoud Abdul Latif used to sit," he said in a fierce whisper.

"The one who shot at Nasser?" I raised an eyebrow.

"*Pretended* to shoot at him. We know this was a hoax now. They gave him special favors by letting him sit in that chair, smoking cigarettes and reading newspapers, while the rest of us were walking in mindless circles around him. And now he's gone. They came to his cell and took him away in the middle of the night. It's all part of their plan."

The guards had taken the professor's pince-nez, and without them he somehow looked both wizened and naïve, like an awkward teen-ager who'd found himself in the stiff-limbed body of an old man. He clung to a well-thumbed copy of George Eliot's *Mill on the Floss* that had its cover falling off and pages tumbling out.

"Which plan is this?" I asked.

"It's circles within circles," the professor replied, barely moving his lips in the morning chill. "The actor has been moved to another stage."

"What actor? What stage?"

It wasn't like my old teacher to speak so cryptically. I wondered if the privations of prison life were starting to have an effect on his fine mind.

"It's obvious now what happened in Alexandria." He curled a lip on which his once-trimmed mustache had grown wild. "This so-called assassination attempt against Nasser was used to justify putting all of us in prison. Latif was only an actor in the setup. He's probably back in Cairo right now, giving false testimony to implicate the rest of us."

"But, Professor." I fell in beside him as we joined the group walk-ing counterclockwise. "There really *was* an intent to get rid of El Rayyis, wasn't there? You had me bring the gun for Osman, before he called it off—"

"Don't be dense, Ali Hassan. They were already onto us. Someone else was informing, whom we now have to find and kill. Think about it. How would they know about the time pencils you bought at the nightclub? Why else would they have had the extra security around the stage? Latif was given a gun that fired blanks. They substituted their fake assassin for our real one, so they could have the drama without the risk. Haven't you asked yourself why no one has seen the film you shot that night?"

I had come to believe Raymond was correct about the delay

between the gunshots we'd heard and the light globe exploding over Nasser's head. The authorities had confiscated the film because the special effect they had planned hadn't quite come off.

"So you're saying we were framed, even though we meant to carry out the plan?" I asked.

"Circles within circles," the professor repeated, like an incantation. "They're trying to confuse us about what's real and what's false."

I glanced around the yard to see who else was watching us. Not just the guards in their towers, but the various factions around us. The Ikhwan walking together in one group, Communists in another, and the ring of Egyptian Jews who had been arrested as Israeli spies coming toward us in the opposite direction. We had all started to turn on one another in our delusions, like members of the famous circular firing squad you hear about sometimes in American politics. But Raymond was refusing to walk. He stood alone in a corner, in his short-sleeved shirt and pleated pants, as coolly detached and observant as he'd been with a camera in his hands.

"The *khayin* is still among us, you know," the professor mumbled.

"Who is?"

"This traitor who spied on us and turned us in."

I was conscious of a group of Muslim Brothers just walking behind us. I looked over my shoulder and saw Sherif leaning on Mustafa for support. My cousin's eyes looked protuberant in his sunken face and his beard had threads of gray.

"We have to root them all out and punish them," the professor said, not noticing more pages falling from his book. "And we need to be very severe about it, so everyone else gets the message."

"Do we know who it is?" I stooped to retrieve them.

"We have a good idea."

A breeze took the pages away before I could gather them. They flew and tumbled toward Sherif and Mustafa.

"I think you know as well, Ali Hassan," the professor said.

"Me?" I watched a page drift over and wrap around my cousin's ankle.

Sherif picked it up and studied it closely.

"Your cousin suggested it's this Christian harlot who was in one of my classes at the university." He rubbed his thumb and forefinger together. "The Coptic girl whose mother was French. You know her quite well. In fact, I think you were in love with her."

"Mona?" I feigned surprise with my eyes and my voice. "Seriously? How could that possibly be?"

"You know as well as I do that the Holy Koran says 'Let not believers take disbelievers as allies.'" The professor shook a finger. "If we *do* find out that it was her, we should bury her up to the neck in sand and throw stones at her head until her face is bloody and disfigured."

I looked up at a plane passing overhead and wondered if Mona had already bought her ticket to America. The rumble and hum made me uneasy. Her father had been transferred to another facility shortly after she visited me. I tried to tell myself there were a number of reasons that could have happened. They could have sent him to a worse place to punish her for not continuing her cooperation. But all the same, there was less spring in my step as I walked alongside my teacher and there was no bluebird on my shoulder either.

"Mona could hardly know enough to inform on anyone," I said. "Someone else must be responsible."

"You know, a lot of people still think it was *you*, Ali Hassan," the professor broke in.

"Me? You think I've been the traitor all along?"

"Why not? We all saw how you ran around screaming like an idiot on the movie set, trying to warn everyone."

My cousin slowly crumpled the page he'd been reading, his eyes never leaving me.

"That was different." I turned back to the professor. "I panicked when I realized hundreds of people could die. I'd never agreed to be part of anything like that."

"However, it's true that you were never really one of us." He looked mournful as he continued his shuffling. "I always hoped you wouldn't turn out to be the weak link."

"But why would I be in here with the rest of you, if I were the spy?" I kept pace. "Don't you think I would have driven a better bargain for my own freedom?"

"Not if you were more valuable to Nasser staying close and continuing to inform on the rest of us." The professor tapped the side of his head. "More circles inside circles."

"I was not the informant, Professor. I swear on it."

"Okay—" He stopped and inspected my face the way he used to stop and inspect in class to find a quote he liked. "I think I have to believe you."

"Oh, thank Allah," I said.

"I think I'll believe you, because I have my eye on someone else."

"Who?"

The professor glanced across the yard to where Raymond was leaning against a wall, nonchalantly watching our circle pass.

"That one," Professor Farid said. "He's always where he should be. Or rather where he *shouldn't* be. And usually with a camera in his hands."

"You think *he's* the informant?"

"Think about it. He's been with you the whole time." He ticked off the circumstances with his long spidery fingers. "He was there when the car struck the imam. He was with you in Sinai. He saw you working on the façade with Sherif. He was at the nightclub when you bought the time pencils. He saw Osman and Mustafa come with you to the houseboat. And he was conveniently in Alexandria when the fake shots were fired."

As we passed where Raymond was standing, I didn't offer even a glance of acknowledgment. Why should I have cared what they said about him? Even if he was no longer a rival for Mona's affections, he'd been a constant irritant since I'd met him.

"We believe he's a spy for Israel," the professor said.

"Interesting." I nodded.

"You've suspected him as well? Why didn't you say anything to the rest of us?"

"Because I couldn't be sure what he was really up to." I slowed down, trying to match the professor step for step.

It made far more sense than Mona being the informant. He'd been harboring secrets the whole time I'd known him. The gold ring that appeared and disappeared on his finger. His fake name and the suspicious gaps in his résumé. The way he took risks filming things that were unlikely to wind up in the documentary. His easy identification of the kind of British time pencil that would have been used in Israel just a few years before. Even the way he'd made casual reference to almost no one ever drowning in the Red Sea, as if he was more familiar with the region than he let on. And most of all, the fact that he had been arrested and imprisoned with the rest of us.

"Think about it." The professor slapped the back of one hand into the palm of the other. "His job making the documentary was probably just a cover to allow him to get in and see our government installations." He dropped his voice. "The guards say he's about to be charged with espionage."

"But wait—" I halted. "If he's a spy for Israel, how would he be spying for Nasser as well?"

"You're getting lost within the circles." The professor looked back at me with a kind of weary exasperation.

"What do you mean?"

"The common goal of Nasser and Israel was disruption and

instability. Our enemies are trying to confuse us by playing all sides against the middle."

"I'm sorry, but I still can't follow what you're telling me."

"Never mind." He cut me off with a chop of his hand. "We're making a counterplan."

"What is it?"

He smiled up at the guards with their rifles in the towers. Then he looked down and reopened the tattered book in his hands, as if he wanted to show me an interesting passage.

"We're organizing an escape," he said in a frantic whisper. "We have Brothers on the prison staff who will assist us when the time comes. And once we're out of our cells and shackles, we'll punish the betrayers and execute them right here in the yard."

"You're serious?"

"It'll be like Judgment Day has come early." He shut the book. "They'll pray for the relief of hellfire."

"Why do you keep talking like there was more than one of them." I stopped walking, and others in the circle passed us. "I thought we were only talking about *an* informant."

"We are. It's just a figure of speech, Ali Hassan."

He rested a hand on my back, encouraging me to start walking in the circle again.

"When we get out, we'll be twice as dangerous to them as we were before we went in," he said. "The terrible things they've done to us in here have radicalized *all* of us. They've turned peaceful little kittens into hungry panthers who will eat them alive as soon as we're let out of our cages."

I noticed how Sherif turned away as he passed us. As if he could no longer even stand the sight of me. Again, I was lost between what was real and what was fake. What the professor was saying was so outrageous and outlandish that I wondered if he was playing some kind of game with me, to see how I would react and reveal myself.

"We'll assign you a role when we're ready to act." The professor put the novel under his arm. "*Insha'Allah*, you'll comport yourself a little more honorably this time."

The next day, guards brought me back in manacles to the office, where the warden and his deputy were waiting with a man I hadn't seen before.

"Good afternoon, Ali Hassan," the warden said. "We are now working with the state intelligence agency. We have been authorized to offer you a reduced sentence to facilitate your ongoing coopera- tion."

"Thank you, Warden." I bowed my head. "But I'm afraid it is still not possible for me to help you until I have spoken to a lawyer."

"Does this man have a lawyer?" the visitor asked.

I am not sure I can describe how much this stranger's presence unsettled me, Alex. For one thing, the warden did not introduce him. For another, he wore sunglasses indoors. His hair was a very deep shade of black, like the varnish on furniture, but a lot of Egyptian men dyed their hair when they reached his age—which I guessed to be about forty. What caught my attention more was the unnatural- ness of his skin tone. He was slathered in some kind of heavy bronzer to make him appear darker than he was. It made the whiteness of his straight teeth more prominent. His slate-gray suit was snug around his shoulders and tucked in around the waist in a fashion that most Cairo tailors could only try to emulate. And I could not help but no- tice that he was quite tall, over six foot four, which was also unusual for countrymen of my acquaintance. The effort to disguise his ap- pearance was so blatant, so almost contemptuously obvious, that it made him even more frightening. As if he was daring someone to question him and give him a reason to show what he could do with all those strong white teeth.

"He'll get an attorney soon enough," the deputy warden said. "The *murderer.*"

He had not spoken to me so sternly since my father began delivering my uncle's pornography. I sensed the visitor was here to put the steel back into the prison staff.

"Forgive me." I turned to the guest. "But I have not been charged with killing anyone. In fact, it's still not clear to me exactly *what* I have been charged with."

"Until now," the visitor said.

"Sir?"

"You fled the scene of a fatal accident. You ran over this imam, Sheikh Sirgani, and then stepped on the accelerator to evade prosecution." His Arabic was very good; if I closed my eyes, I would have taken him for a native speaker. "It was a criminal act. In the West, they call it criminally negligent manslaughter. Here, it may be considered murder."

I stiffened. "Sir, if you are from state intelligence, then you must have known about this accident for weeks. Prime Minister Nasser certainly did. If I'm to be charged, then everyone else involved in the cover-up should be charged, too."

"Do you deny that you were at the wheel?" The visitor grinned, his tinted lenses giving no clue about the true shape or color of his eyes.

"I don't admit anything," I said. "If I speak about this, it will be at a public trial."

He touched one side of his sunglasses and nodded, as if this was more or less what he'd expected.

"Ali Hassan, for your own good, you should cooperate," the warden beseeched me. "It won't be hard. We know you've been talking to other members of the Brotherhood lately. You were seen speaking to Professor Farid in the yard yesterday."

"So?"

"We know they're planning something. Help yourself. You owe them nothing."

"I'm hardly a trusted confidant." I started to lean against a table, my balance compromised by my battered legs. "I spoke to the professor only about literature."

"And this is what you expect us to believe?" the guest asked, his grin widening enough that I could see he had gold caps on some of his back teeth.

"With respect, sir, it is not my concern what you believe but what I'm prepared to say. And I won't say anything to endanger myself or the people I care about."

The warden looked at the guest in a way that told me that he was afraid of this strange man as well. Then the warden grabbed me by my throat.

"You are making a very bad mistake, Ali Hassan!" he yelled as he squeezed my windpipe. "You need to come back to your senses. You're not a fanatic like the rest of them. We know you had a female guest not long ago. Don't you want to get out and see her again before you're an old man and she has forgotten you?"

"How can I tell you anything if I can't breathe?" I gasped.

He let me go and then looked at the stranger, as if this had been a kind of audition.

"You're stronger than you seem, Ali Hassan." The guest pulled his lips back to his vividly pink gumlines. "It's good for a man to master his fear."

I touched my larynx tentatively, making sure nothing had been dislodged.

"But what you discover about life as it goes on is that there is always something *else* to be afraid of." The visitor turned to the warden. "Warden, will you please have them bring in the other prisoner?"

No one said anything for a few seconds, like the audience at the Cairo Opera waiting for a performance to begin. Then the warden glanced at the deputy, who left the room. I became aware of slow shuffling footsteps, rattling handcuffs, and murmured voices. The deputy warden reentered, followed by the sergeant with the bluebird tattoo, who held a baton in one hand and the elbow of Raymond Garfield in the other.

"We know this man was in the car with you when the imam was run down," the visitor said.

"I wish to speak to a lawyer." I turned to the warden.

The deputy warden slammed a chair into the backs of my legs, knocking me into a seated position. When I tried to stand up, the sergeant helped another guard yank my arms back and shackle my wrists.

"Don't tell these morons anything," Raymond mumbled. "They've got no case."

His clothes were now rumpled and ripped. His cowhide boots and silk socks were gone. There was a cut under his right eye.

"Did you say something, scum?" The sergeant poked him in the ribs with his baton.

"I was just agreeing with him about his rights," Raymond said. "I think even in Egypt you have a few."

The warden inhaled, as if trying to absorb the insult. The visitor looked at Raymond and at me as if he were comparing the results of a clinical experiment.

"This man is being charged as a Jewish spy for Israel," the deputy warden said. "He represents the enemy state."

"That's a lie," Raymond broke in. "I'm a documentary filmmaker."

"We have proof to the contrary," the warden said. "Furthermore, since you are both state security cases, we've been keeping track of your guests. The logbooks say the same woman has come to visit both of you. Which means you have competing interests."

Raymond smirked. "That's not true, either. She hasn't been to see me at all—"

"Be quiet now." The deputy warden backhanded him.

It was a glancing blow, and Raymond barely winced. He seemed more annoyed than hurt.

"So now the situation is simple for you, Ali Hassan," the warden said. "You can assist us with our inquiry. Or we will allow this Jewish spy to beat you."

"You wouldn't do that." I twisted my wrists until the skin on them was raw.

"Why not?" The visitor tilted his sunglasses as if he was genuinely interested.

"Because I won't do it," Raymond replied.

He and the visitor stared at each other like they were both trying to decide if they had met before.

"You are saying *no*?" The warden looked around the room, checking to see if the rest of us had heard the same.

"Yes, I am saying no." Raymond made no effort to hide his impatience. "I do not ask you to do my job for me, Warden. So please don't ask me to do *your* job for *you*."

"What's wrong with you, you Jewish dog?" The deputy warden yelled and then aimed his baton at me. "This man Ali Hassan is a filthy son of a whore. He despises you. If he was given half a chance, he would take this rod and beat you to a bloody pulp right now."

"If you're that desperate for confessions, why don't you just start making them up?" Raymond asked, pronouncing the words exactingly. "Or are you worried that will hurt your country's shiny new image as a beacon of liberty?"

"So is this your final determination?" the visitor asked, speaking English with an accent that was strikingly similar to Raymond's. "Are you sure you won't reconsider?"

"*Richtig.*" Raymond snorted.

"Listen to me, inmate." The warden took the baton from his deputy and put a hand on Raymond's shoulder as if he was trying to counsel him. "I want you to understand something. If you do not do what we're asking, we will beat *you* instead. And we will beat you very, very badly, so you may not ever recover. We have done this before, and we're very good at it. Okay?"

"I *do* understand." Raymond blinked very slowly. "But I will not do what I cannot do. So here we are."

The visitor sighed and scratched one of his lacquered temples with a broad polished fingernail.

The warden smashed Raymond across the bridge of the nose with his baton, sending a small geyser of blood into the air.

"*Scheisse.*" Raymond gritted his teeth and shut his eyes again.

"Okay?" The warden held the baton out to him like a maître d' offering a menu. "Now, if you would be so kind . . ."

Raymond touched the bleeding gash, tipped his head, and looked down his nose at the visitor.

"*Nein.*" He refused with an aristocratic shake of his head. "*Ich lehne ab.*"

The warden doubled Raymond up with a blow to the midsection. Then he got behind Raymond and used the baton to choke him until both their faces started to turn bright purple.

"*Inta majnoon!*" the warden shouted. "Look what you're making us do!"

He abruptly let go and Raymond stumbled forward, gulping and clutching his throat. The visitor watched with a hand languidly resting on his chin.

"Okay," the warden said. "Will you be sensible now?"

"*Fick dich.*" Raymond glared at the guest again.

The stranger gave another nod, like a referee allowing a fight to continue; and the officers all fell on Raymond at once, kicking and stomping with unrestrained fury and frustration. After a few seconds, the warden took the baton and got down on one knee, smashing the rod down on the back of Raymond's neck as if he were trying to kill a snake in his garden.

Raymond stayed down, giving only the occasional grunt and groan to acknowledge the force of their blows. The warden took off his jacket, revealing half-moons of sweat under his arms, and then wrung out his cramping-up baton hand before bending down again to administer another frantic flurry of close-range punches to Raymond's head. The deputy warden kept jumping on Raymond's back and falling off. The sergeant grew flustered and then fatigued as he rubbed his bluebird tattoo with the heel of his palm. They were like a demolition crew working overtime to try to finish a project.

"*Khalas,*" said the visitor. Enough.

They backed away slowly, revealing Raymond facedown and motionless. The floor around him appeared to be throbbing from punishment.

The warden sagged against a wall calendar, exhausted, breathing heavily and loosening his collar as if he was about to pass out.

The visitor came over, knelt beside Raymond, and felt for a pulse in his neck. Then he pushed back his sunglasses, nodded to indicate the patient was still alive, and brushed the wrinkles from his tailored suit as he stood up.

I turned my head, not wanting to look anymore.

This foreigner, this outsider, this *kufar*, this filthy *Jew* who might have been a spy for our enemy and whom I had almost dropped off a cliff. There was no reason for me to feel sympathy for him. Spy or not, he was an interloper who never should have been in the country in the first place.

So why did my ribs, neck, and shoulders all throb like I'd absorbed half the punishment myself? The warden dropped the baton, which rolled across the floor, winding up at my feet. Then he bumped into his own chessboard, upending it with a tumultuous clatter.

"Let that be a lesson," he said, kicking at the fallen pieces in disgust before he turned to walk out. "Sergeant, clean up this mess and put things back into order."

June 1, 2015
To: GrandpaAli71@aol.com
From: Nosleeptiljihad@protonmail.com

Grandfather,
I am taking a very big risk in writing to you right now, since my commanders have specifically forbidden it.
I just need to tell you how I feel about what I've been reading.
When we're not praying, training, or working on the videos, we study history in our camp. We talk often about Israel. We learn how they stole the land from us in the 1948 war that your cousin Sherif fought in so bravely. We learn how this theft was justified by religious mythology about Hebrew slaves and a Promised Land, bolstered by this Ten Commandments movie you'd worked on only a few years after the war. It's so odd, so insulting. We learn how these lies that you helped to propagate to justify this theft continue to poison us to

this very day, as the illegal occupation goes on and our brothers and sisters in Palestine keep dying.

Now you're trying to twist my head back the other way with this toxic accommodationist propaganda about a Jew playing the hero and taking a beating in your place. And not just any Jew, but one you yourself suspected of being a spy for the country that stole this land?

It's too much. I'm disgusted from reading this. What am I supposed to do with this book now? Did you make it up to try to dissuade me from the path I am on? Or did you store up these lies for years so you could spring them on me when I was about to become a legal adult?

Abu Suror

P.S. Shayma is gone now, because she got shot while trying to escape from her new husband.

Meanwhile. We have a Jewish guest in our midst ourselves, named Tyler Sommers. At least, I think he's a Jew. And he's not exactly our guest. Anyway, gotta bounce. Bye.

26

When next I saw Raymond, several days later, I did not recognize him. In fact, I could not even tell he was a white man at first. He'd been beaten so badly that his eyes were swollen half shut. His skin was puffy and discolored, with patches of mustard and black. His broken nose was covered in scabs. His old clothes had been taken away and he had been given a galabiya and oversized sandals instead. He was leaning heavily on a crude wooden stick and every few minutes, when he thought no one was looking, he gently pressed his hand against his abdomen, as if his injuries were internal as well.

I ignored him at first, instead preferring to watch the soccer game that was being played between a group of Muslim Brothers and the Jewish spies.

Word had gotten out somehow about Raymond's refusal to beat me, and it had become part of a general lowering of barriers between our groups. Probably this would have happened anyway. Outside the prison gates, these people were, as you say, our mortal enemies. Sherif liked to point out passages from the Koran that described them as pigs and foul, slinking apes. They were everything that the Brotherhood had been formed to oppose: Zionist aggressors, betrayers of our country, liars and perverters of the injunctions God had handed down from the mountaintop. Terrorists, the professor said, at least as much as the rest of us. But within these walls, all that was irrelevant. They were our fellow inmates. They slept in cells in our block and ate the same food as we did. And now it was undeniable that they were tormented and tortured just as we were by the guards.

Gray dirt plumes rose from the men wrestling and scuffling over the bundle of laundry they were using as a ball, the guards occasionally stepping in when the play got too rough and the men fell on top of one another, biting and punching, doing all the things they'd do to our keepers if they ever had the chance. Across the yard, Raymond was trying to light a cigarette as he leaned against a wall, his hands shaking badly. I don't know where he could have gotten the tobacco and matches. Such riches were rare within these walls. It annoyed me enough that he was holding them in public, but that he was unable to use them properly drove me to pure distraction.

I waited until the game became so fierce that no one was taking notice, and then I sidled up next to him by the stone wall.

"What's the matter with you?" I hissed. "Put those away."

"Why?" He tried to shift his weight onto his crooked right leg. "You think someone might get mad?"

I shoved my hands in my pockets, refusing to acknowledge the joke.

"I suppose you think I should thank you," I said after a while.

"I'm not sure I care," he said, trying to light the match again.

"*Yanni,* you know, one more beating would have made no difference to me," I muttered. "I'm used to it."

"You couldn't have told me that before?"

"Again a joke. You're as bad as my father."

"What's wrong with your father? Other than having you as a son."

I scratched the back of my neck and looked away from him, so it would appear to anyone watching that we just happened to be standing near each other.

"Why did you do this, anyway?" I put my hand in front of my mouth, to frustrate any lip-readers in the yard or the guard towers.

"I don't know. Maybe I just have a problem with authority figures. Especially when they have that accent."

"It sounded just like *your* accent. Do you know that man?"

"No. But I know what he is."

"Which is what?" I asked, truly curious.

"Please, Ali, you've heard the exact same rumors that I have about German officers staying on in Egypt after the war and blending in to avoid prosecution." He touched his side again and winced, as if angry at himself for the pain. "It's said that special identities have been created by your intelligence service for the ones with real expertise in science and interrogation techniques that can be useful to this country's security service. I don't necessarily blame Egypt, since other countries have done the same. Including the United States. But I believe the warden's new friend is one of these 'special guests.'"

I glanced at the game, trying to decide if I had a rooting interest. "Then why antagonize him the way you did?"

"I will tell you why not." His sleepy eyes became sharp as razors. "I was born in Berlin in 1921. My father was a proper petit bourgeois, who ran a medical supply shop that sold prosthetic limbs to soldiers who'd been maimed in the first great war."

"What does that have to do with anything?"

"You asked why people like our guest the other day irk me and now I'm telling you," he said. "My father served with such men in the first great war and was awarded the Iron Cross himself, but he never wore it. He never spoke about his service at all. He preferred to take me to the Delphi Filmpalast every Saturday after shul and laugh himself silly at Buster Keaton. Then when I was twelve, he took half our family savings and sent me to live in America with his brother, who had a film lab. And do you know how his fellow citizens showed their appreciation for his patriotic service? They sent my mother and my sister to Auschwitz. And then they sent him to Buchenwald."

"I don't know what those places are," I confessed.

I don't know what they teach you in school these days, Alex, but German concentration camps were not much discussed back then. Especially not in Egypt. To the extent that any of my fellow countrymen talked about the war, it was to side with the Germans, because they hated the British as much as we did.

"They are places that ordinary citizens were sent to and did not come back from." He tried again to light the cigarette, but his hand was shaking too badly. "So when I hear that accent, the spirit of cooperation dies in me."

I grabbed the matchbook and lit the cigarette for him. Fortunately, the players were in a pileup in the middle of the yard and no one noticed. Not even when he took a long drag and started to wheeze.

"Raymond, your lungs sound terrible. Have they taken you to the prison infirmary?"

"Twice. The doctor there is such a quack, I shouldn't be surprised if he had webbed feet."

"A 'quack'?" My English was quite good by then, but this was a new idiom to me.

"You tell him you're pissing blood, and he gives you a purgative." Raymond's laugh turned into a cough.

"Is that what's happening to you? You're pissing blood as well?"

"I was just being figurative, Ali."

I took a quick sideways look and saw his hand linger briefly over his abdomen again. "Are you sure?" I asked. "As soon as your government gets you out of here, they should have you taken straight to the best hospital available."

"Who said anyone was getting me out of here?" He looked genuinely perplexed. "The last time I saw a lawyer from the U.S. Embassy, he said I might be going before a military tribunal. Like the rest of you."

The game had stopped for a minute. The laundry bundle had come apart and had to be gathered up again. The players were standing in a cloud of raging dust, arguing about who should do it.

"How is this possible?" I said. "I thought you were an American citizen."

He took a long, thoughtful drag on the butt. "I'm a resident alien. I never got my full citizenship."

"Even though you were in the United States military?"

"My application got held up." He exhaled a prodigious amount of smoke. "Some questions were raised."

"What kind of questions?" I waved the cloud from my face. "Did someone think you were a spy?"

"A spy?" He squinted incredulously. "For who? The Russians? Do I look like a Communist to you?"

In the prison pecking order, Communists were below even the Jews and the Ikhwan. A group of them were gathered in a corner of the yard, shunned by the rest of the population and not allowed to take part in the soccer game. Not only had they been savagely beaten like the rest of us, they had also had their eyebrows shaved off afterward to degrade and dehumanize them. The cruel irony was that in just a few short years Nasser would become an ally of the Soviet Union, but by then it would be too late for such men.

"No, the great Cecil B. DeMille would never have hired me if I was a true party member with my name currently on the blacklist. The suspicions held up my application, but I was ultimately cleared. I only went to a few meetings anyway. I like a good bottle of wine, clean hotel rooms, and women who shave their legs too much to be a good socialist."

"You know, Raymond, there's a rumor in here that you're about to be charged as a spy for Israel," I said in a low voice.

The cigarette stayed tucked in the corner of his mouth, a slow-burning fuse, without breath going in or out.

"Rumors are just rumors," he said.

"Do they have any proof against you?"

"Other than that time pencil you gave me?" A brief wisp of a smile disappeared in his fumes.

"They must have more than that if they're going to go ahead and charge you."

"Oh, do you really think so?" he said lightly, as if he was parodying the way Henry talked.

I noticed Sherif, the professor, and some of the other Brothers shooting furtive looks at us from across the yard and then turning their backs.

"Raymond, it's no joke." I took a step away from him. "If they convict you of being a spy, they will hang you for sure."

"This I already surmised."

"Then why didn't you beat me when they asked you to?"

"That's a good question." He took the cigarette out of his mouth and looked at it. "Maybe I just thought I could use a friend in here."

"So you allowed yourself to take my punishment for me?"

"I thought you might appreciate it."

I tried to lean back against the wall. But it was farther away than I realized and I stumbled against it awkwardly.

"What you're saying doesn't make any sense," I said.

"Doesn't it? I thought you might return the favor at some point."

"So it's just a matter of horse-trading?" I tried to straighten up.

"Or mutual interest."

From across the yard, my cousin was looking at us and showing Professor Farid a crisscross gesture with his hands, as if demonstrating a connection.

"You know, it would make sense if you were a spy," I said. "All the chances you took with the camera when you were hanging off the edge of the cliff. Those were ammunition dumps in the caves below, weren't they?"

"If you say so." Raymond dropped his cigarette on the ground.

"Those would be good strategic positions for an invading army to know about."

I saw Sherif say something behind his hand to the professor.

"Have you confided any of your suspicions about me to the Muslim Brothers or the authorities?" Raymond asked.

"Not yet. But maybe I should. They say Nasser's judges will give lighter sentences to those who cooperate."

"Then why don't you?" Raymond crushed the smoldering embers with his sandal. "The sooner you get out, the sooner you can be with our female friend. I can assure you, she has no use for me."

"Believe me"—I faced away from him—"I'm considering it."

A bell started to ring, indicating yard time was over. The game ended and the players pulled the bundle apart, taking back their clothes. The Jews went back to their corner. The Communists huddled together. And the Brothers formed a line to head back to their cells. Except for Sherif, who kept staring at Raymond and me while pulling harder and harder on his beard.

"Here's what I think." Raymond rested the back of his head against the wall. "The Egyptian authorities certainly would like to collect evidence of espionage to present to a tribunal. And you could easily give them that evidence by twisting what you've seen and heard. But I, on the other hand, could report that you were acting suspiciously on the film set, even before you gave me that timing device. So it's in both our best interests to improve the terms of our relationship. Don't you think?"

My cousin was still staring and pulling so determinedly on his beard that I thought he might be trying to yank hairs right out of his chin. He seemed almost hypnotized. Then I realized he was working himself into a rage. We might still be family, but we were no longer allies. For the first time, I knew with total certainty that he would kill me now if he had half an opportunity. I took a quick look at Raymond instead.

"So is this friendship or blackmail?" I asked. "I still don't understand why you took the beating for me."

"Have a little faith in your fellow man." He pushed off the wall. "Or look at it this way. I owed you for not dropping me off the cliff."

He saluted my cousin with his walking stick and then hobbled back toward the cellblock.

June 8, 2015
To: Caddygrandaddy71@aol.com
From: Raqqarolla@protonmail.com

Grandfather,
I've calmed down a little since the last email I sent you. Now I can sort of appreciate the irony. Because I've become more acquainted with the Jew I mentioned the last time I wrote.

His name is Tyler Sommers. He claims he's a freelance journalist, but my fellow soldiers don't believe him. They think he's a spy, because he gave two different reasons for being here. First, he said he wanted to interview us about the Kill the Crusader *video game. Then he mentioned he was already in this part of the world to cover the war. I think the truth is that he's just kind of a lonely lost guy,*

trying to get assignments and figure out what to do with his life. But
that makes no sense to a committed jihadi.

Anyway, Tyler is from Montclair, New Jersey, and went to
Middlebury College in Vermont. He's five years older than me and
used to play a lot of the same video games, like Assassin's Creed II
and World of Warcraft. *Other than the stories and reviews that he's*
written for PC Gamer, *I only found three other articles he published,*
two of them on the Vox website. One was about some American
soldiers coming back from the war in Iraq. Another was about a folk
singer named Mandy Prashker, who I think Tyler was in love with.

I'm pretty sure that Tyler Sommers is Jewish because Noah
Sommers in my high school class at James Madison was always
taking off extra time for the "High Holidays," and getting in my face
about Israel and the Palestinians. Also, the third article I found by
Tyler was on something called Jewsinsports.com. But I haven't shared
that with any of my comrades yet.

It's a pretty tense situation right now. Tyler is I guess you would
say our hostage. We're keeping him in a donkey's stall that's been
converted into a cell. My new commanders are in touch with his
parents in New Jersey and trying to get, like, ten million dollars'
ransom. I've tried to explain that even successful American oral
surgeons don't always have that kind of money lying around, even if
they sell their house in the suburbs. But no one wants to hear that at
the moment, so I'm shutting up.

The thing is, I kind of like the guy. He reminds me of Noah and
some of my other friends in Brooklyn. He's a nerd, like I was. He used
to trade Pokémon cards and get beat up by the jocks in the bathroom.
He can recite every word of the rap album Life After Death *by*
Biggie Smalls end to end like it's the Koran. When we caught him,
he was wearing a wrestling club T-shirt that said "Submit," cargo
shorts, and skater-boy Vans, even though he obviously doesn't have

enough athletic agility to wrestle or ride a skateboard. Well, he used to have the T-shirt and Vans. But they got taken away and now my commander wears the "Submit" shirt.

Tyler also claims he has a girlfriend back home, but I don't believe him. Or maybe he just thinks he has a girlfriend.

He's into Spider-Man, like me. He thinks he's like Peter Parker. As if. I guess sometimes I did too. At one point, we talked about doing a graphic novel, with me drawing the pictures and him writing the words. But then my commanders made us take the pen and pad out of his cell.

Tyler's just a really nice guy. Even though I know I should hate him because of what his people have done to our people.

And here's the other funny thing about him. He's seen this movie you worked on, The Ten Commandments. He says he used to watch it every year "on the holiday" with his parents, that it was kind of a family ritual. Only they'd kind of recite the dialogue and laugh at the corny parts. Especially when the Red Sea splits and before that when the lady says, "Oh, Moses, Moses, you stubborn, splendid, adorable fool!"

When I asked Tyler what holiday he was talking about, he said Easter. I didn't believe him, though. Because I know from Noah and parking rules in the city that the holiday of Passover comes around the same time.

So I'm taking a big chance writing to you again, since my commanders have severely restricted our use of computers. So I'm sneaking this message out from an internet café, while I'm supposed to be in town getting a new USB cable for the computer I use to edit videos and send ransom emails in English to Tyler's family back home. I may have to hit the Send button any second, if I see one of my comrades passing by the window.

But I wanted you to know I'm not that mad anymore. Though I am pretty depressed because of what happened to Shayma. I never

really got to know her, because of the language thing and the constant
crying. And my commanders keep reminding me that she's from
a group of unbelievers who are meant to be subjugated. But really
she was just a kid, trying to get back to her family. So that kind of
sucks. Actually, it totally sucks and it's bothering me. But I can't say
anything to anybody here about it. So that's that.

BTW, you still never said how things went with your doctor that
time. I haven't heard from you in a while, so let me know.

Yours truly,
Alex

June 9, 2015
To:Raqqarolla@protonmail.com
From: Bayridgemama475@gmail.com

Alex,
This is your mother. I'm writing in reply to your last email to your
grandfather, which I only just found.

He had a stroke several weeks ago and cannot answer for
himself. It's not clear if he will ever be able to use his computer
again. It's not even clear if he'll ever be able to speak again, or how
much he understands of what's going on around him. His condition
is still a little touch and go, as they say. The manuscript you're
reading may be the only voice he has left to speak to you. We're
praying for his recovery, but it's unknown how much longer he can
hold on.

In your last email, you said you could not be online very much
now. I will be brief, then. Come home. It's terrible what happened to
this poor girl and the business with this Tyler is something you need

to get away from ASAP. In whatever way you need to. I don't know
how much more strongly I can say it. I miss you. Your father misses
you. And your grandfather needs to see you before it's too late.
    Please.

                                                   We love you.
                                                     Mom

27

The weather turned colder over the days after I talked to Raymond in the yard. The guards tried to spread rumors that I was already cooperating, to increase the pressure on me. I was given extra blankets to keep me warm in my cell. I tried to give them to Sherif and Professor Farid in the hallway, but they wouldn't talk to me, so the guard just ended up taking them back. Then I was flagrantly given extra portions of hot soup in front of my fellow inmates in the mess hall. I bridled against this oafish attempt at coercion. But in private meetings in the warden's office, the warden spoke to me more straightforwardly about getting more visits from Mona and my father if I began to inform on Sherif, Raymond, and the others.

"Why hold out?" he asked. "We can make it good for you. If you cooperate, there will be a cell with a clean mattress for the next time your lady friend comes. You'll be spared the gallows for sure. And then, who knows? They may even let you out within a year or two!"

I was up all night, pondering what to do. I still wanted to believe what Mona had said, but I hadn't heard from her in the two weeks since her visit. I worried that if she had gone to America, she might never come back.

But the very next day, a postcard appeared under my cell door with an American postmark and a full-color photo of the Hollywood sign on the front.

Dear Ali,

I'm sitting outside Mr. DeMille's office as I write this. It's not clear if
he is in or if he'll agree to see me. But stay strong, my love. Hold on to
what's best in you. Don't let prison change you. I'll wait until the end
of time if need be.

Yours, with all my heart,
Mona

No more than an hour later, guards came into my cell. The sergeant
took the postcard from my hands and set it on fire. Then he dropped
it at my feet and watched it burn. Of course, they had only allowed it
through to torment me. But the pressure to cooperate faded as soon
as I stepped out into the yard that afternoon. My cousin was waiting.
He fell in beside me as all of us walked in the circle.

"I heard you got a letter today," Sherif mumbled.

"Who told you?"

"We have eyes all over this prison," he said. "We keep trying to tell
you that."

"What do you want from me, Sherif?" I looked up at the high
walls and the guard towers.

"We're about to make our move." He trudged along determinedly,
keeping pace. "We'll remember who was with us and against us for a
long time. Not just you and your father, but the girl. If you talk, we'll
find her no matter what. And then we'll make her suffer. She'll scream
so loud that you won't know another night's rest, even if you're already in the grave."

His warning kept me awake all through the night. I lay there, watching
shadows meld and diverge. Every time I resolved what to do, doubt came
over me. The truth would not necessarily set me free. The authorities could

still keep me in prison even if I testified, while Mona would be in danger as soon as she came back to Egypt to see her father. But staying quiet guaranteed I would be locked up for years.

When the deputy warden and the sergeant roused me in my cell the next morning, they looked like they had not slept much either. Their eyes were downcast and their movements were slow, almost as if they were chastened. They said very little as they hand-cuffed me and marched me past the warden's office and into what appeared to be an infirmary.

I saw about twelve beds, half of them vacant; the others were oc-cupied by quivering figures groaning under wool blankets. On closer inspection, I saw that their IV lines were swarmed by little black fruit flies feeding on the leaking sucrose droplets. The smell of liniments and ammonia filled the air, and a radio down by the orderlies' station was blasting the familiar news introduction "This is Cairo" from the Egyptian Broadcasting Network, a remnant from my old life. There was a great deal of static and distracting background noise from pris-oners yelling in the cellblocks.

I was taken to a private area behind a cloth screen and handcuffed to a narrow steel examining table. I was left sitting there for several minutes.

As I waited, I noticed dots and smears on the screen. At first, they appeared to be squashed bugs, like the ones in my cell. But when I looked more closely, I saw they were specks of blood, bright red as if they had come straight from a human heart and not yet dried.

The screen was pulled back. The tall visitor in the sunglasses and skin bronzer was grinning with his white teeth. A long stethoscope was hanging around his neck, parallel to a red-and-white striped tie.

"Good morning, Ali Hassan," he said, in his good Arabic. "How are you today?"

"I am well, thank you. And you, sir?"

He took a deep breath and rubbed his hands together, as if he had a great deal to tell me, and then sighed as if it wasn't worth the effort. I noticed his palms were pale. He either hadn't bothered to disguise them the way he'd disguised his face, or it simply wasn't possible, with the amount of handwashing required while working in an infirmary.

"Busy," he said, when he finally exhaled.

"Sir, I'm not sure why I was brought here," I said. "I feel fine."

"Yes, I know. That's the problem."

"Sir?"

"Actually, it's 'doctor.' I am called Dr. Abd' al-Qadir Sabri." He grinned more widely, so I could glimpse the gold in his mouth again. "I was telling the warden that you'd gotten too comfortable. And when people are too comfortable, they become resistant to change."

I was mindful of what Raymond had said about his being German. At this close distance, his makeup was even more obvious, almost like American blackface. His smile began to unnerve me, because he patently knew I'd seen through him as well.

"I promise you, Doctor, that I am not 'too comfortable' here," I said. "No one would be."

"Maybe this isn't the right word." He nodded. "Arabic is not my first language, you know. It's not even my second language. Maybe *accustomed* is the word I was looking for."

He took off his sunglasses and put them in his breast pocket. His eyes were gray-blue. They looked alarming with his dyed black hair and his unnatural skin tone.

"Yes, maybe that is a better word," I said.

"Did you hear what I just said?" he asked.

"Which part?"

"That Arabic is not my first language."

"Yes, sir."

"Then you know who I am, don't you?"

"No, sir."

"Of course, you do, Ali Hassan. My previous patient must have told you after our last meeting. Herr 'Garfield.' Which is not his true name either, by the way."

He put his cool fingertips under my ears and began to probe the base of my skull. He smelled faintly of lavender eau du toilette and iodine. His hands were very soft but very strong.

"He's a very intelligent man, Herr Garfield, but not very adaptable," he said as he continued the examination. "Are you more adaptable, Mr. Hassan?"

His thumbs pressed lightly on my Adam's apple.

"I try to adapt to my surroundings, sir," I said with a slightly raspy voice.

"Yes, but how do you do that while remaining true to yourself? How do you 'Hold on to what's best in you'?" He exposed his gums more fully. "Isn't that what the young lady said in the postcard she sent you?"

"It seems everyone is reading my mail." I swallowed, trying to control my murderous impulses.

"Are you upset by that?" His thumbs stayed on my throat while the rest of his fingers burrowed deeper under the base of my skull. "I'm sure you would like to see her again. And she would like to see you. She sounded homesick, don't you think?"

"I don't know. It was a very brief note."

"I feel homesick sometimes," he said. "I miss the Rhine, and the beer, and the high culture of Strauss and Goethe. But there's much I love about my new country. I love the Nile. I love your hibiscus tea. And, of course, I love your history. The royal tombs. The ancient gods and monuments. The culture that brought us writing, paper, accounting, the pyramids . . ."

His words trailed off as he put more vigor into squeezing my voice box. I knew this man could hurt me in more exacting and lasting ways than any of my previous torturers.

"In fact, the only problem with Egypt is the Egyptians," he said.

"Sir?" I held my head up, trying to lessen the pressure of his thumbs.

"You've become stupid and lazy from being invaded so often. You dream that you can be a great people again. But someone needs to wake you up."

He slapped me hard, and I saw a flash of white light.

"How is this part of a medical exam?" I asked, probing with my tongue to see if he'd loosened any teeth.

"I'm testing your resistance to pain, to see if you're as stiff-necked as your friend Herr Garfield." He pinched the underside of my chin. "Don't worry about giving in too easily. He started speaking very frankly about you after about ten minutes."

"If he gave you all the answers you needed, why are you still talking to me?"

He gave a small appreciative laugh. A few small dark hairs protruded from his nose. His general grooming was such that I knew he would be horrified if I pointed them out. But I could not quite see the advantage.

"He's not a well man now, Herr Garfield." He tucked his stethoscope behind his tie. "As you know, he suffered a grievous injury when he fell in the warden's office the other day."

"You refer to that as a 'fall'?"

"Yes. I have diagnosed him with peritonitis. Which can be very serious. Do you know what it is?"

"No, sir."

"It's an inflammation of the tissue in the abdomen, which can lead to sepsis in the blood. It's very painful to the touch, as you might imagine. Perhaps you heard him screaming during the examination?"

I shook my head. "I demand my rights under the Geneva Convention."

"I ski in Geneva." He showed me more of his incisors. "Or at least I used to. Which is a pity. Perhaps I'll take up scuba diving in Dahab instead."

The contrast between his light blue eyes and his tinted skin began to frighten me as much as the sharpened steel instruments on the side table. I asked myself why he would reveal so much if he ever intended to let me walk out of the room.

"Anyway, you distracted me," he said. "We treated Herr Garfield with a new technique I developed back home for treating patients with damaged tissue lining around the organs. We call it the 'bellows.'"

I had not taken note until then of a jury-rigged air pump that sat behind the scalpels, scissors, and tweezers on the side table. It looked more like a household implement or a street musician's homemade instrument, with its concertinaed sides and the long black rubber tube attached to its sharp metal tip.

"The theory is that we fill the body cavities with air and relieve the pressure of the inflamed tissue on the organs." He picked it up and cradled it with a kind of tender pride. "The difficulty is that the pressure of the air on the organs can cause even greater anguish. Unbearable, really."

I started to squirm, as if I could already feel air filling up the empty spaces inside me.

"I've heard the feeling described as your organs swelling up and exploding inside your body," he said.

"It sounds unendurable," I said, as calmly as I could.

"Don't be silly, Ali Hassan. You have no idea what can and can't be endured until you face it."

"But what would be the point?" I asked. "If you explode a man's organs, what good is he as a witness?"

"That's a fair point, I grant you. But most people will say anything to make the pain stop."

"Then why not just make up a false statement and attribute it to whoever you want?" I asked defiantly. "Why bother talking to me at all?"

"Hmm." He put down the bellows and removed a pack of Turkish cigarettes from his jacket pocket. "Another interesting point. You're one of the smart Egyptians. Your new prime minister thinks there are enough of you to make this a modern republic. He hasn't yet realized that democracy is absurd. That people don't really want freedom. That they want to be *told* what to do. It's one of the few things the führer and Dr. Freud agreed upon."

"I want to go back to my cell," I said.

"Too late for that." He hit the pack twice against the back of his wrist. "Unless you want to make a full confession now."

"There's nothing for me to confess."

He took his time unwrapping the pack, removing a cigarette, and putting it in the corner of his mouth. When he cocked his head to strike a match and light it, he looked more like a commoner imitating the manners of an aristocrat.

He let out a thin line of white smoke. "Your loyalty is misguided," he said. "Herr Garfield has already given me a full statement."

"You keep saying that, sir. But if that was true, why would you be quoting my mail to me and threatening me in this way?"

I noticed that he had begun to draw smoke more frequently. The Turkish aroma wended its way inside me, trying to seduce me into second thoughts. I thought of Mona's perfume and the sweetness of anticipating her embrace. If she did ever return from America. My hands writhed, trying to keep from going numb as the cuffs cut into my wrist. I wondered if I was making the wrong choice. Maybe God would make it easy for me if I gave them all that they wanted. But then I would surely not be the man that Mona would wait for.

"No." I shook my head, wishing I could be more certain. "I won't capitulate."

He sighed. "And is that your last word on the matter?"

"It is."

Without extracting the cigarette from his lips, he took off his suit jacket and put it on a hook on the wall. More than a half century later, I can still picture how he smoothed the wrinkles from the fabric as it hung and how the paper burned away without the ash falling.

"Sergeant, may I please have some assistance?" he called out.

He began to roll up his shirtsleeves, folding exactly an inch of cloth at a time. The sergeant and another guard joined us from the other side of the screen. I realized they had been right outside the whole time. Even though I was already handcuffed to the table, they each grabbed a shoulder to hold me down. I strained, rocking back and forth, refusing to let them flip me over.

"Dr. Sabri" took off his stethoscope and placed it on the side table next to the other instruments. Then he began to loosen his tie with one hand, still never taking the cigarette from his mouth. The sergeant had picked up the bellows and begun stretching out the long black rubber tube with its promise of bodily invasion. But somehow I was more fixated on how the ash of that cigarette kept growing without quite breaking off.

I heard the bellows breathing as the sergeant practiced pushing air through it. I braced myself against the table, denying them access to violate me. The other guard went around behind me and grabbed me by the shoulders. I clenched my jaw and buttocks.

Then the doctor plucked the cigarette from between his lips, blew on its tip, and jammed it into my left eye.

July 4, 2015
To: GrandpaAli71@aol.com
cc: Bayridgemama475@gmail.com
From: Raqqarolla@protonmail.com

Grandpa,
I know you probably won't be able to respond to this, but I need to tell you. I'm literally sickened by what I just read.

I'm sorry that the people who did this were so old when it happened. Because I would like to track them down and kill them myself.

For as long as I can remember, I've wanted to ask about your eye. But Mom and Dad always told me not to (Mom, I know you're reading this, so you know it's true). They said you'd lost it because of an accident in Egypt and you didn't like to talk about it. They said it would hurt you if I tried to bring it up. But now that I know the truth, I can't sleep.

I wish I had known all this before. Because then I would have been able to talk to you when I was younger. Now I'm scared that it might be too late. Some bad things are happening that I can't really talk about. We've been under attack from another faction for the last few days, on and off. It's been decided that it's not safe for me to go into town as often for my errands. More drones have been seen in the sky above us, which could be the Americans or the Russian allies *of the regime. Just as bad, I think one of our local informants might have seen me typing in this internet café a few days ago, so I may need to get off right away.*

There's some other really bad stuff with Tyler Sommers as well, which I can't get into now. I made a mistake by becoming friendly with him. I think what you wrote about Raymond might have had an effect on me. Or maybe it was the picture I saw of Tyler and his grandfather from Halloween a few years ago dressed up like Luke and Obi-Wan from Star Wars.

The only other thing I wanted to say is that I'm really sad that these terrible things happened in your life. You didn't deserve any of it. I wish I had known sooner.

I'll write when I have more time and less pressure.

Love,
Alex

28

After Dr. Sabri put his cigarette out in my eye, he took his jacket and stethoscope and left me crying out like a wounded animal behind the screen. It's hard for me to recall much about what happened next, but I can still picture the care he took in rolling down his sleeves and buttoning his cuffs, as if he was quite used to the casual business of leaving his patients permanently maimed or worse.

A nurse came in a few minutes later. She had a cold compress and some kind of smelly antiseptic ointment for the wound. I'm afraid I cursed her with words I'd never used before when she first touched me. I cried like a baby and whimpered for my mother. I realized then that I would be half blind for the rest of my life.

After she was done with the dressing, the nurse held me. I cannot summon that woman's face or the sound of her voice, but I can still feel the tender way she put her arms around me and let me rest my head on her bosom while I shivered. That feeling sustained me after I was thrown back in my cell and all I had to look at were the marks on the wall and the rope knotted around the beam over my head.

Four days later, the door opened and the guards brought in another prisoner. They took off his shackles and shoved him into a corner. Then they dropped a peach on the stone floor and left.

The cell was eight by ten and poorly lit. But it was midafternoon, so shafts of sunlight came through the window bars and found the rotted, lopsided fruit swarmed by flies like a starlet surrounded by paparazzi.

"So, *nu*?" I heard Raymond say.

"*Kos omak*. You go to hell, Raymond. You think this is funny?"

With some effort he cleared his throat. "Pardon me, but I think we already are in hell, Ali."

My right eye gradually adjusted to the light and saw him as he tried to arrange his limbs, straightening his back against the cell wall and resting his elbows on his knees. He looked even worse than before. His color was pallid, except for his still-blackened nose. He looked like he'd lost ten pounds and aged ten years since I last saw him. His beard had gray in it and his sleepy eyes were barely opening now. His arms were thin as breadsticks, and his brow glistened with sweat.

"I heard you were at the infirmary ahead of me," I said.

"Yes. That's so . . ."

He did not smell like a healthy man. But, I regret to report, neither did I.

"Did they hurt you badly?" I asked.

"Well . . . I won't be running in any marathons this year."

"I heard they used the bellows on you."

"Did they?" He attempted to laugh. "Trust me. What they did was enough. I have half a mind to write a letter of protest to the German Medical Association."

He spat on the floor beside him, then wiped his mouth with the back of his hand.

"Damn you," I said.

"Why?"

"*Why?*" I pointed at the dressing over my burnt-out socket. "Why do you think? They stuck a lit cigarette in my eyeball."

"I heard. Everyone is talking about it. But why blame *me*?"

"Because it's your fault. If it wasn't for you, I could have just told them whatever they wanted and been done with it. Instead, you had to ruin me."

"How?"

"Because—" I sputtered like a motorcycle trying to get going. "Because you made me feel obligated, God damn you. With the stupid contract you pressured me into. They had been beating me for *days*. What difference would one more make? I could have taken it. But *no*. My *savior* had to step in and play the big man. You know, I still see through you, Raymond. You're still a low, selfish, worthless snake. I curse the filthy mother's cunt you came out of. I wish you had never been born."

I was shouting so much that whatever remained of my eye's aqueous fluid was leaking out onto the dressing.

"I promise that when next I have the chance, I'll be sure to tear your arm off and beat you with the bloody stump."

"That's not what I meant." I sank into a squat and held my knees. "I'm sure that your mother was a fine and virtuous woman. It just hurts a lot now. I'm at a loss. I don't even know how I'll survive, if I ever get out. I made my living as a driver. Who's going to hire a one-eyed chauffeur?"

"What was done to you was not human," he quietly agreed.

"I never believed people could be so cruel."

"I used to think the same, that there was good and bad in everyone. But after the war?" He held out his thin, bruised arms. "I think sometimes people are touched by something beyond themselves. Not always for the best. They do things that they couldn't have conceived of an hour before. It's how the shoemaker becomes the executioner."

"Then what's your excuse?" I said, remembering to be angry again. "Why couldn't you have just left well enough alone?"

"Don't you mean 'bad enough'? Their intention was to harm someone in that room we were in, and they did it."

"You still didn't answer the question."

"I told you, it was self-interest. Plain and simple. I was trying to manipulate you. That's what movie people do. Even the ones who make documentaries."

"No." My dead eye began to itch. "I still don't accept this."

"Okay." He drew a long breath that sounded like it had to make it past several notches in his throat. "Then what would you like to believe?"

Prisoners in the adjoining cells were moaning and praying to whatever deity or cause they believed in. The Jews, the Communists, and the Muslim Brothers alike. They'd all been forced into the place where even the strongest among us could be broken. And now all were praying for something in the dark to give them salvation, or at least a reason to make it through the night.

"I think God, the Merciful and Compassionate, motivated you, but you're just too stubborn and pigheaded to admit it."

He was silent for such a long time that I was afraid he'd expired. I worried about what to do if I was left alone with his remains. I know Egyptians are supposed to have a special reverence for those who have passed to the next realm. We built the pyramids, the Valley of Kings, the Valley of Queens, and the City of the Dead. But I was pathologically afraid of corpses. I had been the one to find my poor mother after she died from that terrible disease that I was told could linger in the air after she drew her last breath. The shame of running out of that room haunts me to this day. And I was afraid I would go mad if I was left alone with Raymond's body.

"I'm just a Jew with a broken nose and a bum leg trying to follow the eleventh commandment," he said.

"What commandment is that?" I tried to see into his dark corner. "There are *ten*. 'Thou shalt not kill, thou shalt not steal, thou shalt not worship false gods. . . .' Where do you get eleven?"

"'Don't turn your back on a friend.'"

"Oh, so now we *are* 'friends.'" I forced a laugh. "Will you give me one of your good eyes?"

"If you can find a way to take it from me."

His own grim chuckle turned into a hacking cough. He held his abdomen and put his head to one side, presumably so I wouldn't notice him spitting a large quantity of dark blood and pale yellow bile onto the floor. I jumped up and ran to the door.

"Allah." I started pounding on it, pleading for help. *"Il Ha'nil!"*

"Sit down, man." He tried to hold a hand up. "You're making this worse."

"You need immediate medical attention."

"I've *had* medical attention. That's how I ended up in this state."

I went over and put the back of my hand to his forehead. He was burning up. He ground his teeth as his whole body went rigid.

"Is the pain very bad?" I asked.

He grabbed my hand and squeezed.

It's an odd thing, my grandson. Just a few weeks before, I had been inches from murdering him. But now we were like brothers, hanging on to each other, taking whatever solace we could from the presence of another human pulse.

"It's going to be all right." I patted his shoulder. *"Allah, hummagh firliyal katheera mim maa's'iyatika . . ."*

"Is that a Muslim prayer for the dying or something?"

"No," I lied. "I'm just asking for an end to your pain."

"Ali . . ." He bit his lip and crushed my knuckles more tightly. "Don't you dare ask that bastard for anything. Not for me."

"Why not? It can only help."

"Did I tell you *how* I found out what happened to my father?"

"No."

"Then let me." Another wave of pain appeared to hit him, but this time he found a way to briefly get on top of it. "On April 13, 1945, I was with a photographic unit assigned to General Patton's Third Army, when we entered the Buchenwald camp—"

"Are you sure you want to keep talking? It seems to be hurting you."

"Don't patronize me, Ali. You're the one who dragged this sordid business of God into it."

"Okay."

"I'm trying to tell you something about this God that you call the Merciful and Compassionate."

"Why? What does it matter?"

"I'm trying to tell you that I looked for evidence of him in that camp. I looked for him in the truck full of dog biscuits that they kept for the German shepherds while they were starving the prisoners. Then I looked for him in the holes in the walls of the crematorium that the SS left when they pulled out the meat hooks, because they didn't want the Allies to see how they'd hung the bodies up before they burned them. After that, I looked for him in the gold teeth they'd pulled out and left in trays to sell later—"

"All right. Stop. You've made your point."

"But I still didn't tell you how I found out about my father." He seized my hand more fiercely, threatening to break every bone. "I spoke with the prisoners until I found one who knew him. He'd seen my father just three days before. He told me that my father had spoken about me often and dreamed he would get to see me in a soldier's uniform. Unfortunately, on this day the man mentioned, my father had an argument with one of the kapos he was serving in the breakfast line—a man who was nothing but a petty thief in his life before the war. He had been stealing food from other prisoners and taking advantage of some of the female ones. . . ."

He paused and closed his eyes, as if the pain had caused him to pass out.

"Never mind." I started to extract my hand. "You can tell me the rest later."

"No, I need to tell you *now*." He gripped me harder, trying to speak more precisely. "Because my father confronted this man, this gonif, this loathsome *vantz*, who grabbed the soup ladle and attacked him with it. My father was a strong man, but they'd made him weak by starving him. This thief split my father's lip badly and knocked out two of his front teeth. Then my father developed a mouth infection, which was left untreated and spread throughout the rest of his body. The guards determined that he would not be able to do his job at the camp's kitchen anymore without treatment. So they sent him to the gas chambers instead. Less than forty-eight hours before I arrived at the camp. It was just one of those things. About which, God or Allah, or whatever you wish to call this Compassionate one, had nothing to say. So I will not pray for his mercy now. No matter how much it entertains him."

He finally released my hand, and left it pulsing, the joints nearly fused. I remembered what the doctor had said about the course of the infection, and how the damaged organs would eventually be strangled by the swollen surrounding tissue.

"You should stop talking this way," I cautioned. "He's punishing you."

"Then he's too spiteful to be believed in. Or an even bigger egotist than Cecil B. DeMille."

I knew by then that no one was coming to help us. His systems were shutting down. I could see it, hear it, smell it. The sickness in him was trying to get inside me as well.

"Raymond, please tell me what I can do for you."

"Just talk to me."

"About what?"

"About anything . . ." His eyes rolled back in his head. "Tell me about a movie you saw."

"What kind of movie?"

"Any kind." He was breathing more shallowly now. "Just take my mind somewhere else."

"Okay, then," I said. "Do you know *The Thief of Bagdad*?"

"The old one or the new one?"

I suppose it was a little funny, the two of us being cinema snobs under the circumstances. But I was too preoccupied with swatting flies and covering my nose with my collar.

"The one in color with Sabu, Mr. John Justin, and Mr. Conrad Veidt," I said. "It came out just before the war."

"Yes, please tell me about it. Let me hear your review."

I shut my eyes, trying to remember settling into the seats of the Metro when the lights went down.

"Well, it begins a long time ago in a place that never really existed. . . ."

He sighed as if he was going to be dismissive; after all, he was an award-winning documentary filmmaker. But then I realized he was settling into his corner and trying to make himself comfortable.

"There is a white man and a dark man," I said. "And they are in a dirty disgusting prison cell that's a bit bigger than the one we're in now."

"Lucky them."

"One is his highness, the sultan who has been tricked and de-throned by his vizier, who turns out to be an evil and wicked man with a wizard's powers. The other is nothing but a little thief. Less than a commoner. And outside the prison walls, the people are suf-fering and praying for a great liberator—"

"As they always are—"

I heard a sharp intake of breath. If God wasn't punishing him for his defiance, then Nasser surely was.

"Then what happens?" Raymond prompted.

"The thief saves the day. The dark man. Just a boy, really, from a lowly family who were never supposed to amount to anything."

"Go on."

"He steals a key from the jailers and helps the sultan escape from the cell with him."

"And then?"

"And then they set off on their adventure to defeat the vizier and put the sultan back on his throne. . . ."

I was back in the movie theater now, holding my mother's hand and sharing a tub of popcorn with my sisters.

"Oh, so many amazing things happen after that, Raymond. There's a treacherous journey on a riverboat. Then they arrive in Basra. Only it's not like the real Basra, with the traffic and the heat. It's a beautiful place with pink and purple castles and street markets full of magical things and giant sailboats in the harbor. And an even more beautiful princess behind the fortress walls. Of course, the sultan falls in love with her. But so does the vizier, who enslaves the princess and strikes the sultan blind with his terrible wizard powers. . . ."

I hunched forward too quickly, which caused me to feel like the burning embers were still crackling in my eye socket.

"Anyway." I pressed my palm to the wound before I continued. "Again, it's the little thief who comes to the rescue. He finds a genie in a bottle on a beach and makes three wishes so he can help his friend." The more I talked, the more I could ignore my pain. "Then he steals a magic carpet and goes swooping down to save the princess. And then he defeats the vizier and the people are freed and everyone is very happy and, oh, I almost forgot to say, the sultan's sight is restored and he's put back on the throne—"

Raymond had become utterly still. I worried that he had either fallen asleep from boredom or died during my recitation.

"And does this thief get the girl?" he said.

"Oh my God, no, of course not." I rocked back and forth, relieved to hear him still breathing. "Such things don't happen even in movies. But he does get to fly off on the magic carpet in the end."

"So that's something."

I noticed that the other prisoners had gone quiet in their cells, as if they were listening as well. The sun had started to go down. Soon it would be the dinner hour. But it was unclear if we'd be given more than the moldering peach on the floor to split between us.

"Anyway," I said, "I loved this film. I can't believe you never saw it."

His clothes rustled, as if his body no longer filled them. "Who said I didn't?"

"Why did you let me tell the whole story, then?"

"I just liked hearing you talk about it."

I slid down onto my backside and kicked out a leg. In the dying light of the cell, I couldn't tell if he was grinning or wincing.

"I think you're making fun of me again, Raymond."

"I promise you that I am not. I asked you to take my mind somewhere and so you did. I felt like I was back at the Delphi Filmpalast with my father, watching Douglas Fairbanks ride the magic carpet in the silent version. So I thank you. You have my sincere gratitude."

Sometime after that, I fell asleep. My body was exhausted, and my mind had taken in as much reality as it could handle for the moment.

I slumbered as if I had inhaled the Blue Rose of Forgetfulness that the vizier gives the princess in the film. My soul went on a long journey. I dreamed I was in a movie theater. The warmth of my family around me. Not just my mother and my father, but the previous generations in the rows of seats behind me that stretched so far back that I could not see. Mona was in front of me.

In the midst of all this sumptuous opulence, Cecil B. DeMille came up and told me I was sitting in the wrong seat. I tried to find my ticket to show him that I did belong here but found it was gone. He told me I needed to follow him out of the theater. I was torn between obeying him and staying with my loved ones. Then an alarm sounded, telling us there was a fire in the cinema. I looked around for my mother and father, but their seats were empty. So was Mona's. I was alone in the cinema. A jolt of adrenaline opened my eyes.

The alarm was still ringing.

I smelled smoke.

The one bare light bulb in the cell was on. The rotten peach was still on the floor. It was dark outside.

Raymond was curled up in the corner. I could not tell if he was breathing. Someone was frantically banging and yelling about fire outside of our cell door.

"*Akhrogo!*"

There was a great deal of commotion in the hall. Even more people were shouting in the courtyard outside our barred window. I sat up, fighting my way back into a fully wakeful state. My right eye was stinging and tearing up. My throat was burning. I heard sirens in the distance.

"*Gohannem!*" Inmates in the adjoining cells were howling. "*Sa'ed-ini min fadlik!*"

Black smoke curled in under our cell door. It was thinner and a little less toxic than the smoke out in the yard, more paper and less oil, as if multiple fires had been set at the same time in separate locations.

"Raymond, we have to get up," I said.

A cough racked him, but he failed to move. Keys jangled in the cell door. It opened and a fireman stood on the threshold in his heavy yellow and black turnout coat and helmet, holding an ax. I noticed something odd about his posture. He was favoring one leg.

"Ali, *yalla.*" Sherif stuck his head in. "*Yalla beena.* We have to go, right now. Okay?"

July 7, 2015
To: Raqqarolla@protonmail.com
From: Bayridgemama475@gmail.com

Dear Alex,
I have no idea if this is still your email address or if you will ever get this message, but your father and I have exhausted every other way of trying.

Your grandfather is not thriving. I read him your replies about his book and he seems to understand some of it. But his body is struggling and his life force is ebbing. He has not been able to move around much since the stroke, and now the doctors say he has bedsores and fluid in his lungs.

I don't mean to pressure you to the point that you stop communicating. They say it's possible that he can still recover. Greater miracles have happened. But they also say he could take a turn for the worse very quickly. So no one really knows.

I will read your reply to him if you choose to or are able to write back. I understand that it may no longer be in your power to return, even if you wanted to. But you should know that you are still on our minds and in our hearts every minute of every day.

Love,
Mom

29

I gawked at my cousin in his fireman's coat and helmet, unable to believe my remaining eye. It was like a remnant of the dream I'd just been having. Then it dawned on me. This time, Sherif wasn't exaggerating or deluding himself. He and the other Brothers had pulled off the grand conspiracy that the professor had alluded to. Someone inside the system was helping us try to escape.

I pushed up against the cell wall, trying to stand, but my legs were shaking and my lungs were constricting.

"I don't understand." I blinked. "What's going on?"

Sherif came at me with the ax. I was sure that he meant to split my skull open. I crouched down and covered my head with my arms. He grabbed my sleeve and pulled me up.

"For God's sake, get a hold of yourself," he said. "We don't have time for your nonsense now."

Other prisoners were running past us in the corridor, which was full of billowing gray smoke. Another fireman's coat and helmet were lying on the floor.

"Put them on," he said. "We have to hurry."

It was all happening so fast that I could barely make sense of it. Later I learned that it had all been carefully plotted and planned for weeks—the uniforms smuggled into the prison, the fire set by guards who were secretly sympathizers with the Brotherhood—but no one had told me because I wasn't part of the trusted circle.

"You're still my cousin." Sherif answered the question before I asked it. "Blood is blood."

He put his free hand up to my face, as if he was going to pull me close and kiss me. Instead he ripped the dressing from my wound. A rush of ice-cold air seared its way into the exposed socket.

"*Allah!*" I screamed. "Why did you do that?"

"I had to. If someone sees you're already wearing a bandage, they'll know you're a prisoner." He picked up the coat and threw it at me. "Just say you were injured fighting the flames. Pretend to be brave for once."

I looked back into the darkness of the cell, to see if Raymond was still moving.

"Never mind about the Jew." Sherif shoved the helmet at me. "*Yalla, yalla,* we have to go."

I tried to pull the coat and helmet on as he dragged me through the hall. When we got to a bend in the corridor, I saw the sergeant with the bluebird tattoo on his face directing us to the courtyard exit. Now I was sure: the Brothers had more allies and moles in the uniformed forces than anyone acknowledged, or maybe they were just people willing to turn quickly with the tide. Either way, I avoided staring back at the sergeant as my cousin's hand kept pulling at me.

It was an even more hellish scene outside. Fires were blazing in at least four different locations. Thick black smoke curled up toward a half-moon in the sky. I could hear shrieking and smell men getting roasted alive in the cellblocks. Guards and other prisoners were running around like madmen escaped from an asylum who believed themselves to be Olympians.

A searchlight flashed from a guard tower, cutting a bright diagonal through the night, dark smoke ascending into its beam. It found the deputy warden swinging his baton wildly at inmates, trying to drive them back toward the flaming buildings. A loudspeaker crackled. The warden's voice came through the tinny speakers.

"Return to your cells immediately or you will be shot," he said. "This is an order from your prison governor."

A second searchlight went on and crossed toward the first one, finding more guards fighting and wrestling on the ground with escaped prisoners. At least one body I saw was facedown and motionless. I stepped over him and saw it was Osman. Discipline officers rushed out into the yard with German shepherds barking and straining at their leashes. Then I heard the snappish report of a rifle being fired from one of the guard towers.

I was knocked to the ground and separated from my cousin by the crush of men running to get away. A second shot struck the dirt not twelve feet from me. I jumped to my feet with my heart racing and my ears ringing. The second searchlight swept over me, blinding my one good eye and igniting a starburst of agony deep in my skull. My sight returned just as the searchlights converged and crisscrossed near where my helmet lay on the ground.

I grabbed it and jammed it back on my head. Then I turned and found myself face-to-face with the deputy warden, who was still holding his baton. Probably the same one he'd used to beat me and so many others. But in the half second as the searchlight passed over him, I saw that he was alone and no longer so strong. We were just two ordinary men in a desperate situation. If I'd had an ax like my cousin's at that instant, I would have gladly split his head open and then gone looking for the doctor who'd taken my eye. But God had other designs. A surge of bodies pushed us apart and carried me toward the gates leading to the outer yard, which were being opened to allow the fire trucks to come through.

It would be many years before I finally saw *The Ten Commandments,* which Mr. DeMille recovered enough to finish some months after he returned to the States. There's a scene at the end that begins after the one we were filming on the banks of the Red Sea. Moses and his people are being pursued by the pharaoh's army to the edge of the water. Just when it appears that all is lost and a massacre is inevitable, Chuck raises his staff, strikes the ground, and says the line I saw filmed that dusk: *"Behold his mighty hand!"* The waters part and the people are given a path to freedom. I swear to you, my grandson, the same thing happened to me that night. The searchlights missed me. Bullets flew past, some so close that they sounded like mosquitoes whizzing past my ears. The fighting bodies parted, just enough for me to squeeze through. And the lights and sirens of the arriving rescue trucks filled the yard.

I marched briskly toward them, hand over my eye socket, trying to assume the role and posture of a brave fireman. I knew all the other gates to the outside must have been open as well to let the vehicles in. Surely Providence had smiled upon me in this dark hour and given me a route toward my personal exodus. I saw some of the other inmates were up on the roofs of the smoldering cellblocks, waving their arms and crying out to be saved. Somehow, others were pushing a flaming mattress out through the bars of a cell window. A passing guard dog sniffed my leg and tried to lick at the broken sandal under the hem of my coat. Instead of noticing, his master pulled him away.

If I could get outside the gates, I knew that I had a chance. The Siggn was only a few miles outside Cairo. I could get there on foot, under cover of darkness. In my head, I was again chanting "No God but God, no God but God" as I pushed toward the lights shining through the gates. The real firefighters ran by me, lugging hoses connected to the prison's water system. One or two gave me strange looks, but there was no time to stop and question me. A military truck had pulled in behind their vehicles. Soldiers in riot gear jumped out and ran into the yard. They began swinging their rods and beating anyone not in official uniform, clubbing the guilty and innocent alike, paying no mind to the grievously injured.

I was less than twenty paces from the gate now, bodies streaming past me on either side. Red lights atop the pump and ladder trucks rotated in rhythm, throwing alternating blankets of crimson and darkness over the yard. My heart expanded and contracted with the rhythm of hope and terror. I thought of Mona. I thought of my father. Then, for some reason, I thought of Raymond.

It was madness even to consider him at that moment. I'd left the cell door open. If he was well enough to survive, he could have walked out on his own. And if he didn't have the strength, well, then there was probably nothing I could have done for him anyway. If he didn't believe in God, then what was the difference if he died alone? I told myself he was lying when he called me his friend. He admitted that he had been trying to manipulate me. But for some reason, I found myself slowing down as I approached the glaring lights and then, confoundingly, I found I could not take another step.

I heard the warden shouting orders at the guards. In person, not on the loudspeaker. I saw his unmistakable silhouette move in front of the trucks' headlights. He was holding someone by the collar and punching him in the face, as if to demonstrate how it was done for his men. I forced myself to take another two steps forward and saw it was Professor Farid getting shaken like a rag doll while still spitting curses at the prison governor. He turned his head and looked right at me as if he was about to call out my name and alert the others. But then the governor pulled a gun from his holster and shot him in the side of the head.

His blood spurted one way and his body fell the other. The warden looked around as if he knew someone else was out there who deserved the next bullet. I moved out of the light and begged God to help me one last time. I had no idea what to do, whether I should try to sneak past him or go back.

But then the strangest thing happened. A clump of burning wood fell in front of me. A sign. Where it came from, I don't know. It was not significant, compared with all the other destruction around me. But I swear it stopped me in my tracks, the way the pillar of fire would stop the pharaoh's soldiers in Mr. DeMille's film. In strict Islam, we don't truly believe in such Hollywood miracles as water into wine or frogs raining from the sky. We believe that God shows his hand in the small details of life. So when that clump of wood fell in my path, I felt the will of the Divine, plain and simple, blocking me from going any farther.

Sherif ran past me and tried to get aboard one of the fire trucks. The firemen started to yell and point at him. Several guards rushed over to grab him. The ax was pulled from his grip before Sherif could wield it. Then the warden joined the fray, the revolver shining in his hand. My cousin tried to grab it away and they all started yelling. They began to struggle, my cousin wrapping his hand around the gun's barrel. I could have slipped out easily in the confusion. There was an opening of at least three yards between the men and the truck. I could have been out in the desert before anyone missed me. But my feet had taken root in the dirt of the yard. That little clump of burning wood was refusing to let me pass. God would not grant me passage to downtown Cairo that night. Or maybe he had merely caused me to hesitate just enough to keep myself out of the searchlight. Another man ran past me into the light and was immediately shot dead from the guard tower.

A second later, the warden kicked my cousin's bad leg out from under him and sent Sherif sprawling. Then he aimed his pistol down at Sherif's head. My cousin lay on his back and raised his arms, surrendering.

I took off the fireman's helmet and tossed it aside. Then I let the coat slip from my shoulders. God, if he was watching, had spared me. But he was giving me a route as circuitous as the one he supposedly gave the pharaoh's slaves. In a trance, I walked back through the rioters like Mr. Claude Rains in *The Invisible Man,* still evading the searchlights and stepping over puddles made by the hoses starting to get the fires under control. I almost collided with the bluebird sergeant as he exited the cellblock. He looked at me like I was a madman when he saw where I was going back to.

The fire had been largely contained and quelled in our unit. There was an inch of water on the floor from the hoses. I heard moaning voices from behind the cell doors that no one had bothered to unlock. My stomach turned as I realized that what I was smelling was scorched flesh and that it was very much like grilled meat.

The door of my cell was half open, with the key still in the lock where Sherif had left it.

I hesitated before entering. All those years after finding my mother, my fear of seeing another dead body overwhelmed me. My hand shook as I pushed the door open. Darkness swallowed me as I stepped in. Someone had turned off the electricity in the cell. The air was fetid and swampy, like tombs in the flood season. I listened tentatively for the sound of breathing.

"Raymond?"

I could feel the presence of death in that room, as certainly as I felt God's presence protecting me in the yard.

The searchlight through the window bars found his body crumpled in the corner.

I started the prayer for the dead again.

"*Gnug. Dayeinu.*" He coughed. "I'm not dead yet."

His voice sounded low and weak but still retained a faint trace of its customary—and I now believed affected—cynicism.

"Why did you come back?" he asked.

"I thought you'd be bored without me."

"Don't flatter yourself." He wheezed. "You're not that entertaining."

I saw him for a half second, half smiling in a white passing searchlight from a guard tower. His face was gaunt and his eyes were already fixed on a point in the middle distance.

"How are you, Raymond?"

"Oh, I could complain, but who'd listen?"

"Another joke. You wish you were as funny as my father."

He inhaled as if he was preparing to make a dash for the door. "Listen to me now, Ali, there's a mailbox at the Greek Club in Cairo. . . ."

"What about it?"

"It's under the name Paul Leni—"

"Like the director of *The Man Who Laughs*?" I interrupted.

"Yes, yes." He gritted his teeth; this was no time for movie trivia. "Ask for the envelope when a clerk called Ahmed is on duty. It has a passport with my birth name on it and money to buy an airplane ticket to Malta."

"So it's true what they've been saying?" I tried to see him in the dark. "That you've been a spy for Israel all along?"

"If I was, then I'm not anymore," he said. "In here, there's no Egypt and Israel. There's just you and me. And I'm offering you a chance to get away."

"But why?"

He took such a long time answering that I thought he might have passed.

"I don't know. You might still have a future in pictures."

"No, Raymond." I gave him a weary smile. "I think I'm done with that."

I could hear the warden's voice on the loudspeaker outside, speaking calmly and authoritatively, ordering all survivors to return to their cells. The guards were back in control.

"You'll be all right, in the long run," he said so softly that I almost missed it. "They can't keep you here forever. Now be a good fellow and let me get my beauty rest, will you? I've got a date with an angel."

"You? What would you want with an angel?"

His laugh made me want to cry. "Thanks for coming back, my friend. I think I changed my mind about something."

"What's that?"

"I want you to say something for me. Some lines."

"Okay. Are they from a movie?"

He coughed and struggled to clear his throat again. "*Yitgadal v'yitkadash . . .*"

With some difficulty, I repeated what he'd said.

"*Sh'mei raba. B'alma di v'ra . . . ,*" he went on.

The syllables were rough, but somehow not completely foreign to me. Like something I had heard in a dream or a movie. Desert language. Words from the wilderness.

"*Chirutei v'yamlich malchutei, b'chayeichon—*"

"Raymond." I stopped him. "What is it that you're asking me to say here? It sounds like a prayer for the dead. I thought you didn't believe in any of that."

He hunched his frail shoulders, the comedian telling his last joke. "It's such a miracle that you made it back here that I've decided to hedge my bets."

Somehow we got through all of it, with the shooting and shouting outside. The mourner's kaddish that I discovered, years later, was usually only said at the burial and on the anniversary of a Jew's death. I suppose that having a Muslim say the words was better than nothing. Probably he just didn't want to be alone in the end. He wanted someone to see him, so the memory wouldn't just be lost and forgotten like a picture in the sand.

"There, *now* we're even," he said when we finished. "Ali Hassan, you are a mensch."

He turned his face to the wall and said nothing more.

July 14, 2015
To: Bayridgemama475@gmail.com
From: straightouttadamascus@protonmail.com

Mother, Grandfather, Allah,
Whoever sees this,

A lot has happened since the last time I wrote. None of it good.

Tyler Sommers is dead. He tried to escape and they caught him. And then they decided to make an example of him with a video with him. Then they made me edit it. Maybe you've already seen it. It's all over the internet. It's probably even been on the channel 4 news at eleven that Grandpa likes to watch every night after he's done with his old movies.

If you've seen it, then I don't have to describe what they did to him. It was horrible. Not in a movie way, but in a human way that's been giving me nightmares ever since.

This guy was only, like, five years older than me. When I was editing it, I couldn't stop thinking about how he wore Star Wars *costumes with his grandfather and watched this dumb* Ten Commandments *movie every year with his parents. I kept looking at the part where he's supposed to be reading this statement my commanders have given him, but he can't stop his lower lip from trembling. So he just stares straight into the camera and reads in this voice as if he's trying to remember the Pledge of Allegiance. Maybe he just didn't want to believe what was about to happen. Or that they'd somehow do it with special effects and not with a real sword.*

Long story short, I knew I had to leave after that. Especially since a rumor started that I was the one who helped him escape. They found a screwdriver in his cell that he'd used to loosen some of the bars on his windows, and eventually someone figured out that it came from a toolbox I had access to.

I ran away two nights ago and I'm pretty sure that they have sent someone to find me.

I'm not going to lie. I'm really scared about what they'll do if they find me. I couldn't stay, though. Tyler was an infidel and kufar like this Raymond, but I freaked when I realized they were going to kill him even if they got the ransom. That's why I left the screwdriver and prayed he'd get away on his own. But they tracked him down before he even hailed a taxi. And then they made me edit the video and watched my reaction.

I tried to pretend it didn't bother me so I could carry on with the military exercises, cooking, virtue patrols, and working in the editing suite. But I couldn't keep my mind on my tasks. I kept thinking about what would have happened if I never came here, and all the things in Brooklyn that I didn't think I was going to miss so much. The vape shops and storefront mosques on Atlantic Avenue. The Spanish ladies selling churros in the subway. The sneaker shops on 86th Street and the Italian sandwich place where we used to eat, near the Verrazano Bridge. Our Sunday night dinners at Bab al Yemen on Bay Ridge Avenue and skateboarding down by the Narrows. The dudes with their oxygen tanks smoking cigarettes outside the bodegas on Third Avenue and Grandpa falling asleep with the TV on. I guess I'm more American than I realized. Or maybe I'm just homesick and scared. Either way, I need to get out of here fast.

So I'm somewhere else at the moment, near the border. They call this a "safe house," but I don't know how long I'll really be safe here or how much I can trust the people I'm with.

So there's something I need you to do for me right away. I need you to get in touch with Dad's lawyer, Ms. Schulman, and give her this email address. Tell her that I need immediately to speak to the FBI agents who arrested Dad. I have information that they will totally want. But I won't give it to them unless they get me a new passport, money to buy a ticket, and arrange my safe passage home right away.

I don't have time to explain all the other complications. But I want to come back and see Grandpa while I still can. And the rest of you, of course.

Love,
Alex

30

I heard Raymond's last sigh just before the dawn bugler sounded.
I called for the guards to come take his body away, but they left
him with me for several hours while they cleaned up the carnage
in the prison yard.

I did not breathe the air as a free man again until the eighth of June
in the Christian year 1971.

That was when my life began again, which is why I use it as part of
my email address. At ten fifteen that morning, I walked out the gates
of Tura Prison, where I'd been transferred shortly after the riots. I
raised my good eye toward the hazy morning sunlight. I was forty-
one years old. I had been behind bars since I was twenty-four.

A secondhand Peugeot taxi with rusting patches, jittery transmis-
sion, and a dragging muffler sat quivering and rattling outside the
five-meter-high walls. Instead of a chariot with golden wheels and a
leopard-skin interior, this was the vehicle for my exodus.

I got in the back seat and said *"Yalla beena"* to the driver. In his
rearview mirror, the limestone cliffs and caves where I'd worked with
a pick and shovel on the prison chain gangs grew smaller and smaller.
Big rocks into little rocks. I remembered how Sherif once said that
even the bad places make us who we are. He was dead now. He had
been tortured and forced to sign a confession after the uprising, then
held in a cage at the back of the courtroom and made to testify at a
public trial.

He hanged himself with a bedsheet in his cell before he could talk about me on the witness stand. Latif, who had "shot" at Nasser, was dead as well, executed at the end of a hangman's rope, taking any evidence of a conspiracy with him.

But here I was, finally a free man, returning from many years of exile in the desert.

Crossing the city limits, I started to become anxious. Cairo was no longer my Cairo. The streets were crowded and filthy now, the air heavy with the stench of motor oil and failed socialism. Everywhere I looked I saw squalling traffic, exhaust fumes, indolent young men on street corners, women encumbered by too many children and clothes too dark for summer in an African country. Donkey carts broke down more often at traffic intersections; the European clothing stores were mostly boarded up. The old Art Deco hotels and Edwardian-era villas had turned into grime-covered wedding cakes collapsing along the boulevards, the unattended French gardens turning brown in the desert heat. The bistros and sidewalk cafés along the Nile were empty, their Cinzano and Martini umbrellas shredded and infested with crows.

The posters of Nasser were getting covered up and torn off the crumbling walls, replaced by pictures of Anwar Sadat. *El Rayyis* had been dead less than a year by then, felled by a heart attack at fifty-two, which allowed for my "early" release, four years short of the full sentence. Supposedly he had specifically wanted to see me hanged after the uprising. But shortly after I arrived at Tura, I was told by my lawyer that a letter from "an American film company" had been delivered, convincing the authorities to spare my life.

In the modern world, belief is always a choice. So I choose to believe that when Mona went to Los Angeles in 1955 and failed in her attempt to meet Mr. DeMille at his studio office, the long impassioned letter that she left with his secretary managed to reach his desk anyway and influence him. I choose to believe the letter that convinced the Egyptian authorities to spare my life came from Cecil B. DeMille himself. I choose to believe that he remembered me as a dreamer like himself and had tried in his way to help me. For decades afterward, a check for a hundred or so dollars came every year from the production company that his family maintained after his death. How it found its way to me is a mystery that I never quite solved.

And, finally, I *choose* to believe that Raymond Garfield was my friend, even though he was a spy.

Anyway, all of that was done now. Nasser's deputy, General Amer, died in 1967, supposedly by his own hand, after Egypt's defeat to Israel in the Six-Day War. You could feel the collective demoralization in the air four years later, as heavy and tangible as the pollution. Out of shame, the people, convinced that loss was God's punishment for neglecting their religion, had started turning back to faith in droves.

Everywhere I looked I saw more pious beards and burkas than ever before. Mostly it was good, I told myself. God had been good in keeping me alive and allowing me to see this day. But, as Professor Farid had predicted, some of those who were jailed and tortured with me had become far more radicalized and inclined to violence. A few would eventually go far beyond the aspirations of the Brotherhood and fly those airplanes into the towers of the city where I live now and where you grew up.

All of this was still far off into a future that I could hardly even imagine. I was more preoccupied with sadness, as I saw that the Avalon cinema, where I had spent so many happy afternoons, had been torn down and replaced by a small neighborhood mosque.

The taxi came to a shuddering halt in front of a slumping, dilapidated apartment house on Emir El-Din Street. Like most of the surrounding buildings, it had rusting balconies and yellowing rags hanging off the clotheslines. The voices of Koran reciters and Sadat's dutiful minions blared from the tinny apartment radios, in place of

Umm Kulthum and Patti Page. Landlords had not been allowed to raise rents since Nasser took over in the 1950s and so had stopped bothering to maintain their buildings. Urban planning was unheard of. People just threw up their frames without much regard to whether there were schools or a water supply in the vicinity.

I had trouble getting out of the cab. It was not because my body was still damaged from years of hard labor or poor nutrition, but rather because I was unused to freedom of movement. I stopped and looked around, remembering my father, your great-grandfather. That good man who never made it to the Masters Tournament in Augusta, Georgia. For fifteen years, he'd come to see me every week, or whenever he was allowed, even after he lost his job and the government had seized the house behind the golf course in the name of nationalization. He'd never lost faith that I would get out and somehow find the life of contentment he'd predicted, even when heart disease and emphysema attacked his body. He'd finally left this mortal plane two years before, and as I stood on that street corner thinking of him, a tear slipped from my good eye, and I cursed the false prophets whose lies and misguided notions still hung around us like the laundry on the railings.

Just as I began to panic, realizing I had no money to pay the driver, a woman's hand came to rest on my arm.

"It's all right, my love," she said. "I brought the fare."

A part of me still could not quite believe that she had kept her promise and waited. I could not help but notice that her skin looked a little dry and lined now, and that there were dark circles under her eyes, and her yellow hair was streaked with gray. But the sight of her serene profile in a white ankle-length abaya and a black headscarf still enthralled me more than Faten Hamama or Grace Kelly did in my youth.

Yes, Mona had kept her word.

After I had been "sent behind the sun," as they say, and sentenced to sixteen years, I assumed her visits would become less frequent. Yet every other week, she came back with extra food for me to share with other prisoners and money so the guards and nurses would "take care of me."

After all this time, I still wasn't sure why she waited for me or where she got the money. She never spoke of all the suitors she'd had when I was away in prison, though I know there were quite a few. She was pursued by army officers, businessmen, and diplomats who could have taken her to another country. But she simply said she lost interest in having a social life after I was sentenced. She remained devoted to her father until the day he died in his cell. Then she made me her purpose. She devoted herself to helping me get out. She wrote letters. She demanded meetings with government ministers. She eschewed the Paris fashions and the cosmopolitan parties. Instead, she made common cause with the wives of other prisoners, even though she came from a different social class and educational background.

For a time, she even considered exchanging her own faith for mine. She learned verses from the Holy Koran so we could communicate in code, began to dress like a proper Muslim wife in burka and hijabs; and then, after her father passed, she changed her name from Mona to Amina. But in the end, she retained the faith she was born into and attended weekly Coptic services until the day she died.

Perhaps it was true, what she had said when we were both younger: she had always been in search of a purpose that she could open her heart to. She had chosen me, and this was a miracle even greater than the parting of the Red Sea.

She was your grandmother, and I loved her very much.

On that day, she put her arm around me and helped me limp from the taxi into the building where she'd found an apartment for us. It made no sense, except as an act of faith. I was a half-blind former movie critic and chauffeur with a prison record and no immediate job prospects. Yet she acted like I was as wealthy as the Aga Khan. Maybe it was because she knew I needed her so badly that she agreed to join her destiny to mine. The stairway smelled of urine and fruit-flavored tobacco as we ascended to the third floor. She left me to rest against a banister and get my bearings as she opened the apartment door.

There was no furniture inside, just a prayer rug and a golf bag she'd rescued from my father's home, four candles, a Koran, and an old mattress on the floor. I didn't even have a copy of the silly little student film I'd made in eight millimeter. But now a slant of sunlight angled through an open window, and as I heard the chanting of the muezzin from a nearby minaret, dust specks revolved within the shaft in a way that reminded me of the beam from the projectionist's booth on those Metro matinees. And quite unexpectedly, an old, half-forgotten melody stirred in the back of my mind. *See the pyramids along the Nile....*

"God has smiled upon me," I said.

"God is always smiling. Even when we go astray."

"But today, he is smiling a lot."

So this was my Hollywood ending. In a dirty little unfurnished apartment that cost fifty dollars a month, with squeaky plumbing in the bathroom and neighbors arguing loudly upstairs.

We would be married for twenty-seven years. We would live in Cairo for another six months and then move to France, where she still had citizenship because of her mother. Then God would soften the hearts of the immigration officials and make it possible for us finally to come to the United States, where she had a cousin in New Jersey. Then he granted an even greater miracle and allowed her to become pregnant when she was forty-one years old. She gave birth to your father at Kings County Hospital in Brooklyn and lived to see her first grandchild be born as a full-fledged American. I know you were too young to remember her, but she was the finest of women and the shining star of my life.

She waited up for me every night with a cup of tea when I came home late from driving the taxicab with a special license the New York Department of Motor Vehicles granted me for my one eye and the medallion I bought with three other Egyptians a year after I came to America. Then she worked out our finances so we could buy my partners out in 1985 and then sell that medallion for $100,000, which we then used as a down payment for a broken-down Esso gas station on Bay Ridge Parkway. Then she worked beside me at the register seven nights a week, behind a bulletproof glass partition, selling gasoline and lottery cards in her hijab, until we turned the corner, paid off the mortgage on the property, and then earned enough to buy our family our first real home on Colonial Road, made of solid red brick, where it was my joy and blessing to see you come home and grow. So after all those years, we made it over the rainbow and made a small American success of ourselves.

And every Easter, we would watch *The Ten Commandments* together when it was shown on TV. We'd laugh about Yul Brynner and his cigarettes, and Chuck with his beard, and we'd marvel at the beauty of Miss Yvonne De Carlo and Miss Anne Baxter and the parting of the Red Sea. These days, I imagine young people might find the special effects dated and some of the dialogue painful. But it was part of our lives. Every year, we would pretend that we could spot ourselves finding each other among the cast of thousands, which was as close as we'd ever come to having our stars embedded in the Walk of Fame on Hollywood Boulevard.

God took her from me in 1998. Many things happened after that. Some were almost as wondrous as the life I'd had with her. Some, like the day the Towers fell, were as heavy as bricks on the other side of the scale. But I've tried to live as if my heart were as light as a feather.

Not every prayer was answered. And I still miss that woman every hour of every day. But I do not regret anything—not losing an eye, not failing to escape during the fires, not even the seventeen years of my life spent in prison, when I consider that beam coming through that sooty window and the path it illuminated through the long corridor of decades.

"Do you want to pray and give thanks?" Your grandmother pointed to the rug she'd spread before the window.

"No." I shook my head and pointed to the mattress. "I would like to lie with you. I have waited a very long time for this."

EPILOGUE

September 8, 2015
To: GrandpaAli71@aol.com
cc: Bayridgemama475@gmail.com
From: Alexisfire475@gmail.com

Grandpa,
I don't know if you'll be able to receive this message directly, so I've
sent a copy to Mom so that she can read it out loud to you.

I'm on my way home, writing on the laptop of Ms. Schulman,
with the FBI agents looking over my shoulder. A lot more has
happened since I last wrote. I'm not the same as I was when I left. But
I'm not the same as I was when I was over there either.

If anyone would get it, you might. I had to agree to confess
everything I've been involved with to my handlers over here in
Turkey, as part of the deal to get me home. I'm telling them about
some of the things my unit wanted to do to people and places in the
United States. I'm trying not to feel too bad, because now I know you
and my grandmother did some of the same things and had to make
statements of your own. Which made it a little easier for me to make
a U-turn.

I know it's not going to be easy to convince everyone that I'm on
the right side of the road now. I will definitely have some explaining
to do, especially to Tyler's parents—even though I tried to help their
son.

The agents seem pretty skeptical, so Ms. Schulman says I'm
probably looking at a sentence of at least eight or nine years in a

federal facility. Which means I won't get out until I'm close to thirty, but then again it's only about half as much time as you did.

In exchange for signing the cooperation agreement, and because you're housebound, Mr. Foxworth, the special agent in charge, says that he'll write a letter requesting that I get one supervised home visit every two weeks until I start my bid.

So please hang on a little longer for me. I know it's taken me a while to come around, but I'm getting there.

Thanks,
Alex

September 9, 2015
To: Alexisfire475@gmail.com
From: Bayridgemama475@gmail.com

Alex,
Your grandfather says he'll have the kushari *ready and warm seats waiting for you and your handlers on the couch. He hopes that you all like mixed spices and movies long enough to have intermissions.*

Love,
Mom

HISTORICAL NOTE

icture in the Sand is a work of fiction, and most of its main characters are figments of the author's imagination. As always, the mistakes and distortions, intentional and otherwise, are my exclusive property as well.

The background borrows heavily from historical accounts.

In the fall of 1954, Cecil B. DeMille brought the production of *The Ten Commandments* to Egypt to shoot several key sequences in the desert fifteen miles outside Cairo. There had been preliminary discussions with King Farouk about making accommodations to film in Egypt. But by the time a script was ready and the production was travel worthy, the situation had changed drastically in the Middle East.

Six years earlier, Egypt had been at war with the newly declared state of Israel. Its ill-equipped army was soundly defeated, and much of the blame was directed at King Farouk. In 1952, frustrations about the king and the British occupation of Egypt came to a head. A group known as the Free Officers from the Egyptian army, with support from members of the Muslim Brotherhood, staged a coup and forced Farouk to abdicate. General Mohammed Naguib became Egypt's new leader, even though Gamal Abdel Nasser, a young lieutenant colonel, had been the true driving force.

DeMille then struck a deal with Naguib that allowed him to film outside Cairo, using two hundred cavalry officers and their horses to play the pharaoh's army, and borrowing twelve decommissioned air force planes to use as wind machines. In exchange, DeMille agreed to produce a short documentary film about contemporary Egypt and its revolutionary achievements, for the new government to use as it saw fit.

However, things had changed yet again by the time DeMille's ship reached the Port of Alexandria. Naguib and Nasser had become enmeshed in a power struggle, with Nasser emerging as the eventual victor. He met with DeMille and Henry Wilcoxon and agreed to honor the agreements the filmmakers had made with his predecessor.

At the same time, Nasser was dealing with serious issues. Tensions were still high with Israel. Right before DeMille came, thirteen young Egyptian Jews were arrested in the Lavon Affair, which involved spying and acts of sabotage in Cairo and Alexandria. Simultaneously, the Muslim Brothers, who had been more closely aligned with Naguib, were becoming increasingly disillusioned with Nasser's failure to make *shariah,* law based on Islam, Egypt's governing principle. The Brothers' "secret apparatus" hatched a conspiracy to bring down Nasser. The plans included the bombing of roads and bridges and an assassination attempt made against Nasser during a speech in Alexandria. As depicted in the novel, that attempt failed, and newspaper stories the next day mused that the effort had looked so staged that "some people wonder if Cecil B. DeMille came to Egypt to direct the eight bullets, not the *Ten Commandments*." A major crackdown on the Muslim Brotherhood resulted, with hundreds of members imprisoned, tortured, and in several cases put to death. Many historians say the rise of radical Islam, al-Qaeda, and ISIS began in this period.

As in the novel, members of the Jewish spy ring were imprisoned at the same time and in the same facility as the Muslim Brothers. But, according to some accounts, these two groups reached a truce after a

Jewish inmate refused guards' orders to discipline a Muslim Brother by beating him and was, in turn, beaten himself.

The character of Dr. Sabri is also based on historical record. After World War II, a number of Nazi doctors and officials were able to immigrate to Egypt. One of the most prominent was Aribert Heim, also known as "Dr. Death," a member of the Waffen-SS, who killed hundreds at the Mauthausen concentration camp before going to Cairo and living under a false Egyptian identity until his death in 1992.

The Brotherhood's plot against *The Ten Commandments* is a fictional invention, as far as the author knows. It is true, however, that DeMille suffered a major heart attack while directing the Exodus sequence in the Egyptian desert. He managed to climb down 110 feet from the gates of Per-Rameses, and after a period of convalescence was able to return to Hollywood and complete filming on the studio lot, including aspects of the famous parting of the Red Sea sequence that were combined with footage shot in Egypt.

The Ten Commandments was a major worldwide success and won an Oscar in 1956 for Best Special Effects. But it did not win an award for Best Director. It has become a holiday tradition to broadcast it on national television every year around Easter and Passover.

Cecil B. DeMille died on January 21, 1959. *The Ten Commandments* was his final film.

ACKNOWLEDGMENTS

I would like to thank:

Lawrence Wright, Raymond Stock, Samir W. Rafaat, Mona Serageldin, Mahmoud Sabet, Jeff Osborne, Belal Fadl, Khaled Gabry, Amr Gabry, Ahmed Gabry, Ahmed Seddik, James D'Arc, Tawfik Sola, Pierre Cachia, Mahmoud Tawfik, Mona Tawfik, Ibrahim Abdel Meguid, Nina Foch, Haroon Moghul, Tarek Lofty, Gamal Al-Bana, Frank G. Wisner, Arthur Levitt, Peter Bloom, Harold (Smoky) Simon, Elizabeth Keyishian, Kevin Brownlow, Patrick Stansbury, Helen Cohen, Ashraf M. Mobariz, Lawrence Schoenbach, Andrew Patel, Dan Morrison, Naguib Mahfouz, Dr. Nabil Farouk, Maurice Yenni, Katherine Orrison, Mickey Moore, Jim Voorhees, Jeanine Basinger, Francis Ricciardone, Jeffrey Wells, Helen Lovejoy, Stuart Friedland, Barbara Friedland, Alan Weisman, Gabriel Cohen, Fraser Heston, Marisa Silver, George Hagen, Ali Salem, Peg Tyre, Loren Janes, Barbara Hall, Albert Maysles, D. A. Pennebaker, Richard Leacock, Robert Drew, Jack Garfein, Lofti Sherief, Julie Martin, George C. Stoney, Ellen Lippman, Philippa Gordon, Kendall Rose Storey, Eric Pooley, Laura Sanchez, Peter Herbst, Madeline Houpt, Tom Straw, and Angela Cheng Caplan.

I would like to give special thanks to Joanne Gruber for her editorial help in combatting ungrammatical insurgencies. John Ragheb went above and beyond in sharing his insights and showing me around Cairo, especially during the Arab Spring. John was also kind enough to read the manuscript to try to correct my many errors of fact and interpretation.

Finally, I want to thank Cecilia Presley and Joe Harper, Cecil B. DeMille's grandchildren, for their patience, their insights, and their willingness to share memories of their time in Egypt during the filming of *The Ten Commandments*. This book would not exist without their participation.